PIANO
TIDE

PIANO TIDE

A NOVEL

KATHLEEN DEAN MOORE

COUNTERPOINT | BERKELEY

Library of Congress Cataloging-in-Publication Data is Available

Cover design by Kelly Winton
Interior design by Sabrina Plomitallo-González, Neuwirth & Associates

ISBN 978-1-61902-791-6

COUNTERPOINT
2560 Ninth Street, Suite 318
Berkeley, CA 94710
www.counterpointpress.com

Printed in the United States of America
Distributed by Publishers Group West

10 9 8 7 6 5 4 3 2 1

For the damp-haired children
and for the young of all beings in Southeast Alaska,
who deserve an enduring way of life.

CONTENTS

PERSONAE

Lillian Mary Shaddy. b. 1943, Seattle, WA.
Owner/operator, Good River Harbor Bath 'n' Bar, Good River Harbor, AK.

Christopher "Tick" McIver. b. 1970, Skagway, AK.
Carpenter, Good River Products, Inc. Good River Harbor, AK.
Wife: Annie Klawon. Sons: Davy and Tommy McIver.

Nora Montgomery. b. 1973. Birthplace unknown.
Writer, Alaska Marine Highway.

Axel Hagerman. b. 1960, Good River Harbor, AK.
President and CEO, Good River Products, Inc.
Wife: Rebecca Hagerman. Daughter: Meredith Hagerman.

David "Davy" McIver. b. 1995, Good River Harbor, AK.
Father: Tick McIver. Mother: Annie Klawon.

Thomas "Tommy" McIver. b. 2002, Good River Harbor, AK.
Father: Tick McIver. Mother: Annie Klawon.

Howard Fowler. b. 1965, San Mateo, CA.
Surveyor, communications manager, and assistant production supervisor,
Good River Products, Inc. Good River Harbor, AK.
Wife: Jennifer Fowler. Daughter: Taylor Fowler.

Kenny Isaacson. b. 1950, Chicago, IL.

Meredith Hagerman. b. 1995, Juneau, AK.
Father: Axel Hagerman. Mother: Rebecca Hagerman.

Rebecca Hagerman. b. 1960, Bar Harbor, ME. Housewife.
Husband: Axel Hagerman.
Daughter: Meredith Hagerman.

EACH OF THE characters in this book is a creation of the author's imagination. None of them are real people—not even remotely. The author just stood at her little desk and made them up. It will do no good, and probably a lot of harm, to look crosswise at a character, wondering if you have met him or her. You have not.

Not only that. None of the places are factual, and it will do no good to check for them on a map. The author has ranged widely over Oregon and the Pacific Northwest, doing her best to remember a muskeg here, a boat dock there, a sinking skiff in another place, a piling topped with fireweed, a clamflat, a dump. From these glass shards of memory and imagination, Good River Harbor is created.

PRELUDE

HEAVY OVERCAST. RAIN. Wind twenty knots from the southeast. The ferry plowed through the Fairweather Narrows, crowded on both sides by palisades of hemlocks and Sitka spruce. Their branches shredded the fog. A woman in a yellow slicker leaned over the rail, watching until the ship was safely past the buoy that marked a hidden shoal. Hard on the port side, so close it threw spray onto the deck, a creek poured over the broken face of a hanging glacier and twisted down an avalanche chute to the sea. In the black muck beside the creek mouth, skunk cabbage unfurled giant leaves. A bear had been through—probably night before last—trampling the skunk cabbage to dig around the roots, probing into sour mud with lips curled back and teeth reaching tentative as fingertips. Dark water had collected in the sinkholes of its front paws. To starboard, the mountains climbed up and up toward snowfields and granite crags. For three long hours, there was no evidence of humanity except for the buoys and range-markers that led the ferry along the silver sea-path between forested rocks.

So green as to be almost black at first, the forest eventually gave way to lighter green patches along the water, as if a shark had leapt up with pointed teeth to scrape away the trees, leaving only an understory of salmonberry thickets and Sitka alders—dog-hair alders, grown up thick as hairs on a dog's back after the forest was cut to stumps. Some of the cuts were bare to the mud. This, at last, was evidence of human industry. And now the town of Good River Harbor came into view at the base of the mountains.

From the distance, Good River Harbor looked like a string of gulls flying along the water below the mountain range, or a rim of barnacles just uncovered by the tide. One thing it did not look like was a town, but the town fathers could be forgiven for that. The wilderness was desperately steep; the only place to put a building was on a tidal flat that flooded twice a day. So the worthy fathers raised a boardwalk fifteen feet above high tide, a long wooden pier parallel to shore, and along its length, built their houses on pilings. Even the school and the post office were built on a rickety thicket of stilts and piers. The town couldn't be distinguished from the docks, or the docks from the town—almost everything was either tied to a dock or built on it, almost everything grew a thick beard of barnacles and blue mussels. The only structures on actual ground were the remains of an old cannery site on one end of town, the dump on the other, and a little empty cabin at Green Cove. There were no cars, but there were plenty of wheelbarrows and bikes, and a row of beached boats, some more deeply filled with greening rainwater than others, and fine skiffs and seiners nosing into the dock like suckling puppies.

The town of Good River Harbor did not have a real harbor. In fact, it didn't even have a river, and if it had, it wouldn't have been a good one, wandering through the intertidal muck. The town was named after Basil Everett Good, who arrived in 1910 with everything he owned under canvas tarps in a wooden canoe. He aimed to make a living digging clams and selling them to fishermen who happened by. He built a cabin over a stream that drained a ravine and made out all right, until he realized that the real money was not in clams after all, but in salmon. So he signed up to crew on a passing seiner and, for the proverbial bottle of whiskey, traded his cabin to a crew member who was sick of the North Pacific seas.

The town grew and shrank like the tides, as it sold and then exhausted the abundance of the land. In order of date expunged: (1) ancient yellow cedars draped in old-man's beard, (2) Sitka spruce trees six feet across, (3) sweet, feathery hemlocks three hundred years old, (4) king salmon a yard long and fat as dogs, (5) herring dripping yellow eggs, (6) cross-eyed halibut as big as the fishermen's skiffs. The sawmill closed after loggers high-graded the forest and clear-cut all the slopes accessible to logging barges. The cannery closed when the fish could not be counted on. Only forty to fifty people lived in Good River Harbor when the ferry pulled in, not counting the tourists and gunkholers, and a random seiner and his crew—maybe a dozen more souls a day.

The ferry bumped hard into the pilings, shifting the joints of the old timbers. The woman in the yellow raincoat gripped the railing. Deckhands grabbed the lines with boathooks and looped them over the bollards. Old winches cranked the boat to the dock, and the hands wrapped the lines tight over the drum. Bolts clanked and chains rumbled to lower the ferry ramp to the wharf. When the ramp hit the gangway, gulls squawked and shot into the air, as if they had been pinched.

PART ONE
PINK-SALMON TIDE

See here, the urgency of a pink salmon finally coming home. See here, salmon polished to such a sheen that even under an overcast sky the sun reflects on their flanks. They've been gone a year, chasing herring under storm-blue seas. Now they are almost home, so close they can taste it. As they circle at the mouth of the Kis'utch River, their backs darken and their tail stems flush pink. Their flanks streak with white, as if someone had grabbed them before the paint was dry. The backs of the big males grow humped. Their teeth grow long.

On the surge of the flood-tide, the fish throw themselves over the sandbar and press up the stream. In their eagerness to be home, they shoulder each other out of the way, flapping their bodies over gravel bars, swimming sometimes through water so shallow that their humps carve air. Bears wade into them. They toss fish out of the creek to eat later, or they bite out the hump or the fatty brain. More salmon press through bloodied water, like an invading army marching over its own dead.

June 15

HIGH TIDE		LOW TIDE	
2:58 am	18.9	9:28 am	-4.0
4:03 pm	16.6	9:47 pm	1.3

As the ferry pushed into the pilings, Lillian Mary Shaddy spread a plastic grocery bag on the bench at the top of the gangway and lowered herself to sitting. She elbowed a big-bearded man, who moved his bulk over to give her room.

"Who's the woman in the yellow raincoat?" she asked, not expecting an answer.

The woman at the rail of the ferry looked like everybody else in Good River Harbor—baseball cap, wet hair, slicker open in the rain, XtraTuf boots. But the way she was looking around, snapping her head to port, starboard—that would make her somebody new. She wasn't a tourist. A tourist would be running up and down the railing, taking pictures. She wasn't somebody's visitor, because she wasn't waving at anybody and nobody was waving at her. But she wasn't frantically checking her ticket either, so she had planned to come to odd little Good River Harbor.

Lillian tugged her raincoat closed and searched behind her for the belt. No yellow rain slicker for her. Lillian wore a regular department-store raincoat, the kind women wore in Seattle. Carefully, she tied the belt in a square knot that perched like a chipmunk in the cozy place between her bosom and her belly. She adjusted the clear plastic rain bonnet over her hair, which was that day a color called mahogany, and settled her back against the bench. On that damp morning, Lillian felt as groany-jointed as the old ferry, but it's not attractive to complain, and she didn't. She lit a cigarette instead. Smoking in the rain is one of the arts a lady acquires in Southeast Alaska, learning to hold the cigarette between her thumb and forefinger, while the rest of her fingers make a nice little tent. She leaned forward through the smoke to study the new arrival.

The woman's ponytail was knotted up and stuck through the hole in her baseball cap. Sticking out like that, it was as black and wind-smoothed as a crow's tail, and she was skittish as a crow, in fact. But she was tall and long-legged, more like a great blue heron. Whatever kind of bird she was, Lillian was not prepared to say. By this time, the new woman was down on the cargo deck, standing next to a big dog, a pile of totes, and an object wrapped in a blue tarp—a really big object, big enough to be a refrigerator or a shower stall. Lillian took a thoughtful drag on her cigarette and exhaled a long, slow river of smoke.

"The plot thickens," she said to the big man sitting next to her and elbowed him again. He scooted himself even farther away. "Hey, Tick, how about you wander down and introduce yourself. Pretend you're the chamber of commerce. Tell her welcome or something. Or pretend you're a moving company. That's good. Help her with that thing, whatever it is, and find out where's she's going." Honest to God, Lillian thought but did not say, you'd think some people had no sense of curiosity.

Tick McIver was big enough to be a moving company, but he didn't exactly look like a welcoming committee. Lillian had told him a dozen times that he should clean up a little bit—for his own good. Trim that awful orange beard. The thing looked like a stray cat sleeping on his chest. Get rid of those rubber overalls that come barely to the top of his boots. But he protested. He said he cut his overalls off because they're too short anyway, him so tall, and this way they're not always underwater, and he liked his beard, kept his chest warm and scared mice away. And that baseball cap, she'd told him, it looks like it spent the night in the bilge. Well, that's because it spent lots of nights in the bilge, he'd said back.

Tick sighed, hoisted himself to standing, and walked down the gangway to the cargo deck.

TICK WALKED A circle around the new woman's cargo. Somebody who knew knots had tied that tarp up—a single trucker's hitch, no nonsense.

"Whatcha got there?" he asked. Months later, he would think about this time, knowing what he didn't know back then—that he hadn't asked the most important question.

From the gangway, he had thought she looked like a bird. But close up, her face looked more like a fish. Not in a bad way. But her eyes were big and sort of bulgy, and they were golden as a quillback rockfish. That caught Tick by surprise, the big gold eyes. Her face was wide, sculpin-like, and open in a nice kind of way, and when she smiled, she blinked reflexively, as if her eyes and her mouth were connected by the plate of her cheeks, as are the eyes and mouth of a cod. Youngish. Maybe thirty, maybe thirty-five, although now that Tick was forty, he thought everybody was young.

She had a dog with her, a big one, part German shepherd maybe, maybe some golden retriever. The dog strolled around on the cargo deck, sniffing the backsides of every town dog, nosing up to every kid on the deck, looking for a nuzzle or a hug. When the ferry whistle gave a warning blast to signal imminent departure, the dog galloped back to the woman, panicked as a colt. She hushed it with a hand gesture. It sat beside her, whining.

The whistle motivated the woman too. She reached over, yanked the rope's bitter end, and pulled it off the tarp. The tarp thundered as she dragged it to the deck. Under the tarp was an upright piano.

Tick lifted off his baseball cap, smudged the blackflies on his forehead, and settled the cap more firmly on his head. "That looks like a piano," he said. He glanced up the gangway to Lillian, who gave him a big thumbs-up. The new woman laughed, splitting her face with a grin.

"Yep. It's a piano all right. Can you help me get it to the Green Cove cabin?"

"It takes a good high tide to move a piano," Tick protested, even though he knew that this tide was high, a sixteen-footer, high enough to bend the sedges, flattening them in a swirl, as if a bear had wallowed there. High enough to hoist the windrow of rock-wrack another yard up the beach. High enough to launch mussel shells like double-end dories. High enough, Tick knew, to float a boat over the intertidal rocks and bring it right up to the rock ledge at the Green Cove cabin.

"Yeah, I could move a piano, if we did it now, at the peak of the tide," he finally said. "It can be done." Although he was still a young man, he wasn't a man to leap to conclusions. He was capable of leaping to *action* if needed—if, for example, his boat was on fire. But men of the sea are wary of conclusions. "But why?" he asked. It was a reasonable question under the circumstances, but still, in retrospect, not the right one.

"Because this ferry is about to sail off to whatever godforsaken place it goes next, and I don't want my piano to sail with it, and because I bet you're the one who can do it."

The ferry was in fact about to sail off to Bean Point, which was a gloomy godforsaken place in Tick's opinion, and he knew that the people had moved out of that little D-log cabin at Green Cove. He knew of a nice granite shelf slanting up from the beach to the yard, where he had offloaded the logs for that very cabin. He could do this.

He walked across the cargo deck and returned with a four-wheel dolly. He fixed up a lever from a block of wood and a two-by-four and he pried that piano up. He put the woman on the pry bar, and he bent down to slide the dolly underneath. Tick was strong, and easy around water and big things, and before long, he and the woman were edging the piano down the gangway. Couple of turns around piano and post, and Tick had the rope slipping around a piling, and the woman was hanging on to the far end, and Tick had that piano tiptoeing down the ferry ramp like a drunk crossing a log.

A damp-headed boy ran ahead of them, shoving gearboxes and buckets out of the way. The town dogs ran along behind. Then the piano was on the dock, swaying a little. Tick gave the piano a pat and walked down the dock toward the *Annie K.*

Tick had two boats in the harbor—a little skiff and the *Annie K*, a twenty-six-foot landing craft left over from World War II. The *Annie K* was a bucket of a boat, and people compared it unfavorably to their own boats until they needed it, and who doesn't need a landing craft when they have a load of lumber to move, and who doesn't have an inconvenient load of lumber on occasion? With the flat bow that lowers on a winch, landing crafts always leak, but it was dry enough to move a piano, and that is what Tick was going to do. At least the rain had stopped. At least he had the tide on his side. He didn't want to be dragging a load that size over wet rocks, slipping on the rock-wrack.

Casting off his lines, Tick cranked on the engine. He pointed the bow of the boat toward the wharf where the piano and the woman threw long reflections across the harbor. Everything a tide can lift was floating on the polished water. Cork net-floats, a two-by-four, a bloated rockfish— they were all bobbing round down there on the reflection of the town, boats floating upside down and right side up, kids riding down the dock in orange life jackets, reflected upside down on the water beside a floating beer can and tangled kelp.

The challenge of moving a big object by boat brings in the men, faster even than an ancient halibut laid out gasping on the dock. Seemed like every man in Good River Harbor was striding down the ramp. Every one of them started giving directions, pointing here, pointing there, bossing things, even though it didn't look like anybody needed bossing, least of all the piano woman. She stood aside while at least three men stood there on the dock and waved the *Annie K* in. Tick pulled the pins that held the bow closed and engaged the winch. Chains clanked through the guides, the old hinges trumpeted, and the apron of the boat lowered like a castle gate over a moat, bridging the boat and the dock. With men giving hand signals— this way, that way, stop, go, *stop*—they jockeyed the piano around a tight angle and rolled it onto the *Annie K*'s bow. Its sudden weight lowered the bow, and all the reflections bent and rolled. The yellow-coated men shredded into yellow lines that bounced around the breakwall.

The piano secured, the dog and gear totes loaded, the new woman aboard, Tick backed out the boat, and the *Annie K* headed northwest out the harbor, heading for the Green Cove cabin. As he left, he saw the kids and the men and the dogs all headed northwest too, pounding up the boardwalk, then bouncing down the ramp to the trail to the cove. Tick was going to need them, and in Good River Harbor, where men were needed, they would go.

He turned on his depth-sounder and steered wide around Green Point. No doubt the rocks were safely submerged on a tide this high, but he was a careful man with a boat and not one to be taking chances. As he tipped up his cap, his eyes rested on the woman who stood beside her piano on the foredeck. With one boot braced on the bow, she leaned forward into the wind.

That woman doesn't look like a fish or a bird, Tick decided. She looks like George Washington crossing the Delaware. "Row, men, row, damn the ice floes." He considered the similarity. Yep, they could be identical twins, if Washington had worn a yellow slicker, and if George Washington had a strand of dark hair stuck to his cheek by blowing rain.

He stuck his head out of the wheelhouse and yelled into the weather. "I'm Tick McIver. Actually Christopher, but nobody could handle a word that big, so they called me . . . just . . . Tick. Not because I stick to things like a tick. But things stick to me. Even bad luck follows me around like a grinning . . . dog."

His speech ended in a mutter and he bent over the wheel, his neck flushing.

"I'm Nora," said George Washington.

Tick did not speak for the rest of the trip.

Out at Nora's cabin, there was a great deal of dragging around of sheets of plywood. There was a great deal of throwing straps around trees to hold the winch. There was a great deal of cranking. Kids in boots, soggy dogs, men with beards. One may make fun, but these people are very, very good at this sort of thing, and they would get the job done with no delay, no crushed fingers, and not that many beers.

"Up she goes, easy, easy."

"Pull to her starboard side."

"She's turning, she's turning. The bitch got a mind of her own. Kick that wheel."

"Hey, Tick, you got any more rope on that tub?"

"Easy. Easy."

"Barney, you damn dog, let go of that rope. C'mon, this is not a game. Christ."

When the piano rolled off the boat on that grand and momentous piano tide, the assembled town cheered. When it rolled up the ramp onto the porch of the cabin, they cheered again. Then somebody figured out the piano wouldn't fit through the front door. All the discussion and laughter then, the men measuring with the span of their hands, dogs barking at the uproar. Being practical people, the men began calculating how much trouble it would be to pry out the doorframe and chain saw a bigger opening.

But Nora just shoved the piano up under the porch roof, tight against the wall, and toweled it down, pulled a case of beer out of a tote, and threw a welcoming party for herself and her dog, whom she introduced as Chum. Standing, because she had no chair, Nora picked out a semblance of "Amazing Grace." It was awful. She winced and grimaced and even the piano seemed to shudder. Hard to know why a person who couldn't play the piano any better than that would haul it all the way out to the bush, but there are people who just love to carry around a guitar case, so who knows and nobody cared. They all wanted to play her piano under the hemlocks, even people who hadn't touched a key since they were kids. Pretty much all they knew was "Chopsticks." So the kids and the dogs danced to "Chopsticks."

Tick put a can of beer in each pocket and headed back to the harbor, shoving the Annie K away from the beach with an oar. On a falling tide, you can't hold a boat on shore. The tide will drop right out from under you, grounding you, and there you will sit on the mud and rocks for about ten hours, looking stupid.

IN THE MORNING, sunlit yellow fog sagged on the roofs of Good River Harbor and invisible ravens clonked and muttered from the hidden spars. Tick McIver sat on the step of his house on the boardwalk, drinking a second cup of coffee.

Tick was a big man, although he never meant to be and denied responsibility—heavy head, powerful shoulders, meaty hands, beard big and orange. The beard was rumpled, but soon enough he would rummage his fingers through the fur and get it all arranged. His hair he wore in one orange braid down the length of his back. He was big, but he wasn't fat, any more than a tree trunk is fat even if your arms can't reach around it.

That particular morning, he was giving serious thought to seeing what was wrong with the carburetor on his Evinrude, so he'd put on the dirtier of

his two denim work shirts and a huge pair of Carhartt overalls. The overalls
stopped short of his ankles, their rolled hems having been sawn off with
a pocketknife. Logging or fishing or banging nails, you want your overalls to rip when they catch on a snag or an oarlock or a spike in a board.
Tick hadn't got around yet to putting on his boots for the day. So when
he unbent his knees and extended his legs across the boardwalk, the fog
formed droplets of dew on his woolen socks and on two stripes of white
skin stuck with orange hairs.

Tick cupped a hand over his eyes to shield his headache from the light
and squinted in the direction of his big feet. He lived right there on the
boardwalk, and the whole town had to walk past his door to get anywhere
at all, so Tick wasn't surprised when another pair of feet showed up next
to his. Rubber boots and a woman's long legs. He had to crane his neck to
look at her, she had stopped so close to him. All he had was a silhouette
in fog so bright it hurt his eyes. Still, he could see she was tall. Her raincoat flapped off her shoulders and her hair flopped out the hole in the
back of her baseball cap. So it was that new woman. He remembered from
the piano party that the dog's name was Chum, but that morning Tick
fumbled to remember the woman's name.

"Hey, Tick," she said, smiling and blinking at Tick. "Pretty day."

Chum sniffed at Tick's socks.

"Yep. Pretty as a calendar picture," he managed to say back.

Nora sat down beside him. "Mind?"

Tick didn't know if he minded or not. He didn't know this woman who
was now leaning her back on his railing and stretching her legs out beside
his.

"It's really pretty until you look at those mountainsides that have been
cut to mud," she said. But that's all she said, which was good, because he'd
been one of the guys who hauled the choker up and down the mountain,
yarding out the logs, and of course that's not pretty, the stickers and the
sweat. She didn't like the mud, she should have tried dodging trees in that
muck. That was a pretty big silence then. The woman just sat there and
bounced her fist up and down against her thigh.

"Sorry," she eventually said. "When will I learn to keep my mouth
shut?"

Tick didn't know, so he didn't say. Instead, he lifted his beard and scratched his neck. This woman, she just sat there thinking and pounding her leg.

"What the hell," she finally said. "What's the harm?" She turned to Tick, who didn't know the answer to that one either. "Who's the boss of the logging outfit here?"

Tick knew that one, sure enough. "That would be Axel Hagerman, CEO of Good River Products, Inc. Office right there. Axel'll be coming along pretty soon, eight o'clock sharp."

Later, he might have wished he hadn't said that, but it wasn't like Axel was some kind of secret agent, and at the time, he was just being nice to somebody new in town. There is never anything wrong with being nice.

Sure enough, pretty soon along came the president of Good River Products, carrying a workman's lunch box in one hand and a briefcase in the other. That was in fact Axel Hagerman. Axel was a polyp of a man—small, soft, white, roundish now, but capable of many shapes. Just a fuzz of pale hair on his head, hardly more than a baby. He covered his body with the snappiest nautical blues. Navy blue polyester pants, navy blue bowling jacket with the GR Products logo. Under his jacket, his shirt collar was white—white of all things, in Good River Harbor. Indoors and out, he wore a Greek fisherman's hat with a patent leather bill, also navy blue, also emblazoned GR PRODUCTS.

As soon as Axel hit the turn to his office, the new woman jumped to her feet, ran after him, and started in talking. Tick hunched down so he could see between the railings of his porch.

"You're Axel Hagerman, head of Good River Products," she said, as if he didn't already know.

"President and CEO," Axel said, and stuck out his hand. Tick didn't think there was anything wrong with that. She was new to town and Axel was polite to strangers. All the same, he felt the hair prick up on his neck.

She shook his hand, not up and down, but sort of side to side, like his arm was a tiller.

"Nora Montgomery," she said.

So that was her name, or at least what she said. Her ponytail bobbed up and down when she said it, and she reached around to grab her hair.

The way she yanked, it looked like she was trying to stop a runaway horse. That probably would be a good idea, Tick was thinking.

"I've just come in on the ferry," she said. "Got a good view of the logging operation in the old growth this side of the Fairweather Narrows. That outfit is logging too close to the creek." She looked Axel in the eye and he looked at her, and it was like two people bonked heads, you could almost hear it.

"Tick says it's Good River Products running that show," she said, "and maybe you know something about that, being the president and CEO."

Oh god. Tick slumped down behind his railing and buried his face in his hands. Why didn't she keep him out of it?

Axel didn't say anything, but he grew a little taller and stiffer. The hems of his pants lifted off the tops of his shoes.

"There's a pink-salmon run in that stream," she said.

Tick crawled toward his door. He didn't want to see what was going to happen next. Nora raised her voice and lit into Axel again.

"You want fish, you've got to keep deep shade on that water. Warming ocean, they'll need that cool place. And the mud. If you keep cutting those mountainsides, mud's going to suffocate the fish."

Bucked up against his door, Tick groaned. Just on and on, she was explaining it like a professor, like she thought Axel would want to know. She should have had a blackboard, and she could have drawn a bunch of fish floating belly-up with their tongues hanging out and big X's across their eyes. And she could have pointed at them with a long stick, for emphasis.

"And if that salmon run dies off," she said, "what will the seiners do? And who gets the blame?"

Her voice was calm, like a friendly old professor encouraging a stupid student, but it was loud enough to wake the moldering salmon. Tick wished she would shut up. Those aren't the kinds of things you say to a man like Axel.

But Axel just stood there. He stood there in his office clothes, looking at her. The man seemed surprised, and who wouldn't be, yelled at by a woman in town just one week—a week—and they had probably not even said hello more than three times. Crazy, she was saying these things to him—the big, the only, employer in town, living here all his life. That's what Tick would have told her. But Axel didn't say a thing. Not a word.

Instead, Axel turned around, walked down the gangway into his tool-shed, pulled out a chain saw with a forty-eight-inch bar. He grabbed a wedge and maul and his ear protectors and walked up the boardwalk and down the ramp to the Green Cove trail toward Nora's cabin. Nora sort of jumped along after him, still lecturing about fish. Tick snuck along behind, tree to tree, to see what would happen next. Nora's dog, Chum, ran ahead, wagging his tail. That was a dumb dog, if he couldn't sniff the air and know that trouble was coming.

Axel stood there in the forest not ten feet from Nora's cabin and looked all around. That was old stuff in there, three-hundred-year-old spruces and hemlocks. He was eyeballing them, moving around, looking at them with a professional's gaze, tipping his head back to assess the overstory. He picked out a hemlock that must have been three feet across, a couple hundred years old. Carefully, he put his ear-cup hearing protectors on over his cap and adjusted them just right.

"What do you think you are doing? Get away from my cabin."

Good thing Axel couldn't hear Nora anymore, yammering in a voice that got higher and higher. He leaned over and ripped the chainsaw's cord. The motor started on the first pull. That says a lot about a man, when his chain saw starts on the first pull.

Chum took one look at Nora's face and stiffened up. He started growling, way low. Nora grabbed him by the collar. Axel revved a couple of times and pressed the bar against the tree. Blue smoke and wood chips flew out. Nora trotted in circles round the hemlock.

"Stop that."

The chain saw roared in response.

"That's not your tree. Stop right now."

Blat.

"That's a felony. Don't do that. You have no right. What's the matter with you? That's a grandmother tree."

Grandmother tree, oh man. Tick groaned. But Axel acted like he hadn't heard her, which of course, he hadn't, and he just kept working. Chum

lunged and barked. The chain saw snarled. In no time, Axel had carved a
notch a third of the way through the trunk.

Chum threw himself forward with so much force he would have dislo-
cated the shoulder of a lesser woman.

There was nothing for Nora to do but run around shouting. The last
time Tick had ever seen anybody act like that, it was a mother merganser,
and an eagle was rocketing down, talons open. It snatched one chick off
the water, then came back for another one and the next one, until they
were all gone and the mother merganser was circling an empty space on
the bay, whistling soft.

All this time, Axel didn't say a word. He just did his work. Once the
notch was cut, he walked around the tree and made a cut halfway through
the trunk a few inches above the notch.

Finally he turned around, and courteous as a gentleman, he said to
Nora, "If I were you, I would back off."

She shouted, "Like hell! Just stop it. Stop."

But she dragged the dog back a few yards. Axel drove the wedge into
the cut, smacked it one good one, and that tree swayed on its base,
then slowly tipped. It shivered, cracked its length. Picking up speed, it
whomped through the air and slammed onto Nora's trail with a thud that
set her piano humming.

Axel shut off the engine.

The two of them stood there in the sudden quiet, listening to the
piano's trembling chord. They stood there in a gentle rain of pollen and
hemlock needles.

Then Axel brushed the sawdust off his good pants, took off his ear protectors and his cap, swiped his hand over his high forehead, replaced the
cap, straightened his jacket, picked up his chain saw, and walked up the
trail toward his office.

≈≈≈≈

NORA SLUMPED ONTO the stump. "God damn you, Nora," she said quietly.
"What's the matter with you? Why can't you leave it alone?"

Tick couldn't help her there, but oh man, this was trouble. All his working life, Tick had worked for Axel when he had a job to do. He didn't think Axel should have done that, but she shouldn't have chewed him out, and Tick didn't dare take sides.

What Nora didn't know was that there was no future in getting cross-ways with Axel. Tick and Axel had grown up together in this little town, and didn't Tick know. Axel was ten years older than Tick, so he turned into a man and left school when Tick was still learning block letters. But little boys in a one-room school watch the older boys out the side of their eyes.

When Axel was a boy, he lived with old Mr. and Mrs. Hagerman on their fishing boat. It was a steel seiner, but it wasn't fishing because Mr. Hagerman bunged up his back and couldn't do the work. The boat was their house, tied to the dock with rope thicker than a boy's arm and never once untied. On school days, Axel climbed backward off the boat with his lunch box, walked up the gangway, and went to school. Kids would have made fun of Axel, living in a steel box with a straggle-haired woman and a humpback man like in some evil fairy tale, but they were afraid of him. Not because he was big. He wasn't big. He was small and lumpy. But he was tough.

Everybody said Mr. and Mrs. Hagerman weren't Axel's mom and dad, but they took care of him and they probably loved him. Nobody knew Axel's real mom and dad. They were just passing through when he was born, everybody said, and they drowned when he was a newborn baby. Mrs. Hagerman was babysitting Axel then, so she took him in and raised him up. Mrs. Hagerman died before Axel got out of school, and Mr. Hagerman got sent to the Pioneer Home in Sitka. So Axel lived in that cold, steel seiner by himself through the year he was sixteen, but here's the thing.

In that year, he fixed up that old boat, got the diesels running, took apart the winches and pullers, oiled them, and put them back together again, spiffed it all up, painted the decks, mended the nets. And the very month he graduated from school, he hired a crew of grown men, drove an axe blade through the crusted ropes, and went seining for pink salmon. All along, the kid had had a plan. He came back with money in his pocket, and the crew members had money in their pockets, and he started dating the cutest girl in the school, Rebecca Schmidt, who was sixteen too. Then all the boys in the school wanted to work for Axel, including Tick. They cleaned his fish, they cut his logs, they scraped his barnacles off his boats—whatever he had going.

So cleaning up after Axel was nothing new to Tick. And Lord knows there was a dandy cleanup job waiting to be done out at Nora's. He didn't think there would be anything wrong with helping her make that tree into a pile of firewood. But Tick waited until Axel had time to get back in his office. Then he trotted into town the back way, scurried around to his shed to dig out his splitting maul. He picked up his chain saw and a jerry can of gas. He stuck the bar oil in his pocket and rounded up his kids.

All morning, Tick and Nora were out there limbing that tree and bucking it up into rounds. Heavy work with a tree that old, all its years grown tight, layer around layer, a sapling encased in summer winter summer winter like layers of varnish, all those years since the one year when a fleck of a seed blew into the moss on a deadfall's back and the first British man-o'-war explored the dreadful coast—that many years old. Heavy air, fog and sawdust and pollen. Blackflies moved in, and the soft flies they called little bastards.

As Tick worked, he shook his head at Nora and muttered nonstop, "Oh man, aw man, you shouldn't be even breathing ideas like that. It's okay to make a mistake first time you're in town, and you learned a quick lesson, that's for sure. Axel shouldn't of done it, I don't think." The chain saw roared over his words, drowned them in blue smoke. "But you shouldn't of said what you said. No good to come here, just out of the blue, and start a war—especially not with Axel. Nobody's asking me, so I can't say yes or no, good or bad, but it's dangerous to cross Axel, and it's good you learned early. Axel didn't need to do that. Okay. Okay. But you can't even be thinking that I might go against him. I got kids, two kids. I got a wife. I got troubles already, and nobody needs yours. Aw man. You'll have your-self a couple winters' worth of stovewood after it dries, which you were going to have to put by anyway, so maybe Axel did you a favor. If it doesn't start something. Which it probably has," but then the chain saw popped and died, and he fell silent.

Tick tied a thick overhand knot in his beard and tucked it down his shirt. He poured chain saw gas into the tank. He grabbed a beer from

Nora's tote and poured it down his throat. Refueled, the man and the machine roared and mumbled along the tree, dropping rounds, and the piano danced spasmodically, humming away. Teamed up with Tick's older boy, Davy, Nora split the rounds and threw the cordwood into a pile by the back door. Tick's little guy, Tommy, ran around throwing branches into a big burn pile, but then he must have gotten tired of working, because he just ran around.

LILLIAN MARY SHADDY unlaced her sneakers and pushed her stocking feet into old galoshes. She tugged her raincoat on over her apron, flipped off the lights, and stepped out of the Good River Harbor Bath 'n' Bar. She would sit for a while, watch the night come on, let the swelling in her ankles go down, see what she could see. Humming, sometimes letting the words break out, Lillian sat and watched. *And I'll show you a young man with many reasons why, there but for fortune . . .* She pulled a foot out of a boot and rubbed it thoughtfully. *Show me the whiskey stains on the floor.* She wasn't spying on anybody, and she wasn't a gossip. She was definitely not watching for Axel Hagerman, although his house was directly across the boardwalk from the bar. The truth was that when you own the town's only bathhouse and bar, it's your business to keep track of everybody's business. People coming and going in this little town rustle up against each other like the tide, and things get rearranged. Crabs flip on their backs, kelp ties itself in knots, sand fleas snap like sprung springs, and sometimes a stinking murrelet washes in, tangled in fishing line. It's good to keep an eye on a falling tide.

Especially now, with this new woman washed up into town. Already everybody was talking about how she insulted Axel. Poor guy, just trying to make a living. She was trouble. Lillian would reserve judgment until she met her. But that new woman was trouble. Lillian lit a cigarette and held it at arm's length, watching the tip glow in the damp and endless dusk.

And here came Axel Hagerman, home late from the office of Good River Products, Inc. Reaching under her plastic rain hat, Lillian patted her hair into place. She squashed her cigarette out in a pot of blue pansies and twirled it between her fingers to let the last of the tobacco fall onto the soil. Streetlights shone cones of cold light one after another down the boardwalk. As Axel made his way toward home, passing from one light to another, his pale head blinked on and off, marking his progress like landing lights. His shoulders were soft, and his briefcase and lunch pail hung heavy. Under each streetlight, his shadow puddled at his feet.

Lillian flicked open her lighter and drew sharply on a new cigarette.

"Evening," she said.

The unexpected flash on sucked-in cheeks must have startled Axel, because he spun to face her.

"Oh. Evening," he said, and pumped himself straighter.

That's better, Lillian thought. He's a good man.

"How are you, Axel?" she said, smiling smoke.

He paused, as if he were thinking about how he was exactly. Then, without answering, he made a leaning right turn into his gangway and entered the comfort of his house and marriage.

A small wave on the ebbing tide sucked out, took its time to push back into the light thrown from Axel's bedroom window, out and again in. Sucking out, returning, out, and again in, the wave wove a slick rope of kelp, eelgrass, sedge straw, feathers black and torn. The abandoned exoskeleton of a crab rolled end-over-end up and down the beach, losing legs, one after another, water sucking out, pressing in. The water took the crusty legs and offered them back again, carrying them in the line of white foam at the slow lip of the wave. Lillian took her time too, watching the tide, her thoughts fading and returning.

The light went out in Axel's bedroom, and the wave made its way out and in, unseen. Lillian knew these sounds. A tumble of pebbles, down, a flight of pebbles, up. She knew the smells of the evening too—sweet pansies, gooey salt of the rock-wrack, woodsmoke, kerosene lamps, maybe somewhere under the wharf a starfish, dissolved and stinking, maybe a downdraft from mountain snowfields and hemlocks. She breathed them every night. In and out. Now, she heard a woman's soft cry. A man's grunt. Lillian looked up sharply, then turned away. The rhythmic bump and bump, pushing white foam into the dark of it, the cries and the grunts, repeated, repeated.

The lightbulb hanging from a cord over Axel's doorway swung in the rhythm of their lovemaking. Lillian closed her eyes. Axel's wife was giving him a sweet gift tonight, and would you call a man a bad man who takes what is given? The earth gives, man takes. Would you call a man a bad man who takes what mother earth holds out to him in her smooth and stony hand?

THE WIND PICKED UP as night came on, and rain began to fall. Nora flicked on a headlamp and walked onto her porch to watch the squall. Rain came down hard, hitting the alder leaves with such force that they spun on their stems as if they had been slapped. Water rebounded from the alders, from the green platter leaves of the devil's club, from the sword ferns, pinging on the windrows of beer cans left from the party. Wind blew rain hard onto the porch, making tiny craters in the sawdust on Nora's piano.

She did what she could in the storm. Balanced on a round of old hemlock, she drove nails into the beams of the porch roof. There was the devil to pay in that wind, to get the grommets of the blue tarp hung up on the nails, and get the nails hammered flat. The tarp worked hard against her, thundering in the gusts, wrapping around her body until she was soaked to the skin. She chased a bottom corner of the tarp, pulled it tight to the edge of the porch floor, and nailed it down. The tarp slapped and billowed like a loose jib. She grabbed the other corner. Once that was nailed down, the tarp was trimmed neat into the wind and she had created a blue shelter for the piano. Noisy in there, though—the drubbing rain and thrashing wind. Nora dragged the hemlock round over to the piano and sat there, warming her hands in her armpits.

She wanted to play. She wanted to be back in her cabin in the hills above Bellingham, practicing the piano, even if the logging trucks sprayed mud on her window as they carried heavy loads down to the mill, even if their jack-brakes brayed with contempt. She wanted to be backstage with that excitement in her stomach and, in her ears, the song of every instrument in the orchestra converging on A. But there was no going back.

Nora shook out her hands. Was it possible that, in the noise of this storm, she could risk it? Who would hear her? She experimentally played an A-minor chord. It frightened her, the sound of it. There was safety in silence. She knew this, and she wouldn't shed tears over it. Lord knows, the piano was wet enough. She had left herself no choice. Whatever life she lived now would be lived like music—as dependent on discord as it is on concord—finding the energy of it, its beauty, in waves of tension and release, regret and grace, loneliness and . . . and what? Doesn't everything yearn to be called back in? Doesn't everyone long to be part of some whole, some home? She lifted her hands over the keyboard.

If a man had walked through the rain into Nora's clearing that night, all he would have heard was rain popping on alder leaves. All he would have smelled was broken hemlock. He would have been puzzled to see a soft blue glow from Nora's porch and in that glow, the silhouette of a seated woman whose hands flew over the keyboard, suspended in space like angels, making no sound at all.

June 25

HIGH TIDE		LOW TIDE	
0.10 am	16.7	6:44 am	-1.2
1:16 pm	14.3	6:51 pm	3.2

The drone of the outboard motor echoed over the Kis'utch clamflats on the far side of the inlet, as Davy aimed his dad's skiff toward the shore. When he killed the engine, the uproar of the waterfall grew loud again, then came the grind of his hull on gravel as his boat kissed the flat.

"Hey-up," Davy hollered, as he stepped onto the sandflat. He was only a fifteen-year-old kid, but he knew you've got to be polite to a brown bear, let it know you're coming. And you can't just sing out a one-note "hey-up," because your voice might be tuned to the river or the wind, and a bear won't hear it. You've got to pitch it low and squeal up the whole octave, like calling a pig. "Hey-yuuup." And Davy knew not to say, "Hi Bear" or "Bear-anything," because if the bear thinks you're calling it, it will probably come. Bears are very polite.

"No reason to be afraid of bears, as long as you're respectful," Davy told Nora. He held the boat steady as she reached out one long leg, then the other. "Don't want to scare you, but I don't want to lead you into a bear either." That would be a bad start to his new career as a wilderness guide.

When you split wood together all afternoon, lifting that maul over your head and cracking it down maybe ten thousand times each in that stuttery syncopated duet, you get to know a person, and by the time Davy and Nora had split Axel's tree into firewood, they were buddies. He said he would take her to the best place in the whole world, the place across the inlet where the Kis'utch River falls down the mountain into the little pool. A place where the pink salmon come home to spawn. The most beautiful place in the whole world, he told her, a place his mom said was sacred, but he didn't know about that. Nora said she wanted very much to see such a place. So she hired him as a wilderness guide, twenty dollars a day.

"I never guided," he said, "but I've been across the inlet a million times, goose hunting, clamming, whatever, so I'm your man."

"Yep," said Nora, "you're my man." She was nice. "And five dollars extra for boat gas."

"We'll take my dad's skiff, not his landing craft. No point in using all the gas it takes to push that barge around. And we need to go on a rising tide," he told her, "so we don't strand the boat." He wasn't sure how much Nora already knew about boats and water, because sometimes Outsiders can be super dumb.

"You're the expert," Nora had said.

Davy was big Tick McIver and Annie Klawon's boy, born and bred in Good River Harbor. He got his mom's straight black hair, which relieved him, since the alternative was his dad's flaming orange. He'd been growing it long, but so far, his hair only got down to about his chin. To keep it out of his eyes, he walked with his head turned about twenty degrees off-course, and he spent a lot of time throwing hair out of his face by jerking his head. Davy was a lanky kid—legs grown faster than his brain, his dad said, and he better slow down growing and let his brain catch up. One of his dad's dumb jokes.

Davy went to school at the Good River Harbor School, where there were two other people in his grade—Axel's daughter Meredith, who was smart and beautiful, and Curtis Daley, who was a jerk. The food Davy ate came from Good River Harbor or it came in on the barge. So he was made of the Kis'utch country—hot and salty goose breast and clam fritters and thimbleberry jam. Of course, he had seen snowstorms in his years and once drought in the summer, and smoky air. But except for those, most days were cloudy and cool—fifty-five maybe, which was two degrees warmer than the Japan Current that followed the coast. Whether he was walking on the boardwalk or sitting in school, he was always on the water, or at least the water was always underneath him, as much as if he were in a boat. And even though he had worn a raincoat and rubber boots most every day of his life, he was often wet, because the Kis'utch Mountains were the first place the winds made landfall after they crossed the Pacific, and that meant rain. So Davy was made of the Kis'utch that way too—wet and made of water, like a jellyfish.

By the time he was five, he could tell the burrow of a geoduck from a butter clam's by the shape of its hole in the sand, and the difference between a merganser and a loon by the speed of its wings. When he was ten, he was strong enough on the pull cord to start an outboard motor. When he was eleven, he could sometimes get a chain saw going, although chainsaws are tricky. When he was twelve, he shot his first deer. When he was fourteen, he rode on a bus in Seattle with his mom. And the next great event, at age fifteen: his first paying job as a wilderness guide for Nora Montgomery.

While Davy was tilting up the engine, Nora grabbed the anchor, carried it up the mudflat and dropped it behind a log. She had on her yellow raincoat and Davy's hip boots. They smucked into the mud, but that didn't slow her down. Clams squirted in front of her, high as her shoulders, which were high. Every time a clam squirted, Nora laughed. That turned out to be a lot of laughing. She waded into the middle channel of the river and stood there, her arms raised, her face to the sky. Everything was shining from the rain—the mudslicks, the stranded kelp, her raincoat, even Nora's broad cheeks, holding up her big shiny eyes and big shiny smile. Davy stared at her, wondering.

She breathed in noisily.

"Smell the rock-wrack, Davy," she said. "Smell the salt and the cedar."

She made Davy nervous, standing in the creek. It's slippery on algae. Davy thought he should warn her, maybe say something like, "Be careful here, Nora." He practiced in his mind, and then he said it, "Be careful here Nora." But she was out of the river and walking up the mudflat toward the beach rye at the high-tide line. She spooked three eagles off a stranded log and stopped to watch them fly. Davy was glad she stopped, because if eagles were waiting there for the salmon, so were bears.

"Hey-uuuuup," he shouted, and listened for anything moving in the bush.

They followed a bear trail through the beach rye. Bears walk in the same track forever, so they make a good trail, about a foot wide, a foot deep. Davy knew he should be singing. His mom said, "Always be singing." But he wasn't sure which would be more embarrassing—a wilderness guide singing at the top of his lungs or his client surprising a bear. Davy showed

Nora the indentations where bears stepped in their own footprints, going upstream and downstream all their lives.

"Sort of like me," he said, "walking up and down the same boardwalk all my life."

"Be glad for that," she told him. "Could be lots worse." Nora poked with her toe at a pile of bear droppings.

"Sedge," he said. "That's a hungry bear, impatient for the salmon, probably angry at the wait."

"I come on the sloop John B," Davy sang out. "My grandfather and me." Probably it's okay for a wilderness guide to sing, he decided, if it's sort of a manly song, like his dad sings, not like his mom.

They came out of the grass onto the gravel bank where Davy's mom picks beach peas. There's a dike made out of river stones that goes almost across the river.

"An old fish weir. That's wonderful," Nora whispered, and she knelt on the rocks. "How old?"

Davy never could understand why people would whisper in bear country. Here he was, trying to make as much noise as he could, and she was whispering. And actually, Davy didn't know how old the weir was.

"Ten thousand years," he said.

His mom had told him the People made the weir, piling on cobbles and building the weir back up whenever a flood washed it out. Jimmy Pete fished it every year until he died, but that was before Davy was born. He fished on the pink-salmon tide, when the high tide floods over the weir, bringing salmon. Then the ebb tide leaks out between the stones, trapping the fish. Jimmy Pete gathered them in baskets and took them to town. Davy's dad remembered getting fish from Jimmy Pete.

Before long, they lost the bear trail in a mess of corn lilies and cow parsnip higher than Davy's head. Nora moved fast, but following her was easy as tracking a bear. He could see the bush moving around her, and she left a big fat trail of crushed plants and that sharp smell of the broken parsnips. She should stay closer.

"Round Nassau Town we did roam, drinkin' all night."

They waded through the meadow, back into the thimbleberries and blind turns. They hardly got back into the bush before they walked right onto a clearing where bears had chewed out the skunk cabbage roots, battering them into the muck, and scuffed up the parsnips.

"Bear kitchen," he told her. "Got into a fight. Oh, I feel so broke up."

In a few more steps, they burst through the last of the parsnip's stickery stink-smelling leaves and swarming white petals onto a muskeg filled with wildflowers. Nora leaned to cup a spiky blue flower in her palm.

"That's jelch-tache," Davy said. "It means 'raven's odor.' Smell it."

"Smells like an onion," she said, but Davy knew ravens didn't smell like onions, that's for sure.

"They smell like crap and armpits."

Nora guffawed. "I didn't know that," and she skied down the muddy bank and started walking up the river, with Davy following along behind.

Around the next curve, Nora stopped short. There, in front of her, was the side of the mountain, a glistening green wall of ferns and moss-covered rocks. The Kis'utch River dropped through them, combed into a thousand silver threads. Where the water came to earth, it changed from silver into lavender bubbles that dove into a black pool draped with lady ferns. The light was dim and green, latticed with hemlock, saturated with the splash of the stream. Water eddied through the pool, there, cold and clear, and flowed through a freestone pond where the salmon came to spawn.

The current pushed against Nora's boots. Rain dripped off the bill of her cap. Davy walked up beside her and flicked his hair out of his face. She was quiet for so long, Davy thought maybe she didn't like it. When she did talk, he could hardly hear her, it was so noisy by the waterfall. But he won't forget what she said, because she was crying and it didn't make any sense.

What she said was, "Maybe I'm finally home too." Then she reached over and hugged him by the neck and rumpled his hair, like he'd seen her do to her dog. He thought it probably made her dog happier than it made him.

They were following their track back through the corn lilies, almost to the weir, when they heard the grumble of an engine. Davy jerked his head up, listening, and pulled the hair out of his eyes. Nora crouched like a wary raven. Now Davy could see the plane and he was really surprised, because it was Charlie's charter, and Charlie watches the weather. He wouldn't be bringing a plane under a ceiling this low unless it was really important to somebody. Davy listened as Charlie brought the floatplane over the tide-flat, took a hard turn upriver, and flew straight toward Jimmy Pete's weir. Davy ducked without thinking, the plane was that low. It throttled down and kept on course. When he was starting to think Charlie was going to hit the waterfall, the plane banked hard and flew out over the inlet, buzzing them again on the way out. Davy could tell from the engine noise that Charlie was bringing it into the mouth of the river. He hoped Charlie saw the anchor line on his skiff.

Davy listened for the slapslapslap as the plane landed, the falling pitch of the engine, the rev when the plane taxied toward shore. It was quiet then.

"I don't know," he answered, although Nora hadn't asked the question. "Either this is a rich tourist or it's Axel—the only people with enough money to charter a plane."

He looked toward Nora, but she wasn't there.

≋≋≋

SHE WASN'T HARD to track, but he pushed through a lot of devil's club and elderberry before Davy found Nora, crouched under the low, sweeping arms of a hemlock. She'd taken off her yellow raincoat and was sitting on it with her knees in the air. For once, she was not grinning.

"Okay, wilderness guide," she said before he could ask a single question. "Find me the back way out of here."

He led her away from the river, up a blueberry slope into an open spruce forest carpeted in moss. Once they had angled so far that they could no longer hear the river, he circled them back around and broke trail through tangled alder, crawling over windfall, placing their boots carefully on musky duff mined with squirrel dens. Whenever he called out for bears, she shushed him. They were weaving now under cover of alders toward the soft rustling sound of the sea and its bright smell. That's when he felt he could finally ask her what they were running from. But what came out of Davy's mouth was not a question.

"Shit," he said. He swiveled to face into an onrushing noise—a galloping horse, a war drum, a falling cedar, tearing branches off all the trees in its path, the thudding vibration of the hollow duff, and Davy could see the bear, thundering straight at them, slapping away willows the way a skiff slaps waves.

"HEY-UUUUP," Davy shouted. He flapped his arms over his head.

To Nora, "Come close to me, spread your jacket, make yourself big, stand your ground."

And to the bear, "HEY, HEY, HEY."

The bear was so close, Davy could see rims of white around his eyes. He could hear him pant.

"Back away slowly," Davy muttered, and took a first slow step back as the bear charged. Davy tripped on a log and fell flat on his backside.

That's how they were, as the bear pounded past them and disappeared into the brush—Davy sitting stupid on the ground, Nora standing beside him flapping her jacket like the wing nubbins of a nestling crow.

After that, they stayed just inside the screen of alders where the forest gave way to the beach, moving now toward the sound of the river. They were climbing on broken mussel shells across a rock outcrop when they heard a man's voice.

Axel. It's not a hard voice to recognize, kind of sharp around the edges. Davy didn't know if he was doing something wrong or something Axel would think was bad. He didn't even know what he was supposed to be afraid of. But he knew he didn't want Axel to catch him out there guiding for Nora. He couldn't think of anything wrong with guiding Nora, whoever she was, but if there was anything wrong with it, Axel would figure it out. Axel did that, figure things out that are bad. This was a worry, especially if your dad wanted to work for him. And especially if you were a dumb kid secretly in love with Axel's smart and beautiful daughter.

Davy looked out from behind the curtain of leaves. There were two men on the beach, talking. Charlie was standing on the float of his seaplane anchored at the mouth of the river, right next to Davy's boat.

"We're not going anywhere," Davy said.

Nora considered. "You're going to have to go talk to those guys. Find out who they are and what they want. If they're okay, just signal me and I'll come. If they're not, then launch your boat and come get me at the end of the beach."

"Okay about what, Nora?" Davy didn't know why he was suddenly frightened. "What's going on?"

≋≋≋

AXEL DIDN'T SEEM a bit surprised to see Davy, and why would he be surprised, with Davy's skiff anchored right there on the beach. Axel had on his good pants, stuck into the tops of his XtraTufs, and his slick jacket with the zipper pockets to hold his cash, and the same old GR Products watchman's cap. He was about the only guy without a beard in Good River Harbor. In fact, he didn't seem to have any hair at all, any more than a melted candle has hair. Davy's dad said he was the only guy without a beer gut too, and you can't trust a guy who's gutless—another one of his dad's bad jokes.

But Davy didn't feel like laughing. He felt sick.

"What are you doing here, Davy?" said Axel, as if there was something wrong with that.

"Guiding," said Davy, and just about fainted with horror at what he'd said. Because, sure enough, Axel said back, "Guiding who?"

Davy looked around wildly.

"Nobody, I guess," he said.

There was a man with Axel. "Best kind of client," he said. But then he was off and talking.

"Hey, you should have been here a little while ago. Came on a huge bear. Man, did we ever scare it. Said, 'Boo,' and the big guy hightailed it out of here, like he was shot from a cannon. Probably didn't stop running for a mile. Guess he knows who's in charge." And the man began to chuckle, heh heh heh heh, with a sound like an outboard running out of gas.

Davy looked at the man closely. He was nobody he had ever seen before. With short gray hair, tight skin, big ears, the guy's head was a dog's head, smooth and long and gray. He was carrying a daypack and a big surveyor's tape, and he had on XtraTufs, but here's what threw Davy. The guy was wearing a white office shirt, the kind he'd seen in advertisements for photocopiers, and he had on a long diagonally striped tie. Davy stared. It's the first tie he had ever seen in real life. Once he'd seen a tourist in a

bow tie, but not like this. Just above his pocket the shirt said, FOWLER'S SUR-
VEYORS. The guy's sleeves were rolled up, and the hair on his forearms was
the same gray dog's hair.

"This is Davy McIver, from Good River Harbor," Axel said, and Davy
wondered how Axel could make a guy's own name sound like a knife in
the leg.

"Meet Howard Fowler, a surveyor from Seattle. Got him on a project
here."

"Jesus Christ," said Howard Fowler.

He was staring up the beach. They all turned to look.

The bear stood broadside on a thick drift-log, not thirty yards away.
His back was arched and the rough fur on his shoulders flared, a bear of
monstrous size. He swung his immense head side to side, slinging strings
of drool. The sound he made was the exhalation of a coming storm, that
low and elemental, huffing with unmistakable menace.

"Jeezus Kee-rist," Fowler repeated himself.

"I am lord of this beach and all its salmon and sows," Davy translated
in a low voice, as he backed slowly away. "I am the biggest bear and the
baddest bear, and you are peewees. Get out of here before I get mad."

"Looks like that bear changed his mind about who's in charge," Axel
observed.

Howard Fowler stripped off his pack and started rummaging around.

"Got bear spray and flares." Must have been under his raincoat there,
somewhere, not there by the water bottle. He unzipped another pocket.
Not there.

"Jeezus. Jeezus. Jeezus."

"Forget it, Fowler," Axel growled. "Come in close to us and back away."

Shoulder to shoulder, they drew away, backing carefully over a tangle
of kelp, backing carefully over a sand shingle pocked with clam-siphon
holes, backing through a patch of sea asparagus, and then stepping carefully into the river. They pivoted like a marching band and waded downstream. The current slid off their boots, eddying behind them, as they
stepped over the algae-pinked rocks and sea urchins to the mouth of the
creek. Howard lofted himself into the floatplane, Axel climbed in after
him, and Charlie flew them back to town.

≈≈≈≈≈

NORA LEANED BACK in the bow-seat with both arms hanging over the gunwales and her big boots propped on the front bench seat. "Jeezus. Jeezus. Jeezus," she squeaked again, her face split by a great big grin. She sure was cheery, now she knew there was nothing to be afraid of. The boat puttered back toward Good River Harbor. "Those two guys flailing out to their hips to get in the seaplane, and flopping like salmon onto the floats."

Davy wasn't laughing. Tucked neatly behind a log on the Kis'utch beach was the anchor from his dad's boat. He'd had to cast off the anchor line and leave the anchor there, rather than walk back up that bear's beach to fetch it.

Davy dropped his voice into Tick's growl. "*If you're old enough to use my equipment, you're old enough to take care of it.* My dad has only said that about twenty thousand times." His head drooped behind a screen of black hair.

"Hey, wilderness guide," Nora said, sitting up to swack his shoulder. "You did a darned good job showing me the wildlife, finding us a route. You're a pro."

"Should of known the salmon were coming in. Should of known that old bear would be back to play king of the mountain." He tossed his hair out of his face. "But Nora, what were you so afraid of on that seaplane?"

She grinned. "Nothing, turns out. Nothing at all."

Davy slowed the skiff, giving his mind time to work, but for all the extra time, it didn't get much done. So he said, "Tide's high, flooding up under the houses. We could float right up under there. Guides do this in Seattle," he said, perking up. "Put rich tourists on a boat and tour the town."

The putter of the outboard echoed in the sudden dark under the library, and the smell of seaweed and creosote floated thick on black water. There was a constant pock and patter as moisture dropped from the stringers. Metal plates dripped stalagmites of murky minerals and salt. Davy and Nora raised their hoods. He gave her a good tour, steering in and out under the pilings all the way to the end of town, where the docks gave way to a rocky cliff and a boulder beach. That's where the old cannery used to be, but the site had been abandoned for years.

Nothing remained of the cannery but a couple of pilings and a big cedar water tank on a ledge halfway up the cliff. That's where they stored rainwater for the fish processing—a round, above-ground cistern sort of thing, thirty feet across easy, probably fifteen feet high. People in Good River Harbor were proud of the tank, a work of art, they said, made out of cedar staves bound with steel rods, like an enormous barrel. Tight enough to hold water, still tight after all these years. It used to have a pointed roof like a Chinaman's hat, but that blew off ages ago. Then moss grew on the rim of the tank and black stains ran down the edges of the staves. A tiny rivulet dripped from a pipe into the top of the tank, and another pipe leaked water out the bottom. There was a wooden floor, Davy knew, but it was covered deep in spruce needles and duff.

Curtis was over there throwing rocks at the empty tank. Idling just offshore, Davy yelled hey but said he couldn't come throw rocks because he was working as a guide. Then he cut the engine and they just floated.

"The stones bonking against the cistern sound just like the mallet hitting a wooden temple bell," Nora said.

Another rock bounced off the wall. The tank clonked. A raven answered, clonk. "Bull's-eye," shouted dumb Curtis.

"Funny, my mom talks about bells too. 'When it's quiet, you can hear the Earth ring.' That's what she said."

Nora stared at him.

"That was a long time ago when she said that, after I told her how empty our house is when she's off in Seattle, and how quiet it is at night. Listen, she said, because the Earth rings like a bell. But maybe not like a cistern. I don't know.

"But wooee, that cistern isn't going to be empty for long. Axel still owns the cannery site, so he can do whatever he wants there."

"What now?" Nora slumped in the bow.

"My secret girlfriend, Meredith, said that Axel was going to let her mom make the tank into a little community garden—a walled garden with its own little creek flowing through it. Whoever wants to, can grow things there, even high school kids. No deer, no slugs, but piles of flowers or kale, rhubarb, whatever.

"See, that's the kind of person Meredith is," Davy told Nora. "She shares." And he was off—nothing can stop a man from talking about the woman he loves, while his skiff drifts under a rotting wharf and pivots on a pile of floating kelp.

"Like when the teacher decided to teach us justice. Mrs. Brenner had this big chocolate bar—huge. And she said one person would get the chocolate, but the class had to decide who would get it and then why, and no fair avoiding the problem by just dividing it up. So we were stumped."

"Mmm," Nora agreed.

"Finally that jerk Curtis grabbed it, said he gets it because he's hungriest, but we made him give it back. Then we just sat there, looking at the candy and being mad at Mrs. Brenner for setting us up, wishing she would just take her dumb chocolate and go away. Meredith was pretty sad, but all of a sudden, she says, 'Give the candy to me.' Curtis is like, 'What? Your dad's rich. You can get candy whenever you want.' But Meredith is all 'No, no, give it to me. I want it,' and she took it. She said, 'It's mine now, right? And I can do whatever I want with it, right?' That was right. So she unwrapped it, divided it into parts, and gave us all chocolate."

Davy grinned. "See what I mean? She's so nice."

Nora stared at Davy with her mouth gaping. "Davy!" she barked. "Think! How did she get the candy in the first place?" But then she clamped her mouth shut tight as a cod.

"And smart," he added, smiling to himself. "And beautiful."

He yanked the cord on the outboard and steered the boat under the houses and the clanking old Quonset hut. He told her, "That's my house," and showed her the window to his and Tommy's bedroom, tacked on and stuck up on pilings.

"That's wonderful," she said. "Like the crew's quarters on a boat."

"If so, that boat's kind of washed up on the rocks and stove in," he said, and then he was ashamed. But in fact, Davy wasn't altogether sure the town makes a good impression when you see it from below like that. It's sort of an embarrassment, poking around under the buildings, like looking up somebody's skirt. All the pilings are crappy with barnacles and blue mussels, with popweed caught up in them and scraps of line, and there's seaweed dripping off the cross-bracing. Everybody hangs junk there, not just Tick's family—crab pots they're going to fix up and broken oars. Davy wished his dad would get rid of the bike that's been hanging off their back porch for a hundred years, all rusted and the tires rotting off. Tick said he might make something of it, but he said that about everything.

"I've been here all my life," Davy told Nora. "I walk up to my door on the boardwalk, step over that pile of stovewood and the tote with all the boots and halibut jigs, and I'm home. There's the table with the red-checked plastic tablecloth. There's Tommy and Dad. There's never any question. Summer's summer. Winter's dark. School or not school. It's just where I am. I wonder what it's like to be away from home, or even not to know where home is."

Nora didn't answer. Maybe she hadn't heard him, or maybe she was wondering too. So Davy ran her in and out of the docks, right up under the bows of the big boats. The seiners were in, with the guys winching up their nets, coiling the lines, checking for rips. They're all going someplace—into harbor, onto the fishing ground, back out again. But still, they know where their home harbor is. They've got it written on their transom, in case they need to check. But most of the boats at the docks weren't going anywhere. They just sat there under blue tarps, riding lower and lower in the water. Because somebody's going to fix them up sometime and sail somewhere. But why would you? Where else would you go?

All the way out to Nora's cabin on Green Point, there was only the grinding of the outboard. Davy wanted to ask Nora where she came from, but she talked over him, kind of absentminded.

"I'm glad for you, that you have a place," she said. "This spring, I put my piano on the ferry and made myself a promise. Where I go next, I'm staying. The weight of this piano is the only anchor I'll ever have. I'm going to haul this piano up over rocks somewhere, get it fouled in some place I'll never get it out of, and then figure a way to stay. I just want to lead a normal life."

Something about that last sentence came out sort of wet.

Davy cringed. He was going to get in bad enough trouble because he'd left his dad's anchor on the beach. But he didn't do it on purpose; the bear made him do it. He would be doomed if he fouled an anchor on purpose. But he hoped Nora stayed. She was nice. Weird, but nice. So was Chum.

"What are you going to do for money?" he asked her.

"I don't need much money. Sometimes I write stuff for cruise ship pamphlets or ferries. Little pieces about bears or salmon, that kind of thing."

"Well, then, why didn't you just stay home where you were?"

Nora took off her baseball cap, caught up her hair in a ponytail, put back on the cap, pulled her hair through the hole, pulled it to both sides to tighten it all up, tugged down on the brim.

"Do you know what it means to burn your bridges?"

"Sure." Did she think he was an idiot?

"That's what I did."

"Oh jeez," he said. He'd have to run away from home too, if he set fire to a bridge.

"Jeezus. Jeezus. Jeezus," Nora said, and grinned.

HIGH TIDE OR low, hungry or not, but usually hungry, the father and sons of the McIver family always ate dinner at 6:30 p.m. Alaska time—big Tick, and Davy and Tommy—in a tiny kitchen propped on pilings. In her rented room in Seattle, the boys' mother, Annie Klawon, always ate at 7:30 p.m. Pacific time, which is the same time. That way the whole family sat down together for supper, even though Annie had to live in Seattle to work at that insurance place. It holds families together, she always said, to have supper together. Davy once told his mom he didn't know if that counted as "together," with them in Good River Harbor and her being a secretary in Seattle. That made her cry, but she said they had to do it just in case it worked. There's lots of things you do, she said, just in case they work.

Supper for the Good River Harbor McIvers that night was potatoes and venison. Tick tucked his great beard into his collar to keep from setting himself on fire, put on massive mitts, and fished the potatoes and Dutch oven out of the woodstove. They waited just a minute to make sure their mom was seated, then they held hands round the table, little Tommy grabbing however much of Tick's hand he could hold in one of his.

"It's good to be together again," they said in unison. It was a prayer, it was a blessing, it was gratitude, it was relief to count noses at the end of the day and find them all accounted for. Bigger than hope, it was faith in the strength of the circle, the cycle of coming and going and always returning, it was the magic fact that a circle has no end.

"Cha cha cha," Davy taunted, as he always did, to make up for holding hands with his dad and little brother.

They set to.

At 6:45 Alaska time, they were full and the pot was empty.

"Okay, you guys do the dishes," said Tick, which was not that big a deal—a rinse with hot water from the teakettle and a good rub on a towel. "I'm gonna go work on the boat, clean it up for when your mom comes home." He pulled out his beard, gave it a flap, and angled his mass out the kitchen door.

"I'm going to work on the boat" meant "I'm heading to Lillian's," which meant that Davy had to stay home and put Tommy to bed. Six years old, and he wouldn't go to sleep unless somebody lay down beside him—usually Davy. Then, when Tommy fell asleep, Davy had to get up without creaking the bed or bumping his head on the upper bunk, which was where he slept. When it was blowing and the waves broke on the pilings under their room, Davy sometimes fell asleep too and didn't wake up until dark. But he wouldn't fall asleep that night, because he had a lot to think about, especially how he would advertise his wilderness guide business, which had already earned twenty dollars in one day, plus gas money.

Davy tucked the blankets around Tommy's shoulders, like his mom did, and lay down beside his little brother. Pretty soon, their mom would be singing them a song, back in Seattle. Tommy lay still to hear her voice, which he sometimes said he could. Davy, on the other hand, knew it was just the wind in the long lines on the boats, but it would be cruel to say that to Tommy. And anyway, sometimes Davy thought he could hear her too, her singing, even sometimes the words maybe.

He listened with Tommy. At calm dusk, he heard the snick of tide through eelgrass and the hum of a skiff far away and vanishing. In the forest, varied thrushes whistled. So softly the sound came through the woods, it was the silver whisper of Tommy breathing as he slept. From across the channel, the Kis'utch falls murmured like a nursing bear. Now and then a raven clonked. The tide licked a last few pebbles and quietly fell into its own bed.

After Annie Klawon's song was finished, Davy told her about his day, about how Nora gave him a twenty-dollar bill and a five-dollar bill. Or if he didn't tell her, at least he thought hard in his mom's direction, knowing that she turned her face to the north each night and listened. It wasn't really telling her about his day, he was old enough to know, but who else would he tell?

When Tommy cried out in his sleep, Davy reached over to put a hand on his back like his mom did, just the weight of it, so Tommy would know he wasn't adrift. Low tide was breathing whispery now, all the slips and sighs. A moving tide was splashy as a river. A high tide was so still that if you listened, maybe you could hear the vibration of the sea, a shimmering that was almost sound. A low tide was as quiet as it could make itself, pretending to be asleep. Davy listened, but what he heard was men laughing over at Lillian's.

June 26

HIGH TIDE		LOW TIDE	
0:52 am	16.9 ft	7:25 am	-1.6
1:57 pm	14.7 ft	7:33 pm	3.0

For every flood tide, there is an ebb. This Lillian knew. For every pebble beach concealed, there is a mussel bed revealed. For every taking, there must be a giving. This is the way of the world.

The flood-tide was ebbing when Lillian propped open the door of the Good River Harbor Bath 'n' Bar and lit up the open sign. Drawn by alcohol's own gravitational force, or maybe just by habit or boredom, or by the sucking force of loneliness, men began to move in her direction. Lillian watched them come. Four fishermen on a seiner hung rubber overalls by their suspenders on the wall of the pilothouse and strode up the wharf. "I'm heading to the harbor," big Tick called to his boys. He shoved a screwdriver and a Vise-Grip into his capacious back pocket and walked down to his boat. He glared at it, then turned around and walked the gangway toward Lillian's. Gunkholers on the party deck of the sailing vessel Penury drained their martini glasses and headed for the bar. To get there, they all walked past the gangway that led to the cabin of a man named Kenny Isaacson, who would soon be showing signs of thirst.

≋≋≋

"GETTING ON TIME for a drink," Kenny informed Ranger. He spun his wheel-chair toward the door.

Ranger trotted ahead of him and nosed into the streak of light on the doorsill.

"You thirsty yellow dog," Kenny said, and gave Ranger a fond swat on the rear end. Kenny tugged a pine-squirrel fur hat down over his ears, ran his hand over the braids on his chin, pulled on leather fingerless gloves, and they were ready to go.

Kenny had shown up in town about twenty-five years before. Nobody knew where he'd come from, or what he was all about. Not even Lillian knew, although she had ventured to ask him more than once. He moved into a broken-down cabin right there on the boardwalk, and after a while, he was just part of the town—a sort of sullen and fierce part of town. Townspeople tolerated him, even though they might have been a little put off by his manner and his fur hats. But the little boys worshipped him. He taught them to tie a dental-floss noose around the neck of a horsefly and take it for a walk, like a flying dog. He taught the kids to set miniature snares to catch mice and mink, and when they did, he made the skins into hats and wore them every day. They loved him the way little boys love belches, although they were afraid of him, and they followed him at a distance like blackflies follow the smell of sweat.

And tourists loved Kenny, even though they pretended not to see him. He was a tourist attraction all right, sitting there scowling in a wheelchair. He flew an American flag from the back of his chair and a rainbow whirligig off the armrest. Rain or shine, he wore a camouflage poncho and those ridiculous fur hats, and if that wasn't a sight—a guy in a housemouse hat with tails hanging down beside each ear. He braided his chinhair into tight little braids with rubber bands to hold the bitter ends. Lillian had told him a hundred times, "Just shave. Is that so hard? What are you hiding back there under the bullrushes? You're a handsome guy, got a good jaw and nice skin, like a rock-face after a landslide, storm-polished like that, but who can see you under that hat?"

"Har," he always said, as if he were some kind of pirate, and that's the backstory the little boys gave him, that he was a fierce pirate—maybe even Jack Sparrow—who marauded over the seven seas until he got his legs cracked by cannon fire from a British man-o'-war and had to come to Good River Harbor, wearing a disguise that fooled no one. Little boys know things like that.

When he wheeled down his pier onto the boardwalk, men were roaming around the door to Lillian's Bath 'n' Bar like dogs on the scent. Even over the rumble of his wheels, Kenny could hear them yapping. With his arms crossed over his orange beard, big Tick was leaning against Lillian's chalkboard menu. His huge denim shirt erased more of the menu every time he disagreed with somebody. Already he was down to ish *and* chips. Another argument, and there'd be nothing left to eat but ips.

"Har."

"Mighty fine weather," Tick shouted. He leaned over to scratch the sweet spot between Ranger's ears.

Weather wasn't as crappy as it usually was—Kenny agreed with Tick about that—rain finally letting up, sun rolling sideways along the mountains. The guys had apparently been down to see the pile of sawdust and stovewood at the new woman Nora's cabin. That mess was all they could talk about.

"D'ya see that huge hemlock Axel felled?" Tick shouted, and dropped a big hand on Kenny's shoulder. Kenny could never figure out why people think that if you can't walk, you probably can't hear.

"Nah," Kenny shouted back. "But I don't have to see bear shit to know it's there—and it sounds like that Nora woman has made a steaming hell of a pile."

But they stopped talking and got real interested in the clouds, because along came Nora. She was wearing her yellow raincoat and jeans with some kind of tool stuck in her back pocket. Trotting along behind was her dog, Chum.

Kenny called in Ranger. The dog backed up and sat by Kenny's wheel, thumping his stump-tail.

"Don't need any dry-humping today," Kenny warned him. Ranger thumped even harder.

Kenny studied Nora's dog. Chum seemed like a good dog, an overgrown shepherd maybe mixed up with some golden retriever, and that was one point for Nora—that she had a good big dog. Chum ran up to Tick and the rest of the rabble. They all reached down to pat him and scratch him behind the ears. Then he ran back to Nora. He pushed his nose between her legs and shoved his way through, rubbing against her jeans. He ran around and nuzzled in again, pressing his shoulders into her legs and whining until she spread her knees. Nora laughed, leaning over him, rubbing her knuckles into his ribs, fluffing his backside, telling him how much she loved him.

"Tick, look at me," Kenny demanded. "Tell me if my eyes are bugging out like I got smacked on the back of the head with a two-by-four."

Tick's cheeks flushed as bright as his beard. Chum pushed between Nora's thighs again. She sat on his back while he squirmed through and came around to lick her mouth. Kenny grimaced. He could see all those guys trying not to lick their own chops, no different from dogs. Kenny and Ranger followed Nora into the bar and soon enough, Chum wandered in too, and so did Tick, and the half-pint town dog everybody called Lucky, because she was the luckiest Chihuahua that ever decided to chase a bear out of town.

Everybody stopped at the door to pry off their XtraTufs. Lillian insisted on this. Hers wasn't any ordinary bar. It was a bath-and-bar, a place of cleanliness and worth. Brown boots lined up as close to the wall as teenage boys on a dance floor. Everybody hung their raincoats on hooks by the woodstove.

A couple of gunkholer-tourists crowded in, laughing too loud, tripping over Lucky. "Oops. Sorry." Kenny cut his wheels in front of them and growled in their general direction. Just because they own a fancy sailboat doesn't mean they own the place. Kenny could do without tourists, because he didn't like being a tourist attraction himself. There were plenty of nice little houses on the boardwalk, but his was the one they wanted a picture of. Kenny thought that was perverse, being singled out because you're broken down. His cabin was the original—adze-squared spruce logs, fishtail joints, glacier clay in the cracks, fireweed blooming in the gutter, moss on the roof. The door was sort of askew because the front beam gave way, but who needs a square door as long as it opens?

Kenny made his cabin nice, sticking stuff in the window boxes, like plastic flowers and pinwheels, an eagle feather, whatever. Some of the tourists stole his decorations, and some put new things in. A Cleveland Indians pennant showed up one week. But it burned Kenny's butt when some kids on an eco-cruise stole his SOLITARY POOR NASTY BRUTISH AND SHORT needlepoint. Stole it right off his wall. It had taken him a couple of months to stitch it just right. So he wired down his HAYDUKE LIVES sign. Didn't want it hanging in some damn dorm room at Yale.

Shooting pictures of his house was bad enough. But when tourists took pictures of Kenny, he thought that was out of line. They walked by, staring away from him and his wheelchair-o-rama—which was still a kind of staring. Then they came back again, and Kenny could see the little digital cameras they were holding by their sides.

"Philistine," he would mutter. "I'd rather have my busted-up body than your busted-up soul." Muttering always made the tourists rear back and walk away fast, which cracked Kenny up. His shoulders would jiggle up and down under his poncho, as he tried not to laugh out loud, and that scared the tourists even worse. And if he was really ready for a joke, he would put on a biblical voice and shout out something he remembered from way back, and then wouldn't the tourists scuttle. "*And men go abroad to admire the mighty waves of the sea and the circuits of the stars,*" Kenny trumpeted, "*yet pass over the mystery of themselves without a thought.*" Saying the truth in a big voice always makes people think you are nuts. And nutcases scare tourists half to death.

"If it's tourist season, why don't we shoot 'em?" That's what Tick said, and Kenny thought that would be justified. Greatest good for the greatest number.

Once a couple of tourists standing on the dock asked, "How far above sea level are we here?" Course, they didn't ask Kenny. They asked Davy McIver, thinking a teenager's going to know more than a cripple. Poor kid didn't know what to say, he's so polite. Kenny thought he should have said, "Take a step backward and you'll find out." But he said, "Two feet at high tide." Straight as an arrow, that kid.

Sometimes they even ask his dog their questions, so they don't have to talk to a guy under a camo poncho in a wheelchair, just because he's flying a flag and wearing a mouse-skin cap complete with tails. "Does anybody here know where the post office is, hum?" they croon, holding Ranger's snout or scratching him between the eyes. "Dog ain't tellin'," Kenny always said. Made them skitter. Made him laugh.

Lillian hummed over to Kenny's table, gave it a swipe with a rag, and handed him a whiskey. "She's fast, that fat old lady," Kenny said to Tick. "'Whiskey on the rocks. Comin' right up. Quarter for the jukebox. Yes-sirree. Rum and Coke, light on the Coke, and a bag of jalapeno chips.'

Faster she serves them, the faster they drink them, the faster coins fall into the till. Har."

Tick cringed behind his big beard. "Be nice," he whispered.

"Nice." Kenny considered. "How's this? Isn't it too bad that her feet hurt, trundling around like a tub in a gale, and whose feet wouldn't be sore, if they had to hold up that barge all day?"

"I said, be nice. If she heard you talking, she'd unlatch your brake and roll you right off the wharf. Besides, can't you see she's trying to be pretty?"

While Kenny watched Lillian over the slosh of his whiskey, a stranger opened the door. He peeked into a bar probably darker than he expected, but made up his mind and came in. He walked up to the bar and hung one butt cheek on the stool. Kenny had never seen him before. Big ears, gray hair short like a Weimaraner. Murmurs rolled across the room.

"That guy is wearing a button-down shirt and a goddamn tie."

"Is that a noose around that guy's neck?"

"Anybody here need any car insurance?"

Lillian yawled on over.

"I give townies and gunkholers the two things they can't get along without."

Kenny had heard Lillian say this a thousand times, and she always said it fast, as if she were trying to get all their questions over with, so she could ask her own.

"Whiskey is one. A bath is the other. Whiskey in this room. Showers and washing machines in the back. Been here forever, the first place to go up on the boardwalk after the sawmill went in. Been here through the lumber mill, through the cannery, and I'll be here when they figure out the next thing they can sell. Don't miss anything much to speak of, and I don't speak of it.

"Who are you, stranger?"

Kenny swung his chair around so he could hear the answer. But before the guy could catch his breath, Nora sang out from all the way across the room, "Hey, you're the surveyor with Axel over at the Kis'utch River." She sashayed right over and sat next to the surveyor at the bar. Chum crowded in between them. And then the whole room was quiet except for the tourists who kept on guffawing, and then they were quiet too, looking around embarrassed.

Kenny knew that every time a surveyor came to town, another chunk got bitten out of the forest and shipped off to Japan or someplace. Some families got some pocket change, dad working in the woods. Or somebody had to jack up their cabin and drag it off what had suddenly become someone else's land. Or a beach got bulldozed and a dock went in. A surveyor always means winners and losers, usually means money. You don't know. Might be good. Might be bad. Almost certainly smelled of Axel. But what's he gonna take next? Kenny wondered. What have they got over at the Kis'utch River that he could sell? Nothing there but water.

"What's the project?" Nora asked, sweet as can be.

"Axel Hagerman's gonna dam up the Kis'utch River at the old weir, build a big holding tank and a deepwater dock."

"The old weir? Jimmy Pete's weir?"

Every back straightened a little, but Ranger was the only one who raised his head.

"Yup. Then he'll bring in tankers to load up the freshwater from the Kis'utch River to bottle in Japan. Sell it back to California—Good River Glacier Water."

If the surveyor heard Kenny fart, he didn't show it.

"That Axel Hagerman thinks big and he thinks ahead. The more global warming heats things up, the more people will pay for good clean water, and the faster that glacier's gonna melt into money. He's gonna make a killing on this."

The surveyor paused, looked around, waiting for acclamation or even interest. He found neither. Tick leaned way down to scratch his ankle. Kenny fingered his braids. Oblivious as usual, the tourists elbowed each other and snuck more pictures of the stocking feet and dogs under the tables. Kenny watched Nora to see what she would say, but she just looked sort of pop-eyed at the surveyor. Sometimes she can look like a rockfish, Kenny thought, bulgy gold eyes and wide smile from gill plate to gill plate. The surveyor centered his butt on the barstool.

"Can a guy get a drink around here?" he asked.

But evidently, a guy can't. Not right away, anyhow.

"Damming up the Kis'utch?" Nora said, a little too loudly.

The surveyor nodded, not quite so sure.

"There's salmon spawning in that river," she told him.

Chum's ears stood up. He looked at Nora and whined. Then he jumped up with his front paws on her legs and stuck his nose under her elbow, trying to pry up her arm.

"It's okay, baby," she said, and reached down to rumple his rump.

"Good old Nora," Kenny said under his breath. "Gonna start up some trouble again." He sat by himself, laughing silently. His shoulders jerked up and down, until gradually they stilled, the way waves will quiet over time. Waves settle. When all the jittering sinks away, still water glazes over, hard as glass.

DAVY ROLLED TO the edge of Tommy's bed, paused, rolled out onto the floor, and quietly stood up. Tommy lay still, curled into a gently breathing ball. Stepping only on the boards he'd screwed tighter last week, Davy made his way into the kitchen and closed the bedroom door. He didn't need Tommy waking up in the middle of this project. He retrieved the clamshell he'd been saving under the stovewood and found a piece of paper and a pencil. *Dear . . .* Should he write *dearest*? *Dear Meredith, I am a wilderness guide now. I earned twenty-five dollars . . .* It was actually twenty, but with five more, that made twenty-five, so that was not a lie. *I earned twenty-five dollars today. So I guess I'm not as worthless as you thought. You know where to find me.* Should he write *love, Davy*? *Your secret very good friend,* he wrote. Okay, so that was good. He read it again and folded it into a careful wad that he tucked into the clamshell. He closed the lid, looking around for string. There was a tie string hanging from the bottom of his Dad's raincoat. He cut it off and wrapped it securely around the clam. It was yellow. Looked good, like *tie a yellow ribbon round the old oak tree.*

He wasn't supposed to leave home when Tommy was asleep, but what was home, really? Not just these three little rooms held up by posts and luck. His bedroom was connected to the pier and then the boardwalk and then the gangway to Meredith's house. Good River Harbor was home. Staying home wasn't his problem. His problem was that he had to get this clam to a place exactly between his dad, at Lillian's, and Axel, at home. His dad wouldn't come out of the bar until he needed to pee off the end of the outhouse pier, which wouldn't be for a long time, knowing his bladder. With Axel, he just had to take his chances. In winter, this would be easy, but in June, God, it hardly ever got dark. If Meredith wasn't hiding from him, it would be easy to get her a message. Ordinary people just hang out on the boardwalk and talk. But Meredith was, like, not around, and Davy figured her dad had told her to stay away from the riffraff, which he supposed he had been, but was not any more, since he now had money. He grabbed up a fishing pole to give himself an excuse to be on the dock and set out.

A couple of tourists wobbled out of the bar and headed to the harbor. Davy quickly turned into Kenny's gangway and dropped a fishing lure into the last place anyone would expect fish, the eddy where Kenny emptied his pee can and slop jar. When the tourists had passed, he reeled in and walked the last few yards toward Meredith's house. There was no delaying now. A quick glance into the bar, where he saw his dad's broad back and braid, a quick glance at Axel's, where there was no motion to be seen, Davy trotted to the front door, pawed around in the pile of boots for the smallest one—M.A.H., it said—and dropped in the clam. He turned to leave.

The door opened, almost knocking him off the pier.

"Just a minute, big guy."

Damn.

"Thought I'd do a little fishing . . ."

Axel reached around in the boot until he found the clam. He held it the way he would hold a stinking thing, pinched between his thumb and fleshy forefinger. He untied the bow, unfolded the note, moved it arm's length to read. The white of the paper flashed on his white face. He refolded the paper and put it back in the clam.

"I'll say this once."

Davy flipped his head to hide his face behind a screen of hair.

"Look at me."

"Yes, sir."

"You stay away from my daughter, Mr. Big Shot. If I catch you two together, it won't be you who pays the price. It will be your no-good father."

Axel retied the yellow cord and held the clamshell over the water. Opening his hand, he dropped it in the sea. Two fat bubbles, and the clam was gone.

≋≋≋

HOWARD ROLLED UP the sleeves on his surveyor's shirt and loosened his tie. His eyes scanned the room. At the bar, a huge orange-bearded guy twisted an empty beer can into a lump and called for another. Four boys from a seiner leaned on their elbows talking in low tones, looking over their shoulders. The rude guy in the fur hat had rolled himself to a table in the back. Every beefy hand that wasn't holding a drink was under the table scratching a dog. The woman Nora wandered the length of the bar like an overgrown puppy herself, nosing up into conversations, grinning an enormous grin. Looked like she knew everybody and apparently the names of all their dogs and children and whether they liked her to drape a long arm over their shoulders or just nudge into their backs.

Lillian pried open a bottle of beer for Howard.

"Here you go, Mr. Surveyor." As soon as she shoved it across the bar, she eased herself off her feet into a chair. Her body melted over the sides of the seat. With the palm of her hand, she pushed the sweat off her forehead, lifting a fringe of bangs into the air. For some reason, her hair was maroon, her eyelids were green, and she had a rosy spot on each cheek. She wasn't looking at him.

Even though the bar was crowded and everybody was talking, nobody was talking to Howard Fowler, surveyor. He took the beer from Lillian and found a table by himself in the corner. A crowded bar is a lonelier place than the most isolated forest tract he'd ever been in. Better to be by yourself than butt to butt on barstools with people who've known each other for twenty years. Howard had surveyed his fair share of mountains like these, laying out timber buys up and down the West Coast, keeping ahead of the logging camps, and he'd breathed his fair share of the smoke and Clorox smell of bars like Lillian's. When he came home from a trip like this, Jennifer always wrinkled her pretty nose and told him to go straight to the basement, empty his suitcase into the washer, and head for the shower. "You smell like a thirty-nine-dollar-a-night highway motel," she would say, and that was about right. His own house back in Bellevue smelled of new carpet and crayons.

A rack of split spruce barricaded the corner Howard had chosen. It was dark and warm back there. Faces flashed into view when the woodstove kicked up, then fell back into shadow. Raincoats steamed. Dogs snored. Howard drank up the Foster's without setting down the bottle.

"Soon's I knew it, I heard this crashing down the mountain, like a boulder bouncing and falling."

Howard turned toward the voice.

"Sure enough, it's a sow and she's tearing down at me, ripping out the alders, spraying dirt. I go, 'Lordy!' I swing up my shotgun and shoot from the hip. That bear died two feet from my poor gut." The guy's buddies hooted, and he patted his belly, letting his fat cells know they were safe with him.

"Bear tall enough to look in a second-story window."

"The hell."

Another guy looked deep into his drink. "Yeah, so I was riding my bike down the trail, minding my own business, came around a corner and rode right between a sow and her cub. Ah crap, I was thinking. She came after me, snarling and snapping. I lifted up my bike like it was a shield and every time she charged at me, she got a mouthful of Schwinn. Course, then I tripped over backward, and it was a bike sandwich—me, the bike, and the bear. I closed my eyes, sure I was dead, and when I squinted one eye open, the bear was gone. I laid there for a while, thinking am I dead in heaven or are those just the most beautiful clouds I ever seen? Then I wheeled my gimpy, bear-bent bike to the edge of the channel and pitched it in."

"If you'd a been dead, Erwin, those clouds would have been on fire."

Howard laughed along with everybody else.

He leaned back in his chair, starting to enjoy that dark corner, eaves-dropping on the town liars. But sure enough—it didn't take five minutes before the huge guy with an orange beard sat himself down at Howard's table and plunked down two glasses of hooch.

"Stay in this town long enough and you'll learn to love R and R," the guy said, and Howard laughed, even though he didn't know what the guy was talking about. "Rich and Rare," the man said, lifting his glass. "Rotgut and Rumble." He pushed a glass toward Howard and stretched his legs under the table. His socks stuck out the other side, gray wool socks with a red stripe, Wigwams. This boot business was a phenomenon Howard had seen from Ketchikan to Barrow. Like everybody else, this man had left his boots at the door. There was a big lineup of them there, each one identical to all the others. Impossible to know how they tell one pair from another. Of course, if the boots are all the same, maybe it doesn't matter which ones a man brings home from the bar.

"Tick McIver," the guy said, and nodded his head. "Just here for a nip. My big guy is putting my little guy to bed."

"Howard Fowler," Howard said, and Tick laughed. He reached across the table to offer a big, bent-up hand.

"So how's the surveying business, Howie?"

"Fine," Howard said.

"Where you from?"

"Bellevue, Washington."

Tick pulled his chair closer to the table. He had a fuzzy reddish braid down the center of his back and, under a huge beard, a denim shirt with the cuffs cut off, like all these guys who work around water or the woods.

"So what do you do in this town?" Howard said, though he didn't really care.

Tick leaned his chair back on two legs.

"I just try to keep my boys fed," he said. "I'm Tick McIver, Halibut Slimer. Holder of the world's record for best job done on the worst job in the world. Got my rubber overalls and a disposable plastic apron, and bloody rubber gloves."

Howard had worked out of Valdez. He'd heard what a halibut slimer does for a living and didn't really want to hear it again. But what can you do when you're drinking a slimer's whiskey? Howard threw back the whiskey, which was way better than the beer.

"I stand at the conveyor belt with an ulu in my hand. Always noisy in there, storm winds banging the Quonset hut around.

"A gutted halibut skids down the belt, big as a picnic table. I lift the roof of ribs and look right into the hole where its heart used to be. Whatever guts are left, I scrape at, scratching off pieces of kidney and liver and gonads. I flick the pieces into a tray. They got a hose spraying cold water nonstop. Axel—that's the boss—he comes around, presses his face into the cavern, looking for crap, presses his face into mine, yells, 'Keep up the good work.' I told you, I'm a good slimer."

"Congratulations," Howard said, hoping that was the end of the conversation.

"The liver is the worst, Howie. Sticks to the backbone like paint.

"My job is to make the corpse look good. That's my job. Trim around its head, not hurting those bulgy eyes. Smooth the edges of the throat wound. Cut out the anus—people don't like their fish to have an asshole. I give it all a quick spray to knock off the bloody globs, rub it down with the rubber glove to slick off the slime, shove it down the rollers, reach for the next.

"But here's the thing." Tick leaned across the table, pulling in his feet. "Some of those fish are as old as I am. They grow a foot every ten years, so anything over four feet has just about got me beat. All the big old halibut are females. When I get one of them, I trim up the slit in her throat nice and sweet, give her an extra pat, and tell her that she's done a hell of a lot more with her life than I have with mine."

Howard looked away.

"I did a good job. Then Axel fired me. Closed down the line. 'Hard to find halibut any more,' he said, like the fish were hiding behind rocks. Like the fish were playing goddamn hide-and-seek. They mined them out, that's what. Fished 'em till they caught them all. Then what? Then what, Howie?"

He stared at Howard like he knew and wouldn't say.

"Then what?"

Howard didn't know then what. He didn't care then what. What was, he was thinking he needed to pee.

"Where's the bathroom?"

Tick swung his beard toward the front door. So Howard wove between the tables and out the door and sure enough, there was an outhouse on the end of a narrow pier. He held on to both railings and made his way out. No point in taking chances. Fifty percent of the guys who drown, drown with their fly open. That's a fact. Inside the outhouse, he stared down the hole. The tide was swaying down there, seaweed floating by, everything striped with light from between the planks. A big fish jumped straight up, and Howard jumped too, spraying the wall.

When he got back, Lillian was standing there, looking at the empty glasses. Tick was looking at them too, like he was blaming them for something.

"Two more," Howard said, before he could stop himself. Tick nodded approval and started right in where he'd left off.

"Hard to know what to do in a little town without a job. I asked Axel, but he didn't need any help closing down the fish-packing plant. By now, I got Davy and Tommy, my two boys, and Annie Klawon. Annie's my wife."

Interesting name, Howard thought. Haida? Tlingit? He wondered where she was, and why Tick would be drinking alone.

"So I decided I'd scout for stray logs. Towed 'em into town and cut 'em to rounds and split them for shakes. But then everybody had all the shakes they needed, and have you ever tried towing a fifty-foot log, waves knocking the log around? It'll jerk your boat under, sink your stern, and then you're a goner. And Axel was saying those were his logs, saying I was a rustler. It wasn't worth the trouble, fighting about that. You don't win a fight with Axel."

Without lifting his elbows off the table, Tick reached across his face to scratch the far side of his beard.

"Then there wasn't nothing for me to do. Set chokers for Axel's logging outfit for a couple of months, built them some splash-dams to move logs on a flood, then they moved on. All the easy timber was gone, mined that out too. I'd of gone back to work at the mill, pulling plywood, but that's been shut down for years. I poached a lot of deer this winter."

Just saying it outright like that—poached a lot of deer this winter— made him laugh. "Poached a lot of deer this winter," Tick said again, choking he was laughing so hard.

"Finally you're telling the truth," somebody yelled from another table. Tick stopped laughing.

"I wish Annie wouldn't of went. She knew I'd think of something. I told her I was thinking I could be a hunting guide, bring in some dudes, show 'em how to find deer or bear, make a lot of money, set up a lodge."

He paused, staring into the fire.

"That was it for her. She emptied her closet into a tote and hauled off on the next ferry. 'If you're not going to earn a living, I will,' she told me. She moved to Seattle, got a job at an insurance company, sends money for the boys. 'Don't send *me* any money,' I told her. 'I got money in the bank.' Seattle. God. Damn. You can get run over by a bus in Seattle."

Tick sat there for a long time, turning his glass in his hands, round and round, so intent on turning that glass you'd think he was making it out of clay.

"I want her to come home."

Howard cleared his throat, sucked at his empty glass. He didn't know if he should buy Tick another drink, in hopes that he'd fall asleep with his forehead on the table. But a man could go bust buying drinks for every drunk in this dead-end town.

"So anyway, maybe I'll be a surveyor. Any money in that? What's Axel pay you?"

Not much, Howard could have told him. That's a fact. And if he's going to be a surveyor, he better get the hell out of this kind of place, where every boundary line goes straight up a mountain through some alder hell or blow-down Sitka spruce or bear daybed, and the land's rebounding so fast now the glaciers are gone, beaches won't hold still long enough to pound in a stake. And it's not like *he* was home snuggling with his wife or watching TV with his little girl, instead of drinking with a deadbeat in a town that looks like if you cut it loose, it'd drift out with the tide.

"How about this new water-bottling plant or whatever it is—Axel's latest scheme? Any jobs in that?"

"I don't know. Axel will probably hire outside. He says he's got a piss-poor local labor pool in Good River Harbor."

Howard knew he shouldn't have said it before he even got done saying it. The words sailed out into a room gone dead quiet, the way a room will do at just the wrong time. He cast around desperately for a way to take it back. Nobody looked at him, but nobody was saying anything either. Just kind of studying the labels on their beers.

But Tick didn't seem to have heard him. He was staring up at the ceiling, sort of smiling with half his mouth, so Howard looked up too. Any diversion was a good diversion. It was a high bead-board ceiling, glistening amber from decades of cigarette smoke. A couple of long florescent light fixtures hung askew, and over the bar was an old ship's bell, surely rescued from a wreck. Brass, with a short bell rope. Howard looked around, and suddenly everybody was watching him, and it seemed like everybody was sort of wistful about the bell.

"That's an old ship's bell, washed in on a board one blasted winter storm, same storm as washed up a poor fisherman's body. The rope got torn short. Nobody's tall enough to ring that bell," Tick said, and bent his head in sorrow. "But Lillian promises that if anybody can make that bell ring, it's free drinks all around."

Lillian nodded her head in agreement, grimacing. She was probably thinking how much it would cost her, if that bell dinked. The crowd rumbled.

"Go for it, stranger," somebody shouted. The fire dropped in the woodstove and the thrust-forward faces flashed on and off. Shadows danced around, swaying against the cases of beer. By the door, all those empty boots looked like they wanted to go home, get some sleep. But ringing a bell didn't seem so hard. It was a high ceiling, but Howard was a tall man, still agile enough, leaping over blowdown for a living. If he stood on the bar, he'd be most of the way there. He could get a big soup spoon or something from Lillian and reach it up and smack the bell. Take their minds off the jobs they weren't going to get. Show them how it's done. Buy everybody a beer without spending a cent. Seemed like something Tick could have done himself, if he'd had the gumption.

Lillian produced a soup ladle, and Howard clambered up on the bar. The bar was shaky, and the air up there was hot. He had to squint his eyes against the smoke. But he got up there all right, and he reached as high as he could, which turned out to be high enough. People crowded around, cheering. He was balanced to give the spoon a mighty swing, when a half dozen guys grabbed hold of his pants and pulled them down.

"Shit." There he was, standing on the bar in his jockey shorts with his pants around his ankles. A big cheer went up, and he knew he'd been cooked by the oldest trick in the bar. Tick danced around, bent over yowling, and the dogs howled, like it was the greatest joke in the universe, to pants a stranger in your hometown, pulling down his pants just when he was reaching up with both hands, trying to ring the bell.

So he didn't get the bell rung, but Howard did get a free drink, thanks to Lillian. She handed him a beer and patted him on the head.

"Harder than you'd think," she said, "making the bells ring around this place. And don't I know that as well as anybody in this town."

Then she handed out beers as fast as people could crowd in and grab them. This seemed to call for a party, and what was Howard supposed to do? His dark room above the Good River Harbor library, its small window and narrow bed—nobody there but him, no sound but the oddly traffic sound of the Kis'utch River falling down the mountain—that was sounding awful good. But you can't just go to your room after you get pantsed. Howard was sure there was some manhood rule against that. So he got back in line and grabbed another free beer. There was probably a rule against that too, but Lillian was puffing and sweating like a tugboat, working too hard to see who was lining up behind her.

"Come sit with us, stranger," somebody yelled. Howard headed over. Nora got up from the table as soon as Howard arrived.

"Take my chair," she said. "Come on, Lillian. I'll hand out the beer. You sing us a song."

"A song, Lilly, a song," the crowd echoed. Howard looked around wildly, not wanting to be the punch line for another practical joke.

Lillian straightened up and wiped her forehead on the inside of her elbow. She put her hands on her hips and surveyed the murmuring crowd.

"I already gave you free beer," she said. "Why should I give you a free song?" She untied her apron and folded it neatly on the bar. With her thumb and forefinger, she arranged a row of curls across her forehead. People sat down wherever they stood. If there was a chair nearby, they sat in a chair. If not, they sat on the floor or a bottom step or a cardboard box of Fritos. Simultaneously, all the dogs stood up. Cigarette smoke was a blue sky at the ceiling. The chatter drained away. Howard steeled himself for whatever was coming next in this crazy place. And Lillian began to sing.

> Oh my, but you have a pretty face
> You favor a girl that I knew
> I imagine that she's still in Tennessee
> And by God I should be there too.
> I've got a sadness too sad to be true.

Howard stared. There was no end of surprises in this town. The woman sang like an angel. This woman, Lillian, swayed there on her swollen ankles and broken-back shoes and sang the words so beautifully, so . . . Howard thought . . . so significantly, she could have been an archangel singing the coming of Christ. Tick looked proudly at Howard and smiled. Then he leaned back and listened with his eyes closed. The golden pools of Nora's eyes filled with tears.

Howard fumbled for his wallet and laid a twenty on the table. He wanted to be alone, where he could feel what he was feeling. It was eleven o'clock in Bellevue and Jennifer would be checking to be sure the front door was locked, and he had just been pantsed in the bar of an angel with maroon hair. All he wanted was to close the door to his little room, where he could be alone and understand how alone he really was. As Howard passed through the door, Tick was gravely waltzing through the bar with the guy who almost got his gut bitten out by a bear.

WITH BOTH BLACK-GLOVED hands, Kenny pushed slowly away from the table. The seiners managed to scoot their chairs out of the way without looking at him. He maneuvered around the bar and rolled onto the boardwalk. Ranger followed him out.

Rain had started up again. Dusk was finally falling, and the rings on the water do-si-doed in the yellow glow from Lillian's windows. Kenny didn't really want to go home to that black box of a cabin. But he sure didn't want to sit in a crowded bar. On the shadowed boardwalk, though, he felt safe. He would see people coming before they saw him. The tide was coming in under the planks, striped with light. A school of holy-cross jellyfish paraded by. The crosses in their transparent backs glowed as if they'd been blessed. Kenny watched them pulse through the water. Give me a jellyfish any day, he thought. A jellyfish doesn't have a brain at all, and it's smarter than that pack of tourists all put together. And somebody told him a jellyfish can have sex with itself, which is a point in favor of tentacles.

A fish jumped somewhere out in the dark.

Kenny rolled to the railing and looked down. Another fish jumped. Something deep flashed silver. A fish showing its side? Is there a school of fish circling down there? He backed up and pulled in sideways to get closer to the railing.

Somebody was coming up behind him. The boardwalk bounced with each step, and then there was Nora standing next to him. She braced her palms on the rail and leaned over the water. Another fish jumped.

"Pinks," she said in a quiet voice.

It was the first word she had ever spoken to Kenny. Or maybe she was talking to the fish.

"They've come home," she said. He didn't look at her face to see if she was waiting for some response, but he couldn't have thought of one anyway. The reflected yellow light flickered on her jeans. Starting in the place where the jeans puckered into her boots, the light rode up and down her legs, rocking like the water. He felt the heat of her legs on his face and he backed away a little, the way he backs away from a woodstove once it gets cranking.

In a black mass, the fish moved slowly through the water. Glints of white sides flashed back at the streetlights, then disappeared. Sometimes a fish jumped clear of the water and slapped on its side, splashing. Carefully not looking at Nora, Kenny watched the fish for a long time, while their dogs sniffed each other's asses and Kenny tried not to notice that she was there.

Before long, the channel would be crazy with salmon at the mouth of every creek. The seiners would move out before dawn to be in place when the season opened. Then the fish-eating killer whales would infiltrate, squadrons of five or six, with fins sticking out of the water, tall as a man. There would be sea lions hanging offshore, blowing bubbles and farting. Already there were humpback whales, following schools of herring. Kenny would hear their blows rising through the floorboards of his cabin, grunts and sighs like lovers behind pasteboard walls in cheap motels.

Kenny turned and rolled home. That night, like every night, he lowered himself onto his cot, pulled his woolen blankets to his chin. As he listened to the humpbacks breathing, he wrapped his thighs around his blanket. He thought about the sex life of weightless, sighing mammals, what that would be like, floating, rolling, holding a great barnacle-warted beast in his fleshy fins.

June 30

HIGH TIDE		LOW TIDE	
3:21am	16.1ft	9:45am	-1.1ft
4:14pm	14.9ft	10.1pm	3.1ft

illian held a spoon in one fist like a dagger. With the other fist, she held down a salmon carcass that kept slipping off her cutting board. Grinning head on one end, tail on the other, and in between just a spine and a bunch of ribs—there's not a lot to hold on to. She adjusted her grip, taking hold of the backbone where it emerged from the skull. She scraped the spoon hard down the length of a rib, collecting a spoonful of beautiful pink flesh. She knocked the meat off into a bowl, then applied her spoon to the next rib. There would be rich hot creamy salmon chowder at the Bath 'n' Bar tonight, which meant a good crowd for a foggy afternoon.

When Lillian had opened her front door that morning, she had found a blue plastic tote on her doorstep. Ravens hopped around it, jabbing it with heavy beaks. Lillian snapped a dish towel at them, and they hopped away, clonking and grumbling. But as soon as she opened the lid, they were back again, leaping up as well as a raven can leap and stumbling over her slippers. Inside the tote were what remained of three big king salmon and two silvers after their fillets had been removed. The guys from the seiners often caught kings and silvers in their pink-salmon purse seines. It's illegal to sell bycatch, but nothing says you can't slice off a couple of fillets for dinner and give away what's left, especially if you give them to Good River Harbor's goddess of salmon chowder.

Lillian lifted her short curls with the back of her hand, which gave the carcass a chance to slide off the cutting board. "Screw it," she said. She reached for her ice pick and drove it through the fish's eye.

That's when the door opened and Axel slid in. Howard followed him, walking as if his shoulders were tied to his knees, never once looking at the bell on the ceiling above the bar.

"Thought we might talk here," Axel said.

"What," Lillian answered, "your own kitchen table catch fire?"

"You might say." Axel threw a conspiratorial look at Howard. "My sweet wife, Rebecca, is a little riled up today. She thinks it might be better if we met someplace other than home for a while, and Meredith's working in my office."

Lillian washed her hands and poured them coffee. She couldn't remember the last time Axel had sat at her table. Neither man looked up when she put the coffee in front of them.

"I've got a new project, Howard," Axel said. "And I want you to be in charge of it. I'll promote you to assistant production supervisor. How does that sound?"

Howard grinned and leaned forward.

"Set aside work on the Kis'utch River water project for a while," Axel was saying. "Might be a good time to let that one simmer down. There will be time for that. The river's not going anywhere.

"This one is a better idea, and we can move fast on it, have money rolling in before fall. So let's sketch out plans for a bear zoo. Timetable too."

Howard nodded. "Bear zoo. That's a good one." He straightened his tie and pulled a little spiral notebook out of his shirt pocket. He held the pencil over the page. "Bear zoo. Where exactly, and what bear?"

"In that old cedar cistern halfway up the cliff above where the old cannery used to be. Not too big, but big enough to hold a bear or two." Axel poked a short finger at Howard. "And as for the bear, you can leave that to old Axel." Fondly, Axel stroked the top of his head.

"Full moon was last night, which means we'll get good high tides next couple of nights, highest tomorrow midnight. Probably have a half ton of lumber to off-load at the bear zoo site. We need to get that organized and loaded onto the barge to deliver at the midnight tide. A seventeen-foot tide will float the barge almost to the base of the cistern, and the boys can off-load there. Save a lot of hauling over slippery rocks.

"First thing today, you go over and hire Tick McIver as a carpenter."

Howard started to write that down in his spiral notebook but stopped with the pencil in the air.

Axel chuckled. "Tick'll be glad to get on any job I've got going," he said. "Besides, if I give Tick something, he's got something I can take away."

Axel lowered his voice. "It's just a little thing with his scruffy son. First rule of human resource management—give 'em what they want. Then you own them."

Howard, clearly baffled, wrote down the instructions.

"Get him to stage the lumber on the ledge next to the cistern. Sure don't want to wait another month. Want to get cracking on this so I can have tourists there yet this summer." Axel rubbed his furzy head as if he were buffing its shine.

"This might be the best idea I've ever had—making the old water tank into a zoo for wild brown bears. Sometimes I think I'm a genius."

Axel laughed out loud, and Howard joined him. *Heh heh heh*, the same dying motor. Lillian swung her head quickly toward them and just as quickly back to her work.

"Call the eco-tour boats today. I'll give you contact names. Tell them this will be the best tourist attraction in Southeast, work out a good price for them to tie to our new dock. Get a half dozen of them to sign on, won't that be a pot of money, four hundred tourists a day lined up to see grizzlies up close and personal. Refreshment stand, two bucks a Coke."

Howard jotted notes in his little notebook, flipped over to a clean page, and waited.

"Hey," Howard said, as if he'd just thought of it. "I'm really sorry I jumped the gun on telling people about the water-bottling project. I didn't know it was a secret . . ."

"I already told you, never mind." Axel interrupted him. "This sorry-stuff is getting tiresome. Yeah, you made a mistake, and yeah, you're a schmuck, and yeah, I hadn't planned on breaking the news about the water project for another couple of months. Leave it alone." Axel leaned back in his chair.

"If a person's fast on his feet, he can make a glitch work for him, and if I'm anything, I'm fast on my feet. Let Nora fuss about logging next to the creeks or the Kis'utch water project across the channel. I'll be moving ahead on the old cistern out at the cannery site."

Axel raised his coffee cup and clinked Howard's cup. Howard managed a smile.

"That's the thing: You look for opportunities in every direction. If something exists, it can be sold. It just happens that what I'm thinking of selling this week isn't water. It's bears. Water can wait." He chuckled.

"We're going to need a good name for the tank where we keep the bears. Some name that brings in the tourists."

"The Bear Zoo?"

"The Bear Palace?"

"Hagerman's Bear Palace?"

"Good River Harbor Bear Palace?"

"That's good. Classy. 'Bring your kids to see wild Alaskan brown bears. Feed wild Alaskan grizzlies. See a threatened species before it's gone.' Mmm. I like that one. Write that down, Howard. That can be the guts of your advertising campaign. People adore threatened species, and if it's endangered, all the better."

Lillian yanked the ice pick out of the last salmon's head and dropped the skeleton into her compost bucket. She started in chopping onions, but that made so much noise she couldn't overhear anything. She decided that peeling potatoes was a better idea. There was quiet in the Bath 'n' Bar then, except for the squink of the potato peeler and the scratch of Howard's pen. Axel looked around the bar, pointing his nose at the stacked firewood, the smoky light, the neat piles of cigarette cartons. Lillian followed his glance, hoping he liked her place. Axel shook his head.

"I don't know why my sweet wife's tail is in such a knot, Howard. Everything I do, I do for her—for Rebecca. Everything she has, she has because of me. And that goes for the people in this town too. How do they think they're going to eat, if it isn't for Good River Products? Money grows on trees. I told Rebecca that. Money grows on trees. But it doesn't just rain down on you. You have to be smart. You have to work hard to get it out. And aren't I smart enough, and don't I work hard? I'm the guy who figures out how to capitalize undeveloped resources. Then I hire people, and they get paid. 'But sweetheart, you can't squeeze blood out of a turnip,' I told Rebecca. That's what set her off. I thought it was a good joke."

Howard laughed weakly. Lillian smiled too, trusting that the humor would later become apparent.

"Rebecca wanted the old cannery's water tank to be a community garden, of all things. A garden that the whole town would share. For free. Jesus, Howard, I bring her milk crates for her flower gardens. I stack up tires higher than the tide so she can plant rhubarb. I nail gutters to all the railings on our gangway and porches so she can plant flowers. I bring her home a tote-load of fish heads for fertilizer each spring. I help her haul the very best dirt all the way from her special bend in the Kis'utch River. In buckets. On a skiff. The whole damn house is blooming. Bees own the place. Hummingbirds are going to carry us away. I am a very nice man about gardens."

Lillian knew that was true. Their house was buried in flowers.

"But that evidently is not enough for Rebecca." Axel banged his coffee cup down on the table. He reconsidered, picked it up, and set it down gently. Lillian walked over to swipe a rag at what he had spilled and top off his cup.

"Heat yours up?" she asked Howard, but Howard was staring at Axel.

"I love her, Howard. I love it when she's happy and humming. I know she lives for her summer gardens, because winter almost kills her, that darkness, and ice on the shrouds and electric lines. I would do anything for her. But does a good husband have to sit and all the time hear about compost?"

Poor Howard. His head shook, no, and then his head shook, yes, and then it just rolled around a little bit and came to a stop. He held on to his tie for dear life. Lillian wiped her hands on a towel and leaned against the counter. Some days, her heart wept for Axel. Other days, her foot itched to kick his behind. Some things he knew really well. On other things, he was ignorant as a child. It was sad. He wasn't a bad man. He was just clueless, and was that his fault? The greatest mystery in all of Good River Harbor was how two people so utterly different as Axel and Rebecca could love each other.

The parents of Axel's wife, Rebecca, were hippies, honest-to-God hippies. They were gentle people who moved to the bush so they could live in true harmony with the land. Rebecca was a flower child of flower children, a tiny baby cradled on her mother's back in a shawl printed with sunflowers and forget-me-nots. Even back then, her hair was soft and her eyes disappeared into her smile. There was always a flower tied in her hair, a sprig of fireweed or blueberry bells right there in the wave on top of her head. She was so beautiful it made a person ache to hold such a child. Back then, even Lillian—who never let anyone touch her—sat Rebecca on her lap and cradled her in the sun. Without her own child, it was a comfort to her. She taught little Rebecca to sing "*you shall have a fishie on a white dishie,*" even though Rebecca had never tasted fish in her beautiful two years.

Rebecca's parents vowed that they would take only what was given to them by the good Earth and kill nothing that breathed. That makes it hard to live in Alaska, even if you believe that plants don't breathe. Rebecca's mother tended a big garden—spinach and rhubarb, zucchini—and gathered spruce tips and huckleberries, salmonberries, currants. For his part, her father went out in search of the perfect piece of wood. Damned if he didn't find it the first year, a Sitka spruce trunk maybe four feet across and thirty feet long. It had soaked in saltwater for upward of fifty years, part of an old fish trap, before it finally washed to shore.

He cut the spruce into big blocks and stacked them in their cabin. Now and then he would take his band saw and saw off a thin sheet of wood that he would sell to a guitar maker—Martin, Gibson, Taylor. His wood was famous around the world; men journeyed all the way to Good River Harbor to buy a piece of this wood. Half their little cabin was spruce blocks. The other half was a simple kitchen and a dance floor, because Rebecca's father not only supplied wood for guitars, but also played them. When the family wasn't dancing, they rolled out mats to sleep on, all in a pile, like puppies.

So there was money for whole-wheat flour and beans and honey, and sometimes oranges from Outside. Rebecca was raised on good, thick, seed-studded bread and salmonberry jelly. The harmony didn't last, of course. The mother was the one who got restless first and shipped out to Nepal. So Rebecca lived with her dad. When Rebecca was in high school, she seemed to be hungry for something else, maybe something even more nourishing than bread. For a while, she and Lillian sat together in the evenings, struggling through the *Tao Te Ching*. But there was nothing in there that Rebecca hadn't already learned from living in the coming and going of strong tides.

Then Axel came home from his first fishing season, just sixteen, but confident as a man. People called him "successful," and maybe that was the right word. And oh, he wooed Rebecca, the prettiest, sweetest girl in the whole town. He had brought her dried cherries from the Pike Place Market and Brie so ripe it melted onto the paper and fresh corn on the cob—food she had never seen before. Over a beach fire at Green Point, Axel roasted the corn and fed her soft cheese and cherries. And she did love him, not because of the gifts he had brought, but because he had brought them. Because he knew her well enough to know what would delight her, and because he wanted her so desperately to be glad. That was his way, Axel: to decide what he wanted and then figure out how to get it, but that was a good thing, because kindness was the only way to win Rebecca. So that is how they lived, Axel trying to make Rebecca glad, and Rebecca being glad in fact, and loving him in return.

Outside the window of Lillian's bar, the fog had torn into shreds that tangled in the masts. A single beam of sunlight somehow managed to find its way to the back of Axel's lowered head, where it lit his bare neck like a saint's. When he spoke again, Axel spoke with Rebecca's soft, slow voice. His voice was so quiet that Lillian had to come out from behind the bar to restock the packets of ketchup on the tables.

"Rebecca thought the water tank would make the world's most beautiful raised-bed garden. 'The walls will keep out the bears and the deer and the slugs,' she said.

"'Everybody can compost there,' she said, 'and not worry about bears getting into the fish heads,'" Axel crooned.

"'We won't have to chop up our kitchen garbage and dump it out to sea anymore,' she said. She loved this idea.

"'The whole town could raise Nootka roses and honeysuckle, turn the cistern into heaven.'

"'I've never seen her so excited, Howard. That's when I had to tell her it didn't pencil out. I told her, you can't make any money on a community garden. Can't squeeze blood out of a turnip.'"

Axel chuckled. Howard winced. Lillian put more ketchup packets in
the little bowl on their table.

"But God, it was just a joke!

"If we put bears in the old cistern, it's going to turn a profit within a
year, I told her, guaranteed, but she said she didn't care.

"I hate it when she tries to cry and talk at the same time, that little face
all hiccups and sobs. She better get control of herself and learn which
side her bread is buttered on. And that goes for the rest of the people
in this town. Nora Montgomery and that innocent little 'What are your
plans for cutting at Fairweather Bay?' garbage. And Tick better be careful,
pulling off your pants in the bar and then asking me for a job. Cutting up
stovewood for Nora Montgomery, honeying up to her, and then thinking
I should give him a job. And if he doesn't keep his kid Davy away from
Meredith, I'll ruin them both. He better figure out his bread and butter
too. He's got to know there's other people in this town can hammer a nail."
Axel took a deep breath, looked to Howard for an understanding nod, got
it, and plowed on.

"It isn't easy making good when you're an orphan, when your own
mom and dad drown the week after you're born. Yeah, so the Hagermans
took me in, and the Hagermans were good people, but it's not like I was
born lucky. Hell no. I call that born out of luck. I made my luck, and I'm a
better man for it."

Lillian turned away. It pained her that Axel felt orphaned. But she had
learned that Axel was right: You run out of luck, you have no choice but
to make yourself some more. You make it out of whatever you have at
hand. What she couldn't decide was whether there's only so much luck in
the world, so when you make it for yourself, you have to take the ingre-
dients from somebody else. She wondered what had she taken from Axel.

She walked over to refill his coffee.

"It isn't easy when people lean on you," Axel went on, not noticing the
coffee. "It isn't easy juggling all these balls. Because some of them fall.
Nobody wants to tell a guy there's no job left, nothing left to catch or
cut or can. But stuff runs out or costs too much to get. You got to keep
thinking of new ideas. And you got to know how to make those ideas
work. Do a good job of it, have the right kind of brains, you make money.

Some of the money goes to the guy with the brains, but you give most of the money away to the mindless people who work for you. So now Rebecca acts like that's some kind of evil, and sometimes I think, okay.

"Okay, I'll tell her.

"Okay. Have it your way. I'll stop working so hard. See how you eat then. See how long this family sticks together. See how long this town lasts. I'm serious. Who's the one who cares about his family? Who's the one who cares about this town? Who's the one working his tail off to hold things together? And who's the one his own wife despises? How fair is that? This town owes me, and I collect my debts."

Axel stopped to catch his breath. The gusts of his words had pumped up his face, but now it deflated—slowly, like dough poked with a wooden spoon. Behind the counter, the potato water was boiling furiously. The windows had steamed up and moisture beaded on the ship's bell above the bar. Lillian bustled back to turn down the heat. She stirred the potatoes and pulled the salt pork out of the cooler. Soon it was crackling in the bottom of her biggest soup pot. The room was thick with steam and old cigarette smoke and the smell of pork sizzling in its own fat. Axel walked over to open the door.

Howard was saying nothing. He scratched behind his ear. Then he turned another page around the spiral in his little notebook and picked up his pencil.

"What else you got for me, Axel?"

Axel took a deep breath and looked at him with an expression that might have been gratitude.

"Right. Right. We have a job to do. Bear project is going to take a lot of lumber, the way we have it designed. Hope I have enough fir under tarps by the Quonset. Here, make a list of what I need from you." At the top of the new page, Howard wrote, Things to Do for the Bear Tourist Attraction, and made notes as Axel spun off the questions.

"We'll need a dock, but I think we can use the pilings from the old cannery dock. Check on that. A floating dock, and a ramp going up to the cistern. Better put railings on that. It's a long way down to those rocks. Don't want to lose some tourist's kid. On that ledge next to the cistern, a pavilion with a welcome sign and some educational kiosks. You sketch it all out.

"Check on the required number of outhouses. That would be a state reg, I would think.

"Check with Mark Custer. See how soon we'll get the check for our rural economic development grant.

"And—do this quietly—find out how the Alaska Department of Fish and Game permits problem bears."

"Quietly," Howard repeated, flushing. "Can do."

"Check with the Feds to see if we can get mitigation funds for habitat restoration inside the tank."

Howard put down his pen. "Habitat restoration?" he asked. "On the inside of a moldy water tank?"

Axel beamed. "There's money everywhere if you know where to look," he said. The Feds love to give out money to restore habitats, and what habitat more needs to be restored than the inside of a cannery's old water cistern?" But then he stopped short and considered.

"Now there's a brilliant idea. I could give Rebecca the Feds' money and get her to restore a bear habitat inside the tank. That's better than my plan to dump in some construction site debris. She can have all the fireweed and thimbleberries she would ever want. Turnips, for all I care. Compost. Geraniums. Whatever. Bears won't care.

"See, Howard, you've got to be fast on your feet. Sometimes I think I'm a genius—a little slow on the uptake, but a genius. Would have saved Rebecca a lot of crying if I'd thought of this yesterday.

"Okay, so here's the angle on your story. Write it up and get it out. Good River Harbor's famous gardener, the lovely Rebecca Hagerman, will create an ecosystem in the cistern, in a project that will save doomed bears. Perfect. A bear figures out he can get food in town, starts hanging around the dump, killing dogs—that's a dead bear. But we'll rescue the problem bears and put them in the pit. Fish and Game will love us. Tourists on the eco-tours will love us. Eco-freaks will love us. Maybe Rebecca—I don't know. It won't be a Bear Palace. That was a mistake—sounds too much like a circus. It'll be a Bear *Shelter*, like a homeless shelter, only the bears can't leave to go hang out on the street corners, boozing and begging."

Axel stood up to put on his Good River Products hat and jacket.

"Oh, and another thing for your list," he told Howard. "You'll have to be the one to tell Rebecca she gets to make the habitat in the bear pit. She's not talking to me."

As soon as they left, Lillian turned the stove to simmer and crossed to the mirror. Axel has her eyes, she thought, shiny blue, although his were closer together than hers. "Ah," she scolded her reflection. "Don't go there."

But she did let herself wonder if he got his business sense from her. One good tree is seventy-three years of winter rains or 1,060 board feet of lumber or 208 two-by-fours or 6,890 rolls of toilet paper. One good tree is a year of community college classes learning small engine repair; it's a new room on the house for the baby, already grown a beating heart the size of a raisin. One good tree is food on the table or control over a man otherwise bigger than you are in every way. And a glass of cold water— what is that? Life or $2.35, with a plastic bottle thrown in for free. A bear? Bloody death or a good five months of fifteen-dollar admission fees, do the math. One good salmon behind glass in a refrigerated case is twenty dollars times twenty pounds, do the math, four hundred dollars, and a fish head buried in the garden. Oh, the trading that goes on, the choices, the risks and benefits. What will you give for love, what will you give for pride, what will you give for spite, this for that, and who can say that a man is good or bad depending on what he wants in trade?

≋≋

LATER THAT AFTERNOON, Nora shoved up the bill of her baseball cap, leaned back in Lillian's chair, and stared at the bell on the ceiling. Afternoon light reflecting from the channel wavered on the plywood, then broke and bounced in the wake of a passing skiff. When Nora squinted her eyes shut, pink waves danced on her eyelids. She squinted harder. Yellow balls rose from the water and floated off the top of her eyeballs.

"More coffee?" Lillian asked.

Nora winced, then shoved her cup across the bar toward Lillian's apron. She watched her hand pour coffee into a cloud of steam. That was a surprisingly noisy operation, because Lillian was wearing a dozen hoop bracelets that caught and clanked in the folds of her wrist.

"Pretty bracelets, Lilly."

"You could wear jewelry," Lillian ventured. "Soften you up a little. Win you a man." Lillian felt bad about the expression on Nora's face. Her cheeks tightened up and went glassy, and it was hard to know if she was pissed or blue, but maybe she was both. Oh well. Nora was one of Lillian's Improvement Projects, and her IPs were always grateful for her straight talk in the end. All the same, Lillian walked over to the shelf and brought back a little pecan pie in a cellophane wrapper.

"Free," she said.

Nora poked at the wrapper with her spoon. She took a deep breath and changed the subject. "So what have you heard about the new Bear Palace?"

"Axel's on it. In this morning, giving orders to Howard."

"Damn that Axel," Nora said. "Why can't he take a break now and then? He's got the water project on the Kis'utch, and now he's going to set up a bear pit. What drives that man?"

Lillian opened her mouth to answer, but Nora plowed on.

"And why does it have to be me who stops him? I don't want this job. I didn't volunteer. I gave this work up after the last time. I'm retired. Isn't there somebody else in this town? I want to be the one who just minds her own business. I want to play my piano in the woods. That's all I want."

Nora looked up to see what Lillian thought of the whole mess. But Lillian was busy. She had a lit cigarette between two fingers, and she was pulling off her bracelets one by one, which required a great deal of squeezing and pulling of flesh and a final delicacy when the hoop passed over the cigarette and dented the line of rising smoke.

The door opened with so much violence that it banged against the wall. There, silhouetted against the blinding light, stood little Tommy McIver, his legs braced like a miniature gunslinger.

"Well, aren't we the little cliché," Lillian said.

Tommy ran across the room and grabbed Lillian around the hips. Lifting her cigarette in two fingers, she placed her palm against his forehead and pushed him away, somehow not catching his hair on fire.

"My mom's coming home. My dad has a job at the Bear Shelter and my mom's coming home.

"And listen to this. My dad's going to be a carpenter for Axel. I mean, Mr. Hagerman. My dad's going to build a Bear Shelter in the tank at the old cannery site. There'll be brown bears and you can watch them close up and even feed them. And a refreshment stand. My dad says I'll get in free, because he's the carpenter for the Bear Shelter.

"Tell everybody," he ordered Lillian, but he needn't have bothered.

Then he was gone, and the cigarette smoke swirled in the yellow light of the open door.

≈≈≈≈

"KENNY, HOW'M I gonna trap a bear?" Tommy hovered a safe distance in front of Kenny, who was sitting in his wheelchair in the morning sun by the library door, cleaning his fingernails with a pocketknife. He was wearing a new hat he'd made of dried fish skin. He'd sewn the isinglass panels together with red embroidery floss, herringbone stitch, a nice touch. Ranger sat by Kenny's left wheel.

"Don't bother me, midget-boy. I got diggin' and grubbin' to do. Like I said. Look it up on the internet. They got two computers hooked up right here in the library. Learn to use 'em. Artofmanliness.com—everything you need to know to be a man. Now go away."

Tommy took a single step backward.

"Do you think a man-trap? I could dig this humungous hole and cover it with sticks and leaves. And the bear would walk by, sniff, sniff, and whooomph, down in the hole it goes." Tommy said whooomph so emphatically he jumped into the air.

"And then up out of the hole the bear comes in one giant leap and bites off your butt." A big grin spread over Kenny's face, lifting the braids in his beard. He growled suddenly and swiped a hand at Tommy, who leapt backward and teetered at the edge of the boardwalk.

Then Kenny's grin went slack. "How do you trap a bear? If it's this year's cub—no bigger than a bucket—all you need is a dog kennel and a can of sweetened condensed milk, the kind with the cow on the label. Don't make a mistake and get evaporated milk. Open the can and put it in the kennel and your only problem is that the bear won't leave the sweet milk unless you pick up the kennel and shake the cub out like the last Pringle in the can.

"How do you trap a baby hummingbird? With a pot of pansies behind the window. The baby will zippity right toward the flowers, crash into the window, and fall stunned in your hand. You can spring a trap for a crab with no more than a salmon tail on a string. A crab will grab hold with such ungodly stubbornness that you can pull it a hundred feet to the surface. Be ready with a net, because most crabs will let go when they start to see sunlight. But there are crabs who will never let go, ever, even when you swing them over the stove and lower them into boiling water.

"All you have to do is figure out what a thing wants, and then dangle it in front of him. Then he's yours."

Kenny considered. Then he made another swipe at Tommy.

"Kid, I hope you survive long enough to grow a brain. How about you go get me a squirrel instead," he said. "Twenty-five cents for the hide and I'll teach you to skin it."

"Get it how?"

"Like I taught you. Sit real still in a tree and when it comes by, clobber it with a two-by-four."

"Really?" Tommy eyes were big.

"Cripes," Kenny said. He reached under his poncho and pulled out a slingshot. "How old are you?"

"Six." Tommy held up one hand and a thumb.

"Plenty old."

By the time the librarian arrived with her son, Kenny had Tommy shooting pebbles at the *O* on the *Ocean Dreamer's* transom. Couldn't hit the *O*, but he scored a lot of hits on the sailboat's hull.

"You are an evil influence on the children of this town," the librarian said. She was smiling, but she didn't let go of her own little kid.

Ten o'clock on the button, and here came Nora and Chum.

"We have a date, Nora and me," Kenny muttered experimentally. "Every Tuesday and Thursday, 10 a.m., at the library. A date." Then he started to shout, "*Above all, don't lie to yourself. The man who lies to himself loses all respect for himself and for others. And having no respect, he ceases to love.*"

"Shut up, Kenny," Nora said, and smacked his new fish-skin hat. "You do a bad imitation of a nut."

"Dostoyevsky was not a nut."

"Fine."

Chum flounced in front of Ranger, flopping like a marionette with the string tied to its rump. It was hard for old Ranger to keep his dignity. He hauled himself to his feet and started to maul Chum's face. Nora pulled off her boots and they all crowded into the library, two big wheels and two little wheels and two dogs and Kenny and Nora. Tommy stayed put and pinched another pebble into the slingshot.

The place hardly qualified as a library, more like a used bookstore, because nobody ever returned the books they borrowed. Random times, whenever they felt like it, people brought in a plastic grocery sack of whatever books they didn't want anymore, so it worked out. Books were stacked all the way to the ceiling, some on shelves, some just stacked. It was tricky for Kenny to make the sharp turns in such close quarters, with the librarian shouting out avalanche warnings and his USA flag catching on the photo books. But the library had computers and an internet connection, and that's what Nora went after. Kenny too.

Nora was studying up on Alaska things. Marine charts and the rules of navigation. Coho salmon, and then it was marbled murrelets. She wrote natural history pamphlets for the ferries—that was her job. Tourists could take the pamphlets from racks midship and learn things. So every week Nora was taking notes about some species, preferably something about to go extinct. Kenny thought she'd be depressed, but she got all excited about it.

"Did you know that marbled murrelets are shaped like such Milk Duds that they have to fly at forty miles an hour or they fall out of the sky?" she asked Kenny.

She did that. They'd be sitting across from each other at the computer table, quietly doing their work, and then she'd look up, and it was, "Did you know that a marbled murrelet flies from Snettisham to the Geicke Glacier, picks up a fish, flies it back to its nestling, does it again, twice a day, sixty miles each way?"

Kenny thought of himself as up on the animals, at least the dead ones, but he'd never heard of what she told him. Kenny never said "too stupid to live" or "yes" or "no" or "wow." He just grunted and went back to whatever website he was studying. Each marvel—she called them *marvels*—made her grin wider, and each one ground Kenny down, knowing that another marvel was going to be gone before he was a goner himself. Mostly he pretended to ignore her, even though he watched her from under the itchy edge of his cap.

But that day, Kenny saw Nora looking at him when she thought he wasn't watching. He was studying an internet site that showed how to skin a squirrel by turning it inside out over a post—you sort of prop up the body on the post, cut it just right, give a steady pull down on the hide, and get it skinned in one motion. Kenny wondered how mountain men ever figured things out before the internet. But Nora wasn't looking at the video that Kenny was studying or listening to him mutter. She was looking at him.

Kenny watched her looking. She had gold eyes. Maybe they were brown, but in that light, they were gold as a dogshark.

The librarian was hanging around, so Nora held her fire.

"What are you studying today?" she asked, but not like she cared.

"The life cycle of squirrels," Kenny said, then he looked away because he didn't want to encourage her.

Finally, the librarian's kid started to whine that he was hungry. The librarian propped the BACK SOON sign against her coffee mug and left. Kenny thought, here it comes, and sure enough. Nora reached across the table and put her hands on top of his hands, sort of grabbed the back of Kenny's fingerless gloves. He wished she wouldn't do that. He wished she wouldn't look so hard at him. He wished she'd be afraid of him, like everybody else. He shifted his hat down closer to his eyebrows.

"Har," he said.

"We've got to do something!" she said.

"We," Kenny said. It was the only coherent word he could come up with. What the hell was she thinking? They hadn't done anything that needed anything done about it.

"Tommy told me that Axel has hired Tick to build a bear pit," she said in her earnest voice. Kenny muttered something and shrugged his shoulders to keep his back from tightening up.

"Selling refreshments and charging admission to see bears caged in the cistern at the old cannery beach. It's the latest 'Good River Products Rural Economic Development Plan.' Logs, fish, water, now bears. That man Axel never rests. What have you heard about this one?"

Kenny hadn't heard anything about it. Nobody ever told him anything. But he didn't believe in caging things. Better to kill a problem bear than put it in a cage and make it a tourist attraction. Some things are worse than dying. Put something in a cage, and it's the people outside who turn into wild animals, taunting it and poking it with sticks and peeing on it.

On the video, a man's hands in rubber gloves placed the little naked squirrel on a table next to its inside-out skin.

First thing a bear would do, Kenny knew, was try to tear apart the cage, bringing it everything he had. Claws, teeth, brute strength. And when that didn't work, he'd turn his teeth on his own body, scratching and clawing. Then he'd slump down and curse day and night, curse himself for being so goddamn stupid to walk into a trap. Then curse the men with guns. Then he'd curse God. After a couple days of that, he'd be suddenly terrified of God, and he'd shake and cry out and *apologize*, trying to con a deal. But then a little kid would wing a rock at him. That's when he would lose all faith in God.

Nora was squeezing his hands, watching his face.

Kenny yanked his hands away. He rubbed them on his pants.

"Get Tommy to tell you more," Kenny said.

"That's all he knows."

"Get Tick fired up."

The video went back to the beginning. The rubber gloves moved a small knife around the squirrel's shoulders, slicing here and there, just right. The gloves put down the knife. They gripped the hide on both sides and started to pull.

Nora grimaced. "Tick's got his hands full. He can't help us."

A person who already looks sort of like a grunion should not grimace, Kenny decided, but all he said was, "Not 'help us.' Help you."

Kenny looked hard at Nora.

"What is it about you, Nora? Why can't you let it go? The world is fucked. So you came to Good River Harbor. Smart move. Low clouds and constant rain will cheer you up. Yessiree, what you need are twenty hours of darkness and exactly forty-six neighbors—six drunks, seven gossips, thirty-three crack shots, and a cat. If this doesn't make you forget about the world's troubles, nothing can. What did this town do to deserve you anyway, Nora Montgomery, Mary Poppins's evil twin, floating into town in her yellow raincoat whenever we need somebody to fuck things up."

Kenny leered, scrunching up one eye. "Joke," he said. "Har."

Nora's eyes flashed into fire, like propane rings. But soon it was water, not fire, that shimmered there. She closed her eyes and dropped her forehead onto the table. "Yeah. What is it about you, Nora?" she repeated.

While the gloved hands pulled the squirrel skin off the little body again, and then again, Kenny flailed himself. Truly stupid. Deeply, irredeemably stupid. An accursed man, of an accursed species, on a doomed planet. He reached over and lifted Nora's head, awkwardly, by the chin.

"I'm sorry, I'm really sorry. I'd help you. But I don't have a dog in this fight," he said.

"I think you do," said Nora.

KENNY RETRIEVED a fish head he'd been saving in a five-gallon pail on his front gangway. Nora would be a lot happier person if she'd stop hoping so much. He raised his head and shouted, "*Glittering hope beckons many men to their undoing.*" Ranger yowled. A hopeful raven flapped off the railing. A passing tourist grabbed her husband's arm and pressed to the far side of the boardwalk. "Euripides," he yelled. The woman threw him a sick smile. The fish head's smile looked equally sick. "It means, like, pessimists don't go off on risky missions," he muttered at the woman, rolling toward her, trying to explain. The woman scurried away.

He poked a wire through the fish's eyeball and out its toothy jaw, twisted the ends together and wired it to the center of his crab ring. Once he'd tied the line to his porch rail, he lowered it into the tide until he felt it thud on the mud. Then he went inside.

Kenny lived in one room on pilings over the water, there next to the Bath 'n' Bar. He slept on a cot raised two feet off the floor, above the cold air. His only light was a kerosene lamp. His only heat was a woodstove. The roof leaked at a joist, but he rigged up a string that directed water from the leak into a plastic bucket, so it kept his blankets dry for the most part.

The place was adequate, a little damp, dim in the corners. He'd strung a line over the woodstove and got some clothespins, for drying gloves and plastic bags. He had a shelf for the kitchen, which was a washbasin, propane gas burner, and a bottle of the blue dish detergent that decorates every cabin in Alaska. The log walls of the cabin were wallpapered with animal skins, stretched and drying. Field mice. Pine squirrels.

Kenny's important possessions, however, were on the table. He had the full skeleton of a little brown bat. A rock scallop with a kelp holdfast attached. A beaver's front tooth, which was orange. A jar of feathers. A fossil trilobite.

This pleased Kenny, that he had everything he needed and absolutely nothing else. He knew everyone he needed to know and absolutely no one else. He said what he needed to say and nothing more. He knew how to do what he needed to do. He did nothing more than that. Everything he did, he did the way he always did it, and he was proud of that. He smelled like the house, and the house smelled like him—propane and fish. He lived alone. He didn't hope for anything or any fate he didn't already have.

He thought that might be his only virtue.

The bat skeleton could hope that one dark night, its bones would grow stringy muscles under black leather wings, and it would leap away toward the moon. The tooth could hope for a beaver. The feather might hope for a raven's wing. The holdfast could beat itself up with regret, knowing it should have put its roots down on something steadier than a scallop. The trilobite could hope and maybe even pray, "Dear God, in your infinite mercy, let me evolve." It could pray that its exoskeleton would soften like wet leather and pulse long enough at the edge of the sea-marsh that some day—yes!—it would become something—anything—alive and wondering.

Fine. Hope it, for all the good it does. Kenny was done with that.

In low light and gathering blackflies, Kenny pulled on his mouse hat and rolled out onto the porch. There must have been a northwest wind, because he could hear—faint and far away—the stumble-plink of Nora's pitiful piano playing, all the way over at Green Cove. He tossed a gal-vanized bucket into the bay, jerked it a couple of times to sink it, and hauled up seawater. He put the bucket on the burner, flicked a lighter and stepped back. Blue flames shot up the edges of the bucket and settled into a roaring yellow ring. This is the beauty of propane: You can count on propane to light when you turn the knob on and go off when you turn the knob off. That's one difference between propane and hope.

You've got to know when to turn the hope down so low it flicks green and pops off.

He reached over the railing to catch the line on his crab trap. Putting his back into it, he hauled the rope over the roller mounted on the rail. From the weight, he knew before the ring broke the surface that he'd caught a couple already. He levered the trap over the railing. Dungeness, big as dinner plates. The female he threw out first, reaching behind the pinchers to grab the rear of the carapace. She could try to pinch him, and she did, but he knew that the real danger is never from the ones you're grabbing, but from the ones you're not. He pulled out two nice males. These were the old guys, wider than the span of his hand, with barnacles on their carapaces. He laid them on their backs on the railing, where they gasped and bubbled and flexed their muscles, closing their claws on air. They were hoping, that's for sure.

"Hope doesn't do any good, can do a lot of harm," Kenny mumbled at the crabs, "all that random snapping at air. It's sad, that's what it is, all that trying. Try to stay away from sad trying."

He picked up one of the doomed crabs, wrapping one hand around each of its big claws. Fact was, when he had the crab, the crab couldn't get him. He hooked the side of the crab's carapace on the deck railing and pulled hard. There was a loud, crunching crack. The whole back pulled off and fell into the sea, spilling yellow fat. Now the crab really started hoping, and it's surprising how strong a crab is, how you have to hold on tight, because he's arm-wrestling you. Kenny centered the crab's body along the angle of the rail and pressed hard on both sides. The crab cracked into two halves. It went limp, claws and legs suddenly long. The gills lay in beautiful array along the back, like ivory feathers. When Kenny scraped them off and shook the crab over the water, the gills floated away like gulls flying.

Kenny held half a crab in each hand. He scolded the half that had the eyes still attached. "I know you don't have the brains to really hope. You probably don't even try. That's even sadder, to snap and struggle like you're trying but your brains are gone."

The crab's blue eyes had clouded yellow, like a foggy dawn. Kenny's crabs were always dead when they went into the boiling water. This was why he cleaned them first, so they didn't try to crawl out. That kind of scrabbling he couldn't stand.

When the crabs in the bucket flushed bright red, he pulled them out with tongs and dipped them in cold water. They steamed on the railing, cooling—red claws rigid, white muscles of the body in cartilage crisp and brittle as tracing paper.

"God damn it, Ranger," he said dejectedly. "Why do you want me to take these crabs to Nora?" Ranger dropped his nose to the ground and sprang up barking. "All right. But we're not going to stay. Just give her the crabs, turn around, and come home. She scares me, that one, all that fierce hope. And you, dumb dog, you're the worst hoper of all."

July 11

HIGH TIDE		LOW TIDE	
12:52am	17.7ft	6:25am	-0.8ft
0:57pm	6.5ft	6:33pm	0.3ft

"My dad says you're pretty." Davy stole a glance at Meredith's jeans.

"My dad says you're trouble." She flipped her hair over her shoulder.

"My dad says, 'Kiss her, but don't tell your mother.'"

"If you did, my dad would break your neck. Simple as that." She snapped her fingers. "He says if I spend any time with you, he'll kill you and he'll ruin your dad and he'll be very disappointed in me." Meredith giggled, and said it again in her dad's steel-shiny voice, "Very dis-appoin-ted."

For some reason, Davy thought this was hilarious, and he laughed until he had to lean over to catch his breath. Meredith grabbed him by the throat and shook him, like she was going to choke him to death. Her hands felt smooth and warm on his neck.

Davy reached out, gripped the timber above him, swung out like on a trapeze, chinned himself, and dropped back onto the sand. Not every guy is strong enough to do that. Meredith pretended she didn't see, but he knew she did.

This was probably the greatest place Davy had ever found. It's hard to get alone with your secret girlfriend in a town like Good River Harbor, and after that tragedy with the note in the clamshell, the only thing Davy could think of was bribing Curtis to pass a message. Davy said a dollar, but he'd made the mistake of bragging to Curtis that he had a twenty and a five, so it ended up costing Davy all the gas money, but he made Curtis give a money-back guarantee that he'd get the message delivered right, so that was worth it. The message told Meredith to meet Davy on the mudflat under the school right after supper and he would skiff her out to a secret place and show her a surprise.

Davy told his dad he wanted to take Meredith to the clam beach at the Kis'utch River, and could he have the skiff? He had no idea what Meredith told her mom and dad—a lie, whatever it was. Davy couldn't believe his luck when there she was, in her tight jeans and high boots, waiting for him like he'd told her.

He nosed the skiff in. She jumped aboard, pushing them off, and Davy scooted them around Green Point. On behind the point and the cove, there was an old wharf that used to be part of the cannery. It was a big square of planked deck up on cross-braced piers—a deck that might have been wide enough to hold a cabin, but there was nothing up there now but fireweed growing in the gull crap on deck. A storm took out the gangway that connected the wharf to land, so it was just sitting offshore rotting up on high pilings. Nobody went there but gulls. A wooden shelf ran between the timbers underneath the wharf, making a place where a couple of people could sit. But what made it so wonderful was the skirting around the edges of the deck that made kind of a wall, so people on the shelf could disappear if they wanted to—which was really something in a small, nosy town squished between the mountain and the sea.

It was just past low tide when they boated in under the stranded wharf, and the tide would be rising fast. It was going to be the night of the flood-tide of the pink-salmon moon. That's a powerful time, Davy's mom had told him, when the sun and the moon pull from the same side of the Earth. Good and bad things can happen then. Davy cut the engine and tipped it up, letting the skiff coast under the wharf. He tied the boat tight to a piling and held out his hand, very gallant.

Meredith said, "I can get out myself," and vaulted into six inches of water. Right away, she leaned over and started looking for cool things between the rocks, which made her jeans fit her even better. Davy found a sea cucumber. It was long and red with orange spikes, like a punk sausage. He held the cucumber up to Meredith's mouth and pretended it was giving her a kiss. She swatted him hard in the arm.

"Dipshit," she said. "That's the ass end."

He was rummaging around in the kelp, looking for a leather star, so he could rub the garlic smell on her nose, but the incoming tide was lapping at his boot tops. Time to climb.

He showed Meredith how she could put one foot in the angle where the bracing of the wharf is bolted to the piling, then hold on to the brace above her and sort of side-step diagonally up to the next angle on the other side.

"You have to watch your fingers at first, because the mussels and barnacles can slice them easy. Fold your sleeves over your hands," he told her.

The hardest part was almost at the top, where the bracing beams are coated with algae. For that part, Davy stayed under Meredith.

"I've got you," he said. If she slipped, he would put his hand on her pretty bottom to hold her steady.

After the slippery part, it was easy, and she climbed up the last brace, Davy right after her. Under the shelter of the deck and above the high-tide line, the planking was dry and flat. The planks that came down to sheath the wharf made a shadowy, whispery place, completely enclosed except for where storms had ripped away boards. There was a wide shelf there, and that's where Davy had a surprise for Meredith.

They crawled along the shelf, Davy going first to show the way.

"Look," he said, and pressed back against the wall so she could see past him. There were five mud cups stuck to the wall—barn swallow nests. A mother barn swallow sat in each nest, rustling her wings down over the nestlings. In each nest, a row of little round heads stuck out from under the flared shadow-blue wings of a mom. The nestling heads were gray and brown, almost shadows themselves, but when one opened its mouth, its maw was as yellow as a buttercup.

"One, two, three, four in that nest." The moms fluttered their wing feathers and shifted on the nest, but they sat tight, even though Meredith was only a few feet away. Every time a mom shifted her weight, all the yellow mouths in her nest sprang open. Meredith giggled.

"I can hear the babies peeping," Meredith whispered.

"The moms are blinking. They have white eyelids."

Meredith looked at Davy. "That's cool," she said. "This is a cool place."

The wind was picking up and the tide was rising, but it was dry and cozy in their hideaway. The sun, bouncing along the western mountain-tops, shone in under the wharf. Waves were really barreling in, but even the spray couldn't touch them, up on the shelf with the birds. They sat side by side, swinging their legs over the ledge.

"Isn't this a cool place!" Davy said, because he couldn't think of anything else to say, now that he was alone with Meredith. Her hair was long and brown and her eyes were blue as heaven. She was wearing low-rider jeans and a hooded sweatshirt halfway unzipped down the front. Davy squirmed closer to see if there was anything under the sweatshirt. Meredith leaned away and started to talk.

"How'd you find this place?" The question was an ordinary one, but Davy smiled to himself. His dad told him that girls will start to talk when they're thinking about kissing.

"I do a lot of exploring," Davy decided to say, "because I'm going to get myself set up as a wilderness guide."

"In Good River?" She seemed sort of surprised, which surprised him, because where else would he do it?

"I guess."

"My dad wants me to go to college Outside, but I'll do what I want."

Davy sat forward. This might be a problem, because how can you have a girlfriend who doesn't even live in your town?

She looked at him sort of cross, so Davy pulled a joint from his shirt pocket. This was the first time Davy ever smoked a joint with anybody but stupid Curtis and he wasn't sure about good manners with a girl. Do you get it going and then share, or do you offer her first drag? And what if she's worried about germs?—Davy had a hard enough time getting one joint from Curtis, no chance for two.

Meredith looked at the joint. "Is that dope?"

He grinned and nodded. This was the risky part.

"I do dope all the time," Meredith said, and shot him a look through lowered lids. She took the joint between her fingers like a cigarette and put it between her lips. He flicked a lighter, held it out.

"You have to sort of suck to get the fire going," he offered helpfully.

A wave smacked against a piling, splashing water. The wind lifted into their hideout and flowed back out. That was going to be some tide.

She sucked and then blew the smoke out of her mouth.

"Kind of hold it in for a minute," he said.

"There's a lot of bird poop up here," Meredith said.

Davy took off his jacket, spread it on his lap, and gave it a pat. Meredith stayed where she was. It was worth a try. She took another drag. Her words came out in bubbles of smoke.

"My dad says you can get schistosomiasis from bird poop."

"My dad doesn't give a schisto-whatever."

Meredith laughed out a mouthful of smoke. The joint wasn't working very well, but she didn't notice. Davy pivoted on the timber in front of the shelf, rolled onto his stomach, and stretched his arms and legs into space like an airplane, holding himself there, even though it took every muscle he had. Now what do I do? he wondered. Do people just say, do you want to be my girlfriend?

"Boeing 737," he said.

"Doofus," Meredith said, and poked his leg with her boot.

Davy climbed back onto the shelf. She handed him the joint, cold as stone. "Is this how you hold your mouth to suck the smoke?" she asked. She made a face like a gorilla slurping worms.

"No, it's like this." Davy made his mouth into a kiss. Meredith reached her hands behind his head, drew him toward her, and planted a soft kiss on his lips. She drew back, looked into his astonished face, and laughed. Davy reached his hand behind her head, tangled his fingers in her long, soft hair, and pulled her close to him. The kiss was on her lips, then on her neck, then deep in the sweetness of the space behind the half-open zipper. He burrowed his face down into that darkness, kissing. Still holding the cold joint in one hand, he reached his arm around her, lifting the sweatshirt, and ran his hand over the warm smooth arch of her back.

"Is this how you hold your mouth?" she asked, crossing her eyes and sticking out her tongue. Davy surfaced.

"Is this how you hold your mouth?" she asked, putting her finger in one corner of her mouth and pulling. Davy laughed as well as a person can laugh who is smothering a silly little face in kisses. She pushed him gently away.

Davy sighed and smiled. He put the joint in his own mouth. Holding back his hair to keep from setting himself on fire, he lit the joint, inhaled a stream of smoke, then inserted the joint gently between her beautiful lips. He put his arm around her shoulders and settled back against the wharf. It was wonderful, the way her shoulder fit right under his arm and her head rested against his neck. They sat like that for a long time before he got up the nerve to put his hand on the swell of her sweatshirt. The hillocks under his hand were warm and sort of squishy. He closed his eyes. If the world ended right then, if lightning flashed from heaven and incinerated him at that moment, if he had a heart attack and croaked right there and then, he would die a happy man.

A flock of sanderlings blew in. They fluttered around, crying out in their little voices, then cozied up together on a span. They flicked water off their backs, and called kwit kwit until they were quiet. The sun settled down behind a mountain, which turned suddenly black. Meredith whispered to keep from scaring the birds.

"What time is it? My dad will kill me if I'm not home by dark." She looked down at the tide.

"I gotta get home too. My mom's coming on the morning ferry—she's probably already on board—and me and Tommy are supposed to clean the house before he goes to bed."

"How are we going to get out of here?"

The sanderlings startled and flew off, peeping.

Meredith pointed at the water that was slapping halfway up the pilings. Deep shadows pooled under the wharf. Davy could hardly see the skiff. But there it was, dimly green and ghostly underwater, bottom up. It slowly rotated around the bowline that he'd tied tight to the pilings, a knot now ten feet below the tide.

"Oh shit. What a stupid cheechako mistake."

DAVY WOULD HAVE given everything to start his life over. Or go back one day, just one. "Let me do one thing different in my whole life, just one thing. Just one clove hitch. Stupid. I'm stupid. If I have to be so stupid, why does it have to be now?"

"You're always stupid," Meredith yelled. "So what's new?"

He had to think harder than he had ever thought before. But it was like he could either breathe or he could think, not both, and his head was thinking so hard he could have passed out.

"Stupid. That's what."

The swallows were circling around their nests, crapping in the air, peeping like they thought they'd die. The tide was smacking on the pilings. It was a dark tide, like some live thing trying to climb onto the wharf. It got a rough handhold on the barnacles, heaved itself up, and fell off, grunting. It slid a dark hand behind them. It tried again. Darkness spread across the water.

"No. Not swimming to shore," he yelled at Meredith, as if she'd suggested it. Too far, too cold, too rough. "And what would we do on shore if we made it?" soaking wet, freezing, and the tide pushing them against the cliffs or into the dog-hair alder.

"STOP IT."

They stopped yelling and looked at each other, breathing hard.

Davy had brought her out here. He'd tied the boat short and sunk it. It was his job to get her home before her dad figured them out.

"Just let me think," he said quietly.

She pulled her hood over her head and zipped her jacket, tucked up her legs, and huddled back in the corner with her eyes closed. Davy thought she was going to yell at him again, but she didn't.

"Okay," she said instead. "Let's see you think."

"Okay," he said. "Okay."

First thing is, we're safe, he told himself firmly. The tide is not going to come up more than another seven feet. The worse that could happen is that we have to spend the night on this shelf. High tide will be at midnight tonight. Low tide will be at six in the morning. We could wait it out, then muck it to shore at low tide and hike home on the beach. We would be coming down the boardwalk just after our dads finished eating breakfast. Just after my mom got off the ferry.

The horror of this made his head swim. Nobody would be eating breakfast in Good River Harbor tomorrow. Nobody would be meeting the ferry. Another hour and the grown-ups would be asking around, figuring out that Meredith wasn't wherever it was she said she would be, and he wasn't clamming, and the skiff wasn't at the slip, and wherever Meredith was, he probably was too. They'd launch every boat into the darkness, looking for them, scared they were dead. When they found them, they would kill them.

"I'm going to dive down and cut the line."

"No, you're not," she said without opening her eyes. "That water is fifty-six degrees. You know that."

He checked his belt for his knife. A sharpening stone would have been a help, but that's the way it was. He could dive ten feet.

"You can't dive that deep."

"I can. I have."

When he cut the line, the boat would bob to the surface. He was sure of this. He'd helped his dad put extra flotation in the stern this winter. The engine would be ruined already, soaked in all that saltwater. But his dad always kept oars tied into the boat, and once it was afloat, they could climb down, bail the boat, and row home. That would give him time to think about how to tell his dad about the engine.

Once he'd made up his mind, he saw things as clearly as watching a movie. Everything was dim around him, but he could see himself moving like an actor on the Technicolor screen, the colors that bright. He took off his jacket and T-shirt so he would have something warm to put on when he got out of the water. On the movie screen, his chest was as white as a halibut belly. He hoped Meredith still had her eyes closed, but he couldn't be sure. She was sitting up there in the balcony in the dark. He took off his boots, but left on his socks, so the barnacles didn't cut his feet. He wasn't sure about his jeans. Made sense to take them off, but there was Meredith right there, so he kept them on.

"It's dangerous," she said. "If you do this, it'll be the stupidest of all the stupid things you've ever done."

He sidled sideways down a diagonal brace. It shook under his weight. The tide heaved and grunted, slapping up, soaking his pants to the knees. His skin prickled up his crotch into his armpits. The black water reached up, grabbed at his legs, slipped off. A floating gas can rang against a piling. If he didn't get the boat off, the bells of the church in town would be gonging just like that, rousting people from their evening beers to search for two damn kids lost at sea, one of them so stupid they should drown him.

He took a huge breath, jumped feetfirst into the water, flailed to the surface, gasped as if he'd been kicked in the chest, took another breath, folded at the waist, and dove. His hand hit the keel. Kicking furiously, he followed it down to the bow and groped for the rope. The rope was humming, that tight. His hand gripped it, held it steady. He sawed against the fibers. A couple gave way. Damn this knife. How long can I saw without bursting? He doubled over, pushed off the hull, and rocketed back into birds screaming and dark water slapping.

Tread water, gulp air, and back down. This time or die. He smacked his head into the hull, he was pushing down so fast, and felt his way to the bow. With all the strength in his back, he slashed the full length of the knife against the rope. The rope flew apart. The boat reared up, caught him in the ribs, and cracked his shoulder against the piling. He saw the pain of it, a blue explosion, heard a snap. The boat lunged up. A wave grabbed it and tilted it into the tidal current. Davy leapt after it. That explosion again. His shoulder, on fire. The skiff turned bow for stern, then bucked away upside down in a mess of life jackets and buckets.

Waves dragged at Davy's jeans. He reached for the cross-timber. That flash of pain. With his good arm, he reached around a piling and hung on. Splinters dug into his skin. Every time a wave lifted him and dragged him under, barnacles sliced his chest. He scrabbled his legs against the post and grabbed again for the strut, but he couldn't pull up his weight with one arm. He must have weighed a thousand pounds.

"Shit, Meredith."

He felt the bounce of her steps on the strut, and her fist around his belt. As she dragged him up, he scrambled his feet onto the strut. Together they fumbled up the cross-timbers and heaved their bodies onto the shelf.

Sometime in the night, a humpback passed by. Davy heard its blow, like a chest dragged across a deck, then another blow, farther toward Good River Harbor. The dark water shone like it was polished. Now and then, a pod of porpoises leapt by, streaming wakes of bioluminescent sparks. Once a sanderling cried out in its sleep. When squalls blew through, the water rustled against the pilings, in and out, like breathing. Davy held as still as he could to keep his shoulder from catching fire. Salt stung his sliced chest.

When the church bell began to toll, far away and faint, Davy shuddered to keep from crying.

"Meredith," he whispered, but she was asleep.

Somehow his socks and jeans were hung to dry on a crossbeam. His T-shirt was wrapped around his feet. His jacket was wrapped around his legs. He and Meredith were sitting against the side planks. His naked back was against her bare chest, with her sweatshirt around both of them. Her breasts pressed hard into his back. He could sense the warm, slow rise and whistle of her breathing.

He breathed out when she breathed out, breathed in when she breathed in—the sea-wet air, the smell of birds, her hair warm on his neck. He did not hear the ferry churn by in the darkness. He did not hear the cries of the kittiwakes trailing off its stern.

PAN PAN. Pan pan. Pan pan. This is Coast Guard sector five, Ketchikan. Coast Guard sector five, Ketchikan. Time is two two three six. Two two three six. We have a report that a Lund skiff with a red stripe is overdue from Good River Harbor with zero two persons on board. Last seen leaving Good River Harbor, fifteen nautical miles northeast of the Bean Island buoy, at one nine three zero. All vessels are asked to keep a close lookout for signs of distress and render assistance if possible. If anyone has information about this vessel, please contact the Coast Guard, sixteen alpha. Out.

ELEVEN P.M. A tail wind was blowing, so it was cold at the stern of the ferry where Davy's mom had left her backpack. That's where Annie Klawon would sleep, but it was too soon for that. She wouldn't try to sleep until she was exhausted. She had found a dead spot at the bow, and this is where she stood, watching the ferry churn through the dark toward her family in Good River Harbor. Even out of the wind, the air was cold and thick with night-dampness and diesel fumes.

She cinched her hood tight, smiling to think of the fuss and flurry at the McIver household in Good River Harbor, as Tick and the boys cleaned the house. Her big Tick would be trundling fresh sheets back from Lillian's Bath 'n' Bar, probably for the first time since she'd left. Davy would have the broom, sweeping fish scales and hemlock needles out the door and off the deck to scatter on the tide. Tommy? Who knows what Tommy does when he's excited?—dance around, everything but sleep.

The ferry entered Muir's Passage. A chain rattled, a door clanged against metal, and a watchman walked to the bow. The watchman leaned over dark water that rolled under the hull. Navigational markers designate the channel, blinking green and red on a course angling through reefs. But nothing warns of the unexpected hazards—a log boom or gill net, a buoy escaped from its mooring or a boat dead in the water, the engine blown. Shuddering forward at barely ten knots, the ferry wove a drunkard's path through tidal currents and submerged shoals. The watchman suddenly straightened and spoke urgently into the intercom. A spotlight shot from the bridge and jabbed over the water, searching the bow, the forested shoreline, a rock reef. The light came to rest on a green buoy no more than fifty yards from the port bow. Male voices called back and forth. Then the spotlight winked out and the boat moved heavily to starboard away from a place foul with rocks.

Annie Klawon always sang a small prayer of thanksgiving when the ferry left the passage behind and nosed into the empty sea. Outside the passage, there are no horizons, no high bluffs to steer by, no sounds, no stars. Night clouds are indistinguishable from night ocean. The only indication of direction is rain, sluicing in from the west. But in the open sea, you won't stove in your keel on a reef or lurch in whirlpool tides. The open sea was where she was raised, and that's where she felt at home, safest with at least a hundred fathoms under her hull. Long-liners, that's what the Klawons were, pulling long fishing lines from big cylinders, a couple hundred hooks a line, hand baited with chunks of herring. When she was lucky, Annie Klawon's father told her to pilot the boat. That job was dry and warm enough. When she wasn't lucky, she was in the stern, unhooking fish as fast as the lines reeled in screeching, heaving the black cod into the tote, heaving the tomcod, the hake, the uglies, and the sharks overboard. That job was wet and cold and slippery on a shivering, slanting deck.

The watchman left his post. Annie Klawon left her post too and worked her way down the port deck, through the patch of light and laughter thrown from the bar, through yellow streaks from curtained cabins, into the empty dark at the stern. The deck was slick with splash. Her hair whipped across her eyes as she dragged a deck chair into the lee of the life jacket bin and pulled her sleeping bag from her pack. She stumbled backward and braced her legs on the suddenly pitching deck. The boat wallowed through the wake of a ship that had passed unseen long minutes ago. She felt behind her for the chair.

The night before she had dreamed that Tick had lost power in a troller in a gale. His long wet braid was blown across his face and rain was streaking down his slicker. He braced on the deck as wind turned the boat broadside to the waves and dark water poured over the rail. He struggled to start the engine, pulling out the choke, grinding the starter, leaping to check the fuel lines. Davy and Tommy clung to the rails as the world fell away, overwhelmed them, and fell away again. Rain plastered their hair to their faces, blinding them. Sideways to the waves, the lee rail rolled under, waves rose and broke over the weather deck. The figures of her family were cardboard cutouts dissolving in the wind and rain. She knew they were coming to find her. But she pitched past them in the storm, calling out.

Her father had told her that Tick would be taken by the sea. He hadn't said it in so many words, but he never did say things straight out. "If you marry him," is what her father had said, "sadness will come to you." Then he turned and went into his workshop. He had said all that he would ever say about Tick. She tried to imagine how Tick could make her sad. But the only cruel thing she could imagine that Tick could do was to die—that tall, beautiful, capable man with a beard impossibly golden red and hair as long as her father's hair, a braid straight down his back, but the color of dawn, not midnight. If Tick did anything to hurt her, it would be against his will and all his power. And the only force greater than he was, was the sea. That's how she had thought about it then. She had slammed out the door and spent the night with her Aunt Josephine.

She married Tick, but not in the way she wanted. All that winter, her mother crocheted blankets, piles of blankets to give away at her wedding. When Marjorie Klawon used up one ball of yarn, she tied in another and kept on crocheting. The blankets piled up—yellow and green, then green and red, then red and black, endlessly. All winter, Annie Klawon's father worked at his bench, making his tools. He carved the handle of a chisel from an alder limb and a mallet from maple. He would not make gifts for the people at the wedding. Instead, he would carve his only daughter a canoe as long as his arm and he would paint it red, green, black, so that his Annie Klawon would always have a way to come back to her father's house.

Day after day, he went into the forest, touching the trees as he passed through them, looking for the tree he needed. But one evening at the end of winter, her father did not come home, not even after dark, and when they looked for him with flashlights, they found him slumped against the base of a yellow cedar tree, cold as the night. So Annie Klawon and Tick were quietly married by the village priest, with only Aunt Josephine and Annie's sobbing mother as witnesses.

Why did she marry him? Annie married Tick because one day in Hollis, she was struggling with a wooden extension ladder that insisted on tangling in the alders between her family's house and her neighbor's shed. First the legs would snare on a branch, then the rope would wrap around a thicket, no matter how she aimed or tugged. A big man with huge hands came by and said, "Hey, let me help you with that. What's going on?"

"I locked myself out," Annie Klawon said.

The man picked up the ladder as if it weighed nothing. The ladder sprang free from the alders. He was wearing heavy weather gear, but not even the rubberized fabric could hide the expanse of his shoulders.

"Is that door up there unlocked?" The man pointed to the side door on her porch fifteen feet above the street.

"Yes," Annie said.

He lifted the ladder and set it against the porch railing. It was beautiful, how he lifted the ladder and set it against the porch railing. No grunting, no timid tugging to be sure the ladder wouldn't slip. Up he went and over the railing onto the porch. He must be a seaman, to be that graceful in the air. He disappeared through the side door, and before long, he came out the front, where Annie Klawon was standing, staring at him.

"There you go," he said. "But the front door wasn't locked."

Annie knew that. She had already climbed up to the side porch and let herself out the front door. She had been trying to return the neighbor's ladder when Tick came along.

"Wouldn't you love a man like that?" Annie had asked her Aunt Josephine, and Josephine had to agree that it's a good-hearted man who helps first and asks questions later.

"And wouldn't he be a good provider?"

"And isn't it a strong man who can lift an extension ladder out of alders?"

Annie wadded up her jacket for a pillow, tucked the garbage bag tightly around the foot of her sleeping bag, and burrowed in. She would have to be careful what she let herself think about, if she was to have any chance of getting to sleep. Lying on her back, looking into another squall, she began to call up her favorite memories. This is what she did each night in Seattle. After she sang her boys to sleep, she climbed into a cold cot and remembered herself to sleep. She remembered Tick with his legs stretched under the kitchen table and his stocking feet sticking out the other side. He's listening to marine forecasts as he torques pliers to crimp the wire on a fishing lure, or dismantles a spinning reel, every tiny screw laid out on a newspaper, or resolders the wires in the electric plug for the radio. She hears that spattering, and smells the acrid smoke. Sometimes she remembers snow falling past the window, snowflakes big and soft as mice. They appear as they enter the light cast from the kitchen window and then vanish, as if they existed only in that space of time. More often she remembered rain, shiny in the light from the lamps. Or a soft silver afternoon, sitting on the gravel beach at Good River Harbor, her legs braided into Tick's, her younger son, Tommy, climbing over the two of them as if they were logs, her older son, Davy, pitching stones into the sea.

Sometimes, she liked to remember putting Tommy to bed. She ducks under the top bunk and plants a kiss on Tommy's forehead. He reaches for her neck and pulls her to him and kisses her. Then he curls into a ball. She tucks the blankets around the curve of his narrow shoulders. She backs out of the room then, pulling the door closed. The lamplight from the room behind her narrows until only a yellow line draws the contours of her son. Then she sits on the floor by the bedroom door and she sings, always the same song, always the same ending line, "*Tefaay. Aliinghaku::n amsanaku::n. Tefaay.* Through this story, nice weather, clear and calm."

It's quiet in the house then. She knows they are all listening to her sing, Davy and Tick in the front room, Tommy in bed, she at the bedroom door. They listen to water lapping against pilings under the house, a harbor seal's sneeze, the E-flat whistle of wind in the rigging of trawlers at anchor, the Green Point buoy, its moan hushed by fog. She believes that if two people are aware of the same thing, they are somehow joined. When the moon is out in Seattle, or if the air smells of the sea, she looks at the moon or smells the air, thinking maybe her boys are watching out the window the same moon or smelling the same wind. Then she believes that they are together. This is why Annie Klawon tells her boys to pay attention to the rain, the wind. To listen for the voices of the birds.

In the night, kittiwakes circled the ferry. The big spotlight lit their white wings. She could hear their cries, *keit lay day.* But why the spotlight? It was unusual for a ferry to shine a spotlight in the open water past the narrows. A lost ship out there somewhere, or maybe a log raft got loose, or a fishing boat dead in the water. Turning her face suddenly to port, Annie listened closely. She sat up, listening even more intently, but she wasn't sure what she heard. She covered her head with her sleeping bag and closed her eyes.

Annie Klawon remembered what it would be like to come home. She would be at the railing at dawn when the ferry edged into the pilings at Good River Harbor. The ferry would pull into port, and then she would be back with Tick and Davy and Tommy. Gulls would rise from the fireweed that grew on the pilings. The bowman would throw the monkey fist underhand to the pier. The mooring lines would groan, winching the ferry tight against the pilings. Tommy would run down the ramp and wrap his arms around her waist. Davy and Tick would hold back, grinning, then reach their arms around her shoulders and take her pack. The pink salmon would be in. Salmonberries would be ripe and Swainson's thrushes will have fledged. The woods would be full of thrushes learning to sing and new sapsuckers learning to drill a straight row of holes. So many times she's come home. So many times she's left again.

How does it feel to come home? Some ways, it feels like danger, when every part of you is on alert—probing with your nose like a deer, inhaling warily to catch every change, listening as an act of will, willing your shoulders to remember the pressure of your oldest son's hug, willing your eyes to remember the vision of your young son's head, rumpled like a raven with its back to the wind. You have to force yourself to remember everything, knowing you will need to go over those details in your mind again and again. It feels like trying to memorize all the license plates in case you have to tell the police, and the details of every person's weight and height. You have to prepare for it all to be gone.

≋≋≋≋

PAN PAN. Pan pan. Pan pan. This is Coast Guard sector five, Ketchikan. Coast Guard sector five, Ketchikan. Time is zero zero three one. Zero zero three one. We have a report that a Lund skiff with a red stripe has been sighted. The skiff is capsized and drifting two miles north northeast of Green Point. Zero two persons are missing and unaccounted for. All vessels in the area are asked to keep a close lookout and render assistance if possible. Anyone having information about the persons aboard this vessel is asked to contact the Coast Guard, sixteen alpha. Out.

≋≋≋≋

ZERO ZERO THREE ONE. Thirty-one minutes past midnight. As Annie Klawon dozed on the ferry and her son slept in Meredith's arms, a wave surged onto the beach at the mouth of the Kis'utch River. It pushed a line of gravel, then rolled it down again, a great rush of stone on stone. Another wave spilled up the shingle, and this time, a tongue of saltwater crossed the bar. The mix of saltwater and fresh, that sizzle, that sudden shimmer, flooded to the knees of a great blue heron. He lifted one foot, then another, leaving splayed footprints in the mud. He eyed the star-gleam that lit the flanks of minnows. When the stars disappeared behind a squall, the minnows were lost to him. He stretched, lifting his wings. Tide rose around the heron's thin legs, curling into small whirlpools. The heron crouched, sprang, squawked, and scraped the air with his wings.

The high water probed into the roots of the sedges, flowing along voles' beaten-down paths, spreading through soft-bottomed saltmarsh. Black and slick, the water slid around the bend, past a bank topped with horsetails broken under the weight of bears. Geese, settled for the night on Jimmy Pete's weir, startled at the sound of water stealing up through the stones—a whisper, a click. Muttering, the geese pushed to their feet, paced the weir, shook rain off their tails. But the water continued to rise. A goose stalked to the pond and shoved off. Water poured over the weir. With great honking, the flock plowed into the air and dropped into the pool.

This was the flood-tide of the pink-salmon moon. Under the water, the rock yearned upward, as the sun and the moon pulled with their combined weight, and the Earth turned heavily on its axis. Every rock, every pebble, the heavy shoulders of bedrock lifted toward pale light that was just now flowing from the back of the squall. In each granite pore and crack between rocks, water rose. In each cavern, soft water rose. Rock and water, the whole mountain lifted its shoulders into the night. Rock creaked against stone slab, squeezing water upward; water deep inside the mountain lifted toward the distant moon. Stars poured blue light into crevasses in the snowfields and tugged on the ice, spilling water from pools on its pocked slick. Over the lip of the waterfall, meltwater dropped in vertical currents straight toward the heart of the Earth. Falling water caught the light of the stars and carried it, blue and bursting, to the bottom of the pool. There it rebounded, flying apart, spraying starlight on liverwort and maidenhair ferns. The night sounded the groan of the stiff Earth shifting, ancient stone against ancient bone.

Forest duff shifted and the trees themselves lifted heavily toward the starlight. An ancient Sitka spruce, in four hundred years grown heavy-bodied and twisted as a dragon, gradually released its grip on the soil. Its roots clawed for a long moment at the dirt, its branches convulsed, and it toppled into the river. Where it arced down, a cloud of golden needles floated in the night, a mist of starlit needles where the spruce branches had been. The first branches hit the water, flinging up fins of spray, a crackle like water on fire. Then, the top of the tree crashed into the far bank. The tree split its length, and its belly sank into the stream. Water piled against its body, then slid across, turning the rough trunk to beaten silver. Needles drifted down, swirled away. Underwater, blue bubbles traced current lines over and under the broken tree. Water drummed through branches, beating a dull rhythm onto the deeper grumble of the lifting Earth.

As moon and sun rode slowly through that moment, the Earth belled below the deep thrumming spruce, the squealing rock, the clatter of pebbles in water that fell down the flank of the moon-borne mountain. Salmon slid upstream.

PAN PAN. Pan pan. Pan pan. This is Coast Guard sector five, Ketchikan. Coast Guard sector five, Ketchikan. Time is zero one three five. Zero one three five. We have a report that the boat Annie K has a skiff under tow and is proceeding to Good River Harbor. Zero two persons are missing and unaccounted for. All vessels in the area are asked to keep a close lookout and render assistance. If anyone has information about the persons aboard this vessel, please contact the Coast Guard, sixteen alpha. Out.

DAVY SWAM UP through dreams about bees, swam through bees scattered like points of light, but it was a single bee that chased him, buzzing with relentless fury. "Get away!" Davy sat up and then slumped back against Meredith as his shoulder shouted out and reality circled around him, more threatening than any bee. Shadows still filled the shelf under the wharf, but morning glare on the strand threw wavering light into the timbers. The tide had slipped out from under the wharf as the night slipped away, leaving a broad expanse of sand pocked with sea anemones, closed tight. There was no watery sound now, just the soft chirp of feeding nestlings and a buzz as insistent as bees.

"It's a skiff," Meredith said. "They've been coming past all night with spotlights. And look." She pointed at the beach. People were walking up and down the tideline, veering off to peer behind rocks and poke into piles of kelp, checking all the places a young body might have washed up in the night. One man was searching the fringe of alders where a bedraggled teenager might have stumbled, coughing and hypothermic, and fallen on his face.

"This is weird," she said softly. "I've heard that when you die, you leave your body and float up, and you can look down and see the sad people as they look at your corpse and take off your nightgown and wash your naked body. You can see your own naked body."

"Jesus Christ," Davy said. "We're not dead." He paused to consider. "Not yet." He considered further. "Let's see your naked body." But it was a lame joke and it wasn't going anywhere, and neither were they. "I think our best bet is to stay here forever. We could sneak down at night and get clams and sea urchins and eat them raw, and drink from the creek." He turned his head to give her a kiss, but it hurt like hell and he gave it up.

"Davy, look." Meredith whispered. She was pointing to a skiff. A man stood in the stern, scanning the sea with binoculars. "It's Dad."

He must have seen something, because he jerked around, revved the engine, and shot forward. Grabbing a boathook, he clambered to the bow and fished the object out of the water. An orange life jacket, dangling straps. He disentangled it from the hook and pressed it to his chest, holding it like a baby, that tight, that close to his body. Then he fell onto the seat, still cradling the life jacket as if he were sheltering it from a storm. The receding tide pulled him away from shore, but he didn't seem to notice, just held on to that jacket. Finally, he reached into his pack, fumbled with his handheld radio, and raised it to his mouth.

"So now everybody in the Harbor knows that when we went over, we didn't have life jackets on," Meredith breathed.

"Meredith, we didn't go over," Davy insisted, but even he was beginning to imagine a rogue wave, a boat unbalanced by two entangled teenagers, a tragedy, oh God, both of them drowned—two of only three teenagers in the town, fifteen years old and drowned in each other's arms, and only dumb Curtis left to inherit the school. "We are not dead." He glanced toward Axel's boat for reassurance, but found only a man slumped over an empty life jacket, alone in a skiff slipping out to sea.

Meredith looked at Davy. "Do you think you can climb down?" She zipped up her sweatshirt and reached for Davy's clothes.

Together, they managed to get one arm in his shirt, but that was the extent of it. They quit trying and just tied his shirt around his chest, pinning his bad arm to his ribs. Cold, stiff, torn by barnacles, with a dull ache in his shoulder and zinging pain whenever he moved—dragging on wet jeans was simply impossible, although they tried time and again in a space too cramped to stand. Finally, Meredith was able to work his socks over his feet and pull on his boots. "Guess you're going to walk home in your boots and underwear, Davy McIver," Meredith said, and for the first time that morning, began to giggle. But for Davy, giggling just plain hurt, and who could laugh who knew he would soon be dragging into town with his jeans wrapped around his butt like a loincloth?

"Going down is going to be easier than up," Meredith said. "I'll be under you, in case you slip." The barnacle scrapes on Davy's chest screamed as he slid over the edge, reaching with his feet for the beam. But what he was thinking was how ridiculous his legs must look like from below, skinny white legs stuck in XtraTuf boots, dangling and groping around like an amputated octopus. Davy and Meredith were no more than halfway down the struts when they heard a shout. By the time they stood on the sand under the wharf, people were splashing toward them, yelling into radios, and by the time Davy and Meredith reached the shore, the church bell had begun to ring. The glad bronze song rolled down the sun-glazed beach, rebounded from the rocks, and filled the beach like light.

That's how they walked to town, through the light and church bells, holding hands, moving slowly because Davy's shoulder hurt and they had to stop often to tighten the knot that kept his jeans around his hips.

"WHERE ARE YOUR goddamn pants?"

Axel stood at the top of the ramp to the boardwalk.

"Leave him alone, Dad. He's hurt."

"He's going to be hurt before I get done with him. Meredith, get over here. As for you, McIver, if I ever see you with my daughter again, I'll kill you, you damned half-breed. Your father is fired fired fired and will never get a job in this town again. Meredith, get home and get a shower—wash off that kid's filth. Get out of my sight."

Meredith stared at her father. Then she straightened her shoulders, took Davy's face in her hands, and planted a kiss on his gaping mouth.

July 16

HIGH TIDE		LOW TIDE	
4:26am	17.7ft	10:42am	2.4ft
5:13pm	17.5ft	11:16pm	0.3ft

Ⅱ the parts of Tick's outboard motor sat on a tarp on the front porch, stinking of WD-40. Annie Klawon didn't know how Tick thought he could get it going again after Davy sank it. Half the night soaking up saltwater, half the night under tow, it was already starting to rust. Tick was on his knees and elbows, with his face almost to the floor, crawling from bolt to spring, reducing everything to even smaller parts, rinsing them in fresh water, drying them, spraying them, blowing on them as if he could breathe life back into a sparkplug hole. He pulled the flywheel out of the bucket of fresh water, turned it in his big hands, and sat back on his heels. Here Annie was, not even a week back home, and if there was anything left that hadn't already fallen apart, Tick was busy dismantling it.

"It would have been a good job, building the Bear Shelter for Axel," he said. "The kind of thing I'm good at. It would have been all we needed."

She was so tired of hearing him say that. How many times before he gave it up?

"It would have been a good job," Annie Klawon said.

He didn't look at her or make any answer.

"It would have been a great job. But you're fired. It's not fair. It's not your fault. But that's how it is." She was tired of saying that too.

"Don't go back to Seattle, Annie Klawon. Stay home. We can put enough pieces together to keep going."

She used to be so proud of him, how smart he was about working with the pieces. He could do anything, and he would do anything for her. If the back fell off a chair? Why then, the chair was a stool. And if a leg fell off the stool, why, drill a hole in one end for a wrist loop and you've got yourself a fish-whacker. Cut off the other legs, sand smooth the finish on the seat and—hey—a breadboard! Annie has kneaded a lot of bread on the place smoothed by the seat of her pants. And then all those extra chair legs! Three of them! This unexpected wealth! Pile them with the broken-down bike pump and the cracked tote on the front porch.

A mason jar will hold canned salmon until its lip chips. Then sand down the chip and it's a drinking glass, up there on the shelf with the jelly jars and the beer stein that was a coffee mug until the handle broke off.

"Put enough pieces together? Put enough pieces together. See how you are? When will we have more than pieces?" She kept her voice low, so the boys couldn't hear. "There is so much broken in this family. For you people, broken is the best thing about life, a chance to make something new. You people can't wait for something to fall apart or wash up on the beach. Can't wait for the month to go by, so you can cut the picture of a collie off of March and tape it to the wall, where it will hang for . . . How long has that picture been there? Thirteen years?"

"You people?"

Annie Klawon turned and stumbled into the kitchen. Davy and Tommy looked up from the table. These *are* my people, she thought. This is my family, my home—all I have in the world, all I love. If I don't have them, I don't have anything. She sat down at the table to keep from falling, so afraid she could hardly breathe. Is this how families fall apart? Not that you don't have the pieces, but that you don't have the strength to hold them together anymore?

Is this the unhappiness her father knew would come to her? Not the sucking force of the dark sea, drawing her husband down and down, but the smashing force of the brilliant surf, knocking her family to its knees again and again, finally lifting it, dropping it, and shattering it on the rocks.

Tick came in, washed his hands, swiped at a towel, and sat down. She sat on the floor between his legs and rested her head on his knee. It was a rough brown Carhartt knee, stained with oil and fish. His hand was on her hair, heavy as a dead thing. For a long time, while the oven ticked and logs clunked apart in the woodstove, they sat there like that, not talking. Annie felt desperate to say something. The ferry back to Seattle would leave day after tomorrow, and they couldn't afford to waste any of this time together—they had so little. But what was there to say? They had done the math—how much she can earn, how much the family needs. Davy can sell a few hides to Kenny. Tick can keep them in salmon and venison. But now there was probably a new outboard motor. It had cost them almost seven hundred dollars to charter a seaplane to Ketchikan and get Davy's collarbone seen to. Where were they going to get seven hundred dollars, if she didn't go back to work?

There was no other way. She would be back in Seattle, and her boys would be here in Good River Harbor, and it would be only the light from the moon or the smell of the sea or remembered sadness that kept them together. She leaned back against Tick, feeling the bulk of her husband, looking up to find his eyes on her. He watched her like a dog watches a master who is putting on his coat, with that kind of cringing and hope. Annie couldn't see Davy's eyes under his hair, his head was bent so low. His shirt hung loosely over his bad arm, still taped tight to his ribs. Tommy was watching his mother with expectation in his eyes, as if he knew a surprise.

"Is it time to show her, Dad?" Tommy asked.

Tick nodded.

Tommy lifted a cardboard box from the closet floor and set it on the table.

"Open it," he demanded.

Annie Klawon tugged open the flaps. One at a time, she pulled out seven little birdhouses, no bigger than apples. Each one was different, each one made of what Tommy had found in the forest. One had walls of alder bark and a tiny roof shingled with bracts from a spruce cone. Another had cedar walls and a shredded cedar roof. One had a tiny post where an imagined wren could sit. There was one made of hemlock cones, glued together. She held each one, each little home her son had glued together from whatever he could find.

"They're Christmas tree decorations. I'm going to sell them," Tommy said. "I'll set up a little tree at the top of the docks. I'm going to make a lot of money, so you can stay home."

"Dear God." So this was going to be the glue that held the family together, a six-year-old kid, standing alone on the dock in damp jeans and a red sweater, black hair sticking out in tufts, holding a tiny birdhouse.

Who could refuse him money? Even pitiful is a commodity. Heck, Annie thought, let's sell that. Fighting back tears, she turned on Tick, but he was excited too, cupping a tiny house in his hand. If he were to close that hand, he could crush the little house back into pine bracts and kindling. But he didn't. He never would. He held his hand out so Annie could see all the shingles and shutters on the house. It was a big hand with a heavy, calloused palm, and the finger that reached over to touch the tiny stovepipe was gentle and hard as wood.

She turned away and crossed to the oven to check the salmon. Reaching into the heat, she pressed a finger into its flesh. Fish is perfectly cooked when it resists the pressure of your finger, exactly like the fin of skin between your thumb and forefinger when you make a fist.

PART TWO
DOG-SALMON TIDE

From the farthest reaches of the North Pacific, from cold Kamchatkan and Korean waters, the dog salmon find their ways to the mouth of the hemlock-shaded stream where they were hatched. They have grown thick as logs and fat, mottled like the sea-light and alder leaves on the bottom of the stream.

A female sweeps the silt off the gravel while a male swims alongside her. His jaw is elongated, his teeth sharp and protruding. Side by side, they fin and shiver. Already they are dying. Where the skin is torn, gray mold spreads. Their fins tatter. Sometime in the soft night, their bodies shudder and squirt—a stream of eggs, a cloud of milky sperm.

The high tide lifts their old bodies into the grasses where they lie every which way, dying and stinking, shimmering from the motion of maggots eating under their skin. Gulls come first, sinking their beaks into the eyes and anuses. Bears come. Eagles come, mink, river otters. Dead fish sink to the bottom of the creek, swaying in the tide as if they were swimming. But what they are doing is disappearing, the way all bodies disappear, eaten away from underneath by worms. In a few weeks, only a hooded jaw will remain on the gravel, or a spinal disk attached to ribs soaring like the wings of a gull.

August 10

HIGH TIDE		LOW TIDE	
0:58am	19.0ft	7:25am	-3.6ft
1:53pm	17.4ft	7:43pm	-0.3ft

K enny shifted his back. If he slumped in his wheelchair at just the right angle, he could keep rain from spilling off his hat brim down his nose and into his beard braids. Three more hours until morning? He didn't know, didn't want to soak his arm to the elbow by checking his watch. Nothing worse than wet sleeves. Too dark anyway, no sign of light. Noise could make a man deaf, rain pounding on his poncho's hood, smacking on every leaf. Rainstorm had roared in like a floatplane landing. Rain in a dump is the worst, clanging on torn-up tin, ringing broken glass. Bad luck that it would be pouring rain, but what else did he expect? There is nothing to be done, he had told Nora. There is nothing I can do to stop Axel from getting his bear. Nothing will happen but what happens.

So there he was, sitting at the end of the dump road, at the edge of the dump. In dead dark. In driving rain. With his wheels sinking deeper and deeper in the mud. Not his favorite kind of place. But he'd patrolled in the dark before. And at least there would be no rats in a place scavenged by pine martens and bears.

Here is the brave hero, stupid and handsome, setting off with a shotgun to win the fair damselfish by . . . By what? By imbedding a slug in a beer can to scare away a bear? Something, anything to keep the bears out of Axel's trap. Goddamn. Nothing worse than a wet rear end.

He could have dealt with water falling down. But this water didn't just fall. Some force angrier than gravity drove it down. Rain came down so hard it slammed right back up again. The big devil's club leaves threw water in his face. Water ran down his neck, collected in a pool on his poncho. Dripped through onto his lap. Sleep might have been nice, but it was a bad idea. Made his head wobble. Then rain spilled off the hood of his poncho onto his face and he woke up dreaming he fell overboard.

Dark? There is nothing darker than night in a rainstorm, unless it is night in a rainstorm when you are expecting a brown bear. Kenny ran his finger along the barrel of the shotgun, hidden under the poncho. He couldn't see the edge of the dump, but he could smell it now and then, even in the slop of forest smells. Nora would ask him exactly how it smelled. So. Rain on cedar stumps and broken skunk cabbage leaves, rotten in duff like old bananas. Cold sweet Sitka spruce. Mint, unaccountably, or maybe it was stink currant, bruised. Generic salty intertidal. But also diesel fuel spilled from waste buckets and fetid garbage and crab shells gone to spoil and the sharp smell of aluminum cans against the dirt. The stink of men going bad. Kenny decided to breathe without smelling anything, breathe through his mouth.

He could give up, go home. Assuming he could get unstuck from the mud, he could roll down the dump road, up the ramp to the boardwalk, and onto his pier. Shake out his poncho, hang it by the door. That would be cold then, wind against wet clothes. Hurrying, he would roll into the cabin, his wheels throwing mud. The woodstove would be clanking and cooling. He would throw in some kindling and another couple of splits. There would be dry blankets heaped at the foot of his bed. He would wrap himself in a blanket, maybe two or three, not moving a muscle until the whole bed radiated heat. There are people who pitch and kick until their bed is warm. Kenny was not that kind.

Or he could have gone to Nora's. She would have been warm and sleepy when she heard the knock on the door, stretching under her blankets, the way a baby reaches out her arms, pressing her fists to her cheeks, arching her back and bringing her knees to her chest—but maybe not. Maybe she slept like Snow White, still and pale, with her hands folded on her breast. Or maybe she slept all splay-legged like a frog and when Kenny knocked on her door, she would leap up, blinking and popping. Maybe— surely—she sleeps with Chum, who would try to kill anybody knocking on the door at night. She would stumble to the door, dragged by her dog, the dog barking, her yelling at him, and she would open the door and there would be this man with dribbling chin-braids, dripping wet in a poncho long enough to conceal a shotgun.

Dreams. There was no going home. Kenny had promised Nora he'd make sure no bears got hurt. So it was better to be here, patrolling the dump in the night. That was his job. Hell of a job description.

Kenny raised binoculars through the opening at his neck and surveyed the dump. Army-issue night-vision binoculars—never know when you're going to need to see in the dark. Here was the perimeter of the dump, a circle of enormous trees. Their trunks glowed—that lurid green of night-vision glasses. When he followed the trunks up, there were the scattered green pixels of the forest canopy. Still higher, the sky was lumpy green, like algae at the outflow of the village drain. Shit. Rain down the back of his neck. He lowered the binocs to the dump.

The dump glowed just as green. He could make out bedsprings and the angle of an old green refrigerator, lying on its side. Across a distance of a hundred yards, there was a midden of beer bottles, shattered lumber, linoleum scraps. He focused closely on the bear trap wedged between a stand of alder and a twisted bicycle frame. The bear trap that the government trappers hauled up there was basically a big section of culvert mounted on a boat trailer. There were bars across the back end and a barred gate suspended over the front like the blade of a guillotine. It had been hell to pay, getting it up here. Axel's big-shot trappers brought it in on a USF&W barge, rolled it onto the dock, and then rousted out half the population to drag it up the hill and along the gravel path to the dump. They'd been smart enough to tie the tongue of the trailer onto an ATV. So that supported part of the weight. And they'd put Tick's younger one Tommy in the back, to balance it out. But that was a lot of pounds to pull up a hill. And it was only half the town that helped.

The other half went inside their houses and slammed their doors to rant or sulk or mutter on the radio—who knows. Kenny the Black-Hearted Knight, rolled up to the post office, lowered the American flag, and began calling out ruin, like Cassandra howling at the gates of Troy—a convincing enough portrayal of a madwoman to drive the tourists off the boardwalk and onto the dock.

Didn't matter what people thought, least of all Kenny. Axel had convinced the Feds that dump bears were problem bears that needed to be shut up in the Bear Shelter. So what, that he didn't convince everybody in town, didn't even try. He didn't need them. Didn't need to give a god-damn about what they were thinking. It's lucky the people were shut up in their houses and didn't see the big shots shoot a deer on the beach, cut off a haunch, and haul it up the hill to the trap. Left the deer three-legged on the gravel with ravens eating out its eyes and pecking its ass. The kid Davy was the one who scattered the ravens and dressed the deer. Damn the government trappers, setting the trap and going off to bed. They would probably be back bright and early in the morning, drinking Lillian's coffee in paper cups.

Rain drummed on the ground, pinged on the beer cans, patted on the leaves, sang on the glass. Rattled on the refrigerator. Kenny's chin sank to his chest. His eyes closed. A green bear stirred ice cubes with its great green paw and backhanded them off the ice floes. Radio waves cracked jagged ice calves off the Space Needle, they rattled into green seas, green seas, green seas. He swam hard, but green waves dragged him away from shore. The shadow of the wave. Follow me shall mercy and goodness? surely follow me? All the life of my days.

Not ice.

Glass.

Kenny jerked awake and peered into the darkness over the dump. Something new. Had he heard something new? He glassed the garbage dump. There. A big sow rummaging in the beer bottles. Massive side, humped back and lowered head, and maybe the shadow of a cub. Could that be? Damn the focus on these glasses. Yes, a cub. And maybe another? Nosing behind the refrigerator, a little bear with lighter shoulders. A sow with two cubs. Damnation.

The shape of the sow swayed heavily across the dump in his direc-tion. The sow dropped onto her haunches, then rolled over, crunching glass. On her back, with her legs open like a shameless dog asking to be scratched, she lifted a beer bottle between two paws and put it to her jaws. The cubs hurried over, but she rolled onto her side, lifted her great weight, and made her way across broken glass, slowly, jingling and clanking, to the rim of forest. There she squatted on the moss and leaned her back against a hemlock. Then she was up again, lifting her snout to the air, moaning a warning to the cubs. She rose onto her hind legs, swaying, sniffing.

A dump must be a terrifying place for a bear, a place soaked with the metallic smell of humans. Cautiously now, she dropped down next to a stump. The cubs rustled up against her, nosing for a teat. That's how they stayed for a long time, the mother slouched against the tree, the little cubs snuggled onto her ample stomach, pushing against her legs with their back feet, climbing into her glistening fur and nursing while the rain let up and a silver-edged cloud opened for the moon.

Kenny sat perfectly still. Not frightened. He was far enough across the expanse of busted engines, and that was a timid bear. No, not frightened. Cold. Lonely. Okay, he was lonely. A mother bear quietly suckled her cubs—the universal trust of small babies sucking and humming. Behind a rusted boiler, he watched the bears, a lonely, cursed man with a gun across his knees.

If Axel's plan went off without a hitch, that mother bear and her cubs would be in the trap by morning. The trappers would trundle the loaded trap down the boardwalk to the barge, then off the barge at the newly planked dock and up to the old cistern—that Axel now called the "Bear Shelter."

Shoot. Now. Shoot a refrigerator or any damn thing. He waited and watched.

Kenny had called the Fish and Game guys at Ketchikan, left a profoundly profane message on their answering machine. But the guys called back to say that the dump was *federal* property, and the *federal* guys would decide if any of the *federal* bears were going into the water tank, and they would be grateful for the community's help—on a plan that is a model for using forest resources for economic development of rural communities. They've got grant money invested in this—habitat restoration funds—and they want the project to work. And then a couple of weeks later, here came the trappers in their green and gray jackets with all the badges on the sleeves.

Every now and then, the sow grunted and shifted her position, and then the cubs scrambled their paws against her side and pushed into the curve of her belly. Gradually, the sow slumped to the ground, wiggled her rump into the shelter of the rootball, curled around the cubs, and went to sleep. Rain shone on her hanks and reflected off the puddle on Kenny's lap. Dripping steadily from the trees, water plinked on the plastic lid of a broken five-gallon bucket.

Damn Axel to hell. Is there anything in this world that you can't buy and sell or just plain steal? A mother bear and her babies, for God's sake. But why not, when it seems like you can steal everything else or get the government to give it to you free. Trees. Fish. Water. Silence. Just gone. It is all unbearably gone. He waited and watched the sow bear. So comfortable, with her back against the tree. She slept. In the peace of the bears, Kenny slept.

Keening gulls. Smell of garbage. Yellow line of dawn. Metal clanking against metal. Kenny shouted out and threw up his arms. The trap slammed shut. The sow snarled and smashed her shoulder against the grate. Teeth clanged on metal. She huffed and snapped her jaws, slinging saliva through the bars, then launched herself against the corrugated metal. Gulls swirled over the dump, flapping long wings and screeching. The government trappers rose into view in their fresh uniforms, walking up the gravel road with coffee cups in their hands.

QUIETLY, SO HE didn't wake his boys, Tick rolled his great mass out of bed and shuffled onto the porch to piss over the rail. Yellow glassy water. Great blue herons stalking their own reflections. Orange buoy stranded in green sedges. Lap and flush of Kis'utch Falls across the channel. It was going to be a good day. Over the forest beyond town, ravens were up early, circling and yelling their heads off, but nobody was on the boardwalk at that time of the morning. Annie Klawon would want him to row her over to the huckleberry thicket, Tick thought, before he remembered that his wife was gone back to Seattle again. Damn that Annie Klawon.

He leaned back to zip up his fly. Most mornings, he would see her walking home from berrying with a yogurt bin hanging on a string around her neck and old-man's beard in her hair. Berrying was something Tick did not understand. You go out after a deer and you find one or it finds you and you raise your rifle and you shoot it. So that is that, and your family can eat for two weeks. But huckleberries—you pick one here and you pick one there, then you elbow a bear out of your way and you pick another one. All morning, and you might get enough for two pies that your family will eat in five minutes. Annie said it was peaceful, healing work. Tick said the easiest way to find peace was to put your feet up on a stool by the woodstove. And when it came to healing, he wasn't sick. That made Annie Klawon laugh, which was healing even for a man at the peak of his glory.

Tick went round to the back deck to set his crab pot. Crabs would feed his boys well tonight. He set the heavy crab pot on the deck, coiled the rope and tied the loose end to the railing. Then he went into the kitchen for his supply of old bread. The minute he pulled bread heels from the bottom of a plastic bag, gulls lifted off the water and swarmed in. He dropped a piece of bread onto the water. All the gulls swooped over, a screeching mob of clattering wings and scattered feathers. The first gull there gobbled down the bread and flapped off, trailing a couple of others. The rest of the gulls milled around under the deck, hollering their feeding call, the scream of the greedy and hopeful. Tick picked out the gull he wanted and held out the crab pot so it was right over the gull's head. He let the rope slide through his hand. The net pinned the gull to the water, and the heavy ring sank the pot to the bottom, carrying down the gull neat as a pin. Drowned seagull is the best crab bait there is. People say clams, but seagull out-crabs clams every time.

Tick poured a fresh cup of coffee and walked back to his front porch to wait for his boys to wake up. He'd give them another half hour and then roust them out of bed. He sat on the railing, hooked his heels over the bottom rail, and watched the town across the rim of his coffee cup. Gulls swarmed over the dump up the hill, but the boardwalk was still empty. Then Tick was back on his feet. A gunshot, close. Up the hill. What idiot would be shooting so near to town? He settled himself back on the rail, wondering. He listened closely. Nothing. Not even the lap of the tide. Then, a barrage of shots—one two shots three four. Ravens fled past, slashing the air.

Tick spun into his house, grabbed his rifle, and strode toward the gunfire.

He hadn't taken five steps before Axel's government trappers came running down the boardwalk. When they saw Tick, they dropped to a walk, humping along the boardwalk in their shirt-sleeves, as if they had important business—on most days, a cup of coffee and a shit, Tick figured, but not today. Something more on their minds today. They banged on Axel's door until he pulled it open. When he did, they practically fell inside. What the hell? Axel's at six in the morning?

Soon after, Kenny rolled around the corner with a big bundle in a poncho on his lap. A big kid and a little kid ran along behind him, the big one carrying a shotgun. Damned if they weren't Tick's own kids. What the hell were they doing out of bed? And armed?

Kenny went straight to his cabin, and the kids pushed in behind him. Two seconds later, the boys busted out of the cabin without the gun. Tommy ran up to Tick, with Davy right behind him.

Tick caught Tommy on the fly. "What the hell?"

"I found the baby bear and tried to save her, but they killed her."

Tommy grabbed Tick around the belly and burst out crying. Tick looked over at Davy.

"That's about right," Davy said.

"What the hell? Who killed her? What bear?"

"The government trappers Axel brought in to get a bear for the Bear Shelter. They killed her. A cub with silver shoulders."

Damn. Tick knew that Axel needed a bear for his pit. But not a dead bear. What the hell?

"Davy, you got some explaining."

Davy swallowed hard, his new Adam's apple working up and down.

"Really early. We were in bed, but we could hear the government trappers clanking around the woodstove at Axel's, Tommy and me. They clomped across the porch like they didn't care if they waked up the world. Tommy said we should follow them."

"Follow them," Tick said. "You followed Axel's government trappers."

Davy looked at his father out of the top of his eyes. He'd been acting nervy as a beaten dog, since he sunk Tick's boat. Tommy loosened himself from his father's arms and stood his ground.

"So we did that," Tommy said. "We followed them. We waited till they turned onto the dump road, and then I snuck along behind them, like a tracker. But not Davy. He just walked up the road because it was bendy enough they wouldn't have seen him probably. And so what if they did, Davy said. Can't a guy walk to the dump? Which I guess he can.

"We were almost to the dump. We heard a big bang."

"The door on the bear trap," Davy said. "We started running up to see. Kenny was yelling and motoring around, but he couldn't really get closer, and the men were yelling, and the bear was inside the trap, snarling and smashing into the metal. Gulls flew everywhere, so thick they beat their wings on our heads."

"It was scary," Tommy said. "Davy grabbed me and kept me back, but I could see almost down the bear's throat. She shook the bars with her jaws, and I heard her teeth break against the metal, and her nose was all pressed up, and she drooled long slobbers."

"We heard the man with the beard yell. A cub. A sow and a cub. We got a tuber, Larry."

"Two-fer. Two-fer." Davy corrected him. "Like two for the price of one."

"Yeah." Tommy caught at his breath. "The Larry guy yelled, 'far out,' and they high-fived."

"'Axel's gonna love this.' That's what the bearded guy yelled. God, Dad," Davy said. "They stood there drinking their coffee, slapping each other on the back, pretending to be calm even though they were about to shit."

"Real men, those government trappers," Tick said.

Davy studied his dad's face. "Well, they thought they were. They were all excited. The whole trap was rocking. I was ready to grab Tommy and run if it fell over. The sow was slamming and snarling. The cub had backed up into a corner of the trap. I don't think the trapper dudes knew me and Tommy were there, but Kenny did. He told us 'stay back,' which I already knew. The men were trying to figure out how to get the tongue of the trap attached to an ATV, and I had hold of Tommy, and we were staying back."

"That's good, Davy."

"I'm the one who found the other bear cub," Tommy said. "It was right by me, hiding behind a refrigerator. I found it because it was crying like a kitten. It was a little bear with a big baby head, and it was crying like a kitten. I'm the one found it. I showed Kenny and he saw it and hushed me, but it was too late. The trapper with the beard saw it too."

"What'd he do?" Tick guessed he knew how this story would end.

"He said, 'Ho,' real quiet, and he handed his coffee to the other guy without taking his eyes off the bear.

"'That's a beauty.' He was whispering. 'Look at those silver shoulders. Axel's tourists are going to love that.'"

"He never took his eyes off the cub," Davy said. "Even though the sow was about to tear the trap apart. He snuck around the frig. And then, I couldn't believe it. That trapper jumped for the bear. But he missed and smacked onto the ground. The cub ran up a tree. I told Tommy to shut up—he was laughing and cheering for the bear. The other man ran over, pulling his belt from its loops. I'm thinking, is that asshole going to lasso that cub with a leather belt?"

"Oh shit," Tick said. He turned to Davy. "Watch your language, son. Your mother doesn't want you to cuss."

Davy winced. "The bearded man waved away the lasso guy and ran to the tree. The sow was going nuts. God, the way a bear can roar! The gulls were going nuts too."

"They crapped on everything," Tommy said. "And the sow was crapping too. Crap all over."

"'Okay. We've got her treed. Where's the noose?'"

Tick laughed. Davy could do a pretty good imitation of a stone-ass government trapper, crouching down with pin eyes pointed to the bear.

"The Larry guy got a noose from the side of the trap. It was a long pole with wire in a ring at one end."

"What was Kenny doing?"

"Kenny was a stone wall. He said, 'That's enough. She'll come down when she's hungry. Leave her alone.'"

"'C'mon, baby,' the man said. 'Come to Daddy.' "Come to Daddy!" Davy squeaked again. He might make a pretty good asshole government trapper himself. "The guy reached up with the pole and tried to put the noose around the bear's neck."

"But I got loose from Davy, and I grabbed the back end of the pole and I'm pulling and yelling at him," Tommy said.

"Uh oh," Tick said, wondering what Axel would say about another one of Tick McIver's kids messing with him.

"Yeah. Tommy was wrestling the end of the pole and hollering, 'Leave it alone. It's not your bear!'" Davy laughed out loud. "Leave it alone," he said again in a high voice. "It's not your bear."

"Then! The man yelled, 'GET THE KID.' That scared me. The other man grabbed me and I started to fight him, because he was going to hurt the bear. Davy yelled, 'Let him go,' fiercer than I ever saw him. So the man let me go and Davy grabbed me and pulled me back. I would have fought that man. I would have punched him in the balls."

So now Tommy was talking as big as his old man. Annie was not going to like this.

"That's my boy, Tommy," Tick said. "So then what?"

"The man sneaked around and hiked himself up another tree, where he could reach the bear. Kenny didn't like it. He just bellowed, 'THAT'S ENOUGH. SHE'LL COME DOWN WHEN SHE'S READY.' Like he never heard Kenny, like Kenny never said a word, like Kenny didn't even exist, the man reached out the pole and slid the noose around the bear's neck."

"He pulled the noose."

"The cub jumped off the branch. The man held on to the pole with everything he had, and the cub swung out into space, hanging by its neck. Kenny said, 'Jeezus,' but that's all anybody said.

"Gulls were crying and shitting.

"After a while, the man let go of the pole and the cub fell onto the ground."

"It just thudded onto the ground."

"There were hemlock needles falling down, all yellow, like yellow rain."

Tick didn't say anything, watching his boys.

"I was telling Tommy we should go home. But before I could drag him off, he's scrabbling between the men to get to the bear cub."

Tommy buried his face in Tick's belly. Tick had to lean over to hear him. "The noose cut its neck and scraped the skin away. It made its head go all funny, off to the side. I saw the blood and muscle in its neck, Dad. One paw was twitching, like it was trying to get itself up. I knew it was going to die."

Tommy looked up at Tick.

"Kenny held me by the hand and put his other arm around me. I never knew Kenny could be nice like that. Davy came over and got me. Then, Dad? Kenny pointed his shotgun at the bear's head and pulled the trigger. I never heard a sound like that. One boom. One boom. The bear was dead. I knew that because her paw was still and Davy was crying."

"I wasn't crying."

"Never mind," Tick said. "What did the bastards do then?"

"Well, the bearded man said, 'I'd call that a DLP bear.'"

Defense of life or property. Damn them. They were going to say they killed the bear cub in self-defense.

"'Wouldn't you say so, Larry?'

"'I would certainly and officially say so. We'll need the skull and the hide. You got a knife, Larry?' The guy knew the rules. He knew they'd get away with it. He was all jolly, poking the cub with the toe of his boot.

"But Dad, listen to this. Kenny!

"Kenny said to the men, real low and quiet—'Take off your jackets.'

"They were like, 'WHAT?'

"'Listen here,' one man said. Kenny swung the gun his way and the man backed off."

"'Take off your Fish and Wildlife jackets. You don't deserve to wear them.'

"Kenny was sitting there with the shotgun at his shoulder, so they did, they took off their jackets. Kenny pointed the gun to a place in the dump. They put their coats there, watching Kenny all the time.

"Then Kenny shot their jackets. He shot their jackets, right there in the dump. The sleeves jumped up and down. He shot them again and again."

"Kenny said, real quiet, 'Get out of town.'

"The men walked away, sort of mean, like they wanted to go and they always do what they want. Kenny flicked on his safety and gave the gun to me.

"He took his poncho and spread it on his lap," Davy said. "I helped him roll the cub up like a baby in a blanket. He carried it to town. We followed him all the way home. Kenny will know what to do with a little dead bear."

"I should have got the noose away from the man with the beard. I could have maybe. I could have saved the cub maybe. I could have socked the man in the stomach."

Tick started to laugh, but the laughter got all tangled up in his throat.

"You did the best you could," he said, and roughed up Tommy's hair, as if it needed roughing up. "Sometimes that's enough."

Tick could say that. But the best you can do is never enough. He knew that as well as any man. Your best is never enough, but you do it anyway. Tick put his arms around his boys' shoulders. Davy's were almost as high as his own.

"Maybe I did the best I could," Tommy said. "But it wasn't enough."

They walked down the pier to their front porch.

"Stay here," Tick said to his boys. "And I mean it." He hung his rifle in its place, put a quart of diesel fuel and a lighter in his pack and headed out to the dump. He was going to burn a couple of shot-up government-issue uniforms into nothing but ashes and mud.

"AW, TICK, YOU know there's nothing I can do with this cub," Kenny said, tugging on his braided beardlets. He rolled over to stare at the bear laid out on his kitchen table. "We gotta obey the law. We gotta skin it and send the hide and the paws and the head and all the paperwork to Juneau. Law's the law."

Tick smoothed the silver hair on the cub's shoulders. Ranger sniffed its back paw. Hair rose along his spine and he backed away, throwing a reproachful look at Kenny. Tick reached down to scratch between the dog's ears. It was dark in the cabin, except for stripes of morning light that slotted in where chinking mud had fallen from between the logs. The light threw stripes on Tick and Ranger.

"Har. You two look striped as convicts, standing there all stiff and guilty. Guess the law's already got you. Jean Valjean and his scruffy dog, Stupide." Kenny gaped at Tick and shouted.

"*Ce n'est rien de mourir. C'est affreux de ne pas vivre.*"

Ranger padded across the room, put his chin on Kenny's knee, and whined. Kenny noodled a finger in front of the dog's nose.

"You skin out a cub, it's gonna look just like a toddler kid, shiny white skin and blood on its shoulders. Who's gonna eat that, whole family sits down, dad says who wants to gnaw on the baby's dimpled little leg? Organic, dump-raised baby. And why does everybody think I want to be left with the dead things? You think I'm a vulture on food stamps?"

"You skin it. I'm gonna cook it," Tick said. "I'm gonna cook it up with apricot jam and soy sauce, all pretty in a casserole dish and invite Axel over for dinner. You got a pretty casserole dish you can loan me?"

Kenny snickered. That was a lame joke. But it felt good to have some visitors in his house for once, even if one of them was dead.

"You want coffee?" Kenny said.

"Yeh."

Kenny ran his thumb around the rim of his mug, inspected it for drowned spiders, and poured in the coffee. "Sit down?" he said, but that was a joke too. Not a single chair in his cabin. Didn't need one himself, and nobody visited.

"Sure," Tick said, and propped himself up against the wall.

Tick didn't say anything then, just stood there. Kenny tried not to watch him. He was starting to not like this. He was thinking maybe Tick was looking at him or the squirrel skins tacked to the wall or his Marilyn Monroe poster. But it didn't seem like Tick was focusing on anything. He sort of slid down the wall and sat on the floor with his long legs bent at the knees, bringing the coffee mug up to his chin and looking in it, but not drinking any.

"What's wrong with the coffee? God, this business of visitors is making me nervy." Kenny pulled the coffeepot off the woodstove and looked inside, but there weren't any mice or anything floating in there, just the eggshells. He looked up slowly and met Tick's eyes.

"I know what you're thinking," Kenny said. "You're thinking I didn't save the bears. Went up to keep them out of the trap. Didn't do that. Went up to keep them from getting killed. Didn't do that. What a loser. I didn't want to scare them away, Tick. They were like Raphael's virgin and child, sitting there, and then BAM it's like the pietà, with the dead son sprawled across my lap." Kenny struck the table with his gloved fist. "Even if the bears fell asleep, did I have to? Falling asleep on watch? Lots of men have been shot for that. Shoot me, Tick."

The men were silent, the way men are silent.

"What's Nora going to think about this dead cub, and a sow and a cub in the tank?"

"She's not going to like it."

"Hell no, she's not going to like it. She's not going to like me either. Damn. Just when she was falling crazy in love with me." Kenny sniggered. "Yeah, I know. Bad joke."

Tick put a heavy hand on his friend's shoulder, then opened the door. He let in a yellow trapezoid of light. When Kenny spoke again, he spoke to Tick's bulky silhouette. Then to the suddenly dark room and the worried dog.

"That Nora," Kenny said quietly. "You know what she is? What she is, is wind across a fire. Wind across the fires of every person in this town. Whatever you have smoldering, she fans it. Lust. Anger. Ambition. Fear. Loneliness. Hope. What you think you have damped down, just the smallest spark of it left, what you spent all your life shoveling sand on, the wind picks up, the spark glows, a little flame flickers, looks like it might go out, leaps up, then it's a torch. And the hotter the fire burns, the stronger the wind grows, until the wind is a whirlwind and the fire is out of control.

"Loneliness on fire, that's a terrible, dangerous thing. Hope on fire—God save us from the beautiful smile of that wind. Long time ago, I gave up hoping that I could make a woman love me. These are dangerous times, Ranger. Be careful of fires you think are cold."

August 14

HIGH TIDE		LOW TIDE	
4:10am	17.9ft	10:18am	-1.8ft
4:40pm	18.3ft	10:51pm	-0.9ft

Axel Hagerman, CEO, lay in bed with his eyes squeezed shut. It had been a rough week. For one thing, Kenny was parading around with a new bearskin cap. Axel couldn't stand looking at it, a big patch of bearskin like a tea cozy on Kenny's ugly head. Seemed like it was a living thing, the way the fur ruffled in the wind, glossy and catching the light. Whenever he passed Kenny on the boardwalk, that reflected light darted around Axel and touched him, as if the cap were haunting him. Sometimes it swirled in front of him and stopped him cold.

But that wasn't what was keeping him awake. Too much coffee? Maybe, but no. There was something wrong with the night. Axel shifted carefully on his pillow and looked out the window. Dark clouds scudded along, stained yellow by streetlights. The tide was low, but the sea seemed agitated, the way it shrugged and winced. There was enough wind to rock the day-sailors and jangle their halyards against the masts. No sound from the boardwalk, but Axel's mind would not shut up.

He did not like this night. He knew he should have been feeling good. He was juggling a couple of high-stakes projects, and he hadn't dropped any balls yet. The floating dock and the pavilion at the Bear Shelter were almost built. The replacement carpenter from Ketchikan worked almost as hard as damn Tick would have worked. Things looked real nice in the cistern, all according to the landscape plan Rebecca drew up. Hell, it was a genuine fake forest—well, a very small forest—but it had thimbleberries and fireweed. If he could get the sow and cub in there tomorrow—and there was no reason he couldn't—he could have tourists ringing the cash register in a week.

The water project was on schedule too. Axel grinned in the darkness. Could anyone but the amazing Axel Hagerman have pulled that off? He'd made a good decision to put Howard Fowler on that job. And that whole year of work on financing and permits was paying off. The bulldozers were taking down the alder over at the Kis'utch River, clearing the ground for the trailers that would hold the crew. The temporary landing was almost dredged out, so the barges were already getting in. Over at Jimmy Pete's weir, framing was going up for the dam. Axel expected to have concrete poured before the end of the month, the dam pretty well set up before the September storms.

It gave him a good feeling, the buzz of things getting done, men running around, following orders. When Axel heard a hammer ringing steel, an arc welder snapping, a bulldozer grinding through its gears, he felt okay. He felt good.

So what was so weird about this night?

He raised himself on an elbow again to double-check the dark. He could make out the yellow smudge of floodlights lighting up the construction site across the channel. It calmed him to know the bulldozer was sitting there by the river, with the supervisor's trailer alongside it. But the night was too melodramatic—dark clouds trimmed in gold galloped across the moon, engulfing it in darkness kicked up by the onrushing stampede. Ridiculous. Axel lay down and shut his eyes again.

He didn't like this at all. The trouble was, things were going great, then Kenny had gone and shot one of his bears. It didn't make any sense. Sure, Kenny hated the idea of the Bear Shelter. And yeah, he was a certified lunatic. But Kenny was the kind of guy who never did anything about anything, and here he was, going over the edge, shooting a bear cub just to spite him? It didn't make any sense.

Axel ran the scene again in his mind. His trappers get a sow and a cub in the trap, they find another cub, and Kenny shoots it dead. He had told the trappers they should bust Kenny's butt, but they acted like they were afraid of him. Afraid of Kenny's drooping shoulders? "No, no, let it go. We'll take care of things." They were all squirrelly, packing their duffels, practically shoving each other out of the way to climb on the floatplane. It didn't make any sense. None of it.

And then there was his own family. Meredith and Rebecca—his own daughter and his own wife—treated him like the enemy, when it was Tick's kid that got Meredith trapped by the tide. "You're mean to fire Davy's dad," Meredith had said. She had actually called him mean. To his face.

"Davy's dad didn't do anything wrong," she'd said. "Nobody did anything wrong. You're mean."

"No way I'm going to believe that you hot young kids spent the night watching a damn bluebird squat on an egg," Axel had told her. And there was no way Axel was going to believe that Tick McIver didn't know damn well what his kid was doing, grunting around his daughter.

I'm not mean, Axel said to himself. I'm the only one making any sense at all.

But Axel didn't like the feel of the night, not one bit, clouds moving too fast. Wires in the rigging singing like drowned seamen whistling in the storms. And Rebecca lying there with her back to him, her heart pulsing in her neck while she pretended to be asleep. "Vindictive," she had called him. Was he vindictive? Sounded like something a Roman soldier would be: vindictive.

Axel propped himself on one elbow and looked at Rebecca. She was still the prettiest girl in Good River Harbor—not very big, but pretty as a picture. Twenty years married, and she still had those soft freckled shoulders and slender back. He ran his hand around her neck and nuzzled her hair. Smooth and damp. She nudged his hand away with her shoulder.

"Give me something sweet, Mama Earth," he said. She liked that name sometimes, his beautiful gardener, coming to bed smelling so good. Geraniums, hemlock duff. He sniffed into her hair, and then his dick was aching, pressing against his pajamas.

"Tomato leaves?" he guessed—that warm smell, like hot sun.

"Leave me alone." That's what she said.

"Come on, be nice to me. I've had a hard day."

"Leave me alone." She said it again.

Axel rolled her onto her back. Her hair streamed over the pillow. One shoulder had fallen out of her nightgown. Axel reached down to give himself a little more room in his pajamas. He started in unbuttoning her nightgown. Her hands followed his, buttoning right back up again.

"Come on," he said, real nice, and he started over, unbuttoning those damn little buttons. She buttoned right back up, but the hell with that, Axel thought. Maybe a different week, she could have turned him away, but not this one. He grabbed hold of the nightgown and yanked it open, popping off whatever buttons didn't get with the program. Rebecca pulled her nightgown tight across her breasts, turned her back to Axel, and curled herself into a ball like a damn baby.

Axel kicked off his pajama bottoms. He didn't like it, how hard she made him work to get her nightgown up to her waist.

"Jesus!" Axel jerked away from Rebecca as if she were electrified. He sat straight up. The room filled with a tremendous roar. "What the hell?" The bellow came from the water. It echoed off the mountain, bellowed back. The roar rose to a squeal. From every quarter, the night trumpeted and screeched. The channel boomed with a sound like school buses falling off the dock.

It took Axel a long minute to figure it out.

"Feeding humpbacks," he said. White splashes and mighty snouts rose into the night air as the whales lunged and smacked the water. Holding her nightgown closed, Rebecca crossed to the window. Axel flopped back on the bed and only then realized that his heart was racing. Axel coughed, the only way he knew to settle his heart.

But then the noise was coming from right under the house, a roar like somebody starting up a motorcycle, that kind of loud. The house began to shake with the roaring and farting, the blue-smoke smell, the whole house vibrating as if it were going to fall off its pilings.

"Jesus," he said to Rebecca. She was still standing at the window, clutching her nightgown in both hands.

A windowpane cracked its length. A water glass walked off the night-stand and shattered, and still the world roared. Flat on his back, Axel spread his arms and legs and grabbed hold of the sheets. The noise put-tered and then roared again. Do earthquakes make this kind of noise? Landslides? Tsunamis? The moon burst out from behind the clouds and sprayed shards of light into the room.

Meredith rushed through the door. "What is that? What is . . ." She stopped and stared.

Axel stared back at her. Slowly he reached out his hand and drew the sheet over his body. It draped there like a tent fly on a little pole. He cleared his throat. Meredith turned abruptly and fled. She lurched against the doorframe as the house shuddered.

The noise stopped as suddenly as it started. For a long minute, Axel lay sprawled on his back in a dark and a quiet that he did not like at all.

"I'll be back for you," he said to Rebecca. He pulled on his good work pants and went out the door.

≈≈≈

MORNING DAWNED CLEAR, with variable winds.

Lillian shook the old coffee grounds into a five-gallon pail behind the bar. She was saving them for Rebecca to feed to her flowers, which in fact did grow like they were hopped up on caffeine. She poured a hillock of ground coffee into a fresh filter and fixed it into the machine. *My lord, what a morning, when the stars begin to fall.* Lillian was moving slowly this morning, trying to be easy on her hip. It had ached in the night, kept her from sleeping, which was not all bad, because she was awake when all the roaring started, and awake when the light flipped on at the Hagermans' house and Axel flew out the door, zipping his pants. Just like the blessed Mother, Lillian kept all these things and pondered them in her heart.

The door banged open and in rolled Kenny, resplendent in his new bearskin cap. Ranger trotted in after him. A cloud of damp air rolled in with them, and the smell of rising tide. Lillian closed her eyes and breathed. There is no better smell than coffee mixed with salt tide.

"Coffee, Lillian. Quick. I'm exhausted." Kenny stretched dramatically, which lifted his poncho like wings. "It's hard for a guy to get much sleep around here these days," he announced, and looked at Lillian sort of sly.

"Noisy night?" she said. She wasn't going to tell him anything. "Pickled egg today?"

"Roger on the egg, and roger on the noisy night." Kenny positively beamed. "Somebody sneaked under Axel's house with a chain saw last night and notched his piling. That's perfect." He spun his wheelchair in a tight circle. "One more cut and that woodsman would have felled the post and dropped the whole damn house into the drink. I bet Axel's ready to shit." Kenny hooked an arm over the back of his wheelchair and sat there grinning.

"Who did it, old woman?" he asked her.

Ah. "That's a reckless question."

Kenny laughed. Or belched. "A lot of people owe him one," he said.

Ah.

"It could wear a person out—gunshots in the morning, chainsaws all night, hammering all day."

He was right about the noise, Lillian knew. Of course, thirty years ago, the town was all noise, lumber and salmon—the highline squealing and diesel engines grinding, tugboats blasting their whistles. But it got real quiet, real quick, after the cannery closed and the workers moved on. Lillian could sit at the top of the ferry dock and all she would hear was a dog barking maybe, or somebody dropping a hammer on a deck, and ravens sometimes. For years, it was so quiet she could hear the river falling down the mountain across the way, day and night, rustling like that. People didn't say much to each other. Then Kenny rolled into town all grim and silent, hardly even talking to his dog.

But Axel had everything humming and clanking again. When Lillian looked across the channel, she saw bulldozers pushing up the landing on the Kis'utch flats. When she turned toward the southeast, there were hammers clonking that big cistern, men getting ready for the grand opening of the Bear shelter. Turned toward the northwest for some peace, and darned if Nora wasn't practicing the piano on her front porch—a buzz from the forest, like flies at the window.

"Yeah, it's a riot in Whoville," she said. "Nora especially, dink, dink, dink. You'd think, she hauled that piano all the way here, she'd know how to play it."

"Har," Kenny laughed again. The man was Merry Sunshine this morning, propping his Davy Crockett cap back on his head.

"Can't learn to play unless you play," he said. "It's like baby thrushes in the spring. Can't sing worth crap. Can't get the twist at the end of the song. So what do they do? They sing their pitiful songs until they learn. So it's pitiful. So we listen."

"'Für Elise,' a thousand times a day? The worse thing is, the parts she can't play, she plays over and over."

"That's the idea."

Lillian looked at Kenny with her head bent to the side. What demon has taken possession of this man's body? Kenny danced his wheelchair around the table to the window.

"Whoever notched Axel's pilings sure perked you up. And since when do you go on about baby thrushes in the spring?" Lillian frowned at him.

"You are very pretty when you glower," Kenny said. Lillian smoothed the front of her dress and adjusted her face. She did not want glower wrinkles.

"But hark! Here comes the lovely thrush herself." Kenny rolled himself closer to the door and pulled it open.

Nora had chopsticks in her hair, holding it all up in a knot. Her hair was so black it had turned coppery blue in that light, Lillian noticed. You never know, with hair that iridescent, what color it will throw back at you. Nora's arms were longer than the sleeves of her jacket, and when she walked into the bar, she threw her legs out in front of her, more like a heron than a thrush. Lillian thought she should talk to her about that, tell her how to walk like a lady.

Nora reached an arm around Lillian and drew her to her shoulder until Lillian's spine creaked. Lillian shrugged away. "Save that kind of hug for a funeral," she said. In this town, she thought, there was altogether too much hugging.

Nora dropped her arms and plopped into a chair beside Kenny. Chum nudged in between them and Ranger came over to squeeze in too. Kenny leaned over to scratch the dogs, although Lillian suspected it was Nora's knee he'd rather be scratching. You can't be in the bath and bar business as long as she's been without learning how to read people.

Nora reached over and tugged at Kenny's little beards. "Good work, whoever notched Axel's piling."

"Ho now, be cool, old Nora. I'm not saying Tick notched the piling under Axel's house. I'm not saying he didn't. I'm not saying I know who did it. Not saying I don't. But if I did do it, I'd be proud. And if you did it, you should be proud. Dangerous business, though. Nobody better say any-thing, because Axel will have the cops in here on the next flight, haul the suspect onto the backhaul in handcuffs. Willful destruction of property, reckless endangerment."

Nora spit out her breath. "Doesn't matter that he practically dropped a tree on my piano? Is that reckless? Is that endangerment? If that wasn't willful, then *nobody* has a will and we're all just flapping around, responding to the pain, like gaffed halibut. How come Tick and Axel can both do the same thing—notch a pole—and Tick's a criminal and Axel's not? I'm sick of this—all my life . . ."

She stopped herself.

"Hey, hey," Kenny said into the sudden silence. "I never said Tick notched his piling, and maybe he didn't. Understand? But whoever did, that's a crime. A perfect crime."

Kenny leaned back and laughed, lifting his little beards into the sunlight. "When I passed Axel's cabin and saw all the two-by's he's got nailed up to reinforce that piling, I about bust out laughing."

"Hunh," Nora snorted, but there was no energy in her. Without waiting for Kenny's shoulders to settle, she launched back in.

"Doesn't matter that Rebecca ran away from home last night?"

Lillian's head snapped around. "I don't believe it. Be careful what you say."

"Last night. She pounded on my door in the middle of the night. Barefoot. In her nightgown." Nora grabbed for Lillian's hand, but Lillian shook her loose. "She asked if she could stay with me, Lillian. Said she didn't feel safe with Axel anymore."

"Nothing, not even a dead codfish, is safe with Axel. So what's new?" Kenny did his best imitation of a dead cod, which was pretty good, complete with the cod's little chin-barb and frown.

For a long time, the only sound in Lillian's Bath 'n' Bar was the giggle-chortle of percolating coffee. Nora stared at the floor. With his index fingers, Kenny twirled his little beards. Lillian watched the coffee blurp. Steam filled the space between them.

Nora shook her head, as if she were in fact the cod, trying to throw off a treble hook.

"So, Kenny. I've been looking for you."

"Hey," he said, sort of surprised. "Looking for me?" But then he was back at it. "All that vibrating knock your piano out of tune again? Or did you lose out on some beauty sleep last night? Or have you been sawing logs?" Kenny apparently thought that was pretty funny, har har, but Nora apparently did not. She rocked back and forth with her hands rubbing her thighs. Chum nosed under her knees.

She was looking out across the water. Behind the dredge anchored off the mouth of the Kis'utch, a front loader ground over the flat, shoving broken trees into a pile. A couple of men in hard hats hammered at the plywood forms that would shape the concrete for the dam. There were snapping blue sparks over by the office trailer, and even in town, the smell of burning metal sharpened the air. Behind a thin line of smoke from a slash pile, the Kis'utch Mountains climbed up to the snowfields, and the river tumbled into the industrial site.

"The salmon," Nora said flatly. "And the bears," she said, as if she'd been making a list. She grabbed Kenny's arm.

"That cedar cistern is too small for any bear. It's cruel. Kenny, you can help the bears. You're a hero."

Kenny's eyes went wide.

"I'm not a hero," he said sorrowfully. Then he wobbled his head around and raised his voice to a shout. "I am only a little soul carrying around a corpse."

He grinned expectantly at Nora. "That was Epictetus."

"Quit farting around, Kenny. I'm serious."

"Call in your Zeus, Epictetus," he yelled wildly. "Call in the southeast gale, flip the cottonwood leaves white-side up, throw the eagles into the air, bend the hemlocks, lift the water, and save my sorry soul from the serious lady."

Nora went on as if he hadn't said a word.

"I've been thinking about when Axel's men bring the trap down to the bear tank, line the doors up, and open the gate on the trap, what that'll be like for the mother bear, Kenny, thinking she's free, galloping out into the open, running smack into the far wall, what that'll be like when she figures out she's only traded a little trap for a bigger one. How will she figure it out? What'll it feel like when she does?"

Lillian looked over to Kenny for his smart-aleck answer, and it seemed for a while that he was trying to think of one. He grinned, but his mouth was working like he couldn't shape words.

Nora prompted him gently. "What will that feel like, trapped in that moldy pit?"

Kenny's grin faded. He jerked his arm away from Nora's hand, swiveled his chair, and backed away from her. Something terrible had come over him. Pushing with his arms, he crouched his back to get his weight over his bent legs and finally stood, crooked and off-angled under his poncho.

He stared at Nora. "It's evil to put a living thing in a cage," he whispered. "It destroys them."

"Yes," she said quietly. "I can imagine."

"No," he said flatly. "You can't."

Kenny closed his eyes as if the light hurt him. His legs began to tremble. He groped behind for the arms of his wheelchair. Nora moved quickly to help him, but Ranger jumped to his feet and barked sharply. Growling deep in his throat, he held Nora at bay until Kenny was able to lower himself into his chair and wheel away from her. Together, the man and his dog passed through the door into the bright light.

Lillian rested her back against the doorjamb and watched Kenny pump his arms to turn the wheels, his head bowed over. Ranger trotted along beside him, casting a few dark glances over his shoulder. When they reached the cabin, Kenny tugged the door open and pushed himself in. Ranger followed. The door shuddered against the frame as Kenny pulled it closed.

≋≋≋

KENNY BACKED HIS chair against his door and sat with his eyes closed.

A hero.

No hero wants to be a hero.

He spat on the floor. All I know is a hero is afraid of the sound of rain, tick tick like rats scrabbling against tin. It's only rain coming. It's rain. Or claws on soft wood and teeth in a jaw narrow as needle-nose pliers, scraping teeth on bone. Day and night, the snapping and tapping. A hero is afraid of the dark too, because that's when sleep sneaks up and throws a hood over his head and forces mud into his mouth, stinking mud and stinging ants. And when his mind is thick and dark, defenseless, that's when sleep sends the child soldiers and long-dead grandmothers and cold fingers that walk across his neck and pinch and pinch. A hero wakes up screaming, with rats chewing his nipples. A hero squeezes rats with his bare hands until blood squirts out their noses. How many rats, marching through the dark, a fucking phalanx, falling back, ticking claws. Better awake in the dark than asleep. Better anything than asleep. A hero sleeps in mud and his dreams are pathetic. He is a little boy left out in a school-yard when all the other children have gone in to their books and the doors are closed and locked and it is getting dark and no one hears him pounding on the door. A hero wakes up crying and wonders if he is dead.

"Ah, Ranger," Kenny sighed, nudging the dog with his foot. "Bark if I'm dead."

Ranger lifted his chin and barked sharply.

"Wrong answer," Kenny said, and closed his eyes again.

Ranger climbed to his feet and put a paw on Kenny's knee.

A hero makes the stupid, stupid mistake of believing in something. Anything. Love. Loyalty. Terrible mistake.

I don't have strength for all this and you too, Nora. I'm doing the best I can. Stay away from me. You don't know. Do you know? You don't know. You've been looking for me? Why? What do you want? And what about you? Why are you so afraid to do anything, Nora? What have you got to lose? Where do you come from, Nora? Why do you come to me?

Ranger whined and wagged his tail.

Kenny let his head fall back against the door. The room was quiet except for the scrabble of a gull on the roof. He heard its ridiculous feet slap the tin. Suddenly, Kenny pulled out his knife and spun across the room. He dug at the mud chinking between two logs until the point snapped off the blade. Then he dug with the broken blade until a section of chinking sprang out and clattered onto the floor. Ash and clinkers and clay. Prying at the edge of the opening, he popped out another piece. When a bar of light gleamed between the logs, he stuck his knife blade into the light and twisted. Soon he had cleared enough of the chinking to let the outside air flow in. He pressed his nose to the opening.

Woodsmoke, mildewed rope, maybe a trail of thyme and yeast, where a woman had walked by.

That's all he believed in. That and nothing more.

He liked being an end-of-the-roader, and wasn't this the end of the road, this broken-down shack at the last stop on the last ferry? He liked the name he'd chosen. He liked his ugly beard. He liked being crazy. Up until Nora came, he'd liked being alone, even though he'd thought a little sex would be a good thing now and then.

He reached one arm across his body to knead the muscles in his shoulder and settled back in his chair. The warmth from the stripe of light crept slowly, slowly up his face. Finally, he took a long breath and blew it out through a crooked grin.

Ranger ventured to let his tail slap back and forth on the floor.

Kenny threw Ranger a sly look.

"If I was going to be a hero, which I am not, as you know, Ranger, I would be a hero dog. Rin Tin Tin or somebody. A dog, yeah. Then Nora would ruffle up the hair on the back of my head. And hold my muzzle with both hands and kiss me on the nose. And slap me on my flanks and murmur goofy baby doggie words into my pricked-up ears. I'd rescue any kid for her then, capture any robber."

Ranger gave him a long, long look and flapped his tail experimentally. Kenny's shoulders dropped.

"Are you laughing at me, Ranger?"

Ranger's tail stopped abruptly.

Kenny leaned down to slap him on the butt. "Smart dog. We'll laugh last, Ranger. You and me." The tail started up again.

"But we're not in the hero business. I've learned my lesson. Har. Learned it the old-fashioned way."

Kenny gripped Ranger's lower jaw and looked him in the eye, smiling and fumbling his beards while he found the words. He nodded: Aeschylus. *He who learns must suffer. And even in our sleep, pain that cannot forget falls drop by drop upon the heart, and in our own despair, against our will, comes wisdom to us by the awful grace of God.*

Har.

He wrenched open his door and howled at the only person he could see, who was Lillian, watering her pansies. His terrible voice echoed over the boardwalk and into the dark spaces underneath. "In our own *despair*, against our will, comes wisdom to us by the awful grace of God."

Lillian looked his way, smiled, and gave him a weary thumbs-up.

August 21

HIGH TIDE		LOW TIDE	
11:58am	13.1ft	5:21am	1.7ft
11:36pm	15.0ft	5:35pm	4.5ft

There's nothing a man does that lasts. Lillian knew this, if anybody did. A man makes his plans, plots it all out, builds his big buildings, thinks he's changed the world. But a few years go by and everything on his blueprints is decaying in a skunk-cabbage swale. Roofs cave in. Floods undermine the pilings. Down it goes. Alders grow over it, erasing every trace. Nothing lasts. When you have a choice between betting on a man and betting on an alder, always put your money on the tree. Only good thing about the human race is that nothing it does outlasts the alders.

This was Lillian's time for thinking, when the last paying customer had swayed out the door and pissed into the sea, and lapping water was the only sound to be heard in Good River Harbor. Lillian poured herself a glass of whiskey—not too much, not too little, not too expensive, but not the rotgut that Tick drinks. After she'd circumnavigated the room, snapping off lights, she waded through yellow rectangles thrown across the floor by streetlights on the boardwalk. Yellow beads glowed on the windows, gathered themselves into runnels, and rivered down the windowpane. She dug one shoe off with the other, sank into a chair and, grunting, lifted her feet onto the windowsill. Her ankles were swollen and her feet bulged around the shape of her shoes, the way a ball of dough only gradually releases the shape of the baker's fist. Lillian leaned over to knead the sorest of two sore knees.

A long day and a long night with a crowded bar and everybody giggling like kids about Axel's notched piling. Lillian sighed and raised the glass to her lips. Her lipstick left a kiss on the edge. She leaned forward, trying to see through the window, but all she could see was herself. It always surprised her, the fat old lady who peered at her from windows and mirrors, the soft round chin, as layered as a croissant, and the cheeks that drooped below her jawline. The old lady's eyes were bright blue, yes, but they floated in watery pink seas. The whole face was yellow-tinged and speckled, but that was surely the treachery of the window's reflection. Which is real—how you see yourself or how the vengeful mirror reveals you? She rubbed her chin, which more than one man had described as cute. It made her teeth feel tired and uprooted to think about that. Made her whole jaw ache. She washed the whiskey experimentally around her mouth.

One thing she knew, if you're a man getting old, don't look at an old salmon, growing that monstrosity of a jaw, teeth so big and jutted out he can't get his mouth shut. And if you're a woman getting old, for god's sake don't look at a salmon hen. Because there it is, the old thing dribbling red eggs even while her flesh is molding off her back, scratching dirt to make a redd, fraying her tail to a bloody stub. And the male squirting and leaving. Squirting and leaving—that's guaranteed.

Lillian stared across the dark channel to Axel's construction site. The yard lights illuminated the bottom of the rainsquall that was sliding down the mountain. As the storm descended, the lights over the equipment yard disappeared first. Then the lights in the office trailer dimmed out. A red pickup truck under a security light faded to pink and vanished.

Oh, there's a lesson in that for somebody like Nora, so upset about the dam and water project. Everything a man makes starts falling apart as soon as he pounds the last nail. That's the difference between Father Time and Mother Nature: He knocks things down, she grows things up. Lillian shook her head. Nora needs to know that Axel's not the first one to build on the tideflat at the base of the Kis'utch River, and he won't be the last. Used to be a whole town there. Lillian herself used to own a business in that town. Gone. Everything gone. She would tell Nora about that. Nora needed to know that. Put her mind at ease, settle her down.

Lillian sipped the whiskey in the dark and listened to the rain hit the window and gargle in the downspout.

"Sing for me, Lilly," the men would say. "Sing me a beautiful song. Do I have to get down on my knees?"

They did then. The men walked on their knees with their hands praying as if she were an angel, across the parlor to the base of the stairs where she waited for them. Men walked on their knees. "A song, then," she would say, curling her hand over a man's hair, stroking under his chin. She sang for them.

"Summertime."

The first words quieted them, the rough men. Even the snuffling dogs jerked to attention, sat back on their haunches, and stared. She sang slowly, as if this were the first time she had tasted the honey of the words. She sang with her eyes closed and her arms straight at her sides, her hands open and turned to the men. They thought she was an angel. She wore a white gown with feathers at the hem and let her hair fall over her shoulders. Golden curls down to her waist.

"One of these mornings, you're gonna rise up singing. Then you'll spread your wings and you'll take to the sky."

They cried then, the men. You don't know, when a man pays for a woman, if he wants his mama or his girl or an angel in a white dress.

"Ain't nothing can harm you, with mama standin' by."

That was back when timber crews worked the woods around Good River Harbor, yarding spruce logs down to the sea, penning them inside log booms and dragging them with tugboats to the mill. Back when choke setters and sawyers crowded the docks and each day crews moved higher and higher on the mountain. Back then, there was a little town at the mouth of the Kis'utch River, across the channel from Good River. The town fathers of Good River Harbor made Lillian run her business over there across the channel, over with the Indians and the clams and the stills. Her building backed up against the bank of Jimmy Pete's pond—a two-story frame shack propped by two-by-fours onto a ridge of boulders. On slow nights, Jimmy Pete would come and sit by her woodstove, drink her whiskey, and tell her how it used to be, about the Tlingit village and the songs.

I'll tell Nora my story, Lillian decided. I should think about how I might put it into words, what I might tell her. She needs to know. Axel's got the bulldozers over there now, pushing the rocks around, but those rocks have been pushed around before and will be pushed around again, and the trees grew up over the land and it was the bears' land again. That's what I'll tell her first.

The only man Lillian ever loved was John Shaddy. Oh, he had plans. Nineteen years old and he had plans. He was a Wisconsin boy, on his way north. If north was his direction, then north was Lillian's direction too. They hopped from logging camp to logging camp at every river along that wet green coast—Astoria, Aberdeen, Prince Rupert, Hydaburg, Wrangell, Juneau, Hoonah. John set chokers on giant trees. Lillian stood in clouds of horse flies and ground up venison for loggers' sausage. For four years, she cooked in logging camps—mosquito-plagued summer forests, bear-infested autumn forests, sea-rimmed winter forests, one after another.

John was a handsome man with a silky yellow beard and muscles so big in his arms he never could get them down to his side, walked around sort of spread out. At night, they tucked up tight under the blankets and made love and talked about their plan. They would go until they came to a place where two roads crossed and that's where they would stop. They would open a roadside inn with red-checked curtains and a sign held up by a carved bear. John would build the kitchen and the guest cottages, and Lillian would cook and sing for the customers.

In Hoonah, a yellow cedar rolled on John. Everybody knows how it happens. Choker setter on his knees reaches a cable under the log, the log gives way. Lillian's beloved John went whistling off to work with his buddies, and they carried his body home on a stretcher made of saplings and flannel shirts. He's buried there in the little cemetery grown up in alders, around the corner from Hoonah's ferry dock. So much for a man's plans. Lillian got on that ferry and rode from little town to rundown little town, until the end of the line, where she got off. Good River Harbor was the last stop.

Even back then, running her business, Lillian listened to the river. A sawyer's grunts were loud in one ear, but the river was louder in the other—that's a clean sound, water rushing always to another place. When the sawyer lifted his prickly chin, groaned, and called out to God, she imagined she was riding a log along the river, floating into a place with deep shadows and monkeyflowers blooming. By the time the river floated her to sea, the sawyer was pulling on his oily trousers. He flipped his suspenders up with his thumbs and let himself out the door, leaving a twenty-dollar bill on the bed. The next man came, the one who hauled deadheads from the river and sawed them into salty stovewood, the man with splinters in his hands and the smell of sweat and cedar in his beard. The machinist, with red hair between his legs—the one who kept the donkeys oiled and cranking. Then the harbormaster, with cold damp hands.

Lillian didn't know exactly how or when it happened, but just once, she conceived and bore a son. He was a beautiful child with a furze of hair so blond it might have been white. She named the baby John Shaddy, and she gave him away to a man and woman who lived on a seiner. They changed his name to Axel Hagerman, and that was that. That was a secret between her and that man and woman, nobody else, and that was that. That mistake is what it is, she had had to tell herself more than once. Grief is healing, so grieve. But regret is poison. No looking back.

After that, Lillian had walked upstream every morning to a shallow pond ringed with boulders. It was just a little pond, rushes and dragon-flies, even in the rain. Sitting naked on a rock, she smeared herself with blue mud from the glacier, then washed it all away—the mud and the smell of the men.

In the summer of 1959, heavy rain fell on the snowfields. There'd been a lot of snow, and the rain melted it fast. Water rose in flood in the muskegs, then broke through the logjams and thundered all at once down the mountain. Lillian heard it coming and ran with the men to high ground. It wasn't the falling force of the water that destroyed everything, but its lift. Back-eddies rose into town and lifted every building—the mercantile, the hotel, the shacks where the loggers lived. The flood smashed into the log yard, rolling logs off the piles, turning them into ramrods that took down the walls. Wrecked everything and washed the wreckage away.

The flood lifted Lillian's shack and carried it downstream, upright and entire. She watched it go. It lodged against a rock, turned, and slowly came apart, boards springing up like herons. She watched it happen, nothing to be done about it. A curl of tar paper peeled off the wall and rolled under a wave. Her mattress rafted downriver. The bedspread swirled away. It was a lovely bedspread—red sateen. In an hour, nothing was left of her life but one of her shoes. She found it in the mud. Shiny patent leather, but the sole was gone.

Townsfolk salvaged the timbers of Lillian's shack, sawed them even and hammered them onto a log flattened by a chain saw. It made a good bridge over the Kis'utch until the next high water took it out.

"And what of you, Lillian?" she asked herself fondly.

"Me?" She downed the last of the whiskey and smiled at her reflection, which smiled back.

"I have spent the rest of my life washing the stains out of men's clothes and drowning men in booze." Her reflection leaned back its head and laughed.

"But I'll tell Nora about the flood. I'll do it tomorrow. That should cheer her up."

≈≈≈≈

THE BEAR BOLTED out of the trap through the door into the cistern, then braced to a stop, swinging her great head and stumbling over her cub, he was that close to her rear legs. She raised her snout, swaying back and forth, then rounded back to the door just as it slammed shut. *Where is the smell of the other cub, the musk of milk and moss?* The slam brought her up short. She rose on her hind legs and stretched to full height, pawed the air and roared.

"Drop that bar across the door and chain it good."

The sow brought her head low, stiffened her front legs to raise her shoulders, and turned the full expanse of her shaggy flank toward the place where the shouts of men thudded into the wooden wall. She huffed and stamped, shaking her head, slinging saliva in long strings. Metal chains rapped metal. Moaning, the bear lunged along the side of the cistern, looking over her shoulder. The cub galloped along behind her.

This way, she extended the distance from the men, but even as she directed her course in a straight line, the wall turned her in, and in, and the farther she ran, the closer she came again to the smell of men and metal. She slowed, circled her cub, nudged him with her nose, then launched her weight against the door. A dull thud, shouts from men.

"She'll kill herself against that wall."

She reversed direction and quickened her pace, but the farther she ran in the curve of the cistern, the closer she came again to the smell of men. She smashed her shoulder into the door, then raised herself on back legs and let out a fearsome roar. Her claws tore against the wood.

"Stay back. Stay back," men shouted.

She turned and galloped back the way she'd come. Each time she ran into the smell of the place the men had been, she stopped so suddenly that her paws skidded in the gravel and dug holes into the dirt. Finally, at the farthest reach from the door, she slowed, gathered her cub under her flank, backed into a rank of transplanted alders, and crouched by the wall.

A hank of deer meat fell on the bear's hips. She lurched and spun around. *The smell of blood, the smell of men and metal.* She leapt from another thud, as a second chunk of meat dropped beside her. She backed from the meat, snarling. The cub sprinted away. *Iron-red blood smell, crushed bones, gun oil, the salty-sour smell of men.*

"She'll eat when she's hungry, I can money-back-guarantee you that."

Backing farther into the alders, into the crackle of branches and flutter of falling leaves, she lay down heavily, her eyes on the group of men leaning over the edge above her. Mewling, the cub followed her in, circled her, nudged at her belly. As the cub took shelter beside her, the sow growled, a long steady unbroken growl, the rasp of rising wind.

Ravens lined the rim of the tank, black against gray sky. They clonked and clattered, flapping strong wings to hop sideways, turning their heads to get a better look at the joints of deer. One raven spread its wings, hopped up, tilted, and dove. Flaring to arrest the dive, he landed with an extra hop next to the joint. He eyed the meat with one eye, then the other, hopped closer, looked in both directions, and stabbed at the meat with his hard beak. The bear watched, her head between her paws. A bald eagle soared overhead, banked sharply, then flew over again, lower this time, clattering. By the time the rain stopped, the birds had stripped the deer joints to clean white bones and only one raven remained, pecking between her toes, mumbling to herself. She flapped away as the men approached on the viewing platform.

"With the cub, we might want to raise the price. What's a cub worth? I mean, in the wild like this?"

"What do you think? Fifteen dollars a person? Twenty?"

"Are we charging by the person or by the hour or by the bear? And is it just the sight of the bears we're selling, or is it the whole scene—bears and eagles and mountains, a package deal?"

Exhausted, the bear slept with her chin in the mud, a wild dark empty sleep. Rain blew in at dusk, coursing off the bear's shoulders. She rolled to her feet and began to walk.

Broken rock, sulfurous mud, beach grass dead and decaying, gravel and gasoline. Sniffing under the door—the salt-air beach, driftwood rimed with shipworms, wave-windrowed kelp, broken clamshells, the body of a storm-drowned murre, hopping with beach fleas. She raked her claws against the door. Then she stalked around, around, around the cistern. Off gravel onto broken rocks, slick with algae, then dirt and fireweed, back to the place of the bones, still there, shiny in the rain. Mud, fallen beach grass, gravel and gasoline, the place of the men, sea-smell, gravel, broken rocks. Algae-slicked mud, fireweed, bones, mud, beach grass, gravel and gasoline, the place of the men, sea-smell, gravel, broken rocks, mud, the place of the meat, mud, beach grass, gravel and gasoline, the smell of men and tide rising among blue mussels. She did not find her second cub. There was no smell of her in this place. What there was: not her smell.

From time to time, the bear raised herself against the wall, reaching with her front paws, raking deep scratches as she scrabbled for purchase. Along the wall she paced, then lifted to scratch claws on cedar, and sank down and paced some more, and up again. She sniffed the ground. Then suddenly, she began to dig. Dirt and gravel flew past her face. A young alder toppled against her shoulder. Mud spattered the wall as water drained into the hole. Then her claws raked against the wooden floor. Again no way out. Even under the earth: no way out. Finally, the bear squatted in the hole, her haunches in mud, her chin resting on her front paws. Sometimes she turned a paw over and licked the bloody torn spaces between the claws, the flakes of wood and embedded stones. But as dark closed in, she sat without moving. Her cub nudged her hard in the flank, and she rolled over to let him drink what he could suck.

Remember. Spruce tips, arnica, cedar stumps crumbling into the place of the balsamroots. High meadow laced with the burrows of mountain voles, tubes of excavated dirt lying where melting snow had laid them.

Remember. Nests of newborn mice. Fresh deer kills, slippery with ravens and marten. Clear trout-flecked water under banks of moss. Under the highest, oldest spruces, the place of the huckleberries. Two cubs, musky and suckling. On a small wind, each remembered smell.

BY THE TIME he found the perfect tree, Davy's back was soaked with sweat and his neck itched from all the duff and moss that stuck to it. It had been a steep climb up behind the big old cistern, alders in there, bent over by avalanches, and the spongy stumps of felled spruce, hard enough to climb over with two good arms, really tricky if you don't quite trust the other one yet. And he couldn't trust the carpet of moss that covered the ground under his feet. Wherever a log had rotted out or a bear had undermined a stump, the carpet gave way, sinking him to his knees.

The tree he found was exactly what he needed. It was a western hemlock with limbs like a ladder, maybe the only hemlock left among the alder. He climbed one-handed to a place where nobody could see him, but he could see out between the branches, right down onto the viewing platform over the Bear Shelter. Davy didn't want Axel or anybody to know he was anywhere near the cistern, but man, he wanted to see Meredith. Even just see her. He had it figured she would visit the bears sometime that afternoon, and even if he had to wait half the day, that was okay with Davy.

For the best view, he needed to be just a little higher. He pulled himself to the next branch, and then he had to stop to think this over, because somebody had been in the tree before him. There was a plank set just right across the branches to make a steady seat. The plank hadn't been there long—no hemlock needles dusted it, no cobwebs or spiders, no tiny hemlock cones. It was like a deer stand, but who would hunt for deer right next to the old cannery site, when you can get a deer on Green Point whenever you want? More like somebody wanted to get a free look at the bears in the cistern, cheat Axel out of twenty-four bucks.

Davy hauled himself onto the plank. This would be a great place if you wanted to shoot a picture of the bears. Almost below him and off at a little angle, the sow was sitting in a hole she must have dug. She didn't move, so maybe she was asleep. Her cub was tucked up beside her, sitting in a mud puddle. She'd torn out a whole bunch of fireweed. It must have been a bad scene when they put her in the cistern. But nothing was happening now. Davy leaned against the trunk, settling himself for a long wait.

A carpenter he didn't know was hammering siding onto a kiosk. It made Davy sick, knowing that if he hadn't got Meredith stranded, big Tick would have been the carpenter pounding those nails. Each hand-built detail of the Bear Shelter—the ramps and platforms—flooded him with shame. Davy's dad hadn't driven the screws in the gangway that spanned the distance from the dock to the pavilion. He hadn't pounded in the footers that held the Bear Shelter pavilion onto the rocky shelf beside the cistern, or figured out how to build the observation platform so it wouldn't blow away. Like everything else, the observation platform got built without Davy's dad.

The carpenter crossed the pavilion to get another one-by-four. Somehow it all was happening without big Tick McIver, which made Davy's mouth go dry, at this evidence that the world could go on without Tick McIver, that anything good could happen without his dad. And that his very own screwup had taken his father completely out of this world. He felt like a lonesome murderer sitting in a goddamn tree. He squinted his eyes and tried to summon a picture of Meredith.

Approaching on the trail from town, a small woman in a red sweater climbed the ramp to the Bear Shelter pavilion and paused to look around. Her hair was tied up in a bandana, but Davy knew it was Meredith's mom. Rebecca Hagerman. He would know her from any distance— one, because she was so small, but also because of the way she walked, which was courteously, stepping lightly, nodding her head, as if she were friends with the bushes. She crossed the pavilion to the door in the cistern where they'd loaded in the bears. She stopped there, and maybe she was listening for the bears, but it couldn't have been only that, because she threw a quick look at the carpenter's back and then she moved in close to the bar that was levered across the door and fingered the lock. Finally, she climbed the path to the observation platform and looked over the rim at the bears.

Davy pulled himself out on the limb to see her more clearly. It was odd, the little squeaks she made, like a mew gull. It took him a couple of beats to realize she was crying. Davy had sunk so low, he hadn't thought a guy could feel any worse, but this was worse, all right, a mother crying.

Rebecca Hagerman straightened suddenly and pulled back from the edge. Davy pulled back too, because here came Curtis and a couple of kids he knew, jiving across the pavilion and bounding up the path to the observation deck.

Curtis leaned over the railing and dropped something on the bear. It hit the branch over her head and bounced onto the mud. Probably just luck, Davy figured, that the next thing he dropped bounced off her snout. The bear shook her big head.

"Does anybody have any more pennies?"

Davy ground his teeth. That stupid Curtis.

The bear hauled to her feet, shook her shoulders, huffed, and turned sideways to the voices. She drew her shoulders high, lowered her head, swaying it back and forth. Hair stood up along her neck. A stream of watery crap plopped onto the fallen alder leaves.

"Boy, if I ever came on a bear displaying like that, I'd be shitting my pants too," Davy muttered. "That's a pissed-off bear." Another penny bonked against the wall behind her and she backed away.

"Quit it, you dipshit."

It was Meredith.

She looked beautiful, climbing the path. She had on her gray hooded sweatshirt, open halfway like she does. Her jeans were shiny and stuck tight to her legs. She ignored her mother and leaned over the bears.

"I brought her huckleberries," Meredith said. Her voice was beautiful. And wasn't it just like Meredith, Davy marveled, to think of something nice like that?

"I brought her huckleberries," Curtis whined in a sick-sweet voice, and Davy could have popped him one. But Meredith whacked Curtis in the arm and he laid off. Meredith poured the huckleberries over the edge. Huckleberries bounced off the bear's head and fell in the mud between

her paws. The sow moved away. But the cub nosed around in the huckleberries. Then he rolled on them, rubbing his back in the dirt.

"Huckleberries are to eat, you silly bear," Meredith said. She draped
her arms over the railing. After a while Curtis and the others got bored
and left, but Meredith stayed there, watching the bears. Davy thought
she looked sad, the way she stared out, and maybe it was because of the
bears. But maybe she missed him. Davy knew she didn't think it was fair
that her dad fired his dad, because her mom told his mom so. Her mom
had cried and cried about Meredith gone missing. But in the end, she
said Davy did the best he could and they weren't drowned and that's
what counted. And she said that was just mean to fire Davy's dad—even
though it's good, she said, to keep Davy and Meredith apart for a while,
to let things simmer down. Davy wondered what that meant, to let things
simmer down. Maybe Meredith told her mom that things were pretty hot
between them.

Davy cupped his hands to his mouth and gave his secret raven cry.
"Gaaaa. Gaaa." Meredith turned around and looked up the mountainside.
There were lots of real ravens around, cawing away, so Davy thought he'd
better do it again. Meredith looked straight at him then. She ducked her
head and waved her hands in front of her face, as if she were brushing
away flies.

It might have been a warning. Then Davy was afraid, but he didn't
know what of.

He stayed in the tree for a long time. Finally, Axel came and Meredith
went home, although Rebecca stayed on, leaning over the bears in her
bandana and her flowered skirt. By then it was getting toward dusk, and
Davy thought if he didn't get home himself pretty soon, his dad would
report him missing again, and then he'd be dead again.

He'd climbed down the tree and was backing down the mountainside
through the alders, slipping on the branches, when he heard somebody
bushwhacking up toward him. It was probably a person, because a bear
would make more noise than that, and a deer wouldn't make so much. He
slid down behind a stump. The branches kept cracking in his direction.
If it was a person, it was a big person. And it was coming at him. Davy
pressed the side of his face into the rotten stump and gathered his arms

close to his body. If the person kept coming, this would be no hiding place at all. The footsteps tromped past him and then paused.

"Dad!" Davy said, and stood straight up.

Tick jumped and spun all in one motion, swinging the muzzle of a rifle toward Davy.

"Jeezus, Dad," Davy yelled, and dropped on his face in the duff.

Nothing happened. A jay cried an alarm call and nothing happened. Davy lifted his head.

There stood Tick with his beard flowing over a camo jacket, his mouth open and his Marlin .444 hanging from his hand.

"What the hell you doing? God, Davy, I could of shot you, popping up from behind a stump like a goddam shooting gallery." Big as he was, Tick was shaking. "Don't you ever, ever, ever surprise a man with a gun. Whoa, if I'da shot you point-blank with a rifle this big, you'd be nothing but red mist." Tick closed his eyes.

"Yeah, but Dad, what are you doing up here with that gun?"

"Thought I'd . . ." Tick was stumped.

"What could you shoot from up here?"

"Thought I'd get us a deer liver for supper," Tick finally said.

"Yeah. Deer liver.

"But that would be a lot of trouble, wouldn't it?"

Tick shook his head again, as if to clear it, and then he had to sit down, right there in the ferns. Davy sat beside him, leaning against his dad.

"I guess let's us two go home and open a can of ravioli," Tick said finally. "That would be a better idea."

"Yeah," Tick said again, almost to himself.

"That would be a better idea."

August 22

HIGH TIDE		LOW TIDE	
		6:07am	0.9ft
12:39pm	13.9ft	6:21pm	3.6ft

Howard Fowler—formerly Howard Fowler, surveyor, but recently promoted to Howard Fowler, director of communications for Good River Products, Inc.—stood at his office window. He still couldn't believe how quickly Axel had promoted him. "I need new blood on my team," Axel had said, and Howard understood how this could be, since Axel had sort of bled out a lot of former employees. "I need a good mind on my team," Axel had said, and Howard could understand that too, being proud of his good mind and his wife always telling him that he was too smart to be just a surveyor. "You have a good rapport with the community, Howard," Axel had said. Now that was hard for Howard to understand, considering that the last time Howard talked much with any of them, he had his pants around his ankles on Lillian's bar. But he did understand that Axel had a public relations problem, and he was happy to help out, happy with the new salary, happy with his office.

This was the first real office he'd ever had, so even though it was just a construction trailer, he kept his computer desk tidy, his business cards squared up, his tie neatly knotted, and his office philodendron looking good. He reached over to pick a dead leaf off the potted plant. Because the trailer sat right there in the construction site at the river, Howard always knew whether the water project was on schedule and who was working hard, who was screwing up, and what was going to need explaining.

Howard glanced out the window each time he heard an outboard motor. Unfortunately, his Time Management Seminar hadn't told him what you do when you've got a meeting scheduled for 8 a.m. and all the people you're supposed to be meeting with are hanging around at the top of a wharf a hundred yards across the water, scratching dogs, shooting the breeze, gazing out to sea—doing everything but checking their watches.

He'd come to the site early, set up the PowerPoint presentation, put on the coffee. Axel was trusting him to do a good job with this meeting, which was a lot of trust in a surveyor who was promoted to communications director only last month. Axel had sent Howard up to Anchorage the week before to take some workshops, hone his people skills, get his confidence all ramped up—because confidence is everything—but he was feeling a little skittish. All the same, he'd learned that *Communications = community + relations*. That was his first PowerPoint slide.

Howard understood that Axel had a lot riding on this. He hadn't objected when the townies demanded a tour of the Kis'utch River construction site. Told Howard, set it up. Don't volunteer more information than you need to, make everybody sign a waiver, in case they trip over a clamshell and sue him. So that was fine—a good chance to get the town lined up behind the project. Howard didn't tell Axel that his own wife was the first one to sign up for the tour, which was just weird. He thought there might be quite a communications issue in that household.

Howard looked across the channel. No progress on that front. He toggled over to email. Twenty-four new messages. He searched for anything from home. If it weren't for Jennifer's emails, he wouldn't last a week in this town.

> Taylor's playschool is putting on The Three Little Pigs, and she's going to be the middle-sized pig. She's got a little rubber pig nose with an elastic string. She loves it. Won't take it off, even to sleep. She's so cute, you should see her. I'm sewing a curly tail onto her pink pajamas.

Howard chuckled. He lived on Jennifer's emails, breathed them in. *I can just see it*, he typed, *Taylor asleep in her new big-person bed, cheeks all pink, arms thrown out, the little pig nose squashed into the blanket.* Howard hoped Jennifer tiptoed in and took the nose off before Taylor suffocated.

> She's been practicing her line. She's only got one: "Oh no, bad wolf, don't blow my house down."

Last time Howard talked to his little girl on the phone, he told her he'd seen a real wolf from the floatplane, but Taylor said, "Oh, Daddy, that's just in movies." Whatever. Real or animated—it didn't matter. He would protect his daughter from wolves and winds and anything else that might blow down her house.

He checked out the window. Odd, how on a perfectly clear morning, a strip of fog hovered over the river at shoulder height. One end of the fogbank lifted slowly and floated there, reared up like a sea snake. But here the townspeople came, finally. They were all piled into Tick's work-boat, standing in the bow. Howard picked up binoculars. Seven or eight of them, looking cheery enough. Better go down to the landing and help with the boat, he decided, because they do that here, run over to haul around each other's anchors. If they see you in the library, they might not even say hello. But come toward land in a boat, especially if the wind is blowing, they run over to keep your skiff from scraping on the gravel or bumping into a piling. As Howard watched from the beach, Tick lowered his bow and they all walked off like some Committee of Inspections.

First off the bow was Axel's wife, Rebecca, no taller than Howard's armpit. He had met her before. When she smiled to say hello, her cheeks crinkled up into her eye sockets. How she could smile and see at the same time, Howard could not figure. He remembered that her hair was long and brown, but she had it all bound up in a bandana for the tour—not exactly dress-for-success. Her head nodded reflexively, as if everything was yes. He shook Rebecca's hand firmly, covering the handshake with his left hand and looking her square in the place her eyes were buried—the way they taught him in Interpersonal Communication: Five Minutes to a Trusting Relationship.

Nora next. Yellow raincoat, jeans, some sort of tool stuck in her back pocket—socket wrench? But what's she been twisting? That woman made Howard nervous. So friendly and everything—she had her hand over his before he could put his over hers. But she was intense, always looking around, always thinking something, and Howard never could figure out whether she was beautiful or just bizarre. Her face changed fast as the weather. She could flash a smile that would make puddles steam and disappear. Other times, the puddle would shrink into the ground if it knew what was good for it. She looked Howard straight in the eye, just as he was looking her straight in the eye, a game of chicken, and then they both flinched.

"Welcome to corporate headquarters," Howard said, and smiled the rueful little smile he had been practicing, sweeping his hand toward his

Airstream. "Things are just getting going. We threw up that wharf just to get stuff in. Next time you come out, it'll be more impressive."

Couple more people. The postmaster with his arms crossed on his chest. The man and woman who lived on the schooner *Fairwinds*, wearing matching red bowling jackets, for God's sake, with FAIRWINDS stitched across the back. A random kid with black hair. Last one off the boat was Tick McIver, with his orange beard swinging off his face. He slung a long leg over the gunwale. He was carrying the anchor up the beach, which saved Howard the trouble of deciding if he would shake the hand of the man who had humiliated him in the bar—after he'd sprung for Tick's drink.

They all crowded into the office. Howard called up the PowerPoint presentation he'd prepared.

"Been reading email messages from my wife. My daughter's going to be the pig in a play." The personal touch. Howard congratulated himself. "Thanks for coming over. I'd like to share our vision for this project. We at Good River Products are proud of our plans for the future well-being of the community."

No response. Rebecca was nodding at him, yes, yes. The rest of them stared out the window. He walked over to close the mini-blinds.

"So if you'll direct your attention to the screen? And you just interrupt me whenever you have a question." He ran the cursor up to start and pressed enter.

"Can we do this outside," Rebecca said. Was that a question or a statement?

"I have prepared a PowerPoint presentation."

"Such a beautiful day."

So much for the PowerPoint.

"Sure thing," he said. Howard remembered to press the sleep button on his laptop to keep from running out the battery and let them go out the door first.

They all crunched over the gravel to the clamflat, stretched out empty and gleaming at low tide.

"The wharf's just a temporary fix. We'll be dredging a channel here and putting in a boat basin for the barges and tankers. We're going to need rocky fill for the dock. The engineers say that if we remove the top-fill from that slope, we'll find readily accessible basalt. This can be quarried at recoverable cost, since the Forest Service has agreed to waive . . ."

Damned if that big guy Tick wasn't crouched down in the sand, digging wildly with his bare hands, scraping away a hole that was filling with water as fast as he dug. The kid was helping him. He straightened up, holding a bulging clam that looked sort of like a yam with a droopy penis sticking out of one end.

"This is a geoduck," Tick said. "It's a clam. Some people call them horseneck clams, but this thing doesn't look like a horse neck to me." He smirked. "Pretty good to eat. And maybe you wonder how a geoduck breathes, under the sand."

Howard nodded stupidly. Damn.

"See, it has this siphon. Looks just like a penis. It pushes that up through the sand. You seen that?"

Howard didn't know. When would he have? "Yes," he lied.

"You can dig geoducks at low tide." Rebecca spoke up, all excited. "Just bring over a skiff with a couple of garden shovels and a couple of kids, and in less than an hour, you can have as many as you can eat. You got to skin that penis thing. Put it in boiling water for forty-five seconds and then the skin will just peel right off. Slice it crossways, pound it good with a mallet, and fry it up. Squeeze in some lemon and throw in some butter and half a clove of garlic and let them sizzle a bit."

Do these men think of nothing but sex and the women only of food? And who would eat such a thing, skinned or not? Howard's mind flashed to the beef Wellington Jennifer made for their anniversaries. A special meal, candlelight, sex.

Focus. Focus on your outcomes, Howard reminded himself.

"The kids will have good jobs over here before the year is out. They'll be too busy raking in the dough to think about digging up clams." That was good. Howard chuckled. Keep it light. Talk about the good of the children, but don't get too personal. He tried not to look at Nora, but whenever he did, she was looking straight back at him.

"Over here." Howard turned and walked them through wet grasses to the weir on the old Indian allotment the company had leased. "This was a coup, by the way, how Axel smooth-talked the Indian bureau-crats on that lease." Almost as brilliant as getting the environmental impact statement done before the salmon came back to the river. Howard chuckled, but before he had taken five steps toward the weir, his pant legs were soaked to the knee. He should have insisted on the PowerPoint.

Carpenters had finished nailing up plywood forms for the concrete pour. "This will be the front wall of the collection pond, built right here across where the river is now. We'll dig to bedrock, then build up about twenty feet above grade, rock and concrete, make a nice sturdy reservoir. The river will fill up to about here." Howard put his hand up under his chin to show the depth, only realizing from their stares that his gesture looked a lot like he was slitting his own throat.

He pulled out a handkerchief. "Excuse me." He blew his nose, because what else was he going to do?

"Pipes will carry the water about three hundred feet to the dock. We'll take the water in tankers to a bottling plant in Japan, ship it back to Cali-fornia to sell. *Glacier Water from Good River Harbor.* Quite a vision."

Howard smiled in the general direction of the townies. But that damn Tick was digging into a bear poop with a stick.

"Blueberries," he said. "Rock crabs. But mostly salmon. This time of year, the bears eat mostly the brains, leave the rest for the gulls." He picked up a gooey bone splinter for everyone to admire.

Howard rushed on with his planned speech. "If you're interested, the Environmental Impact Studies are all on file in the office, including the seismic reports on the quarry, and the restrictions on the covenants for the allotment land." Howard knew he was jabbering, but what was he sup-posed to do? "You'll find that the papers are all in good order. Axel worked on that for a full year before we even came on site, in close coordination with the congressional delegation."

Rebecca looked up sharply, showing her eyes. "Axel's been working on this for a year?" Rebecca shot a glance at Nora, and Howard was glad he wasn't between them to intercept that one. He'd be collateral damage, that's for sure. He thought of Jennifer, and how much luckier he was than Axel. Rebecca just might be a house on fire.

As if Howard hadn't said a word of any interest whatsoever, Tick kept right on talking about the salmon.

"The seals will eat the stomachs, biting big gashes in their sides. And sometimes, bears will stand here and bite out the salmons' humps while they're swimming upstream."

"The covenants on the allotment land . . ." Howard said, because it was all he could think of to say. Suddenly, Tick was nudging him.

"It's important for you to know what salmon do," Tick said, with a level of sternness Howard had not seen before.

Howard ran a hand over his mouth. What was he doing there, manager of communications, standing in muck, being lectured by the prince of defecation?

"Oh, we'll take care of Mother Earth," Howard said. "This entire area will be a nature reserve. There will be no hunting of bears or deer, no fishing for salmon, no clamming. Total protection. Total. Very enviro. Don't you worry."

Howard beamed his warmest smile toward Rebecca. "Anyway, Mother Earth is a tough old gal."

Rebecca looked away, staring out to sea. "If the Earth were your mother," she said in her sweet little girl voice, "she would grab you in one rocky hand and hold you underwater until you no longer bubbled."

HOW QUICKLY THAT had gone sour. Howard loosened his tie and leaned back in his new Naugahyde chair. He knew there was nothing Tick or Nora or any of them could do to stop the water plant. That wasn't the issue. Axel had covered all his bases; you could count on the front office of Good River Products. So why did he feel so shitty? Honestly? He wanted them to be grateful—for the project, for all the trouble Axel and he and Good River Products were going to, to develop the channel. That was it. He wanted them to like him. He wanted them to understand he was on their side. Good River Products was doing it *for them*.

"I'm not a monster," Howard said to his potted philodendron. "My little girl doesn't think I'm so bad." In the evenings, when he's home, she settles into his lap with a book, all cuddled tight in pink footie pajamas. He reaches around her with both arms and takes her little fuzzy feet in his hands, and brings her up into a little ball that fits exactly in his lap. Nothing in his life makes him happier than that—that he can provide the people he loves with that kind of shelter and safety. And with this new job, this new income, it will be even better. When he gets home, she will crawl into his lap with her little piggy nose on its elastic string, and he will gather her in his arms, lean over her, and say, "Little Piggy, Daddy will never, ever, let anyone blow your house down. That's why Daddy works so hard," he will tell her, "that's why I have to be away so much, so we have enough money to build a house out of the strongest bricks in the world."

Howard's eyes fogged up, but he shook it off.

"For how good you Good River Harbor people are with your hands, you are surprisingly dim when it comes to business." This was what he should have said when Tick was going on about fish. "You could have it all—that's what you don't understand. You can mine the mountains and the seas and the rivers, and the Earth will just keep growing more trees, growing more fish, and do any of you think the rain will stop falling? That's the miracle of water: It falls from the sky! It melts from the glaciers! It's yours for the taking, world without end, amen."

That's exactly what Good River Products was doing, taking it. Trans-forming the unused resources of the Earth into wealth—for everybody: Power-Point slide seven. The more money there is, the more money there is to share around. Give Good River Products a couple more years, and this channel will be swimming in money. And this was just the beginning, selling the water. If those people were smarter, they could figure out how to sell the goddamn air.

Howard clicked the email icon, looking for a message from home. Nothing new.

Sometimes he was as frightened of wolves as any of the three little pigs, even though he would never tell Taylor. Frightened of brown-skinned people in the cities, poor and rude. Of cancer. Of getting old and sick. Of radical environmentalists taking control of the government. Of the weather, so violent. Of not being able to give Taylor what she wants, of having her unhappy. In a dangerous world, you need money, because money is the only thing that gives you the power to protect yourself and the people you love. His PowerPoint presentation had a nice section on this, the benefit to the families. Instead he got Tick's clam penises.

Oh well. When he got home, he would read to Taylor about "silver bells and cockleshells and pretty maids all in a row." He'd tell her that he has seen a cockleshell, all fat and chalky, dug right up out of the sand by one of his new friends. And he would be able to tell her stories about her teddy bear too. The way its nose pokes out its big round face. That makes it a brown bear, he would tell her. He would tell her that he's seen a real teddy bear's baby—saw it from a boat just last week—big head and button eyes and round, fuzzy ears sticking up above the grasses, the little bear swaying on its hind feet, its paws curled over its fat tummy. Right there, on the beach.

She would think he was making it up, but he would say, no, no, someday I'll take you there and you can see all this for yourself. She would giggle and snuggle into his lap, and his heart would almost break. How long would it be before he got to go home? All he wanted to do was go home.

≋≋≋

WHEN THE TOUR of her husband's water project was over, Rebecca climbed back onto the *Annie K* for the trip back to town. She was glad she'd gone over to the dam site to see for herself what Axel had planned. She moved to the edge of the boat to watch as they approached town and the house that she designed and Axel built for their family. That was her home, her only place on Earth, before she fled to Nora's. She felt her whole body pulled toward it. What is that force that draws an animal so strongly back home? The Kis'utch River salmon swim to the Oregon coast or make a wide arc to the Russian Kamchatka Peninsula—two, three years, two thousand miles. Suddenly, all they want to do is go home. Even when the water from their river is diluted in the salt sea, they can smell it, some combination of hemlock roots, melted snow, rotting alder leaves, glacial till, and the bones of their mothers, the flesh of their fathers, the breath of the winters away. For miles, they home in on that smell, finally bursting upriver on the rising tide. They will create new life in the place they were born, or they will die trying. Some succeed. Some come all the way home, only to find that their home has been destroyed or denied to them. These die at the mouth of the river with their eggs still in them, or leak eggs into the mud, red and doomed on the gray glacial silt.

Not just salmon—hummingbirds, geese, frogs, sandhill cranes, humpback whales, songbirds, wounded soldiers, and children at the end of the day when the air turns suddenly cold and woodsmoke drifts over the tide. Suddenly all they want to do is be home.

She knows that, but who can explain it? And who can explain the desperation? Who understands why a salmon launches its body over the rocks of a waterfall again and again and again until it gets past or batters itself to pieces? Nothing but dying will stop a salmon from going home.

With the free edge of the bandana, Rebecca swiped at tears as the workboat took her toward the harbor. Then her shoulders straightened. So here is the greatest mystery. What kind of person would dam salmon from a river? What kind of person would cut the salmon off when they are moving most urgently, stop them just short of home after they have traveled a thousand miles to get there? Who could do that? Who could deny them? Hundreds of fish, struggling upstream? How could that ever be right, in what morally corrosive world? Dam a river, and salmon will throw their bodies against the dam until their faces are white with torn flesh. Then they will fin slowly in the cold tailwater, stinking and dying like drunks outside the door at the Greyhound station.

≈≈≈≈≈

AFTER TICK SHOOK the last of the shrimp into a five-gallon pail, he stuffed a new tomcod into the bait cage on the shrimp trap and snapped shut the lid. Poking a fillet knife through the wires, he slashed at the cod's belly until it dripped intestines. He shoved the trap a little farther over the bow of the skiff, so the cod didn't bleed into the boat.

"Got to keep a boat clean so the bears don't come sniffing around," he told Nora. "They'll chew on your gas cans and hoses, just for fun."

With his boot, Tick shoved away a tote full of coiled rope. Then he checked the knots and tilted the trap into the water. "Stay free of the lines," he ordered. As the trap sank, the rope lifted in curls from the tote and dis-appeared underwater. Forty fathoms of lead line, and then the last of the line slid overboard and flipped the buoys out of the boat.

Tick picked up a shrimp that was flicking on the floor of the skiff. He hooked it on his fishing line and cast it out. "You catch your bait, then you use the bait to catch a mess of shrimp, then you use one of the shrimp to catch more bait, and you hope that in this whole process, you get some-thing to eat." He put his rod in the holder, settled himself between the oars.

The day had been calm, but light winds were starting to crinkle the water and turn the whole channel to used tinfoil. Tick reached behind to start the engine, remembered he didn't have one, pulled on an oar to head them into the wind. He turned to watch Nora.

"No. Like this."

Tick let the oars rest on the oarlocks while he reached into the bucket of shrimp Nora had between her knees.

"Put your whole hand around the head. With a shrimp this big, you can't just hold it with your thumb and finger and your pinky in the air. See all those spines, that whole ridge of spines along the back? See that spear out the front? You don't want to give it any room to wiggle or it can poke a hole in you. You got it. Wrap your whole hand tight around it, like you're holding the handlebar on your bike. Same thing with the other hand—grab the tail. Now twist, like you're wringing out your undies."

Tick watched her face, because he knew what was going to happen next. The head end would twist off just fine. Then the beheaded shrimp would muscle around, flapping in her hand, surprisingly strong, like it's trying to get away. A shrimp has more sense in its ass than its head. But Nora just twisted the head off, heaved it overboard, dropped the tail in a ziplock bag, and reached for the next.

"One," she said. Tick had promised her four dozen shrimp if she would teach Tommy to play a song on the piano.

"What song?" she had said.

"Annie Klawon said any song. But Tommy wants 'Ninety-Nine Bottles of Beer on the Wall.' Both hands."

"Deal."

So the deal was done. After the official tour of the dam site, Nora had gone out with Tick in his little skiff to help pull up the trap. Tick put shrimp traps deep, at least thirty-five fathoms. But in fjord country, that's only a hundred yards offshore and that's a good thing, he thought, especially if your son sank your outboard and turned your skiff into a damn rowboat. It was embarrassing to row out from town, everybody watching. But everybody knew that Tick was still working on his Evinrude and expected it to be running any day. At least he'd got his winch back to working. All that lead line, he wasn't going to be hauling it in hand over hand.

Nora was twisting the heads off shrimp, tossing the heads overboard, counting the tails into the bag, hardly looking at what she was doing. All the time, she was watching Tick.

"What," Tick said.

She didn't say anything.

"You don't need to be thinking how'm I doing without a job. Everybody's thinking how'm I doing. I walk down the boardwalk, everybody says, how'm I doing. Order a beer, how'm I doing. Open the door, somebody's left a zucchini or a loaf of warm bread. No job. No wife. No outboard. Kid in trouble. Fine. I'm doing fine. Except for that look. That gives me the creeps.

"I'm fine," Tick said.

"Good." Nora said. "That makes one person in this town."

Then she let loose. Tick grinned and leaned his bulk away from her. For a lady who didn't say much of anything except nice, always smiling and hugging, she had a bunch of not-nice to say. The Bear Shelter was not fine with her. The water-collection dam on the Kis'utch was not fine. It was not fine, the way Axel treated Tick. Tick's grin faded back into his beard.

"Firing you because of what Davy did is not fair. Sins of the son visited on the father—on the whole family—which I don't think even God would do, even though God is mean mean mean and He definitely takes sides. If God and Axel got in a wrestling match to see who's meanest, they'd bite off each other's ears. So there's God saying, 'What? I can't hear you!' which at least gives Him an excuse for never answering."

Three more shrimp met their maker.

It was not fine the way Axel treated Tick about the Bear Shelter.

It was not fine the way nobody, not Kenny, not even the bear, and definitely not Nora Montgomery was standing up to Axel.

"I'm tired of ignoring Axel's bulldozers. I've tried. I've tried picking berries. I've tried reading a romance novel. I've tried teaching my dog to dance. But all the time, the roar of those bulldozers drown out the river while the salmon circle in muddy water, and I'm sick of it."

Tick was glad he wasn't a shrimp, the way she was tearing off their heads. He was glad he wasn't Axel. Or Kenny. He was pretty sure the only reason she wasn't laying into old Tick McIver himself was because she thought he notched Axel's piling, which maybe he did and maybe he didn't, but whoever did, did a good thing.

"Every place I've lived, people came and wrecked, cutting the old growth, strip-mining the ore, filling marshes for subdivisions. That's not making a living. That's vandalism. That's theft. That's murder—except that people call it enterprise. They didn't have to. If they'd thought about it, they could have found a gentler way to make a living on the land. But no, they wrecked every place I've lived. Why? Because no one stopped them. What did I do? Nothing. I trucked my piano to the next place. So they came and wrecked that. Finally, I got sick of it. You have to do something after a while, don't you?"

She studied a big shrimp loaded with eggs. "Good luck," she said, and tossed it overboard.

"What we need is an act of God."

"Not quite sure whose side God is on, Nora," Tick said, surprised by this whole conversation.

"An act of God, like a lightning strike. Or a flood!

"Here's the thing, Tick. Lillian told me that once there used to be a whole town across the channel, on the clamflat at the base of the Kis'utch River. Right where Axel's dam and the water exportation dock are going in. Lillian had a business where the construction office is now. There was a huge flood—warm rain on the muskegs and snowfields—and the Kis'utch thundered down and wiped it all out. The whole town. Wiped it off the face of the Earth."

Tick knew that this was true.

Nora lifted her head from the shrimp bucket and stared across the channel at the Kis'utch clamflat. "That's all I'm hoping for now. A huge flood to tear out the construction site. Pray for rain. Forty days and forty nights. C'mon, God!"

She cupped her hands around her mouth and shouted to the sky. "A flood, God! Another big flood. No, not a *rug*, you stupid. A *flood*."

"Hell," Tick said. "You want a flood, why don't you ask *me*?"

She stopped yanking off heads and stared at him.

"What."

"You teach Tommy to play some songs Annie will like, I'll make you all the floods you want. Something good. Nashville."

"What are you talking about?"

"Meet Tick McIver, splash dam maker."

"What."

"Making floods is one of the things I used to do. I made a good living. I built splash dams. The timber company falls some trees up high, drags them over to dam up a stream at the top of a hill. Rain comes, the dam makes a reservoir. You load the reservoir with floating logs from the cut. When the reservoir is full of water and chock-full of logs, you lever out the key log in the splash dam. Bam, the dam gives way. The whole thing—water, logs, the whole pond—comes screaming down the hill. Look out below! When the tidal wave settles, you got your logs delivered right to your dock."

Nora didn't say anything. But she was starting to show some mercy to the shrimp. She weighed a small one in her hand, then threw it overboard.

"That's a beautiful thing," she said, "that shrimp floating down." Tick looked over the side—long pink antennas waving thank you, God, blue bobble eyes, spidery legs, stripy pink scales. One lucky shrimp. Unless something ate it on the way down. It had a long way to go.

"How much would it be for one splash dam, a big one, just above the Kis'utch Falls?"

Tick looked up at the ridge where the river broke through the granite and fell to the clamflat. Any shithead could build a splash dam up there. He'd built dams in lots worse places than that. Above the falls, the Kis'utch ran through a narrow gorge, so the dam could be small and tight—hard work, but could be done in a couple of days. There's plenty of muskeg in the basin behind the gorge, so the water would have room to build up.

Lots of water up there, draining steep snowfields. The waterfall was so noisy, nobody would hear chain saws. A flood is an act of God—who can blame God? Who can handcuff the Holy Ghost? The more Tick thought about it, the more he thought he might be able to drive a good deal.

"That would cost you four songs," Tick said. "But right and left hands on both songs. Not just the tune. Chords too. Why not?"

Nora raised her face to the clouds. The swell rocked the boat, sent waves of light across her face. Shrimp tails flicked and popped in the bucket. Tick reeled in his line, found nothing on his hook, cast out again.

Nora sucked in a great breath. "Okay, so I'll tell you why not."

Tick looked into her face and leaned away. "Ah. Maybe you shouldn't tell me, Nora."

Nora plunged on. "Last place I lived, Weyerschafft decided they'd log the hills up the river behind my house. Cut them to stumps, three-hundred-year-old trees. What's a person to do, when every day you watch trucks rumble down the hill and across a little wooden bridge right in front of your house, carrying the giant corpses, red bark chipped off, scarred, blue numbers spray-painted on their butt ends?

"I had a jerry can of lawn mower gas. I had a lighter. I had all night. What more did I need?"

Nora pulled on her ponytail. Broken light from the sea scattered across her face.

"When the truckers hauled up to the creek the next morning, the bridge was still smoldering. I didn't know they would be that angry, so then I was really scared. Before the Feds could figure out who did it, my friends helped me load my piano on the ferry and I just took off, figuring I'd go until the ferry stopped going, and then I would get off. I'd stop making trouble. Model citizen. That piano would be my anchor. I'd get it tangled up there in the rocks until nothing could wash me loose, and that is where I would stay. Then I would have to mind my own business. I would have to keep my mouth shut."

Tick started to hum and play his fingers over his knees.

"No, Tick, you bastard. I can't do anything. I don't dare make any more trouble. They've got a warrant out on me. Arson. Mandatory four-year sentence for using fire to destroy federal property. They'll find me out. I got my piano holding me down, and I can't even play it." She looked up at Tick. "But I *can* play it, Tick. I can play it beautifully. But if I did, they'd be on me—the Feds. Better mark of identification than a tattoo. So I teach kids to play with three fingers.

"This is my home now. All I want is to mind my own business."

"You don't seem real good at minding your own business."

Nora took a halfhearted swing at his chin. "It's hard," she protested, but gave it up.

"You're a good man, Tick McIver. It's really too bad I'm reformed. But I'll teach Tommy the songs anyway."

The tip of his rod bounced. He grabbed it, pulled it up sharp. Started reeling. The thing fought him for a while, then it was all dead weight. A bad sign.

"Rockfish," he said. "Halibut fight all the way. Rockfish die halfway up. Pulling them up from forty fathoms gives them a hell of a case of the bends. Eyes bulge out of the sockets. Bladder pops out their mouth." He held it out to show her. It was a bright red fish with quills standing up on its back and a white thing sticking out its mouth like a swollen tongue. Tick laid it in the bait bucket. There would be rockfish for supper at the McIver house that night.

Tick expected Nora to be gazing into the fish's googly eyes, saying "isn't that wonderful," but she didn't even look. She was all business, twisting shrimp. The wind had laid down, and the water was flat and shiny as glass, except where shrimp heads hit the water, eyes all big and surprised. Toward the horizon rose seven columns of mist, the exhalation of feeding whales. The channel reflected the whole Kis'utch Range upside down.

"Good place," Tick said.

"It's like we're floating in our boat on the top of the mountain," Nora said, "up there with the snowfields, all bent and wavy. You'd think it's a perfect reflection, but the blue is more blue than really, the green is greener, like the reflected world is made of stained glass with light coming through. Like church. Good place for an act of God."

Tick squinted into the water. Nora was right. When a flock of white gulls settled onto the channel, another flock flew upside down to meet it. Each gull sat on the rump of an upside-down one. Whiter than white. But all the gulls lifted off, just like that, screeching, and swam toward a ruckus on the water a boat's length away. Great bubbles the size of washtubs blurped up and burst. "Hang on!" Tick grabbed the oars, spun the boat, and stroked away with all the strength in his back. Nora ducked under the thunder of a terrible roar.

The sea in their wake bulged and broke apart and up rose the humpback whales, with all the majesty of their great size. Their open mouths were caverns, dimly lit and terrible, engulfing fish and sea. Nora threw her head back to see them, they were that high. They fell back between thunderous walls of waves. Water poured from their baleen. Tick's oars grabbed immense bites of water as he rowed. Waves rebounding from the whales' crusted flanks lifted his stern and pushed his boat away. The whales slammed their tails, stunning the herring, then leapt on them, openmouthed, and swallowed them down. Nora crouched in the boat, hanging on, squinting, while sunlight dove deep into the sea, bubbled up, slammed down again, rebounded in violent arcs. Gulls swarmed and screeched.

Then came again the roar of the feeding whales and Tick's answering halloo. "I told you this was a good place," he shouted. Broken herring finned away from the echo into the ambush of the whales.

Tick rested on his oars. Grinning, Nora rested her back against the stern. A whale rested beside them on the glaze of the sea, lifted by the calming water of its own wake. It blew a great breath. Sunlight silvered the spray. There were many whales. They all sucked bright day into their lungs, blew it out with the sound of a rock slide. Then there was silence except for the whispers of murrelets and the flicks of the fins of wounded fish, fluttering in small circles. Already, the sun had melted the rough water, skinning it with silver. Gulls swayed on the swell, and even the sacrilegious gulls were silent.

A whale folded its back, slowly unfolded, and levered its flukes into the air. The tail stood like a black jib, streaming water, then sank as the whale dove to a seam below the reach of the sun. Water slipped into the space the whale had pressed on the sea. One by one, other whales raised their flukes and dove. The gulls, still silent, waited still. They knew that in their own time, the whales would begin the hunt again. The water rose and fell in meditative breath.

August 24

HIGH TIDE		LOW TIDE	
0:59am	16.2ft	7:20pm	-0.3ft
1:43pm	15.4ft	7:33pm	1.9ft

Just before midnight, a bulge of sea rolls smoothly past Good River Harbor. It's the flood tide of the dog-salmon moon, the highest tide of the month. On its dark currents, it carries a lost gill net, drifting unmoored. These are the dangerous nets, detached from human intention. A dog salmon nudges into the net. Her head slides through the mesh, but her body is too wide to pass. She backs away. The net snags her gill plates. The fibers dig into the feathery red tissue, deeper as the salmon tugs to get away. She curls her body and snaps it straight, yanking at the net until her blood pinkens the sea. There she hangs by her head, caught by gill plates bright and round as the moon, cratered with the moon's shadowed seas. More salmon nudge into the net, flashing silver as they struggle to escape. A school of salmon weaves through the kelp forest, approaching the net, wary in the night. Salmon and salmon and salmon nose into the net that seizes them more tightly the more they flail. The nets bulge and recoil. Silver tails swirl.

Tasting blood, a salmon shark sways close to the net, singing his rough flank against the fibers. He snatches off a thrashing tail, snatches another. But then he veers and noses into the net. He catches first a tooth, then pushing forward, catches another. The shark whips his head from side to side, savaging the net, driving the falling scales into silver swirls. He vomits salmon tails and trailing intestines that sink through the currents. A gray cod snaps up the falling pieces and pushes into the net, where she finds her own death. Heavy now with the dead, the net slowly sinks until it settles, swaying on the floor of the sea.

A hermit crab reaches tentatively for torn flesh. Dungeness crab move in, scuttling sideways. A small sculpin thrusts its spiked head into the red tissues and spins, tearing off flesh. The water is cloudy with sea-fleas and shrimp eating the soft meat under the silver skin, nibbling around the bones, a cloud of eating. Hear the tick of small teeth, the click of small claws. Spot-shrimp stalk in on spidery legs, following their orange prows. Long antennae reach toward the dying and the dead. Bubbles pop from shrimps' mouths and stream toward the moon. When the banquet is finished, there is no flesh, only skeletons and strips of white skin, swaying.

Without the heavy flesh, the net rises again on its floats. Listen now. Skeletons with silver skirts ride the ghost net, hissing. Strips of skin swirl. Plated heads grin. The ghost net floats past the town on great tidal currents, gathering bones.

THE GHOST NET slipped under the Annie K, which was tied up at the brand-new dock at the Bear Shelter. Tick sat on his bow under the dog-salmon moon—a full moon pale and pockmarked. He studied the joinery where the pilings met the planking. He could of done a hell of a lot better work. But never mind that, like Annie Klawon said, that's gone, and the moon really did look like a dog salmon's belly. Yep, he decided, with the same rim of pink where the curve fell away and the same shadowy spots and rays. White clouds floated across the night sky. Their reflections rose and fell, stretched and shrank on the swell. Tick sat on his life jacket locker, leaned back against the cockpit window, and watched moonlight move over the waters. If it weren't for the windshield wiper gouging his back, the bow would make a great reclining chair. The boat swayed on a long swell that made the ropes creak on the cleats—more than likely a wake from a ship too far away to see. He clasped his hands across his great beard.

There was no place Tick would rather be than on the bow of his boat, tied to a dock on calm seas on a God-glorious night like this. The dock was so new it still smelled of sawdust and creosote. Even if Tick wasn't the man who dropped his piney pants on the floor after every good day's work, glad to hear the thud of money in his pocket, he admired a guy who could pull off a project like this. Axel had brought in a lot of men and moved fast—crappy work, but done on deadline. The dock was plenty big enough for the eco-tour boats that would put in there and send passengers up the ramp to the pavilion. Pavilion. Tick guffawed. That's what Axel was calling the wooden platform they'd built on the shelf of cliff next to the cistern. Passengers would pay their money and crowd in under the Good River Harbor Bear Shelter sign. Tromping across the pavilion past the refreshment stand, they would climb the path around the back of the cistern to the observation deck. That's where they would lean over and watch the bears in the pit below.

Except for the security lamp over the door where they'd prodded the bears into the tank, only moonlight lit up the site. New-cut plywood shone under the moon and even the old water tank gleamed like an oil slick. In the morning, kids and their folks in brand-new Bear Shelter sweatshirts would lean over the edge, throwing salmon heads to caged bears. The sow and cub would shy into the ditch they'd dug behind a thimbleberry bush and lie still. Camera flashes would bounce off the rain-shine on their pelts. Tick pulled at his beard and considered.

He'd seen the posters stapled to walls all over town. GRAND OPENING, 10 A.M. FREE ADMISSION FOR GOOD RIVER HARBORITES, FIRST HOUR ONLY. THEN TWENTY-FOUR BUCKS, KIDS HALF PRICE. When Axel set his mind to something, he got it done. Tick rearranged his back against the Annie K's windshield and snapped open another beer.

He would think about calm seas, Tick decided. He would think about the moon. He would think about the pull of that moon, like a silver seiner hauling up the highest tide of the month. He wouldn't think about Axel or his dead bear. Instead, he would think of dog salmon charging upstream to their spawning beds. He would think about Annie Klawon, dreaming in Seattle. He wished she were here beside him, right here, leaning against the windshield, tucked under Tick's arm. He could smell her hair even now, the black strands tangling in his orange beard. Cedar. Kelp, maybe.

"Don't think about the bad things," she would say. What do you notice about this night? What is true of this exact moment in time? She would have talked about the smells. She would have talked about the way a high tide has no smell, like a special kind of olfactory silence, every smell hidden and hushed.

"High pressure in the gulf will linger through tomorrow. Tonight, winds calm. Light winds becoming south ten point zero knots by morning. Seas two feet or less, mainly west swell. Pressure thirty-three and steady. Tomorrow, light winds becoming west ten point zero knots in the afternoon. Seas two feet or less. Visibility ten miles."

Tick grinned. The steady low voice on the marine radio was so precise, so sure. Annie Klawon was afraid of the prideful forecasts—"As if anybody really can know what the wind will bring, let alone calibrate the future to the tenth of a knot," she had whispered. But the radio told a comforting story, bringing order out of the watery chaos, safe seas, the blessing of calm winds. Tick wouldn't have been surprised to hear that solemn voice just come out and say it straight: "The moon will make its face to shine upon you and be gracious unto you, both now and forevermore. This is NOAA Weather Service WXJ twenty-five, on one six two point four two five megahertz. Update at 6 a.m."

Tick had been glad to help when Kenny asked for a ride to the Bear Shelter dock. He knew how hard it would have been for Kenny to get down the boardwalk stairs, along the town trail, and up to the pavilion in that little wheelchair. Kenny was stuck between town and the dump, unless somebody delivered him somewhere else. And even then, the boat had to be a drop-bow or have a pretty good gangway. Kenny told Tick he wanted to go at midnight, to catch the high tide. At low tides, the gangway from the floating dock to the pavilion would be too steep. But on this night of the dog-salmon moon, the tide had lifted the floating dock so high the gangway was almost flat. Tick had lowered the bow, and Kenny pushed off onto the dock and on up the gangway to the pavilion.

Tick squinted up the platform. He could see Kenny hunched by the door to the cistern, a sharp silhouette under the security lamp. A strange and wonderful man, Kenny. Sort of a self-appointed scientist, studying all the animals. An old-fashioned natural philosopher, Nora said he was. That means he likes animals best when they're dead or at least on their way to extinction. Nora said that Kenny had been studying the life cycles of squirrels. But he's been reading about bats lately, she said, coming to the library early to be there when it opened and staying all morning. Bats and man! Fruit-eating bats! Rare bats of the world!

When he'd asked Tick for a ride, Kenny said he was looking for one of those rare bats, thinking its range might extend this far north. He thought that if it was around, it might be attracted to insects coming to the bright light over the door to the bear tank. He was excited on the run over, leaning forward in his wheelchair, talking away, happily mourning the loss of bat habitat and cussing out white-nose fungus.

Tick tried to remember exactly what Kenny had said on the ride out. "White-nose fungus hits a cave, next thing you know, it's dead bats lying a foot deep on the floor." He might as well have been talking about the coronation of the queen, he was so keyed up. He had printed out a page from a website that described the bat he was headed out to look for. He'd unfolded the paper and waved it in Tick's face, but it was too dark in the boat to make it out.

So there Tick was, sitting on his boat in the middle of the night, waiting for a weird guy to get tired of waiting for a bat that might or might not even exist in Good River Harbor. Made sense to him. How could it not?— it was a warm, sweet night and bats are as good a reason as any to stay out late.

He scanned the moonlight for flying mammals. If Kenny wanted to see his bat, he should move into the darkness, instead of sitting there right under the security light. And he should be quiet. But all of a sudden, he was making a lot of noise. Tick sat up. He squinted into the distance, trying to make it out. But he was too far away to see anything more than Kenny's lumpy silhouette. The sound coming from that direction was scratchy, like a big grasshopper's up-and-down song.

It sounded like somebody fiddling away on a busted violin.

It sounded like someone sawing away on a chain.

"No," Tick shouted. The word hit the side of the cistern and slammed back in his face. Kenny looked up. Tick leapt from the boat and sprinted up the gangway.

"Don't!"

Kenny turned back to sawing, faster then. Tick heard the chains fall away even before he got to the welcome sign—a rattle and a heavy clank.

"Don't do it."

Tick pounded past the sign, past the refreshment stand, leaping over their shadows black as holes in the planking. He could see Kenny lean forward and pull open the door to the pit. Not too late to slam the door shut. Not too. Late. Slam the door. Damn it, running in slow motion. If only he hadn't worn boots. Damn these boots. Now, almost, another step and then leap for the door.

A small shape ran into the light and disappeared in the shadow of Kenny's wheelchair.

"No."

A black mass hurtled out the door. Kenny's shadow tangled in the darkness of the bears. The whole dark mass cartwheeled off the pavilion. Tick dove, trying to grab a wheel. The wheelchair fell, tipped sideways, disappeared into black space. A terrible crack and rattle of metal on rock, clatter of bears fleeing over gravel, snap of breaking branches through the forest, and then nothing but the slowly settling echoes.

"Mother of God," Tick whispered, but then he was screaming. "Kenny!"

Tick ran down the gangway and skidded down the pilings to the rocky strand below the cliff. He couldn't hear anything but blood in his ears. He couldn't see Kenny. He ran across the rocks, slipped on the rocks, fell on the rocks, damn those rocks.

The security light threw Tick's big shadow across Kenny's poncho. Tick leaned out of the light, but oh God. Blood was running from Kenny's mouth. The bones of his skull dear God. All busted on the rocks, brains oh God. His twisted neck. The security light in his startled eye.

Do something. What do you do? Tick's howl echoed against the mountain. Tick pressed his fists against his mouth to quiet himself and fell onto the rocks beside Kenny, but dear God. There was nothing to do.

So quiet. A single wheel still turning.

Tick ran up the steps to the pavilion, grabbed a two-by-four from a lumber pile and slammed it against the interpretive sign. THE KINSHIP OF LIFE smashed and toppled. Tick swung again. The glass on the USE CAUTION AROUND BEARS display blew to bits. The two-by-four levered out of his hands and thudded against the cedar tank.

"Damn that Kenny." Tick leaned over and vomited, cradling one hand in the other.

When he could breathe again, he wiped his mouth on his sleeve and closed his eyes. The door to the cistern. He should close the door to the cistern. He crept to the opening. Not a sound came from inside. Not a breath of wind. Not a killdeer's call. The air smelled dank. He stared at moisture beading on the sawed link of chain. Starlight trickled down a link, paused, then grew into a drop as round as an eye. The drop gave way and rivered to the next link. Another drop formed and fell away. Already Kenny's eyes would be wet with dew.

Tick walked into the cistern. Its mounds of dirt lay cold and white under the moon, as cold and white as snowbanks. He stepped out between the pale trunks of dead alders. In the puddles of their shadows, they held all the loneliness of the world. He stood, quiet and empty. He stood. In the quiet of that white night, he heard moonlight drip down the cedar walls.

There were bats, he slowly realized, lots of them. Kenny had been right. The moon cast their shadows over the ashen mounds. One darted toward Tick, then at the last minute veered away. Another sailed past his ear. He felt the bats more than saw them—breath on his forehead. He could see the shadows of big moths too. A whisper and a moth disappeared.

"Kenny, Kenny, if you had told me the truth, I could have helped you do it right. I could still catch a bat for you, Kenny, if you ever really cared about bats. If I lift my hand into the air at just the right time, like a catcher's mitt, I could grab a bat out of the night. I could hold it in my fist and bring it to you. You could extend its wing, and we would see through the membrane and touch the claw at its elbow. We would look into its face." Dear God a horrid face. Eyes afraid and bleeding, and the face pushed all to the side.

The black shadows of the alder limbs were perfectly still on the cistern walls.

Tick turned and ran to the door. He needed to tell people. He needed to tell Nora. He needed to tell Lillian. She would know what to do. He couldn't wait until morning to tell them. In the morning, Meredith would come to open up the ticket booth. There would be a line of people waiting. They would be disappointed that the bears were gone.

The cistern's door squeaked as Tick slumped against it and slid to his haunches. The pale wing of a moth drifted through the light and settled on the planks. One wing fell, bitten off at the base, then another. They fluttered down, soft as ashes. Tick lifted his hand to catch one, but his reaching pushed it away.

Nora was still awake, working at her plywood desk in the light of a kerosene lamp. For many minutes, Tick stood outside the window and watched her. The smell of that kerosene—dark and musky—and the mewling of the Green Point buoy, they confused him. Marine charts were spread over the desk. She held one finger at a place on a chart. With the other hand, she typed with one finger. The keys ticked, tick-tocked. She looked happy. Suddenly afraid for her, Tick fled and ran instead to Lillian's and pounded on her door.

Soon enough the church bell began to ring, sounding the alarm. People flew from their front doors. In the storm of rising shouts and running feet, banging doors and outboard motors, Tick stood on the boardwalk, as unmoving as a piling in a flood tide. He stared over the inlet. While he watched, the hemlock trees slowly rose to touch the bottom of the moon.

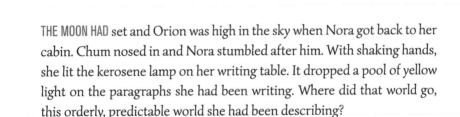

THE MOON HAD set and Orion was high in the sky when Nora got back to her cabin. Chum nosed in and Nora stumbled after him. With shaking hands, she lit the kerosene lamp on her writing table. It dropped a pool of yellow light on the paragraphs she had been writing. Where did that world go, this orderly, predictable world she had been describing?

"RED RIGHT RETURN" IS THE PRINCIPAL RULE OF NAVIGATION. THAT MEANS THAT AS YOU ARE COMING INTO PORT, YOU KEEP THE RED NAVIGATION MARKERS ON YOUR STARBOARD, OR RIGHT, SIDE. THE GREEN MARKERS STAY ALWAYS TO PORT. IF YOU ARE HEADING HOME BETWEEN THE RED AND THE GREEN LIGHTS, YOU ARE SAFE FROM SHOALS.

IN NARROW CHANNELS, THERE ARE SOMETIMES RANGE-MARKERS TO HELP MARINERS NAVIGATE THE DANGEROUS PASSAGES. RANGE-MARKERS ARE WHITE MARKERS—ONE NEAR, ONE FARTHER AWAY.

IF YOU STEER A COURSE IN SUCH A WAY THAT THE WHITE MARKERS ARE LINED UP, SEEMING TO MERGE INTO ONE, YOU WILL AVOID THE SHOALS.

Crying out, she tore the page from the typewriter and crumpled it against her chest. Chum barked sharply. "Oh, Chum." She fell on her bed. Chum nosed at her face. She pulled the dog over her like a rug and trapped him in her arms. He lay still, barely breathing. "Oh dear God. Kenny, oh dear Kenny."

"Come back," she whispered. Chum whined and struggled to escape. She held him, whispering urgently. *It's dangerous. You can't be sure. You can't trust the bottom of the ocean not to heave up in shoals. It does that, it heaves up a shoal and the ocean breaks against it. Your boat will be lost. You think buoys don't come loose from their moorings. But they do. Buoys come loose from their moorings and float into the wrong places and you follow them, you trust them, and they take you onto the shoals. You think the numbers on the chart will keep you safe, even on a dangerous sea, foul with rocks. But maybe there is no chart. Maybe you believe in it, but it doesn't exist. Maybe there are only the sea and the rocks and the wind. Or maybe there is a chart but it's made up or wrong, and how would you know? A blinking light can be near or far, you just can't tell. Light bends. It gets lost in the fog. How can you find your way? And sometimes you think it's a lighthouse but it's a star behind a wave. You think you're on the right course but it's wrong, and how do you know until you hear the terrible crying and waves smacking rocks? You have to keep going, or you lose steerageway. Even if you don't know where you're going, you have to keep going or the seas will turn you broadside. You have to keep going, even in the dark, you have to steer by the foghorn, but how can you trust the moaning sea? Can you steer by shame?* Kenny. Oh, Kenny, what have I done? What have I done to you?

Chum howled, but the sea was silent.

PART THREE
COHO TIDE

~~~~~~~~~~~~~~~~~~~~~~~~~~~~~~~~~~~~

Oncorhynchus kisutch, the coho salmon, squirts her eggs at the head of a riffle in the small tributary of the river. Cold water flows through the dark spaces between grains of gravel where the eggs have come to rest—a hundred red beads among the gray stones, sparks of life in the dark. Over time, months and months, the red fades, and each globe takes on the shape of a tiny fish with a yolk sack on its belly. More translucent than stray light, smaller than a spruce needle, it shivers there in the interstices of the stones, absorbing the nutrients it carries in its sack. When it is fully a fish, grown to the size of a hemlock needle, it wriggles up through stones into the moving water.

How it comes to be, that the onrushing, taut-muscled ferocity of a coho salmon grows from a sliver of light in water-washed darkness, who can say? But there it is, leaping at the end of a whistling line, a hook in its jaw, and a silver flasher twisting light. Listen to the thud as its heavy flank strikes the wave.

~~~~~~~~~~~~~~~~~~~~~~~~~~~~~~~~~~~~

August 28

HIGH TIDE		LOW TIDE	
3:13am	16.2ft	9:19am	0.1ft
3:32pm	16.6ft	9:39pm	0.7ft

H oward watched out the little window of his room over the library. A strange guy lets a bear loose and gets his skull broken for his trouble. So what do the people do? They make a casserole. The guy's dead, so they put water on to boil and dump in noodles. It's like it's the only thing they know how to do. A whole parade of women wearing hot mitts carries casseroles over to Kenny's house, their men in tow. So who's going to eat all that salmon loaf and potato salad? Do they think about that? It's not like Kenny's hungry, for God's sake. Or like he has a grieving wife and kids sitting on his couch, crying over family pictures.

The women bucked up against Kenny's front door, which was closed up tight. They could have let themselves in. Kenny had put a super-duper new padlock on the door, but then—to make sure of the point—he'd told everyone that the combination was K.E.E.P., as in KEEP OUT. So people respected that. You could see each one of them thinking—Nobody home. Hmmm. Well, we'll eat this ourselves. No place to sit on Kenny's gangway. No dishes or silverware. When the women realized this, they sent the kids back for forks and plastic chairs. Soon, people were lined up along the boardwalk to Kenny's, eating from paper plates filled with casserole. Men looked around, then went home and came back with six-packs. The post-master came by with an accordion in a suitcase and it was a party, there on the dock, in silvery light under low clouds.

Howard knew this wasn't his party. But being alone wasn't much of a party either. He pulled on his jacket and walked over to Lillian's. He was the only customer in the whole place. He sat by the window, nursing a cup of coffee, knowing he should check in with Axel. Lillian bustled around, swiping at red eyes with the edge of her apron. She closed down the popcorn machine, piled up a platter of hot dogs, pulled down the shades. The whole place was submerged in darkness.

When Lillian opened the door, Howard turned his head against the glare of light. She stood there, silhouetted with her hot dogs. "If you have another cup, leave the money on the counter," Lillian said, and left. Howard dropped his forehead onto his crossed arms and closed his eyes.

That was exactly what he would do, sit there alone, have another cup of coffee, listen to "Good Night, Irene" from the accordion outside and "Yellow Submarine" from the jukebox inside, all the time thinking he really should stop by Axel's, let him know the breaking news.

He had called Jennifer in the middle of the night last night, as soon as he heard about Kenny. He woke her up, and she was frightened until she learned that he had called, as people do, to tell her that someone else had died.

"Kenny," she had said, wondering. "Did you know him? Was he a friend?"

"No. I didn't really know him. Nora was his friend. Tick McIver." He paused. "Maybe Lillian."

"He must have been a good man," Jennifer said.

"No. I wouldn't say that."

There was a long pause. He heard Taylor crying in the background. The phone would have frightened her too.

"Listen. Jennifer. I'm sorry I called. I don't know why I called. I just thought you should know. I thought I should pass along the news, so you would know."

"No. No, you should always call, any time day or night, I like to hear your voice and know you're okay. You okay?"

He had been okay, until she asked. Then he really wasn't.

"Yeah. Fine." He had to get this call over with. "You go back to bed. I love you. Tell Taylor I love her too." That's when he started to weep, holding his hand over the phone.

"I love you too. And I'm sorry about your friend."

He'd hung up without saying good-bye.

What was the matter with him, calling his wife in the middle of the night? He walked over to Lillian's coffeepot and poured himself another cup of lukewarm coffee. Maybe that was it. Maybe when people cry because someone's dead, they're crying because they'll be dead too someday, and they cry out of terror and pity for the people who love them. That's what, maybe. Maybe he called Jennifer to say that he was still alive, but someday he would be dead, and he was sorry about that, really, really sorry that he would have to leave her alone and really, really sorry for Taylor, to be making it alone in the world without a father, and who would keep her safe? Maybe all he wanted was for Jennifer to say, "Howard. Howard, you're alive. You called me, so you can't be dead," and maybe that's what she was telling him, and maybe he cried with relief, about that fact, that he was alive. Briny night, full moon, taut seas, dead guy shining in the rocks—that's when you would call the one you love more than anyone else in the world and tell her that you are alive. And why wouldn't that fact make you cry? Close your eyes and weep with gratitude and relief.

Howard went behind the bar, helped himself to a splash of whiskey for his coffee, and laid three dollars on the counter. He really should get over to Axel's. But it was comfortable behind the bar, with a little warm steam and the rattle of a clothes dryer coming from the door of the laundry.

Howard had had only one real conversation with Kenny, and that—he realized with a start—was behind that very bar. Lillian was washing the floor. It was afternoon, and the sun was warming up the wet wood and raising the stink of Lysol. She'd put all the chairs up on the tables, so Kenny had rolled behind the bar to drink his cup of coffee. His hair was still wet—from a shower, Howard had guessed. Howard poured himself a cup of coffee, and because there was nowhere else to sit, he pulled a chair alongside Kenny.

"Mind?"

Grunt.

That was the extent of the conversation for a long time. Lillian went on shoving and lapping at the water with a long mop, humming away, there is a balm in Gilead, her hair protected by a plastic accordion rain hat.

Out of the blue, Kenny looked out the window and said, "So, surveyor-person, what do you think of Good River Harbor, now you've got it all measured up?"

Howard was not going to say *anything* remotely offensive. He was not comfortable with this man.

"Beautiful place. Friendly people. Different from any other place I've been."

How could Kenny have taken offense at any of that, Howard wondered. He was bewildered and sort of offended himself by the face Kenny was making, like he smelled a garlic pickle. But it turned out Kenny was just thinking.

"I've thought a lot about what makes it different," he said, and Howard had about fallen out of his chair. Who was this man and was this the start of a conversation? He couldn't be sure, because Kenny was clearly directing his remarks to some ghost outside the window.

"Don't mean a damn thing, our lives," Kenny said. "How hard we try, whether we suffer or don't. We're not part of any plan."

Howard didn't take the bait Kenny was clearly dangling in his face.

"You know Sisyphus?"

Howard might have and might have not, so he said, "Sure."

"Condemned."

Howard flinched when Kenny pulled a knife out of a sheath on his belt and started scraping at a pile of candle wax on the bar.

"Condemned. Zeus made him push a huge rock up a hill each day, when all it did was roll back down again each night. Slowly up each day, fast down each night. He had to keep doing it, but it didn't mean a damn thing."

The story was starting to come back to Howard, vaguely and from the distant past. But the last thing he expected was a philosophy lesson from a guy with a Buck knife and a mouse-skin hat, although it made sense later, of course. Out of the corner of his eye, Howard saw Lillian straighten up and lean on her mop, listening.

"Everybody in the world has his own rock. Big fucking lichen-crusted rocks in this town. And everybody's got his shoulder to that rock, shoving it up the mountain. After a while, people get pretty attached to their rocks, think they're the greatest. But here's the difference."

Kenny was working more and more intensely on the wax, pushing the blade of his knife with his thumb.

"Every time the people in this town get their rocks to the top of the mountain," he said, "they sit down and look at the view. Har." Kenny clearly thought that was pretty funny. His shoulders shook like an engine starting up. "That glacier valley over there, that arm of the sea. And some of the people, some of them even climb up on their rocks and sing a song." He poked the point of his knife toward Lillian. "Yep. Music. That's the mistake Sisyphus made. While he was on top of the mountain, sitting beside his rock, catching his breath, he should of stood up and let out a song. Should of sung loud, so Zeus could hear him. *I go to the hills for the sound of music!* Wouldn't that have made Zeus rage?

"Har.

"Probably would have aimed a lightning bolt right between Sisyphus's ugly eyes."

Then maybe he was laughing or maybe he was hawking, but the conversation was clearly over. Kenny had winked broadly at the ghost out the window, drained his cup, and rolled out, still laughing.

≋≋≋

WHEN HOWARD FINALLY got over to Axel's, Axel was sitting alone at his dining room table, making to-do lists. He poured Howard a glass of wine. He poured himself one too, which kind of surprised Howard, who thought he was strictly a coffee kind of guy.

"You'd think Kenny was some kind of *hero*, instead of a criminal, the way those people are *acting*," Axel said. "Who's stopping by my house to say they're sorry about the losses to the business?—bears gone, picnic pavilion wrecked, grand opening canceled. We're going to have to act fast, or this whole Bear Shelter business is going to sink like a stone. You're the community relations guy. Get in touch with the press. Seattle. Juneau. Anchorage. Tell them about how he snuck in at midnight and cut the chain. Tell them about how he had a lookout in a boat at the harbor. Tell them about how he vandalized the *interpretive displays*. Tell them we're, um, looking into a conspiracy, how somebody practically *felled my house*, how they had the piling notched before I scared them away. They'll ask about what we're going to do next. Tell them that

we are going to keep our commitment to provide shelter for imper-
iled bears. Axel Hagerman is not going to be intimidated by a gang of
eco-terrorists."

Oh boy. Howard thought maybe he'd wait until the next morning to
write the release, to give Axel time for second thoughts.

"What are the lawyers saying?"

"No real liability issues on our part," Howard said. "Easy case to defend.
Harm caused in pursuit of an illegal activity is presumptive evidence of
contributory negligence. Nobody to blame but himself. You can sue his
estate for damages, but that's an empty pocket."

"Good. Sue him. We'll get the house at least, and we can tear that down,
sell the pier for somebody else to build on. What else have you been doing,
Howard, for community relations?"

Howard cringed. Axel was either going to like this or hate it, but you
don't need a special seminar to understand that it's important to project
an image of caring.

"I issued a statement expressing Good River Products's condolences
to the town for the loss of a friend and neighbor. Pinned it to the bulletin
board at the post office."

Axel looked up sharply. "Neighbor maybe. Friend? Not so much."

"I told Nora that as an expression of sympathy, we would cover funeral
expenses, fly the body out for cremation, fly the ashes back for burial."

"Umm. What'd she say?"

"No thanks."

"No thanks? That's two thousand bucks, easy."

"A long time ago, Kenny told Lillian he wanted to be burned on a big
funeral pyre on the beach, so that's what they're going to do. They got his
body wrapped in a tarp and cooling on ice down with the salmon in the
hold of a seiner tied up at the dock. Tomorrow they're going to burn him."

Axel glared at Howard.

"Report them to the police and to the Environmental Protection
Agency. That's a crime and an air-quality issue. And it's *sick.*"

"Too late. Nora already called around and got the permits."

Axel went to the window. The setting sun glared on the glass. "I'll Fly
Away"—banjo-accordion duet—leaked in under the closed door.

"If they invite me to their pig roast," Axel said, "tell them I am otherwise engaged."

Howard felt sorry for Axel. The thing was, nobody would invite him to the funeral. It's sad, Howard thought, how people don't like the man who does them favors. Quickest way to lose a friend is to give him a job or give him a promotion he doesn't deserve. Tells him who's boss. Makes a guy feel bested. Howard suspected that the only reason people tolerated his own presence is because they pulled down his pants in the bar and then turned his PowerPoint presentation into a discursus on clam penises and bear poop. They showed him who's boss, so he's okay. The other thing is, you don't like the man you fear. These people suck up to Axel when he's on top of the world, but any sign of weakness, they're on him like weasels. He'd had a run of bad luck, and already they were saying it was his fault that Kenny was dead. If it weren't for Axel, they were saying, Kenny would still be alive and farting among us. And that's not all that the people were saying. Axel didn't know the worst.

Howard reached for Axel's glass and poured him another drink. Can you fire a community relations man for bringing bad news? He was sure Axel would. And maybe Howard didn't care. Right now, he wanted to be home. That was all. He knew that's not how a corporate executive is supposed to feel, but that's the way it was. Somebody dies, a normal guy wants to be home.

"So," Howard said.

Axel looked at him with narrowed eyes. "So. What?"

"They found a congressional Medal of Honor in his things."

"Kenny? The guy with the mouse-tail hat? The dead guy?"

"Yep. The crippled guy. When they found the medal, Nora went to the internet and looked it up. Put in the name of the medal and the date and up popped the whole story. Took her two seconds to find it, and people are saying she already knew. Born in Chicago, 1947. Real name is William Kenniston. Dartmouth grad. Philosophy. He was an Army Ranger, a prisoner of war in Vietnam. Kenniston. I actually think I remember reading about this, decades ago. He had a horrible time of it. When the Viet Cong captured him, they put him in a cage. To fit him in, they bent his legs until they splintered. They left him in the cage in the center of the village.

People cursed him, poked him with sticks between the bars, urinated on him. Seven weeks he endured this, and then the Viet Cong abandoned the village. They just left him and ran. Rats were a plague, chewing on him. He survived on rainwater another week until Special Forces found him."

Axel let his breath out real slow, sucked in his wine. "He was a strange man. Not much use for people."

"Yeah, well. That might explain it."

Axel went out the side door onto his deck. Howard followed him out. It was getting toward dusk. Howard knew that at home, Jennifer would be tucking Taylor into bed. First Teddy B. Bear. Jennifer tucks the blankets up under his floppy arms. Then Taylor. Jennifer smooths the hair back from Taylor's forehead and kisses her.

A thick fog had moved in over the harbor. Across the channel, the yard light at the site was just a faint glow. The signal at the end of the pier blinked a big pillow of light. Howard could barely make out the green light at the end of the breakwall. The only person on the dock was Tick McIver, wobbling on his long legs toward the fish-cleaning table. Still, the music played on at Kenny's party and laughter sank into the fog.

"Call the press," Axel said slowly. "Tell them that Good River Products expresses its sorrow and sympathy at the death of an American hero, and the . . ." He paused. Howard could tell he was making this up as he went along.

". . . and the particular tragedy of Kenny What . . . What's the guy's name? Kenniston . . . that would lead a man who defended his country so . . ."

"So courageously," Howard said.

Axel threw him a look. ". . . so effectively, to engage in acts that are deeply harmful to the American way of doing business. Uh, make that the American way of life."

Axel cranked open another bottle of wine and poured himself a glass.

"Are you sure you want another glass, Axel . . . ?" When Alex didn't answer, Howard took out his notebook, and got it down while it was fresh in his mind. It's true, Kenny did Axel some real damage. Kenny did mean to let those bears go. You can't accumulate capital if you can't prevent theft, and that was a theft. Before he put the notebook back in his pocket,

Howard flipped to the front cover, where he'd pasted last year's Christmas portrait of his family. There were Jennifer and Howard, smiling, and Taylor in a red velvet dress. Howard stared out over the railing on Axel's porch.

"Axel!" he said suddenly. "Where are Rebecca's flowers?"

There was nothing there. The deck had been heaped with flowers—flowers in pots on the railings, flowers in planters on the stairs, flowers hanging from the rafters and climbing up the posts from planters under the house. Used to be, a man had to claw his way through Rebecca's vines and leaves out there, like George of the Jungle. But the deck was clean and empty. Howard leaned over the rail to look under the deck. Not a flowerpot, not a pile of dirt.

"When she left, she took the wheelbarrow too," Axel said, and turned away.

≈≈≈≈

TICK PUSHED BETWEEN the flocks of people at Kenny's and teetered in front of the fish-cleaning station, which the women had commandeered for a table. Leaning forward slowly, carefully, he studied the empty, encrusted casserole dishes and half-empty liquor bottles. He lifted a half gallon of Jim Beam up to where the sun would have been, if fog hadn't flopped over Good River Harbor and settled itself like a nesting gull. The sun wasn't going to tell him how much whiskey was left in there. He sloshed the bottle. Good enough. So he stuck it into his shirt and aimed toward the harbor. He picked a halting path between conversations.

"Kenny sure bunged up Axel's bear-o-rama."

"Somebody's in deep shit, but I can't figure out who."

Tick spun off the bear-o-rama person and ran right into the next.

"Think Tick knew?"

"Why'd Kenny smash up the place?"

Tick looked hard in the face of the person who asked. "I don't know," he said, and wandered off, shaking his head sorrowfully.

"I'da taken a gun."

"I'm gonna hunt down that sow and kill her good."

Tick stopped to stare. Kill her? Who?

"Where's Axel?"

"What's Axel saying?"

Pushing the whiskey bottle deeper into his shirt, Tick looked wildly around for Axel. He was nowhere to be seen, but he could be anywhere, and nobody much could be seen in this fog.

"What's that Kenny got for brains?"

At this, Tick stopped for a long pull on the bottle, because in fact, Kenny didn't have *anything* for brains. His brains were scattered on the beach, getting pinched up by gulls that probably thought God had sent them a special blessing. Tick flinched as a banjo sprang into action.

"*I'll fly away, oh Lordy. I'll fly away.*" The music shoved Tick toward the harbor. "*When I die, hallelujah by and by, I'll fly away.*" That Lillian sure did sing like an angel, and the accordion player was Gabriel himself.

The anchor lights on the masts in the harbor swayed. Tick grabbed a light pole and hung on. Fog made the lights into fuzzy yellow balls. So thick the fog erased the edge of the docks too, and Tick stumbled between the disembodied bows of boats that rested against the dock.

"*To a land where joy shall never end, I'll fly away.*"

The dock suddenly stopped, and Tick slammed on the brakes, unsure where the planks had gone. Nothing in front of him but a patch of gray velvet sea and a five-gallon bucket on a post at the end of the planking. He swayed and burped as a bilious wave lifted his shoulders. He grabbed for a piling, but he was wobbling so violently it took two tries to get hold. As he reached for the bucket, he completely forgot why, turned it over and lowered himself to sitting.

"Flying apart," he whispered, wondering. "Everything's flying. Apart." There was no answering explanation from the rising tide. "Seen this kind of thing when the planks pop off an old dory. Soon's one pops, another one goes. Dangerous. Axel's dangerous. I'm scaring myself too, the shithead ideas I get."

He fumbled with his suspenders, trying to release the whiskey bottle.

"Why'd you have to go be a hero, Kenny? Makes the rest of us look like losers. And if you had to be a hero, why'd you have to go get yourself killed? Come on back, Kenny. Drinks on me. Come over to my place. Annie Klawon's gone off. Boys dancing at your party. Place all to ourselves."

Still there was no response, but the fog began to turn lavender as evening came on and the tide sank under the dock.

"Found the bottle of tequila in your woodpile. That's gone by now. Thought you wouldn't mind. We're missing a good wake, you and me, people singing in the fog. Real thick out here on the docks too. Can't hardly find my own mouth."

There was silence on the docks, then, and vague music on the fog.

"Holy shit, Kenny. You under there?"

The reply was a nasty growl and the crunch of teeth crushing bone.

Tick rolled off the bucket onto all fours and pressed his eye to the space between the planks. The dock shifted under his weight. The sudden movement made his head spin.

"Kenny?"

A heavy body bashed into the planking and growled again. Tick jerked back. It smelled hellish down there, like rotting fish. He swung his head toward a great splash and ruckus at the edge of the dock. From the folds of the tide, the pallid carcass of a halibut slowly rose and, with a great growling and smacking, slid onto the float under the planking of the dock.

Tick put his eye to the crack again. In the dim light, the halibut skeleton's grinning head, its smashed eye, the knobby spine and stiletto ribs— they all passed by like a film reel, and Tick found himself eyeball to eyeball with a river otter. It snarled.

Tick jumped back. "Do that again, I'll piss my pants."

He sat back on his haunches and gripped the spinning planks. How could he shoot that otter without blasting a hole in the float and sinking the dock? Before long, the line of thought dissolved into the fog. Tick fumbled for the bottle and found it safely next to the bucket.

"Sure is a pile of people over on your gangway." He took a slug, for Kenny.

"Pretty dark in your cabin.

"Nora was there. All by herself. Leaning on the wall. Her face was white as a flounder. Shivering like a dying flounder too. You know that, Kenny, how it shivers down its fins when you run a knife down its line?"

Tick waited to see if Kenny had anything to say about that. The river otter moaned. Water hummed along the planking of the boats. The tide was running hard.

"'This is all my fault,' that's what old Nora said, but she was a liar. I said it was all my fault, and oh then she was pissed.

"'You did the best you could,' she said. 'Even if it wasn't good enough to save him, it was still the best you could do and how could you know what Kenny was up to, even if I could have figured it out if I wasn't such an idiot, and even if you had figured out what Kenny was doing, how would you know what the bear was going to do . . .

"'If I wasn't such a coward.' That's what she said, Kenny. 'A slinking coward.' She kind of choked then, Kenny. 'That Kenny was a good one. He was a prince. And look what I've done.'

"A prince, Kenny. She called you a prince." Tick's sudden laughter collapsed into sobs. "If it was anybody's fault, it was Axel's for putting the bear in the tank and for using a cheap chain on the lock.

"God's truth. If Axel wasn't such a cheapskate, you'd still be here, Kenny, stinkin' up the boardwalk, that's what I told Nora, negligent homicide, that's Axel, cuff him and fly him out of here. Ask me, you took a bullet for Axel. Bear should have went for Axel. But you won't see Axel saying thank you any time soon. That's what I was saying."

The first of the sunset was seeping out of the fog and spreading across the water. On the sinking tide, seas pulsed against the pilings, slow and steady and dark red as a heartbeat. As if each impact bruised the sea, the Green Point buoy moaned again and again and moaned again. Tick rolled onto his back and groaned.

"Oh God, I'm sorry, Kenny. You know it was my fault. Coulda shot the sow and cub that afternoon, I was ready to, had it all set up. Knew you wouldn't like that, but that's not why I didn't. You know why I didn't shoot 'em? Chicken. That's what I was. Davy shows up, that was just an excuse to go home. Didn't want to go to jail, boys sent off to Seattle. You'd've told me, 'aahh go on, shithead. Shoot 'em. Put 'em out of their misery.' But it's different when there's us two thinking up crazy things.

"Crazy things.

"Yeah."

The otter went back to chewing.

"That was a good one, you and me, notching Axel's cabin." Tick's chest guffawed, but his throat closed against the laughter. "Yeh. Good one. You got the ideas and the balls. I got the chain saw, no ideas, no cojones. A perfect team, Laurel and Hardy, that's us. Now I guess it's just Laurel. Or Hardy.

"Crap.

"Up at your cabin, I rummaged in your woodpile until I found your stash, hah hah knew that's where it would be, poured Nora a stiff one. She wouldn't take it, so I drank it myself. To be friendly. It was awful quiet, Nora just standing there in your cabin with her eyes closed sometimes and sometimes open, sort of staring, party going on outside.

"'There's lasagna,' I said, and even stupid me, I knew that was a stupid thing to say to old Nora, who was just standing there. Standing . . . that's all.

"'We're going to give him a good fire.' Nora said that. Out of the blue. I said, 'What?' She said, 'You can help,' so I said okay." Tick rubbed his eyes, saltwater on his hands. "Shit. My job? Getting dry firewood from everybody and loading it onto the *Annie K*. Then I guess we'll load you on too, unless you want to ride out to the bonfire beach in the seiner."

For a long time, Tick lay stiff on his back under the cold hand of the fog and waited for Kenny to make up his mind. As if they were uncomfortable, the boats in the harbor shifted and the lines creaked.

"Don't want you too froze, or you'll just smolder."

"*No more cold iron shackles for my feet.*"

Tick lurched up straight, then quickly laid back down, gripping the edge of the dock. The sound came from another world. His head reeled.

"What's that? What, Kenny?"

But it was the music up on the boardwalk, and the accordion solo trickling down through the fog and an electric guitar joining in, bwaa. Tick sucked on the bottle and settled back down.

"So listen, damn you, Kenny.

"Nora must've loved you something else, Kenny, cuz she's furious that you went and died. 'We need him.' She said that. 'The world needs Kenny. What a waste! What a terr-i-ble waste.' Like you were toothpaste or something, all squoze out for nothing.

"Aw, sorry about your brains, Kenny."

Tick wished the otters would quit their chewing. All that smacking and the fog sinking and the night falling until there was only a narrow crawl space between the fog and the bones.

"And I was getting nervous, up there in your cabin, because there came Lillian, and all your buddies huddling in the dark was starting to look like a freaking committee meeting. Freaking. Committee. What we gonna do first? What we gonna do next? Couldn't figure out why Nora was acting like I was in on something. Did everybody know I notched Axel's piling? Did they know about the Marlin .444, how I was gonna put the bears out of their misery? I was getting out of there, and somebody knocks on your door.

"It's Rebecca Hagerman, peeking into the dark.

"Ah shit, I'm thinking. I am so busted.

"But what's the crime in being the friend of a dead guy? I'm tired of thinking, am I doing somethin' Axel won't like? Screw it. I was drinking a dead guy's tequila, and in walks the wife of the guy who probably killed him—I mean, yessiree, if you think about it. Is she gonna arrest me? She looks around, kind of letting her eyes get used to the light . . . I guess squinty is what she always is, kind of checking out who's there and who isn't, nodding yes yes. But she's crying, Kenny. That little nose is red as a bug. She says, 'I brought Kenny a petunia,' and damned if she didn't. A purple petunia in a little green pot. Nora grabs her in a big hug and says Kenny would be so glad to have the petunia, and I thought yessirreebob. Kenny would be so glad to have a petunia, so he could pee in the pot at night and wouldn't have to go out and pee over the side. He'd pee until the poor petunia keeled over and died. Then he'd throw it overboard."

Pee. Tick rolled to his knees and stumped like a penitent to the edge of the dock. He leaned his forehead against the bow of a Boston Whaler and fumbled with his fly. Where he pissed into the bay, tiny jellyfish flickered like candlelight. Had he been in this place before? He had, maybe a long time before. He struggled to remember. He knew the sound of the wine pouring into the chalice and the pressure on his knees, and he knew the hand on his head and the smell of candles burning. He knew the sound of a hundred people trying to be quiet. It was the rustle of water when the tide had fallen and stilled.

"How can you stand it, Kenny, to lose this? How can you stand it, losing night tides and wet docks? What's it like when it all disappears? Just, suck, gone.

"Ah man, I'm going to lose it all. Lost you. Lost my fishing trawler a long time ago. Lost my job. Lost my nerve. I'm going to lose Annie Klawon. Then I'm sure to lose my boys, Tommy crying for his mom in the night. How pitiful is that? Davy coming home smelling of dope and not saying where he was at, and why should he say anything to a shithead father can't hold anything together?"

Hand over hand on the light pole, Tick raised himself to standing. He rebounded from bow to bow along the dock, until he got to the edge of the falling tide under the dripping cross-timbers of the town, to the hidden places only vaguely revealed, the rotten bases of the pilings, the gaping holes in the mud where soft things retreated. The slow slug of waves, the tick tick of barnacles. Fog opened in front of him as he stumbled along, and fog closed behind him, the way music will do, or water. Not night, not day, not alive, not dead, the fog absorbed everything, digested it into something vague and formless and yellow—the air and the soft mud, the stinking shame that emanated from every step Tick took, the deflated kelp, the vague yellow shame of the world.

August 30

HIGH TIDE		LOW TIDE	
4:19am	14.8ft	10:22am	1.9ft
4:33pm	16.1ft	10:51pm	1.3ft

"Here, get your hands off me."

Tick had Lillian under the arms and was about to hoist her from the wharf onto the deck of the *Annie K.* Great God almighty, if he would just leave her alone, she could climb on board under her own power. It had been a while since she'd got herself in and out of a boat, and her knees didn't work like they used to, but that was no reason to treat a lady like a crate of pigs. Besides, why would a woman want to hang on to a man when there was a perfectly trustworthy railing right there in front of her? She stuck her good slacks into her boots, tugged down her hat, held on to the railing, and hauled herself onto the boat.

"See?" she said to Tick, and poked him sharp with her elbow. He'd been standing by, hanging on to Lillian's raincoat as she hauled, the way a longshoreman holds the rope to guide a pallet that's being on-loaded by a crane—sort of off to the side and ready to jump if she gave way.

Once Lillian and Tick were on board, Tick pulled the *Annie K* next to the salmon seiner where they were keeping Kenny on ice. He and the fishermen went into the fish-hold and brought him out. Kenny was rolled up in a blue tarp, tight as a burrito, so with a couple of guys holding the tarp at one end, and a couple holding the other, they didn't have any trouble slinging him onto the *Annie K.* Kenny was plenty cold. The breath of the guys fogged when they leaned over to set him down by the wheelhouse.

The *Annie K* was a heck of a hearse, that old rattletrap boat with greasy rags thrown in the corners and splinters and moss-bark all over the deck. But Kenny couldn't have asked for a more beautiful funeral-parade route. It'd been misting all morning, but as the *Annie K* left the harbor, the sun came out, and every fleck of rain glittered.

Lillian looked over the stern. The people of Good River Harbor had turned out to honor Kenny's last journey. They stood bunched up on the ferry dock, reflected upside down on the water. All of them were turned on their heads—the men and women who stood silently on the dock to watch the *Annie K* leave, the children riding bikes past green, pink, blue houses, the postal clerk by the flag at half-mast. As the *Annie K's* wake rolled under the town, the town and all its people stretched and narrowed, stretched and narrowed, then slowly rocked themselves together again. When a stray cloud drifted over the town, the reflected figures shivered under light rain.

The *Annie K* rounded Green Point and motored along the shore, past Nora's cove, past the headland, then along alder shores. The sun paraded in and out among the clouds, sending down rays like roaming spotlights, pointing to the spruce forest, then the clear-cut hill. A layer of low clouds bisected the mountains, so the mountaintops floated up there like green and white balloons.

"Don't you be grumbling, Kenny," Lillian said to the blue tarp. "I'm tired of hearing you complain that the sun spoils your complexion. Shut up and enjoy it just for once."

"HAR!" Tick yelled from the wheelhouse, making her jump.

Propping her hip against the rail, Lillian buttoned up her raincoat, tightened the knot on her belt, and pushed her hat down tighter. She had chosen the hat because it looked good with her eyes. It was a cloche she had knitted herself from yarn she unraveled from a blue sweater. She pulled a couple of curls down over her forehead. Then she stood braced in the bow beside Kenny, watching the coves and headlands go by.

Lillian had dressed up in honor of the fact that she was the preacher and the choir for the day. Nora and Tick had appointed her. They needed a preacher, they said, to say some holy words over Kenny's ashes and they needed a choir to sing a hymn. Lillian thought that was appropriate. She had been doing laundry for twenty years, washing men's dirty clothes. How much harder could it be to clean up their snotty, soot-stained souls? Absolution might even be easier than washing Carhartt overalls, which takes some muscle, getting them out of the washer, all soaked. But who knows? It might have been smart to start off her soul-cleaning business with somebody easier than Kenny was going to be.

Poor old Kenny. Lillian pulled her eyes away from the blue tarp. On the day he died, Kenny and Ranger had rolled into the bar, just as they did every Friday morning at ten. Ranger sniffed at the door to the laundry, rolled his eyes, and lay down with his chin on his paws. Evidently, he did not approve of what was about to happen. Kenny shoved a dollar in the can, helped himself to a clean towel and bar of soap from the shelves, chose a hunting magazine from the slanting pile, and shut himself into the laundry and shower room. After a while, Lillian heard the hot water clank on, and after many more than the five minutes he had paid for, she heard it clank off. Then a lot of scuffling, and three out of four quarters dropped into the coin receptacle on the washing machine. She heard Kenny pound on the washing machine the way he always did, trying to make the fourth quarter fall.

"Just jiggle it," Lillian had yelled. It pained her now to know that those would be the last words she said to him.

There had been no response, but the washing machine rattled violently on its screw feet. Water poured into the machine, and Lillian went back to her accounts as the machine sprayed and spun. She knew that Kenny would be sitting in the steamy laundry room, white and naked and skinny as a tomcod, reading about rifles. Naked as a tomcod before the eyes of God, while the machine washed every item of clothing he had been wearing, which is about every item of clothing he owned—with the notable exception of his hats. The machine spun and squealed and finally clanked to a stop. Then dimes dropped into place and the dryer bumped and thumped.

There is no place in the Bible—Lillian knew, because she had looked. There is no place in the Bible where Jesus or the Apostles or anybody says, please God, tighten the screws and oil the bearings on my soul. Nobody says, glue these splayed soul-joints and clamp them tight. Oh no. When people's souls need attending to, what they need is a good washing. *Dear God, wash my soul clean from sin.* Water is holy, and the person who runs the Laundromat is doing the Lord's work, even though the carpenter got first billing. Lillian didn't have much use for God, or vice versa, she guessed, but it mattered to her that Kenny was clean when he died. She hoped that when she died, she would be fresh out of the shower and that she would have had time to arrange her hair into curls pretty enough to please the angels.

Tick nudged the *Annie K* into the beach, jumped out, and dragged his anchor up the strand. He'd chosen a wide gravel beach encircled by a forest, a good distance and downwind from town. Nora had her little team working hard. She was splitting wood, bareheaded in her yellow raincoat, her hair stringy and stuck to her back. She had already split an enormous pile of kindling, and she was still going at it. Tick had been in and out of town with the *Annie K* all day, collecting the firewood people donated—milled wood ends, broken shipping pallets, quartered rounds of hemlock and spruce. It was three miles out of town and a mountain of firewood, so that was a lot of hauling. Lillian ran a practiced eye over the stovewood. Two, three cords, maybe more. This was going to be some fire. A small woman with her hair tied up in a red bandana was kneeling in the gravel, hammering together a sort of lattice platform from poles cut from alders.

Rebecca Hagerman, Axel's sweetie, Lillian said to herself. I'd heard she defected.

Rebecca looked like she'd been crying. Her nose was always unattractively pink, but it wasn't usually that pink. She was smiling over her work now, and her head was bobbing, even though hitting a nail square on the head was apparently a work in progress. Lillian wondered what Axel thought about his wife working with Kenny's funeral crew. She guessed Axel didn't know what Rebecca was doing, partly because she'd moved over to Nora's, but mostly because he had decided not to care. That was one of the talents Axel had developed early, a talent that other people had to work all their lives to perfect—without even breaking a sweat, he could decide not to care.

Now that the guest of honor had arrived in his blue tarp and the clergy-and-choir was present, everybody was there who was invited. Lillian turned her head away as Tick leaned down to unwrap Kenny from the tarp. When she heard the familiar thunder of a tarp being shaken, she turned back. Nora was folding the blue tarp as carefully as if it were a soldier's flag, and Kenny's body lay on the gravel, wrapped head to toe in his camouflage poncho. Two ravens marched over and stood by like an honor guard.

"Let's get to work," Tick ordered, and the ravens lifted off and soared to the edge of the clearing. First, they built the structure that would hold the body, setting a platform on thick green poles. Tick and Nora struggled to get Kenny up there without unrolling him. The platform was head height, and the last thing they wanted was to roll him out onto the beach, half thawed. Once he was safely loaded, they stuck the pinwheel and the little American flag from his wheelchair into a chink in the wood near him. Nora had brought along the hat he'd made from the bear cub with silver shoulders. Crying quietly, she tucked it under his head.

Tick brought over a bucket for Lillian to sit on, bless his heart, get the weight off her feet while she watched. They built four big piles of kindling near the corners of the platform. Then they loaded on the firewood, stacking it under the platform in a teepee higher than Tick's shoulders. People had picked out good wood, nothing punky or wet, and that's one thing you can say about the people in Good River Harbor, they have good judgment in firewood. Tick had held back probably another half-cord to feed the fire if they needed to. He ran around the pyre, getting things set up just right, pouring a slug of diesel fuel at the corners. Then he went back to the *Annie K* and brought out four propane torches.

Tick gave out the torches and made one last check. Then he sent Nora around to one pile of kindling, and Lillian and Rebecca to the others. He looked over to Lillian to see if the preacher was ready to issue the call to prayer.

The preacher stood up and smoothed the front of her raincoat.

"Light him," she said.

They all knelt down and set their propane torches to the kindling. It struck Lillian to the heart, to see Kenny's friends down on their knees like that, bent over like they were sinners, not arsonists. Starting at that moment, she missed old pickle-face, missed him hard and bad, like she would miss the sour pleasure of coffee in the morning if it died and went to hell. White smoke rose from the four corners of the pyre. Everyone backed away to watch it catch. Before long, smoke was sliding up the side of the firewood, and then flames licked up through the pile. Yellow smoke seeped through the platform and curled around the edges. Soon Lillian could hardly see the poncho in the haze. If they can't get a fire hotter than this, she fretted, they should have brined and smoked him.

A new wind sucked the fire into the center. Suddenly, the pyre erupted in flame. Smoke rose straight up. The loose edge of the poncho flapped violently. The stars and stripes waved. The pinwheel spun madly. Flames shot up twenty feet. The edge of the poncho blackened and melted onto the pole. Lillian backed away. The pyre was all on fire now, burning like a torch. Kenny sizzled. Everyone backed even farther away, pressing toward the cool forest behind them. Ashes shot into the sky. The air above the flames was clear and shimmering, the fire was that hot.

One of the poles on the platform burned through and dropped a corner of the platform deeper into the fire. Sparks and cinders flew straight up. A scrap of poncho, seared at the edges, sailed toward the sky. The fire roared and snapped. Each time it fell into itself, Tick ran toward the fire, threw on another log, and raced away before he melted his raincoat. Above his orange beard, his face was bright red. Another pole burned through, sending up a shower of sparks. The noise of that fire was terrifying as a train in a tunnel. The heat of it backed them against the trees. They all shifted out of the smoke.

A shotgun went off, so near that Lillian almost crinked her neck, flinching. Then another blast. She grabbed hold of Nora and cranked around. There was Tick, the gun to his shoulder, shooting into the air. He shot it off again. He stopped to reload.

"Twenty-one gun salute," he said somberly. "Eighteen to go." He fired them all off, three at a time, stopping to reload, sending buckshot into the ocean, into the trees, into the fire, blam, blam, blam. Lillian's ears rang from the shotgun blasts and the roar of the fire.

She couldn't see anything of Kenny. Her eyes were watering from flame and shimmering mountains—yellow flames, orange flames, sometimes a feather of blue, a burst of black smoke, a spiral of white, then the silver air and the flames. Who knows how long the fire burned? After a while, Tick stopped throwing on logs. He joined the others on boulders at the edge of the beach and watched the fire settle into itself. A wind came up from the northwest and the fire came to life again. Flames raced up and down the logs. Gray smoke blew over the water. Then the fire settled itself into a flickering burn. Evening came on, with yellow streaks behind the mountains. The cold started to flow from the forest. The fire felt good. They moved a little closer—to the fire, to each other, to Kenny's warm ashes.

The tide began to rise. The leading edge fingered under the fire. White ash lifted on the curl, a sheen of ashes that swayed and spread across the water. A river of ashes seeped out on the current, flowing across the ocean and vanishing in the slick of last light. The tide lifted burning embers and drifted them away, smoking and sparkling yellow. The fire whistled and whispered as water rose under it, and smoke bubbled up and burst. Lillian realized it was time to sanctify the moment.

She settled her cloche and curls, stood up, and made her way over the gravel to the upwind edge of the fire. She waited until Tick paid attention.

"Dearly Beloved," she said. Everybody was looking at her. Nora put her arm around Rebecca. Tick straightened his shoulders. Out of her coat pocket, Lillian pulled a bottle of the best brandy behind her bar. She uncorked the bottle, moved as close as she could to the fire, and slowly began to pour. Beautiful blue flames licked over the log—blue as moonlit midnight, blue as muskeg lakes, blue as crab eyes. As she poured, Lillian looked toward heaven and began to sing.

"Sunset and evening star," she sang.

"Stop!"

Lillian was so startled she tweaked her bad knee. Tick had already started toward her. He cradled the bottle in his big hands and looked at the label. "You drink the host," he said soberly. "You don't pour it on the ground."

He had wrecked Lillian's holy moment, after she had practiced it, the gestures and the silken tone. But she was feeling dry herself. So they drank the brandy. They sat by the fire, like people would sit around any campfire, and passed the bottle as the tide crept in and floated the ashes away. The brandy opened Lillian's throat. After a while, she stood up, lifted her arms the way she'd practiced, closed her eyes, and began again to sing.

Sunset and evening star, and one clear call for me,
And may there be no moaning of the bar, when I put out to sea.

When I put out to sea, when I put out to sea.
And may there be no moaning of the bar, when I put out to sea.

But such a tide as moving seems asleep, too full for sound and foam,
When that which drew from out the boundless deep, turns again home.

Turns again home, turns again home,
When that which drew from out the boundless deep, turns again home.

Lillian waited a long moment, then lowered herself onto her five-gallon pail. She lit a cigarette. The only sounds then were the snap of the fire and the whisper of water and ash.

"Damn that Kenny. Damn him to hell." Tick was blubbering, so he could only croak out the words. He has a way of turning the mood, Lillian could say that for him.

"Hellfire's going to be an anticlimax," Rebecca said softly.

Lillian figured it was time to exert some ecclesiastical authority. "No more talk of hellfire. The only sins Kenny committed were pigheadedness, grumpiness . . ." She stopped to think. ". . . and corrupting the youth. None of these are mortal sins, last time I looked."

"Shitheadedness. And lusting in his heart," Tick choked. "And lying to his friends," he added, with some degree of resentment.

"He was kind to dogs," Nora pointed out.

"That will turn the argument for St. Peter," Lillian decreed. "That and the fact that he had more courage than all of us put together. And he died playing what he thought was a good trick on the world." She ground out the cigarette with her boot on the sand.

So the issue of salvation was settled. Lillian nodded to Nora, who had prepared the benediction. Lillian had chosen her because she was the only writer among them and she would work hard on it and say something good. Nora pulled a piece of paper out of her raincoat pocket and unfolded it in the light of the flashlight Tick held.

"You're free, Kenny. So, go. Float into snaggle-top spruce trees and settle on the shoulders of disappointed ravens. Rise on the upslope winds to the snowfields. Dust the blue ice and bog orchids. Spread your ashy wing across the water. Drift with the torn kelp. Sift slowly down in the dim saltwater, past bulging yellow eyes watching. Suck into the gullet of a great ugly sculpin, and stick to the tube feet of the blood-red star. Rise again with the roaring whales. And when the salmon come, go home with them. Go home to the place where they die. That is the place where life begins again."

Nora refolded the paper and pushed it into the embers. It caught and flared. Kenny's friends murmured.

"Roger that."

Lillian wasn't expecting to be touched, but that part about going home? That did it for her. This time, she didn't mind when Nora wrapped her long arms around her and dragged her damp hair over Lillian's face.

Night covered the cove like a raven's wing, and still they sat. Tide fluttered in. Lifted, the Annie K nosed into shore. Tick picked his way through the dark to pull in slack rope. When he lifted the painter from the water, it trailed a skirt of sparks. Tick threw down a loop of rope, drawing an answering loop of sparks that flashed and popped so sharply they almost crackled.

"You in hell after all, Kenny?" Tick hefted a rock and tossed it in the drink. In the place it disappeared, a splash rose like a circlet of flame.

He tossed in another stone. Small creatures in the sea—bioluminescent algae, dinoflagellates, jellyfish—flashed blue, flashed white. Nora waded in. Small sparkling lives swirled around her feet. Rebecca held Lillian's hand and led her into the water. That's how it ended, Kenny's funeral. Silhouetted black against a black night, four friends slowly, sedately, danced in the tidal swash and the flash of small lives. Ashes stuck to their boots.

September 9

HIGH TIDE		LOW TIDE	
1:35am	19.3ft	7:47 am	-3.0ft
2:07pm	19.2ft	8:11 pm	-2.6ft

So it was decided. That quickly. On an early morning walk in the intertidal to hunt for sea cucumbers. On a day of scattered clouds and minus tides, with a skiff running down the channel and an eagle watching the kelp beds for crabs. By two people standing ankle-deep in water beside a log polished silver by winter storms, it was decided. Is this how it happens, as routinely as day turns to night?

All the week before Kenny died, Nora and Tick had been talking big, hanging out in her kitchen while Tommy practiced the piano and Rebecca washed old wine bottles for salmonberry wine. But all their talk had been hypothetical, a silly joke they shared.

"If we wanted to wash away the plywood framing for the dam, we would need just the right flood—not too big, not too little. We would be trying to save the salmon, not wreck the place." Nora.

"We could time it to a flood-tide, water rising up, water crashing down, yeehaw." Tick.

"We would have to figure out how nobody gets hurt. Just stuff, right? Just the dam." Rebecca had walked over, drying her hands, and they all three solemnly shook on that.

It was just fun, a charade, nothing real. They laughed, their uproarious little committee.

Then Kenny died. That was real.

On the beach, Nora leaned over to pick up the empty carapace of a crab. The outer surface of the shell was ruddy and knobby. But inside was luminous, opalescent, lavender.

"Look at this, Tick," she said. "You tell me why this is so beautiful in its hidden places. What's the use of that, what's the survival value in that, to be beautiful inside, where no one will ever see until it's dead and gone?" It made her think of Kenny, but that was no surprise. Everything made her think of Kenny. "Kenny told me about that philosophical problem, called it the Problem of Unnecessary Beauty."

Tick took the crab shell in his big hand. "Yeah. The guy was full of philosophical problems."

"Do you remember that night at Lillian's when Kenny told us the story of Abraham from the Bible?" Nora went on.

Tick snorted.

"God said to Abraham, 'I command you to kill your son, your only son, the one whom you love—Isaac,' Kenny said. 'Take him to the mountain, tie him to an altar, pile sticks around him, slit his throat, and set him on fire.' So being a man of faith and obedience, Abraham did what God said. But just when he was bending to cut his son's throat, an angel appeared. She told Abraham to let Isaac go and sacrifice a ram instead. Which he did.

"'So was Abraham a good man or a bad man?' Kenny demanded. He drew his knife then, right there in Lillian's bar, and held it to his own throat.

"'Jeezus, Kenny,' everybody was yelling. 'Put the knife away.'

"'HAR,' Kenny said, and drove the blade into the table."

Nora settled herself on a driftwood log with her knees to her chin and her arms wrapped around them. Abraham was a good person, wasn't he? She had asked Kenny, but he wouldn't say. It's a good person, who does what she thinks is right, even if she loses what she loves the very most. Even if she wrecks her chance for a normal life? Even if she destroys stuff. Isn't that true? Is that true? Or is that just stubborn and stupid? Her eyes were huge and bright with yellow light reflected from a glaze on the sea at the Green Point buoy. She inhaled the smell of the cove—hemlocks and salt-crusted algae. God, she loved this place.

"Shit, shit, shit, shit, shit," she said. "Here I go again. I guess we really are going to make that flood. This one's for you, Kenny." And because Kenny couldn't answer, Nora answered for him, not shouting as Kenny would have done, but murmuring quiet as the tide. "When you were called, did you answer, or not? Perhaps softly and in a whisper?"

"Kierkegaard," she told Tick, and grinned. Tick grunted, and sat down so hard he lifted Nora's end of the log. Chum barked sharply, then jumped off the log to snuffle under a coil of kelp.

"That splash dam has to go in this week, before the rains start to fall on the old snowfields," Nora said. She looked hard at Tick. "You all in?"

He rubbed his forehead with his beard. "I'm in. I'm stupid, but I'm in. For one damn time, I'm putting myself in charge. All my years in the Harbor, I tried to keep my tools oiled, my propane tanks full, my pantry stocked," Tick said. "Didn't always get it done, but I knew I had to try. That's what you do when you know it's all going to end. You keep your chain saw sharpened, and you stay alert, because you know you won't get much warning. Then, sure enough, it's over and that's that. Don't know how many times my life has ended, Axel laying me off, Annie Klawon heading back to Seattle. Five? Six? And each time, I think how in the name of the ever-lovin' God am I going to get my life started up again, but I got to. I just do."

Nora closed her eyes. Didn't she know it?

Tick whapped her solidly on the back. "But this is no end, old Nora. For once, we got ourselves a beginning." He looked around. "Where are the trumpets? Shouldn't there be trumpets? Gonna make a world that doesn't have to end all the time, used up and shut down.

"I can build a splash dam across that little opening in a day, maybe two. That might be bragging, but close enough. I know how to fix the dam up with a key log, so it only takes one person on a pry pole to break it open." Tick stopped. "Who's gonna be on that pry pole?"

Nora took a deep breath. "That would be me," she said.

There were no trumpets, just young ravens yakking, kelp blades swashing in a falling tide, and a single thrush whistling. That was it.

From the curve of ancient logs that rims the cove on the far side of the point, they could see the lines on the beach that mark each level of the receding tide—a row of clean gravel, then the line of green eelgrass laid down by the ebb tide, then a windrow of white clamshells, then a band at the edge of the water—broad brown blades of kelp. Past that, there was clear sand in shallow water.

Nora leaned back and rubbed her eyes. "Those five tide lines are laid out like the lines of a musical score," she said, pointing to the lines of shells and seaweed on the beach. Tick looked up. Five lines there were, and sea stars clinging like quarter notes to the places they had landed when the tide went out. Chum's footprints ran in and out of the lines. A black raven stood in the eelgrass strip and pecked at a clam.

"It is all so ordered and inevitable—as if God were trying to find the language to tell us something. Or to make us feel something, some emotion. If only we could learn to read that music. The notes are written right there on the gravel. There is a divine score. The universe is a madrigal, and it's beautiful and true and complicated, all the parts moving together in these changing relations through time, and we're all part of it—I just know this, that we're part of the music—but we can't quite figure it out, no matter how hard we try, *and we do try,* but we play our parts wrong and what could have been so beautiful is ugly and mean. It's so sad."

"Shut up, Nora." Tick flipped up his beard to cover his eyes.

"We're all trying to find that resonance, the hum in our bodies that tells us we are exactly in tune with the planet, and sometimes we do—enough to make us long for it every day. We tune ourselves too high this way, too low that way. We come so close, but that's the worst dissonance, to be close and get it wrong. Don't you think that when even a five-year-old kid can hear when harmony goes sour and change his fingers until he knows it's right, *just from the sound of it,* that the rest of us could figure it out? You have to try something, and listen. Why is that so hard for us?"

Tick covered his ears. Nora lifted her head. She listened more intently than she had listened in her life. Under the slow pulse of the sea on stones, under the mutter and squeak of unseen lives in the kelp, she heard the rush of her own heart, not beating against a wall—the way it always had—but flooding, as a wave pours down the beach.

She squared her shoulders and stood up to retrieve the bucket. Tick stood up too, and they walked down to the water, where they would find the sea cucumbers they were hunting.

"Okay, so we should get started. Who knows how long it will take for the reservoirs to fill. And the first salmon are already staging at the mouth of the river."

They skidded along the slippery edge of the bay, trying to put their boots on the rough grip of gravel. Eelgrass is slippery, and kelp blades are even worse.

"It's time." Nora nodded. "I dreamed the salmon's dream again last night. It was dark and it was raining. I was trying to get home. But everything stopped me. I couldn't find shoes. I looked everywhere, in my file cabinets and suitcases. Just tore them apart. And all the time I was looking for my shoes, I knew I only had ten minutes before the bus left. I ran to the bus, in snow, in the dark. Snow now. I don't know if I found my shoes. The last people were getting on and they looked back at me and frantically waved me in, but I had forgotten my suitcase, and when I went back to the house, it was locked, and when I ran back, the bus driver said, 'Where to?' I didn't know. It was written on my ticket and I couldn't find my ticket because it was in my coat, but the coat was in the closet and I went back home and I was pounding on the door of my apartment, but how could that be, because I was home, but I had to get home. I couldn't and I had to."

She had told Tick about the salmon dream several times before. She believed that salmon have the same dream as she does, and swallows, and college students, and every homesick goose, all trying to get home, all feeling that panic when you have to go home and everything conspires against you. She thinks this is the dream of the world. "We're all one big dream of going home," she said, "and it's a nightmare."

Water lapped at their boots, reminding them that they were supposed to be gathering dinner. Still they stood there. Chum waded out and then looked back, waiting for them. The tide was rising. It straightened the kelp and pulled at the fur on Chum's belly.

"I'll check the tide tables and set the date," Nora said.

She couldn't believe the words were coming out of her mouth. She felt like someone else, maybe someone she used to be.

"And Tick, I'm going to talk to Axel one more time. We have to give him a chance to do the right thing."

"How many chances does a dick get in one lifetime?"

"One more."

SO THAT WAS that. Nora checked her watch. "I need to be careful of the time. I want to get back to tuning that poor piano before Tommy comes for his lesson. God, Tick, it's hard to keep things tuned up in this place. It's not like you can get every tone right in itself, they have to be right in relation to each other. That's the tough part. Constant struggle. Then the weather changes."

They waded in the tide up to their boot tops, stumbling over rocks hidden by kelp. Under the kelp were all the sea cucumbers they would ever want. For a good dinner, they needed five of the astonishing things—short, fat phallic echinoderms with orange spikes poking out every which way and a crayon-red body. In the water, they're fat. But when Tick draped a sea cucumber over his hand and lifted it out of the water, it stretched to twice its length on both ends and rolled away, a stretchy pouch of water almost too insubstantial to hold. Tick pushed his sleeve back up, reached into the sea, and pulled up another sea cucumber. Nora offered the pail.

As they hiked up the trail from the cove, they heard Tommy playing Nora's piano. Chum ran ahead, barking. Nora had told Tommy to chord with his left hand and play the melody with his right. He had mastered the melody, but the chords were coming more slowly, so it was an oddly limping song he played, with long pauses when it was time to switch chords. He sang along, accompanying himself, patiently waiting for the chord to change before he picked up the next phrase. Nora laughed. It felt good, almost like a fairy tale, to walk with a big woodsman from the moss-fragrant forest into a clearing where a little boy was playing the piano rather badly on the front porch of a log cabin. How can a life like this last forever?

Rebecca was sitting on the porch next to Tommy, sorting leaves from a bucket of red huckleberries, nodding her head in time with the music. Nora went straight to Tommy, rubbing his head and praising his song. Then she leaned over his back to watch him play. That's how they went through "Motorcycle Cops." Tommy was racing through it as well as he could, asking when they would get to "Jingle Bells," and what would be the song after that?

It seemed like a good thing, this trade—a flood for a song, a song for a flood—the power of water for the beauty of music, the beauty of water for the power of music.

"Dashing through the snow, in a one-horse open sleigh."

Nora was playing the song, with Tommy on her lap and his hands on hers. Tick pulled a plank from Nora's lumber pile and leaned it against the porch. He drove a nail all the way through the board. Reaching into the bucket, he pulled out a sea cucumber and impaled one end on the nail.

"O'er the fields we go, laughing all the way."

The sea cucumber hung there on its stake, getting longer and longer, stretched by the weight of the water collecting at its aft end. Tick snipped its skin at the bottom. The water drained out. With a fillet knife, he slit the sea cucumber stem to stern and opened it. There were the five long, white muscles that they were going to eat. Sliding the knife under one end of each muscle, he stripped them off, one and then another. Then he slit each muscle lengthwise, ending up with ten strips of meat and a limp sack of skin.

"What fun it is to laugh and sing a sleighing song tonight."

While Nora and Tommy worked over the chords, practicing the switch from C to G, Rebecca turned on the propane tank and went inside to cook. While the oil heated in the skillet, Rebecca dredged the sea cucumber strips in flour, salt, and pepper. She cooked them fast, until they were golden. They ate them with their fingers, the four of them, sitting on the planks of the front porch in the gleam of the day. The sea cucumbers were salty and good.

Hold on to this memory, Nora reminded herself. Let it settle into your mind, the sweetness of this point in time. Step back and see it from a distance. Try different angles, front view, rear. Chew slowly, and hold the taste on your tongue. You will look back on this very day and wonder what happened, and you will need to remember the sound and the taste of it, and this crazy, awful thing, that you will give up this home, what you love the best, so the salmon can find their way home.

"Which do you think my mom would like better," Tommy asked. "'Go Tell Aunt Rhody' or 'Angels Watchin' Over Me'? The dead gray goose maybe, or angels? Nora says I get to choose."

Rebecca reached around his shoulders and pulled him close. Her eyes disappeared in her smile.

"May it be angels," she said.

AFTER SHE MOVED out of Axel's house, Rebecca had trudged up and down the boardwalk, nodding yes yes, pushing wheelbarrows full of plants from her house to the bear pit, a load of tomatoes just turning red and then back again for Shasta daisies and back for lilies, and back for petunias and zucchini. She planted them every which way in the bear pit, sticking them in piles of dirt as if she didn't care if they lived or died, until her house was stripped bare and the bear pit looked like a community garden planted by a committee of zombies.

But Rebecca had come alive while she lived with Nora. She had laughed like a schoolgirl while she stuffed a rotten salmon into a sculpin's mouth. Tick thought it was a silly trick, risky and useless, but she said, no, it was almost perfect and the only thing better would be if it was a bear's paw. And then she laughed and laughed, until she started to cry. Nora went over and hugged her, and Rebecca put her little face into Nora's shoulder and sobbed. Sobbing still, she went back to the sink and started in again twisting a knife into the sculpin's jaw, trying to work it big enough to take in the salmon's tail. She swiped at her tears with the back of her wrist, because her hands were disgusting. At midnight, she had snuck down the boardwalk and dropped the fish in Axel's boot.

Nora laughed as she pulled out her tuning lever and opened the piano. Rebecca came out and sat cross-legged on the porch beside her.

"How's the Axel Improvement Project coming?" Nora asked as she bent to her work.

"How's the piano tuning?" Rebecca replied. "About the same constant struggle?"

"You said that right," Nora said, as she turned and tuned, turned and tuned, stopping only to wave away blackflies.

To tune a piano, it isn't enough to get each string to sing out, loud and true. It has to sing in relation to the other strings. You turn, tiny turns, tiny turns, to get middle C right. But each tone has three strings. So you mute two of them with narrow rubber pads. You have to be able to make them silent; it's the silence that allows you to hear that glorious moment when the middle C vibrates with the middle tone of all things, the center of time, the hum of tide through a sea urchin's spines, the golden mean that is the exact middle between two extremes, the way courage exactly cuts the difference between recklessness and cowardice. You find that center if you listen when everything else is quiet. Then you bring those other two strings into the shimmer of that tone. It is a shimmer—you feel it in your body, you feel it with a surety that this is the way the world was meant to be.

Okay, so that's what you do first. It's hard to explain, it's complicated—imagine finding that center, how that feels. Then D has to be right in relation to C. Tiny, tiny. Right turn, tighten, sharp. Left turn, loosen, flat. Tiny change. And E has to be right in relation to D and C, all the way up to the next C, and that gives you the temperament. Well, that's just the start. But it's good, because now you have the reference, that's what you need, the eight true tones.

Now you find the octaves, matching D to D and E to E, you find the miracle, the notes that are the same and not the same—an identity so obvious in your ear that even monkeys can hear it, even babies. And what you hear is the pulse of melded frequency, one frequency and another that is double it, or half. You have seen this if you have seen a wave overlap a wave that is rolling to shore, a convergence like a zipper, the sides of a zipper converging as they race along the shore, until there is one wave, a wave so clear and blue you can see light through it, and sometimes the dark form of a harbor seal. Convergences, all the way up the piano, all the way down. Tiny turns. Tiny changes.

It takes hours. And then the day darkens and the sky descends and the piano breathes wetter, cooler air, or the sun flashes between clouds. The world is as new as if it had been created at that moment, and that is the world in which the piano now has to resound. You keep the tuning lever always in your pocket, the way other people always carry a pocketknife, or pliers or a Bible.

Nora gave the piano an affectionate pat, packed up her tools, and went into the house. Rebecca stayed for a few more minutes on the porch. She smelled her hands and smiled.

"THAT'S IT," AXEL said. "That is entirely enough."

Notching his piling, wrecking his bear shelter pavilion, stealing his bears—fine. Just fine. But the rotten salmon in his boot, that was going too far. The fish was so far gone that it was just a mass of slime and maggots, barely held together by moldy skin, pocked and fuzzy. That was disrespectful. That was taunting him. That was poking him in the eye with a stick. And that was something he couldn't stand, being poked in the eye with a stick.

It would have made more sense for him to wash his boot out on the deck, where he could use the hose. But Axel was determined that no one—not one person—would have the satisfaction of seeing him scrubbing. So after Meredith left for his office, he put the boot in the kitchen sink, half filled it with hot water and poured in a good slug of bleach. Then he pulled on rubber gloves, grabbed a scrub brush, and went to work. It's not easy, scrubbing fish slime out of a boot. You have to reach all the way to the toe, and that's a tight fit. And where the brush doesn't fit, you have to sort of scratch with your fingers. He scratched and scrubbed, then held the boot closed at the top and shook it, sloshing the water around. When he had rinsed it, which he had to do quickly because bleach eats neoprene, he leaned down and gave a test smell. He threw the boot against the sink so hard it jumped out like it had a foot in it, kicking water onto the floor.

"Now we're playing for keeps," he said to the boot, as he pulled it out of the sink. He cranked the heat up so high under the teakettle that it rattled and buzzed. He would go after the smell and the slime with boiling water and just hope he didn't melt the damn boot.

Axel could have believed it was just kids playing a joke, maybe one of Meredith's friends, stuffing a huge dog salmon into his boot on the porch. The salmon might have washed up on the beach, stinking, with its stomach bitten out by a bear, and some kids might have found it and thought, hey that's cool, and they could have carried it up on the boardwalk and thought, hey that would be fun, let's stick the fish in this boot. But why his boot, when every single person on the boardwalk left his boots by the front door? They had probably ninety boots to choose from, and it would take some guts to choose the boot of Axel Hagerman.

No. This wasn't a joke.

Axel poured in the boiling water, careful that the boot didn't bend over and empty a load of scalding water onto his socks.

When he was young—he didn't remember how young, but just starting school—somebody stole his lunch box, took his lunch, and replaced it with a bear's paw. People find bear paws sometimes. Dogs bring them in from hunters' gut piles. He would never forget opening his lunch box, hungry for the sandwich that would be there, and finding instead that paw. A big furry hand that ended abruptly in a trail of tendons and broken bone. A bear paw is a terrible thing—not the claws so much, even though they're scary—but the monstrous puffy black pads. They are rough as sandpaper, and thick as moose hide, which makes sense, and you think it's one thing to be slashed by claws, clean and neat, but what a bear could do to your face with the roughness of the pads! Take your cheeks down to bone. Axel shook the paw into the tide and sat on a rock under the school all during lunch period, so no one could see that he didn't have anything to eat.

That was the worst part of it, that he didn't have anything to eat, and if he had gone home, Mrs. Hagerman would have said, "Do you think halibut sandwiches grow on trees? Go back and find the person eating it and take it back." She would have been right, because there wasn't extra bread on that seiner, and you can't make halibut out of thin air. So he didn't tell anybody how hungry he was, and one good thing he can remember is that he didn't cry then. Not one sniffle. He wanted to throw away the lunch box too, and tell Mrs. Hagerman he accidently dropped it and the tide carried it away, but he wasn't a liar and that was the other good thing.

When school was over and all the kids and the teacher had gone home, he took the lunch box into the school bathroom, locked the door, and washed it and washed it until it smelled like raw metal. That's when he cried, but that was okay.

Axel poured the boiling water out of his boot and went back to scrubbing and scratching. And here's the part that got him. Whoever put the fish in his boot took the trouble to catch a sculpin, pry open the sculpin's mouth, and stuff in the whole tail of that salmon. It looked like the little fish was swallowing the big one. This was a message. Axel knew a message when he saw one. A small ugly thing has got you gutless creature by the tail.

That's what they were saying. This was not a joke. This was a threat. That takes some guts, to threaten Axel Hagerman. He smelled again at the boot and went back to scrubbing.

He never learned who stuck the bear paw into his lunch box, even though he watched people carefully to see who was laughing at him. But he would find out who left him that dead fish.

Who are my enemies? He ran names through his mind, making a list. Who's jealous of me? Who have I fired lately? Who hates my projects? Who loved Kenny? Who have I outmaneuvered? Who have I ruined or driven out of town?

It turned out to be a long list. Axel crossed the kitchen and locked the back door. First thing, he needed to protect himself and his family. This was a blood threat. He needed a security guard. Somebody local, with his ear to the ground. He ran the names of possible hires through his mind. It was pretty much the same list as the enemies list.

War games can wear a man down. If you keep looking over your shoulder to see if somebody's going to stab you in the back, you can't look forward, can't get anything done. He knew he needed to outsource that job, get somebody to watch his back. Rebecca said his work was making him brutal, but that was a woman speaking. He had to remember to take everything she said with a grain of salt. "Brutal" she had said—actually, more than once. That was hardly fair.

"A rapist," she had said when he got back home the night somebody notched his pilings. "You can rape the mountainsides. You can rape the channel. You can rape the whole beautiful town. But you will not rape me."

Axel slumped into a kitchen chair and looked around. He could hardly recognize his own kitchen without windowsills messy with pansies and counters buried under egg cartons spilling dirt and whatever sprouts. You can't rape a mountainside. That is illogical. He would have told her that, except it would have been a waste of time, trying to reason with a woman. Rape is where you say, I'm going to take something that you don't want to give me, and I'm going to take it whether you want me to or not. It's sort of like armed robbery. But the mountainside doesn't say no, I have a headache, or no, you can't have these trees. The mountainside doesn't say a damn thing. A mountain doesn't think like a mountain or anything else. It's a pile of dirt, for God's sake. Limestone and dirt. Granite. And when you take the trees, they grow back and the mountainside has its damn trees, even more than it had before, and more deer than it ever saw under the closed canopy. Besides which, if the mountainside loved you, which let us presume for the sake of argument it *said* it did and *promised to forever*, it would *give* you the trees. It would want you to have whatever you wanted. You can't rape someone, if they really love you.

Axel stood up, tucked in his shirttail, and put on his dress shoes. Let it go. There is no reasoning with her. He shouldn't have torn off the buttons on her nightgown. That wasn't nice. He knew better. That wasn't who he was. But she should know that wasn't who he was. She should know him better than that. He was sorry, but she should know he was sorry.

And then, after Kenny got himself dead, she called him a killer. But was he a killer? She was throwing her clothes into Meredith's old red wagon, and he was trying to tell her. He was *sorry* Kenny was dead, he would *never* have killed him. He didn't do it. He didn't do anything. All he was trying to do was run a business, and is that a crime? "Where are you going?" he'd asked her. "I'm going where I'm safe." But she was safe with him. What's he supposed to do? He was trying every way he knew how to do what he was supposed to do, which is make her happy and keep her safe. He was trying every way he knew how. She should know, he was trying every way. All he wanted was for her to be safe and happy. All he wanted.

He sat at his kitchen table, put his face in his hands.

All he wanted was for his girls to be safe and happy. He was trying as hard as he could. And wouldn't they love him for that, how hard he tried?

He wiped the dishcloth around the sink, wrung it out, blotted his face, and hung the cloth over the faucet. He didn't need to wipe up the water on the floor. He'd already soaked it up in his socks. After he'd straightened the kitchen and locked the back door, Axel walked out onto his porch. He tugged at the front door to make sure it had locked behind him and made his way toward the office of Good River Products. Howard was sitting on the bench above the ferry dock, resting in the sun. Axel stood in front of him. That forced Howard to stand up. They walked together to the office without saying a word.

Once he'd closed the door to the office, Axel told Howard about the fish in his boot.

"We've got an enemy," Axel said, surprised at how good it felt to say *we*. "To protect ourselves and our work, we need to think this through very carefully." Axel studied Howard.

Howard was looking sharp in his brand-new Good River Products jacket. He clamped his hand over his mouth and closed his eyes. He bowed his head and shook it slowly back and forth.

"Ugly situation."

"Absolutely. Ugly.

"We need a security guard. Be best to have somebody from Good River Harbor, somebody the people trust. Who do we have?"

Howard sobered himself up and considered. He cocked his head and considered again. There was a lot of considering to do.

"Well," he finally said. "Tick McIver needs a steady job." He put his hand back over his mouth and kneaded his cheek.

"Oh for God's sake, Howard," Axel said. "Right, Howard. Exactly right. I'm going to hire the guy who probably hates me the most, hire the guy whose son sneaks around with my daughter, the best friend of the guy everybody thinks I killed. Hire this guy to protect me and figure out who's messing with me, when he's probably the one, and if he isn't, he knows who is. Tick McIver, security guard. Right."

There was silence in the Good River Products office then. On the roof, two young ravens hollered back and forth.

"Yikes," they said. "Yow."

But the two men just stared at each other across the desk.

"Howard, that might be the best idea you ever had."

"Put a guy on payroll, you own him."

"I tell him what to do, and if he doesn't do it, I fire him and his family doesn't eat. 'Find a way to put a stop to this vandalism,' I'll tell him, 'and you'll keep your job.' Won't that put him between a rock and a hard place."

"A very large rock and a very hard place."

"You go hire Tick, Howard. I don't want to talk to the guy. And put an engine on his half-drowned skiff. He might need it."

September 18

HIGH TIDE		LOW TIDE	
10:33am	12.4ft	3:45am	3.3ft
10:16pm	13.2ft	4:17pm	5.6ft

Axel sat on the edge of his desk so he could look down on Nora, who was perched on a folding chair backed against the wall of the Good River Products office. He poured himself a cup of coffee, gestured in Nora's direction with the pot.

"No thanks."

He set the pot down and took a thoughtful gulp.

"You're a pretty girl, Nora, and you live by your conscience, just like I do," he said. "I admire that. You speak your mind, and I admire that too. In a different world, we could be a team."

It was sort of sweet, really, the meeting she had called, Axel thought. Her first mistake was agreeing to meet him at his office. That shifted the balance of power right there, him sitting on his desk, her clinging to a chair like a robin about ready to fly out the window. Her second mistake was that she didn't have a bargaining position. She didn't hold a single card. Under those circumstances, Axel was moved to tell her the truth, and he did. He wanted her to understand that he was not a bad or stupid man.

"I'm sorry about blocking the salmon," he said. "I really am. I like to watch salmon spawning as much as the biggest eco-freak. If I thought I would be hurting salmon populations, I'd shut down. But my operation isn't going to hurt the population. It's not like there aren't other rivers and other spawning beds up and down the channel. No way we're going to run out of rivers. That's like saying Antarctica is going to run out of igloo ice."

Nora stared at him, openmouthed. That wasn't Nora's most becoming expression. Axel smiled. He hadn't really meant to throw her off-balance like that. She seemed to be thinking hard.

"That's good to know," she said. "So okay. The point is that there has to be some way to make a living off the land without wrecking it. There has to be some way to take what the land gives us, and give back what it needs to be even healthier—the way the salmon do, that way. Our job—you and me, working together—is to imagine how to do that."

"Salmon give back by dying," Axel said. "You volunteering?"

Ooh, that was nasty. Axel tried again.

"Nah, just joking. Tell me what you have in mind." He really was trying, but he did not get that Nora Montgomery.

"Okay, so here's an idea." Nora pulled at her ponytail, and Axel had the impression that she was really trying too, in her muddled way. "You go ahead and put a small dam on the river. You pull water out winter and summer. But when the silver salmon come in to spawn in the fall, you leave the water in the river, open the dam, and let them swim upstream. In the spring, you open the dam again, to let the fingerlings run out to sea."

Axel let the room refill with silence before he answered.

"That puts me at half capacity," he said.

"Which is more than you need to make a living," she said.

"I don't want to make a living." Axel gazed at her over the rim of his cup. "I plan to make a killing." He leaned back and chuckled. But when he saw her face, he froze.

"You've already made one killing," she said quietly.

"Now that's uncalled for."

"Unless you count the bear cub, and that makes two."

"Now that's enough." Axel stood up.

"Of course, if you count the salmon . . ."

"That is the end of this discussion."

"That is the beginning," she said. She stood up, which forced Axel to look up to her.

"Is that a threat, because if it is . . ."

"It is not," said Nora. "It's a warning."

Axel threw his hands up in mock dismay.

"It took God a whole week to make this world," Nora said. "He likes it, said lots of times that it was good, and it was good, and it was good. If I came to work every day and plotted how to wreck God's good world, I'd be keeping my eye out for lightning strikes. Earthquakes."

She walked out the door, not even bothering to close it behind her.

"Fire and brimstone." She threw that one over her shoulder, and something in her voice made Axel follow her out and watch her stride down the pier.

As soon as he closed the door, he slammed his cup on his desk. Coffee sloshed on his blotter.

"The beginning," he repeated. "The beginning of what?"

He crossed to the window.

Calm seas. Flat calm all the way across the channel. A few squalls out toward the narrows, but nothing that would reach him there. God on his side. Axel fell into his chair, then abruptly returned to the window. *A day this calm makes me think maybe life is playing me for a sucker,* he thought, *pulling away from my punches to throw me off-balance. Wouldn't that be something. Sun coming out. Water calm. Nora weak as a wienie. Muhammad Ali ducking so fast, George Foreman falls on his face.*

As he stared at the water, a black knife blade rose out of the channel, sliced a long gash through the surface, and sank. The wound slowly closed. Then another black knife blade, closer than the first, cut a long incision through water that winced and ran. Water shrank away as another knife rose slowly up and began to slice the surface. Gulls screamed. They swarmed to feed in the open wounds. And then there were five black blades, each as tall as a man, cutting the channel into strips. They veered suddenly in Axel's direction, and he fell back from the window.

Dropping into his chair, he forced a laugh.

He'd seen killer whales a thousand times before. They always appeared like that, those dorsal fins like scimitars sticking out of the water, and the rest of the great beast hidden, the way an army of cavalrymen thrust their swords over their horses' heads until they seem to be a sea of swords advancing. Nothing to be frightened of, unless you're a coho salmon, and then you're good as dead.

Axel went back to the window. There was nothing there, just the sea as flat as silver plate. Gulls floated, as if nothing had happened. The reflection of the mountains stood still, *as if nothing had happened.* The perfect peace of the calm sea. If Axel hadn't just seen them, he would never know there were huge black beasts circling their prey twenty fathoms down.

Suddenly restless, he walked out his gangway, gripping the deck rail, and looked toward the boardwalk. Somebody had a marine radio on at the other end of town. Axel could hear the urgent pattern of a man's voice. From down at the dock, a hammer echoed against a metal hull. Tommy mangled a song on the piano out at Nora's. Beyond that, there was only the quiet of the channel, and the purr of the Kis'utch waterfall.

How is this possible, that the sea can calm so quickly and completely? Events could engulf a man's hopes and plans—the way water closes the gap where a man has fallen through, the way the present closes over the past, the way death closes over life—and leave no trace at all.

Axel walked quickly back to his office, shut down his computer, turned off the lights, locked the door, and turned toward home. The head of a harbor seal rose from the calm sea. With red-rimmed eyes, the seal stared at Axel's retreating back. When Axel turned the corner to his house, the seal sank out of sight.

Who does she think she is, telling *me* what God does and does not like. God likes a man who loves his daughter and his wife so much that he spends his whole life providing for them. Who does she think she is? Who is she? Who . . . is . . . Nora Montgomery?

Axel swerved one hundred eighty degrees off course and bustled back to his office.

He opened the computer and then set about pacing around the desk while the machine took its sweet time to wake up.

Finally, *dink*.

He plopped into his chair and went to work, pudgy white fingers poking keys, reaching like inchworms for the letters, enter, search, scroll, enter. If she is planning some fire-and-brimstone thing, she'll have done it before, someplace else. Outstanding warrants. Pacific Coast? Washington? Oregon? Getting closer. No, dead end. Try this. Eco-terrorist. Federal. Closer. Closer, closer, no. Woman. Closer. Bingo. Logging action. That would be her.

She burned up a goddamned bridge.

Well, well, well. A bridge to a logging site. The face in the photo was hard to mistake. Forty-five minutes of searching and he was sure enough. Axel's white face puffed into a smile. He reached for the phone.

≈≈≈≈

"HELLO, BELLINGHAM D.A.? . . .

"Axel Hagerman, Good River Harbor . . .

"Yeah. Good River Harbor . . .

"Alaska. Doesn't matter where it is. Listen . . .

"No. Southeast. Listen . . .

"I don't know your stupid brother-in-law. Do you know how big Alaska is? Listen . . .

"For God's sake, will you listen to me? I've got your fugitive.

"Yeah! Now you listening?

"No, not the rapist, Goddamn it." Axel threw his pen at his desk.

"The eco-terrorist. The woman who burned down the bridge to keep the logging trucks from hauling out the Nooksack timber sale.

"Nooksack. Arson . . .

"Yeah, I'll wait."

. . .

"Yeah, that's the one. About five years ago.

"No, not blond. Her hair is so black you can hardly believe . . .

"Yeah, okay, blond. I'll be damned.

"Concert pianist? Hell, no. She can't play the piano any better than a five-year-old kid. Come on. Focus!

"Right! That's the one. I'd say five foot ten or eleven. I don't know. She's thin. Thirty? Thirty-five—I don't know. Eyes like a . . .

"Yeah. Fish! That's the one. How soon can you get a deputy up here, slap some cuffs on her, and get her out of my sight forever?

"No. She's not a flight risk. She's gotta stay right here, at least until the next piano tide.

"Piano tide. Right.

"Oh, for God's sake, because she has a piano with her, and you can't move a piano without a good high tide.

"Jesus Christ. Trust me on this. You can't move a piano until the tide lifts . . . Forget it.

"Look, just come and get her. I guarantee she'll be here.

"What do you mean, low priority?

Axel plucked at the top of his head.

"You Bellingham granolas soft on terrorism?

"You'd come and get her tonight if you knew she had another crime planned, I betcha.

"No, I don't have hard proof of another crime. Which side are you guys on?

"Okay. You guys just sit in the office down there, coddling criminals. I'm going to set a trap for this little lady. Catch her red-handed. I'll be back in touch."

Axel thoughtfully pushed the off button and walked to the window to scan for the killer whales. He, Axel Hagerman, father of one, husband of another, president and CEO of Good River Products, enemy of eco-terrorists, had a sudden new interest in killer whales.

≈≈≈≈

"ALLOW TO REMAIN on hair for twenty minutes, then rinse thoroughly." Lillian squinted at the Lady Clairol box to be sure of the timing. Did she get all her roots? She checked in the mirror. What a sight, hair dye glooped all over her scalp, and the dry hair sticking out in stiff curls.

"You look like a Brillo pad that just scraped a stew pot," she chided herself fondly. But it would be worth it. She loved the brightness of the new color they called "autumn auburn." Lillian was quite sure that she was the only woman in Good River Harbor who took the trouble to keep her hair looking young. She could name half a dozen women who didn't need to look so old, if they just took a little trouble. In fact, she could do this for them, start up a little color salon, if she got tired of the bar.

She shook out the plastic bag that came in the Clairol box and put it on like a shower cap over her hair, clipping it in place with a clothespin. Now she would get a fresh cup of coffee and wait. It was cozy in the bar with the rain pouring down outside.

And wouldn't you know. The door to the bar scraped open.

"I'm closed," Lillian yelled. She darted into the laundry room and cracked the door.

"That's okay." It was Nora with a couple of others. "We just want a cup of coffee," Nora called out. The people dragged their chairs up to a table, and one of them rustled around behind the bar, clinking cups and pouring coffee. "Anybody want cream and sugar?"

Apparently so. There was more rummaging and then Nora called out, "Lilly, where do you keep the cream?"

"There's a quart of milk in the beer cooler," Lillian yelled back, wondering how she was going to get her cup of coffee without showing her head.

"Leave the money on the counter." First things first.

"And pour me a cup and leave it inside the door to the laundry. Sugar. No cream."

It was warm in the bathhouse. Lillian settled her chair by the door and sipped the best coffee in any harbor bar in Southeast. She paid attention to the amenities that made a bar more than just a place to pour down drinks. She pulled an old National Geographic off the shelf. Gorillas.

Nora clumped back to the table with their coffee and they started in on the weather, which was not much to talk about—clouds sitting down on the mountains, rain showers blowing through now and then. Lillian knew Nora's voice. And Howard Fowler's. But it took her a minute to figure out the third voice. Rebecca Hagerman—this was a voice Lillian didn't hear much in the bar. Turned out to be kind of a committee meeting. Lillian drew her chair closer to the door.

"There's been too much trouble in this town," Nora was saying.

Lillian swallowed hard to keep from laughing out loud. Nora should know. She was about ninety-nine percent of the trouble herself.

"People taking sides. People getting hurt."

Yeah, getting killed must hurt, Lillian thought. Poor old Kenny.

"Well, I agree it's time for reconciliation." That was Rebecca.

Howard was not saying anything.

"Time for people to come together to celebrate the values we all share—a healthy community, people helping people, making music together, making a life in this beautiful place."

Lillian smothered another laugh. Were they reading off a script?

"Let's have a community potluck," Nora chimed in. "Everybody comes—the people in the town, Axel's employees out at the Kis'utch water plant site, Axel, everybody. Food, games, music."

"The values we all share." Lillian harrumphed in a fair imitation of Kenny. If he were hiding back there by the washing machine, he'd be bent over laughing. "*The values we all share. Let me count the things we value,*" he would say. "Dead fish. Foster's beer. And then there's, um, BIG dead fish. Um, LOTS of beer."

"And fireworks," Nora was saying.

"We get to know each other, eat and drink and dance and laugh together. It will be a healing time. The potluck will go down in history as the time when Good River Harbor came together again into a community."

"What do you need from Good River Products?" Howard said. It was the first thing he said, and Lillian thought it didn't sound like a very friendly response. What's the matter with him? You'd think he'd jump at this. It sounds like the end of the resistance to everything Axel's doing. He's the public relations guy; he ought to be encouraging that.

"I'll bring down my popcorn machine," Lillian hollered out, to set a good example, "and set up coolers of beer. Take a beer, put a dollar in the slot in the can."

There was a startled silence.

"That's great, Lilly," Nora yelled.

"See what I mean, Howard," Rebecca said. "Everyone pitching in."

"The only thing we need from Good River Products is buy-in, or co-sponsorship, or whatever, so we're doing this as partners," Nora said, "to get everybody involved. Get your employees to put their names on the sign-up sheets for setup and cleanup, running the games. Get them to come to the potluck. There can't be a single person left at the construction site. No one. Not even the night security man. That's the whole point. If you can empty out that place, get everybody to the potluck, that's all we need from you. That's essential. We'll turn out the townspeople."

Howard apparently was considering. He's a good man, that Howard, Lillian thought. Solid family man.

"I imagine Axel will want to leave a security man on site."

"Oh, the big spoilsport," Rebecca said. "Tell Axel not to spoil the fun. Let everybody come." Lillian was surprised by what Howard said next.

"We can do this. Maybe Good River Products can supply the fireworks. We're shipping in explosives for the quarry, probably be easy enough to get somebody to put a show's worth of skyrockets and aerial shells on the barge.

"And we got a new man on site, Mike Sorenson. Do you know him? He's a great guy. From Forks, Washington coast. And he plays the banjo like God would, if He gave up trumpets."

Rebecca nodded yes yes. "Mike Sorensen joins the band. We're going to need dancing music. Let's get some lists started."

Back in the laundry room, Lillian grinned at her reflection in the mirror—dancing music.

So then it was down to work. Nora wanted the party to be on the coho tide, the highest tide of the month, "to honor the natural world." Howard didn't see a problem with that. In fact, that could be a nice phrase for the press release. Coho Day. They'd need to round up blue tarps in case it was raining. Howard thought he could put a man on that.

"I'll need to check everything with Axel," he said. "Um. Unless you want to, Rebecca."

She shook her head, yes yes, but what she said was, "No, no. You go ahead." Didn't sound like Rebecca wanted to talk to Axel about anything. They made a list of the lists they'd need.

That was Lillian's twenty minutes, so she went back and rinsed out her hair. It looked pretty good, a lot lighter than mahogany, with nice reddish overtones. She towel-dried her hair, fluffed up the curls, tied on a fresh apron, and went into the bar to make more coffee.

"You're looking especially pretty today, Lilly," Nora said.

"A person can try," Lillian said, hoping Nora would get the point.

By this time, they must have had the plans all laid, because Howard was sitting back with his stocking feet on a chair. He's educable. First time he was here, he didn't know enough to take off his boots. He was telling Nora and Rebecca about his kid and his wife.

"Jennifer told Taylor I live in the movies with the whales and the bear cubs, so she wants to come to visit. I'd like that more than anything in the world, because if they could just see this place, they'd love it, and they'd never want to leave. It's not good for a man to live in one place, and his family to live in another. I mean, I can do it, because it's my work, but I think about my girls all the time. I asked Jennifer before to come, but she said, 'If I wanted to go to a place without hot water or indoor plumbing, I could go to India.' That sort of hurt, but I told her it's not like that, it's beautiful and you can always heat the water and Lillian has hot-water showers. But now I'm thinking, invite them for the Coho Day party. Let them see what a real community is. Maybe Taylor could ride Tommy's bike, when he's not using it."

Howard was talking on and on about his kid while Nora made supportive noises and Rebecca looked sad. Pretty soon he was pulling out a photo of them all at Christmas. Poor guy. Lonely is his middle name. Howard Lonely Fowler, surveyor. Howard Pitiful Lonely Fowler. Howard Pitifully Hopeful Fowler. Lillian hoped his family came to town for the potluck. She hoped they liked it here. They'd probably add a little class to the place. Just as long as they didn't think they could take Kenny's cabin and fix it up. The town wasn't through remembering Kenny.

Lillian shook the coffee grounds into the compost bucket and added fresh to the pot. While water gurgled up through, she walked out the front door with the compost. A cold, gray day, sort of blustery, rain pouring down like Noah's flood. Standing under her eaves, she deadheaded the pansies, throwing the spent flowers into the sea. The nasturtiums were still blooming, but the plants were getting leggier and leggier. Summer was about done with. She gave each plant a shot of coffee grounds, thinking it might perk them up.

≋≋≋

HOWARD SAT ON the ferry-dock bench beside Tommy McIver. He reached over and patted down the crest of black hair that always riffled up from the back of Tommy's head. Tommy was wearing a T-shirt and jeans tucked into one boot and hanging over the other.

"You warm enough, Tommy?" Howard asked. Just because it wasn't raining at that particular moment didn't mean it was warm.

"Sort of cold," Tommy said, and skooched over until his side pressed into Howard's. Howard reached out his jacket and enclosed Tommy in its flap like a mother bird. They sat there together, absorbing each other's warmth, watching a seiner back out of the harbor in a cloud of gulls and diesel exhaust. It thrilled Howard, honestly, how much Tommy seemed to trust him and seek him out. Maybe Tommy knew that Howard was a father and thought that fathers can always be trusted, or maybe Tommy sensed somehow that Howard was as lonely as he was. "He's a half-breed kid," Axel had told Howard, "but still, he's smart and friendly—in an annoying sort of way."

"He's a kid," Howard had said back, "and he misses his mother." Sometimes Howard surprised himself, and this time, he had clearly surprised Axel. Howard reached down and tucked Tommy's errant pant leg into his boot.

"I'm going to piano lessons," Tommy confided, showing Howard his lesson book. "I already know how to play one song, and I'm learning another one."

"What song can you play?"

"'Ninety-Nine Bottles of Beer on the Wall.' Now Nora's teaching me 'Motorcycle Cops on Guard.'"

"Well, let's hear it," Howard said.

Tommy unfolded a cardboard representation of two octaves of piano keys and set it on his lap. Howard reached over, turned it right side up, and steadied it. With his hands on the drawings of the keys, Tommy moved his fingers up and down as if he were playing. Middle, pointer, thumb, pointer, middle, middle, middle. He sang at the top of his lungs.

Motorcycle cops on guard,
Chase the cars that speed.
Every driver must watch out,
Traffic laws to heed.
Stop on red and go on green,
That's the safest way.
Motorcycle cops on guard.
Laws we must obey.

"That's pretty good," Howard said. "Nora must be a good teacher." He wasn't sure how much the movement of Tommy's left hand had to do with the song, but the melody hand seemed right there.

"I practice on this," he said, "but it's more fun to play on a real piano."

"Tommy, what does that mean?" Howard ventured to ask. "Stop on red and go on green?"

Tommy looked surprised. He thought for a long time. "Some places, like if you go to Seattle where my mom is, there's red squares and green squares, like in a game," he said. "If you get on a red square, you have to stop."

"You are one very smart kid," Howard said.

"Yes," said Tommy, as he folded up his paper piano and gathered his lesson book. "I'm going to learn three more songs, plus my two, that's five songs that I can play for my mom when she comes home." He worked that out on his fingers to be sure. "It's going to make her really happy. 'Jingle Bells' is next. My dad's trading Nora for lessons." Tommy smiled up into Howard's face, as if this was the most wonderful thing in the world.

"That's the most wonderful thing in the world," Howard said, because it was. "What's Nora get in the deal?"

Tommy considered. "The first song, she traded for four dozen dead shrimp. I don't know about the next," he said. Then he was off, down the boardwalk toward Nora's.

Howard leaned back on the bench. He knew that before long, he would hear the broken notes of "Motorcycle Cops" vaguely and endlessly from the forest at the edge of town. He hoped Tommy's mom would come home soon. He really did. He hoped she liked the songs. And whatever Nora got in the deal, Howard hoped it was exactly what she wished for.

Howard pulled his pocketknife and a small block of maple from his jacket pocket. He was carving a baby bear for Taylor. He pressed the knife into the wood, using his thumb to guide the angle. It was hard for him to imagine that his Jennifer would want to move here from Bellevue, give up her friends and committees. But he'd been thinking about it more and more, especially if he kept getting promoted. He was already associate project manager, as well as community relations specialist. They could buy Kenny's cabin from Axel, raze it, and build a two-story log house with lots of windows framing that million-dollar view. Jennifer would like Rebecca. Maybe she'd like Nora—that was a harder call. Taylor could go to school over the tideflats with the twelve other kids. She could look out the window and see bears rolling boulders to find crabs on the beach, and then she'd believe him about what it's like to live in Good River Harbor. Jennifer had told Taylor that her father was living in the Discovery Channel, and sometimes he felt that he was, out there with the starfish and the whales.

He stretched out his legs in the dim sunlight and looked up and down the boardwalk—a sweet, soft, silver day. Fireweed had blown to seed, leaning out over the tide. When Jennifer and Taylor came to visit, he hoped it was a day like this. The sun had brought everybody out. Mrs. Chambers wobbled by on her bicycle, coming from Lillian's bathhouse with her hair wrapped in a towel like a turban. The postmaster was practicing the guitar, sitting in the doorway of the post office. Down the way, Jeanne and Dave Berkowski and all three of their grown kids were sitting on stacks of lumber, leaning over cigarettes in the sun. The ravens were plonking and belling, gulls muttering. Dogs flopped on the boardwalk as if they'd sprung leaks. It surprised Howard how much he felt at home.

Things were even settling down at Good River Products. Axel had a lead on a new bear, a young male that was nosing around the dump at a hunting lodge out of Eagle Cove. "That bear's either headed for a bullet or salvation at the shelter," Axel said. The guy was starting to believe his own propaganda. Now that was the sign of an effective communications person. Axel had pulled a couple of men from the water-bottling job to do the repairs to the Bear Shelter pavilion and the cedar cistern. No need to root out the flowers Rebecca planted there, he told Howard. Let the bears do that job. What a guy.

A column of smoke rose from the slash pile at the construction site across the channel. Mike had his bulldozer moving rock fill across the riverbed. Howard could see it backing and pushing, trailing black smoke, hear him shift gears. The water-selling project was still on schedule. And what gratified him most, as community relations specialist, was that all the muttering in town about freeing the bears or saving the river for the salmon seemed to have died down, now that Kenny was dead and gone. That sure knocked the stuffing out of Nora and Tick. They didn't say much to each other, at least not when Howard was around them. And Nora seemed on edge and somehow thinner, although she was thin to start with. Now that Rebecca was boarding with her, Nora seemed to be doing a lot less agitating and a lot more of what the women in Good River Harbor like to do—berrying and making jam and collecting everybody's old wine bottles, setting up to brew black currant wine. And now the potluck, the party that would celebrate a new start.

Boats creaked on a low swell in the harbor. The spars and masts swayed. Ordinarily, Howard would need to be out at the work site. But Axel hadn't called him in yet, so he wasn't in any hurry. Through half-closed eyes, he watched Tick paddle a canoe from behind Green Point. Crossing the inlet, he nosed into the bank at the far edge of the clamflat, pulled out a chain saw and a peavey, then hauled the canoe onshore and hid it behind the rocks.

≈≈≈

REBECCA AND TICK scrambled like bears toward the Kis'utch Ridge, holding on to roots and pawing over rotted logs and head-high ferns. Tick carried a chain saw and a peavey that would lever logs around. Rebecca carried an axe, using it as an awkward alpenstock. Her foot slid off a root that skidded her down a muddy chute. Reaching to stop her slide, she grabbed the stinging spines of a devil's club, snatched her hand away, and grabbed for the rootball of a lady fern. It came loose from the duff, spraying hemlock needles that stuck to her cheeks and hair. She came to rest, lodged against a stump.

"You bust anything, Mrs. Hagerman?" Tick looked back over his shoulder.

Ever since Kenny's funeral bonfire, Tick had been Rebecca's friend, crazy as that was, Tick and Axel's wife. Maybe she had been a little bit drunk on Lillian's brandy, or maybe funerals are the sort of occasion when you want to clear the air, not let your sins linger around you for everybody to smell, like cigarette smoke in your clothes. For whatever reason, Rebecca had walked over to where Tick sat on a log watching the last flames flutter in the coals. She perched next to him. When he inched away from her, she inched after him, until it was stay put or fall off the butt end. She remembered the hellfire smell of that moment, probably spruce smoke and dioxin from Kenny's plastic poncho.

"I'm really sorry, Tick," she had said. "I'm sorry about how rotten Axel has been to you. Giving you really crummy jobs and then laying you off all the time, so you're always struggling, and you're always depending on him. And I'm sorry that all I've done is try to make that look pretty, decorate it all up and pretend that's the way the world was meant to be. That makes me even worse than Axel. How can I make it up to you and all the other broken men?" Thinking about it later, she decided there was in fact a bit of brandy in that question.

"Here's to me and all the other broken men," Tick had said quietly. For a long time, he rubbed his thumb against the palm of his other hand, stroking his life line. What he said next was like a blessing, the cool of holy water on Rebecca's forehead.

"You're not the stink-bait in that pot, Mrs. Hagerman," he said.

Rebecca had looked at him closely then, maybe for the first time, certainly for the first time in the golden light of brandy. His cheeks were pink under his orange beard and his eyes an astonishing blue. His shoulders were broad and his hands were huge and capable. She wondered what it would be like to be touched by those hands, what those hands would feel like on her hair, on the back of her neck.

"I'm not sure," she said back. "I haven't done anything to check Axel. He was rotten to fire you for what Davy did—and Meredith. They were in it together. And if he hadn't put a bear in the cedar cistern, it couldn't have charged out and killed Kenny." She had known she was babbling, but it pressed on her, that she was the only one who could move Axel off course, and she hadn't.

"Aach," Tick said. "We'll fix up Axel, we broken men. You ever see a halibut corpse after the sea-fleas and bent-back shrimp get done with it?"

She hadn't.

"It's a skeleton as spidery and white and clean as the day it was born."

Tick stopped climbing and looked back down the mountainside. He called again. "You okay, Mrs. Hagerman?"

"Nothing broken," she answered. "Everything covered with mud."

"Well, then, get a load off," he said.

She grabbed her hair in a fist and stuffed it down the back of her rain-coat. She retied her long skirt in a knot at her waist and started up the slope again. She could not have been wetter. Clouds dropped rain. Thim-bleberry leaves and sword ferns batted rain into her face. The waterfall drenched the air with fine fern-scented rain. But every step gained up the mountain made her feel lighter on her feet and clearer in her mind. The air was sweet in ways she had forgotten, broken bracken ferns, and when she crawled under the trunk of a giant tree that had fallen across the slope, she caught her breath at the fragrance of decaying cedar and hemlock boughs broken by snow. Tick had disappeared above her, but it was easy to follow the trail of gouged dirt he left in his wake. Every once in a while, he yahooed, and Rebecca yahooed back, not knowing if he was calling out to frighten bears from the track, or to make sure she was still following along.

Before long, Rebecca scrambled over the shoulder of the ridge and found herself on the easy walking of a rock ledge. Then suddenly, they were at the place Nora had said she would recognize by its beauty—a place where the Kis'utch quieted in a tarn before it pushed through a narrow rock opening and plunged off the mountain. She would help Tick build a splash dam here.

Their little act of God team had been careful not to attract atten-tion. They never let anyone see all three of them talking together, and Rebecca was careful not to be more than just polite to Tick in public. That morning, she had wandered through town with a berry bucket, chatting with her neighbors, then turned conspicuously into the forest. Once she was out of sight, she cut downhill back to Nora's house. Nora called Tick on the marine radio, saying she was cutting firewood and needed help with a chain saw that was acting up. Since everyone in town eavesdrops on radio chatter, no one was surprised when Tick walked up the board-walk with his chain saw and turned toward Green Point. Hidden from town by the point, Rebecca crossed the channel in Nora's yellow kayak. Tick followed in her canoe.

The rainclouds scattered. On the ridge, Rebecca stood with her face to the breeze, taking in the sudden space of it, the vast sky falling onto the rocks. The morning sun flared on muskeg ponds that reflected spruce copses and mountaintops. Between the bogs and rocky outcrops, plants grew low and springy, forced by the winds to hunker down, forced by the frost to spread every leaf flat to the rays of the sun, and who knows what forced them to bear fruit? But every plant, the mountain blueberry, the bog cranberry, the kinnikinnick, was flush with berries. Every berry held a drop of dew, and every drop of dew held the sun in its slipping grip.

When Rebecca looked down toward Good River Harbor, she saw only clouds heaped like pearls. She knew that somewhere under there, neighbors rewired radios or corrected children's spelling, looking up only to grumble at the foul weather. They seemed far away and unreal, as if, when Rebecca stopped imagining them, they would all dissolve into the drizzle, hallooing as they lost color and faded away. She pitied them, that under the fog they had no idea there was a heavenly blue sky just a hundred feet straight up.

Her heart beat in her ears, and whether it was the altitude or the astonishment of being in this place, she did not know. What would Axel say if he knew she was going to help blow out his project? The likely answer made her catch her breath. What would he think of her if he could see her here, standing on a mountain ridge with an axe in her hand?

On a fallen log, a pine squirrel squeaked an alarm call and leapt for cover.

I wish he could see me now, she thought, with mud in my hair. I am strong in ways he never could imagine. I have friends who trust me. I have hard work that I believe in. I do what I think is right. Who is brave enough to rip the nightgown off such a woman?

Rebecca stood on a boulder, spread her arms, and turned like a prayer wheel. Around and around she turned. Every turn was a prayer for the chance for a new beginning. Her boot slipped off the boulder and she had to throw herself into the grasses to keep from rolling an ankle. She sat in the blueberries, laughing.

"You okay, Mrs. Hagerman? Jeezus. You looked like Julie Andrews dancing up there on that rock, except you got mud on your pinafore.

"*The hills fill my heart with the sound of music.*"

Singing in an appalling falsetto, Tick pinched out his pant legs like an apron and pranced around. Rebecca giggled and then she was singing too, and she was spinning again.

"*My heart wants to sing every song it hears. My heart wants to beat like the wings of the birds that rise, from the lake to the trees.*"

Tick laughed and went back to work. His chain saw sang against a hemlock. His voice roared along with the saw. "*Like a lark who is learning to pray.*"

Rebecca dropped onto the rock and studied her hands.

"Listen to me, Axel," she whispered. "I will send you trials. I will not sleep in your house. I will cram dead fish into your boots. I will strip you of art and flowers. I will wash away your dam. I will make you afraid. I will take away one thing after another until you figure out what you can live without, and what you can't. And then you'll know how to love your family."

She raised her head.

"It's glorious up here, Axel. Why have we never seen this meadow?"

That small cirque held all the beauty and sorrow of autumn, a few yellow leaves on wind-stunted willows, cottontop grass, horsetails beaded with rain, the seedpods of wild iris and penstemon. The stream passed under moss pillows and spilled through cascades of hanging bells gone to seed. There behind the ridge, Rebecca couldn't hear heavy equipment moving rock. When Tick turned off the chain saw, the silence was a holiness she almost remembered—water flowing onto rock and the stillness of the mountain. The words she wanted to say to Axel tumbled through her mind.

We'll come back here when it's over, Axel. You'll sit beside me and never once think about how you could market the meadow. You'll think about how beautiful it is, and how strong I am, and how blessed you are, to be in this place with the woman you love. We'll tell the story of the flood God sent into the valley to save your soul.

We will make love then. It will be awkward, our rubber raincoats squeaking and sticking together. We will laugh and tug at the endless layers. "Is there no end to this tugging and pulling?" you will moan. "Is there any way to pull off a boot but to hop and yank?" But then our clothes will be in a pile on the blueberries and we will stand naked in our woolen socks. You will stroke my hair away from my cheeks and hold my face in your hands, using your thumbs to wipe the dew from my eyelashes, and you will say—maybe you mumble this into my hair—you will say, "We can find a better way, Rebecca. There has to be a better way." And we will make love in the thin air, with the valley dropping out from below us, and the ache of grief will expand in your heart—every mortal loneliness, every broken plan, the terrible danger to every child—until your heart bursts. And when you lay back in the blueberry bushes with my body melted into yours, you will be sobbing. I will stroke your face and shush you.

The pine squirrel chirred. Rebecca jumped and then laughed at herself. She sure could spin a story, weepy enough to make even herself cry. Ought to be a romance writer. Make some money. Rebecca blew her nose, and then she went to work. She hooked her axe over a branch and dragged the tree to a growing pile at the opening in the rocks.

≋≋≋≋

"I DON'T GET it, Ranger," Davy whispered. "I really don't get it. Mrs. Hagerman climbing to the Kis'utch Ridge with my dad? Why isn't she picking berries and making wine with Nora? What are they doing, dragging those little trees over by the creek? My dad does lots of weird things. But this is weirdest. Dad and Mrs. Hagerman? Cutting down trees and piling them by a creek? Is it going to be some kind of garden hut?"

Ranger evidently didn't get it either. He kept close to Davy and whined.

Davy grabbed his muzzle and whispered in his ear. "Better be quiet, Ranger. Last thing I need is for them to know I've followed them." He actually didn't really follow them. He'd been sort of keeping an eye on Mrs. Hagerman lately, weekends and after school and such, making sure she was safe, thinking he'd show Axel he was responsible after all. Meredith's mom didn't always make good decisions. Like who would go berrypicking without a bear spray? When Davy saw her heading out like that, unprotected, he got his dad's rifle and called Ranger to follow him, and they walked into the forest behind her, keeping their distance. In case she needed help. Ranger was the world's best dog, and once he understood that Davy had inherited him from Kenny, he heeled close and minded. He was brave, and he would let Davy know if there was a bear around, and then Davy would feel sorry for that bear.

But the thing is, Mrs. Hagerman didn't go into the huckleberry patch behind the post office. She started that way, but then she circled around through the forest and came out at Nora's. Davy and Ranger almost got found out then, because Chum came bouncing into the bushes where they were hiding. Nobody even noticed. That proved Davy's point: Something could be following Mrs. Hagerman, and she wouldn't even know it.

Davy couldn't hear what was happening at Nora's. They were talking real quiet. Since when does Nora talk quiet? She's always yahoo this and yahoo that. Davy was thinking, this is so weird. And then Nora went back in the house, and Davy crept around to the bay, where he could watch Mrs. Hagerman paddle her kayak across the channel. She didn't have a float coat or anything.

Ranger and Davy snuck back to the dock and got his dad's skiff. That was a pain, having to row that old thing, but close to town, he didn't want the noise of the outboard motor Howard had loaned them. Once he'd rowed past Green Point, he started up the engine and crossed the channel.

A kayak and a canoe were hidden in the trees at the far edge of the clamflat. Two boats. That threw him. And two sets of boot prints, one big and one little, going up the mountain. He took a different route, so they wouldn't see Ranger's tracks or his. It wasn't easy, climbing up roots with a gun, but Davy could do it, even with his shoulder only just healing, and it wasn't far. When he heard voices, he dropped behind a rock and peered over. The first person he saw was Mrs. Hagerman. The second person was his dad.

A pine squirrel chirred in alarm.

"Sit," he whispered urgently to Ranger. "Stay." The commands clearly bewildered Ranger, but he did as he was told.

Davy watched Rebecca and Tick for a long time, but they didn't do anything, like kiss or anything. They just hollered and sang to each other and pranced around and joked and felled sapling alder, like they were best friends. Are they best friends? And who is Julie Andrews? And why does she go to the hills? What do they need to build, way up there?

Finally, Davy signaled Ranger and they crept away, so he could get the skiff tied up at the harbor before his dad came in from pretending he was helping overhaul a chain saw. Why would he do that?

By the time his dad came striding up the boardwalk from Nora's, carrying an empty jerry can, Davy and Ranger were hanging out on their front porch. Davy looked carefully at the sawdust on his dad's pants and the mud on his boots. Tick looked carefully at Davy.

"Well. Took all afternoon, but we finally got Nora's chain saw going. Gummed-up carburetor. Had to take the whole thing apart." Ranger wandered up and sniffed Tick's boots.

Davy didn't know what to say, so he didn't say anything.

I should ask my dad about what I saw, he thought. But then he'd know I was spying. I would tell Meredith if she would ever hang out with me at school, always running off with the girls, giggling. She's smart and she would know what's up. I wouldn't ever tell Tommy anything. He'd just blab. Maybe Howard Fowler—he's a nice man who knows things. Maybe I should ask him. Probably everybody knows about this but me. But it might be a mystery. Maybe I've discovered a dangerous secret and I shouldn't tell a soul. Just Ranger and me, protecting Meredith's mom's secret. I better keep my eyes open.

ANNIE KLAWON CHECKED her watch. Almost eight o'clock in Seattle and still Tick and the boys hadn't called. They almost never called on time, but a half hour made Annie wonder. Every Friday, she got off the bus from work and walked to University and Fourteenth. There was a pay phone in a booth next to the coffee shop on the corner, and some plastic chairs where she could sit under the awning and be sheltered from the rain while she waited. At exactly seven thirty Alaska time, Tick was supposed to gather the boys at Lillian's and call the Seattle pay phone.

Sometimes, there would already be someone on the phone when Annie got there. Worse, sometimes a person would walk up just at 7:28 and punch in a number. Then Annie would pace, trying not to listen, while some balding professor argued endlessly and unkindly with his wife over whether it should be Italian or domestic Parmesan cheese he picks up on the way home, or a high school girl explained in pained detail what a dork her mother was, what a complete jerk, to yank her cell phone, which she didn't have a right to do, and that's stealing, and as soon as she ended this conversation, she would call the police and report her mother, who was a thief. Worse yet, some people spoke gently to their lovers—"Tell me how you will love me"—as Annie ground her hands into her ears.

But today, there was no one on the phone and still the phone did not ring. Rain was falling hard. Already the day had turned dark. In the glare from shop windows, red leaves ran like rafts down the gutters. The yellow lines of the coffee shop's neon signs reflected in the windshields of parked cars. She turned her back to escape cigarette smoke that seeped from the noses of teenagers at the next table. Diesel fumes sank into a blue pool behind the Fourteenth Street bus. Annie caught the scent of woodsmoke from someone's chimney, and then the wind picked up, sending leaves spiraling, and she could smell the lively air of the sea.

At home in Good River Harbor, summer is over when the berries of the mountain ash turn bright red and the wind swings around from the southeast and the salmon come home. Coho salmon push up the Kis'utch River to the pool with the lavender bubbles. Highbush cranberries are ripe. Annie used to hike to clear-cuts with her cousins to gather the berries in five-gallon buckets. She gathered stink currants too. Every house would have a jug of stink currant wine fermenting behind the woodstove.

Eight fifteen.

When they call, she thought, it will be like always. She will talk to Davy first, who will answer all her questions in the same flat voice—he's great, his shoulder is great, things are going great. No, no news, no new clients for his guiding business. No, Dad couldn't get the outboard to run yet, but almost. Then Tommy will get on the line and talk and talk as if he were sitting on her lap—telling her about the playing-card clicker he made for his bike and singing "Jingle Bells," right on the phone. Tick will be last. He'll say he's doing fine and the kids are doing fine, the same old song, and then he will say, "Come home, Annie Klawon. I miss you. The boys miss you. We can make a living here."

If Tick didn't call in five more minutes, she would call Lillian's phone, but that would be a last resort because then she would have to pay for the call.

She went into the coffee shop and poured herself a glass of water. The air in there was hot and steamy. Water ran across the floor from umbrellas propped by the front door. Parents in three-hundred-dollar rain parkas leaned over their children at the counter, buying them a paper cup of cocoa on their way home from daycare on a rainy day. Annie brought the news section of yesterday's *Seattle Times* outside and tried to read it, but how can you read when you don't know where your boys are?

She dug for change and called Lillian's bar. It was Lillian who answered.

"Annie Klawon! It's good to hear your voice. All's well in Seattle?"

Just hearing Lillian's voice made her crazy with worry. "Where's Tick, Lilly?"

"I don't know."

"Where's Davy?"

"I wish I could help, Annie, but I don't know. Last I saw, Tick was over at Nora's with a jerry can of chain saw gas. I'm guessing he's cutting trees."

"At Nora's?"

"Yeah. He was. I don't know where he is now. I don't know about Davy. Haven't seen him today. Tommy's riding his bike up and down the boardwalk, happy as a clam. You shouldn't worry. Everything's going fine for them. Tick's been smoking salmon."

When the silver salmon come into the channel, skiffs troll slowly past the town. People pull in three, four coho, as many as will fit in the propane smoker on their back porch. While they brine the fillets, they soak alder chips in fresh water. Then they light the propane, put the pan of wood chips on the burner, load in the fillets, and soon the smell of warm salmon fills the air. It's smoky, sweet, and salty. When the salmon smoke sifts through the hemlocks and sinks onto the intertidal stones, there is no more beautiful smell in all the world.

"Have the sandhill cranes been flying?"

"Just a few, so far. I heard them bugling last night."

Annie Klawon had missed seeing the cranes last fall and the fall before that, sandhill cranes tangling their lines as they staged to fly south. They kettle into the sky before dawn, circling up and up, gargling like wet trumpets. She would not be there to hear them this year. She would not be there to lie in bed next to Tick, to hear him breathe, to hear rain on the cedar shakes, hear the sea rising under the house, hear the sandhill cranes flying home. She would not be there to know the woodbox was full and sweet salmon were smoking and the children were safely sleeping—to be warm under the quilt, to be slowly aware of coming light, to think of the first cup of coffee with Tick and a second cup with friends.

"Anything you want me to tell Tick?" Lillian was saying. She waited.

"Annie Klawon?"

There was a long silence on the phone.

Father, send me a carved canoe. Raven on the bow, beaver on the stern. Send me a canoe with a flying hull that will cut the waves and curl their froth into long gray feathers. Send it, Father, on the wind that lifts the cranes. Here is the sadness you told me would come.

"Annie, is there anything you want me to tell Tick?" Lillian's voice was a little softer than the first time she asked.

"Tell Tick I'm coming home. I'm coming home to stay."

If Lillian hesitated, Annie did not notice.

"That's a good thing, Annie Klawon," she said. "That's a really good thing."

September 20

HIGH TIDE		LOW TIDE	
12:03am	14.2ft	5:36am	2.0ft
11:58pm	15.0ft	5:58pm	3.4ft

Meredith stuck her head out her front door. "Shut up!" she yelled to Tommy and slammed the door shut. The kid was driving her crazy, riding his bike up and down the boardwalk in pouring rain, singing at the top of his lungs.

"All day, all night, angels watching over me, my lord. All day, all night, angels watching over me."

Every time he got to the end of the boardwalk, he screeched his bike to a stop and no matter where he was in the angel song, he yelled out, "Stop on red." Then he yelled, "Go on green," and off he sped. "When at night I go to sleep, angels watching over me."

Tourists thought that kid was cute. It made Meredith want to puke. They held up their cameras and shot videos while he went speeding by in his red sweater with his bed-hair sticking up. They gave him a dollar the next time he came by, and then he was singing and riding his bike and eating an ice cream bar he bought from Lillian. Tourists probably read in a guidebook that they should tip Indians if they're going to take their picture.

Tommy pedaled by again, this time practicing his syncopation, hitting the brakes on the short notes and stuttering through the song. "WATCH in' O ver ME."

Meredith opened the door again. "Shut up!" she shouted, and found herself looking straight into the broad face of Lillian Shaddy. Lillian was standing there in her Seattle raincoat, with a couple of damp curls sticking out under a blue cloche hat. She had pinned a corsage of yellow silk carnations to the collar of her coat, where they sagged under a load of rain. She had hot mitts on both hands, and she was holding out a pot.

"Hello, Meredith," she said. "I thought with your mother gone off, you and your father might like some salmon chowder." She paused, then added confidentially, "and a lady does not shout."

Of course a lady doesn't shout, Meredith thought, confused, but what does a lady do when somebody shows up at her door in hot mitts? Clearly something was expected of her, but this was a new problem for a house where very few people knocked on the door and the ones who did weren't coming to give her something.

"Thank you." Meredith said. Was that all you did? "Would you like to come in?"

That's what her mother would say, Meredith knew, but it wasn't what she wanted to say. She groaned when Lillian bustled right in the door and crossed to the kitchen to put the pot on the stove.

Lillian stood expectantly, dripping on the kitchen floor. Now what?

"Would you like a cup of tea?"

Lillian smiled encouragingly, as if Meredith had got her lines right in play practice, and she crossed the room to hang her coat on a hook by the door. The old woman tugged her sweater closed across her belly and held it tight. Meredith didn't like tea, and she didn't like talking to old people, especially not fat old women wearing lipstick, and she didn't like talking to strangers, which Lillian practically was, even though she'd seen her every day of her life, and she didn't like people telling her whether to shout or not, and she had no idea how she was going to get Lillian out the door again. But when Lillian sat down, put the cup to her pink lips, and asked, "How are things for you?" Meredith found that all she wanted to do was tell somebody, anybody, how things were for her, which was totally crappy.

"All I'm allowed to do in this town is go to school in the week, and look out the window on the weekend, and all I can see is this stupid kid and the broken-down cabin of a dead man. I'm practically a prisoner in this house. I wanted to move out to Nora's with my mom, but she's like, 'Oops, nope, no room, sorry—you're best off with your dad.' Work at the office, helping Howard Fowler all day Saturdays. Call about this bear, call about that bear, type up a news release about the new bear. And then I have to stay home all night. I only see Davy McIver out the window. I'm sick of him, too. He's started carrying a rifle through town and sort of swinging his shoulders like he's a big shot. Tourists take pictures of him, too, probably, going, 'Oooh wilderness, must be bears nearby. Even the half-witted teenagers are armed.'"

Lillian nodded, which made Meredith feel somehow good, that there was another human being who knew how pathetic her life was.

"Can you believe I listen to the marine radio for entertainment at night? How pitiful is that? Sometimes I get to watch a video on the computer at the office, but mostly it's just, 'Coast Guard sector Juneau, Coast Guard sector Juneau, vessel calling mayday please state your position.' Like you're going to be reading your GPS while you're sinking. Five eight glub. Then Nora calls on the radio—'Tick, come out to help me start my chain saw.' If Tick would just stay home, maybe his kid Tommy would have something else to do than disturb the peace. Teach him to change the sparkplug on a chain saw.

"My mom might think about coming home sometimes too, instead of all the time living with Nora. She even went to that funeral, where they barbecued Kenny on the beach. That was so gross. Came back smelling like greasy smoke and talking about redemption. 'Mom, you are gross,' I said. Dad was mad she went, but she said, 'From now on, I guess I will decide what I do.' Oooo. Sassy. Thought he was going to yell, but he seemed too tired."

Whoa. Maybe she shouldn't be telling Lillian all this, but Lillian didn't seem all that interested. Just went over and poured more hot water in her cup like she lived here.

"It's grim around here, dad's all grim, no flowers. Mom even took down the paintings in the house. Never said anything, just took them all down one day and stacked them in the corner. 'Not my room,' I said, and she said, 'Okay.' Maybe I will go to that boarding school in Sitka. Might be a cheerier prison than this one.

"'Be glad you have a job,' my dad says. 'You're not a prisoner. You're an employee, and you're better off than your friends, who are just hanging around being useless. And besides, you'll want to do well in school.' Like that's supposed to cheer me up."

Meredith stopped talking long enough to make sure Lillian understood how definitely not cheery that was. Lillian gave a twisty smile, then turned toward the door, where Tommy's song was going by again.

"All day, all night, angels watching over me, my lord."

Even in the house, there was no refuge from Tommy. The song swelled and faded like a train whistle. Meredith ran to the door, pulled it open and yelled.

"ALL DAY, ALL NIGHT, DEVIL CHASE ME OFF THE DOCK, MY LORD."

She knew she shouldn't have done that, not right after Lillian told her not to shout. But that would be good—she could see it so clearly in her mind's eye. *Stop on red!!! but he doesn't, and he and his dipshit bike and his ice cream bar just sail off the end of the wharf and disappear forever, nothing on the water but a glob of vanilla.* Meredith laughed out loud.

She saw Lillian grinning across the table—not at her, but at something farther away. The feeling was strong enough that Meredith looked over her shoulder to see what was making Lillian seem so soft and glad, but there was nothing there.

"I like you," Lillian said suddenly, as if she'd just decided. "You're funny. And you're pretty."

"You remind me of me when I was a girl."

Meredith stared in horror. No way. Could that be right? Had this town turned her, Meredith Hagerman, into somebody who would turn into Lillian? Things were even worse than she thought. She pulled at her hair, determined never to cut it, but maybe she was truly doomed.

"Well," Lillian said. "I didn't mean to stay. Thank you for the conversation and thank you for the tea." She picked up her mug. "And Meredith? You might think about tucking your hair into a ribbon so people can see your pretty eyes." Her chair made an obscene grunt as she pushed away from the table.

Meredith stood at the door and watched Lillian walk up their gangway on feet that seemed too small for the job. At the intersection with the boardwalk, she stopped and lit a cigarette. Lillian was probably crazy, that's all. That happens to old people, they get crazy and imagine crazy things. She turned to put away the tea mugs before her father got home and figured out she'd had company, and he would never in the world believe her if she said it was Lillian. And then she'd be in worse trouble than since Davy messed up so bad and got them both in deep shit—not like Davy didn't try to do the right thing and there's nothing wrong with that, but what a mess, and what a wienie.

And now this stupid mystery.

The day before, Meredith had opened her desk at school. There was a clamshell with a string sticking out. When she pulled on the string, out came one of Davy's stupid notes.

Dear Meredith, I have uncovered a mystery. It is about your mom and my dad. Meet me on the rocks under the school on the day of the potluck. I'll be there with my dad's skiff. Meet me exactly when the men go down to the dock to set off the fireworks—that way, nobody will hear the outboard. Wear boots and rain overalls. Your (very) good friend, Davy

Meredith snorted. Just because we spent the night together half dressed under the wharf, do we have to be very good friends?

She read the note again.

So what's he talking about, his dad and my mom? Not likely. And what's the mystery? The trouble is that Davy always tells the truth. So something's up. I already know my mom's not acting normal—Mrs. Barbecue Hagerman. Mrs. Black-Swamp-Gooseberry-Jam Hagerman. Mrs. Hum-All-the-Time-and-Don't-Even-Bother-to-Comb-My-Hair Hagerman. I don't know what's up. I just wish it wasn't Davy who's going to tell me.

≈≈≈≈

AXEL SAT DOWN at his desk, pulled out a piece of paper, and began to think. What did he know about Nora's next crime?

It would be arson. *ARSON*, he wrote on the paper. Everything fit. All the bottles Nora had been collecting for salmonberry wine? For all that bottle-gathering, he hadn't been seeing much berry-picking. And all the chain saw gas Tick had been carrying over to her place? For all that gas-carrying, he hadn't been hearing much tree-cutting. Molotov cocktails, for sure, and enough gas to soak the place. Hell, she practically confessed—be careful of fire and brimstone, she said. Axel had no idea what brimstone was, but he sure knew what she meant by fire. And then, arson seemed to be her MO, judging from her burning down that bridge.

The target would be the water-bottling site on the Kis'utch. *KIS'UTCH RIVER CONSTRUCTION SITE,* he wrote. Axel didn't have any doubt about this either. Nothing much happening at the Bear Shelter, and she'd already hit that. Nothing at all happening at the logging sites. No, it was the construction going on over at the Kis'utch River. She hated that as much as she loved the sloppy salmon. She practically confessed that too—coming with her plan to close down for the salmon half the time. She didn't get half, so she was going after it all.

The date? It would be during the potluck. *POTLUCK: OCT. 1.* This was a no-brainer too. God, either Axel was one very smart detective, or she was a dumb, dumb criminal. And that she was not. At first, he'd thought the potluck idea was jim-dandy. Hah—a jim-dandy way to empty out the site, so she wouldn't get caught and she wouldn't kill anybody. She might be an arsonist, but she wasn't a murderer.

But when? She would choose her time carefully. A smart arsonist would throw firebombs when the fireworks were blasting away. Nobody would know the difference. They would ooh and ahh at the spectacle, never figuring it out until the buildings were in flames and the trucks were exploding. Hah, Axel thought. Maybe he should go into crime, he was so good at planning it.

The co-conspirators? Axel stopped to think about this. He leaned back and crossed his feet on his desk. He felt good. Okay.

Number one? Tick. Big orange-beard himself. *TICK?* he wrote. Tick was an interesting problem. He was Axel's security guard and needed that job. That argued against his being a co-conspirator. He was in love with Annie Klawon and he doted on his boys. That argued against him. But he was an idiot and a horse's ass. That was a point in favor.

Number two? Kenny. Well, sure, Kenny was dead, but he might be the brains behind the whole thing. Axel made a note on the paper: *THINK LIKE KENNY.* Then he thought better of it, and crossed it off.

Anybody else?

Rebecca had been living at Nora's. She could be indoctrinated, like those women with Charles Manson, twisting their sweet souls to the dark side. *REBECCA?????* But no, she would be afraid of a plan like this. He crossed her name off the list, then went back and wrote a heart next to it, to make up for drawing a line through her name.

Axel walked over to the window. Rain tingled on the harbor. It watered down the bright paint on the sailboats and seiners and softened the spruce trees on the far side. Frayed ends of clouds draped over the mountains and dragged in the wind channels. Axel felt tingly too, that same shimmer. He wished he could tell Rebecca what a genius he was.

Now. What about Howard? No point in spoiling Howard's fun now. He was so excited about Jennifer and Taylor coming, he wasn't thinking straight anyway. Axel decided that at the very last minute, maybe fifteen minutes before the guys went down to light off the fireworks, he would tap Howard on the shoulder, tell him to corral Tick and get his ass over to the construction site. They would be there to greet Nora when she arrived. He would loan Howard his revolver, in case Nora got ugly. That would impress little Taylor—that first night in town, her dad corners a criminal.

Axel sat in his chair, folded his paper into a small square and tucked it in his "to do" file. Wind must have been picking up. The Green Point buoy moaned.

≋≋≋≋≋

BEST TICK COULD figure, lining up the post office flagpole with the Kis'utch River, he had about two hundred thirty feet under his hull. There ought to be at least five big halibut down in that hole, sitting there looking stunned. Which they always do, being fish. You'd think pretty soon one of them would want to bite a nice fresh herring with a hook stuck through its spine. Up and down, up and down, Tick lifted his rod and dropped it—bump the sinker on the bottom, lift it five feet, bump it, lift it. "Come on, sweetheart. Look at that herring, swimming up there, sinking, twisting onto its back, flashing its belly. That's one sick puppy, easy pickings. You tired of busted-up herring? I got a bucket of octopus tentacles I can feed you."

Tick needed a freezer full of halibut, and a smoker full of salmon too, before Annie Klawon got home. It might have been smarter to trade his splash dam for venison instead of songs, he thought, if Nora could've shot a deer without popping her dog one. Got himself kind of behind the old eight ball, making a dam instead of going after fish. Didn't exactly expect Annie Klawon to come home so soon. She said she was lonely for the smell of smoking salmon. That puts a man in a hard place, it does. "Yeah," Tick said when he called her back on Lillian's phone, "that's the world's best smell," and sucked deep, like he could smell salmon, and about choked.

"Come on, sweetheart. Don't just nibble." Ah. That hard sharp tug, and Tick tugged back, and then it was like being hooked to a Chevrolet. Pull up, crank away, pull up, crank away, lose ground when she makes a run for it. Pull up, crank away. Two hundred feet of line he had to bring in. This was a honey of a fish, dragging him out to sea. Crank, pull. Pull, crank. Finally he got her almost up, but when she saw the skiff, she took a run straight down, stripping line off his reel. "Son of a bitch." The reel handle spun around, cracking into his thumb. He grabbed the whole thing and started cranking again.

"I don't need a free bath," Tick had told Lillian.

But she said, "Yes you do, and so do your boys. I'm not going to have Annie Klawon come home to this."

Nora said, "Take this jam. You don't want Annie Klawon to come home to this."

Rebecca'd been over, dusting and sweeping. "So Annie Klawon doesn't have to come home to this."

Davy said, "Dad. What. Is. Going. On!"

"What Rebecca is doing is called 'dusting' and 'sweeping.'"

"Cripes," Davy said. "Why is Rebecca doing mom's job?"

That boy scared Tick, he had so much to learn about women. "Son," Tick had said, "Go out and get us a deer."

"I guess I will," Davy said, kind of sad, and took the rifle and off he went.

So Tick had been running around after halibut. He'd been thinking he could trade some for silvers. And Nora had promised to help him cut and haul wood, fill the woodshed. By the time Annie Klawon got there, she was going to think she landed in a movie set. Wilderness cabin, with strong, handsome husband with a freshly combed beard. Fine husband in a clean shirt, and two strong, handsome, clean children, one of 'em singing "Jingle Bells." There would be a clean oilcloth on the table and thimbleberry jam on the shelf. And all the empty whiskey bottles would be sunken in the clean blue sea.

Finally, the halibut was coming in. When Tick got it close to the boat, he gaffed it and dragged it up. But he clubbed it good before he hauled it in. Too many fishermen have been knocked out of their boats by a pissed-off halibut. Tick wouldn't pull the halibut into the boat until its eyes were crossed.

"My mistake was, I thought I didn't have anything to lose," he said to the fish.

What a jerk. And now I've got myself in a fix, where I really could lose everything—Annie Klawon, my boys, my new job, my cabin—just to save some salmon spawning beds. Or just to piss on my boss. Maybe that's what I'm doing. Or just to yuck it up with people I want to be my friends. Or to keep my promise to Nora, because wouldn't she twist my tail if I didn't. I don't know why I'm going to flood out Axel. "Forty-eight shrimp tails for one song," I said, and that was a good deal. "A splash dam for four more songs." Now when I hear Tommy sing and poke his fingers against that paper piano, I am so afraid I almost vomit. "Jingle Bells" puts me in a cold sweat. "Angels Watching Over Me" will be the end of the line.

The dam was holding. Rain was coming down hard on the old snow. The reservoir was filling fast. Their only weather worry now was that there would be more rain than they needed, more flood than they wanted. But there was nothing to do about that. God ran the rain-machine.

The potluck promised to be a foot-thumper. Tommy would play the cardboard piano and sing for his mother. Annie Klawon would laugh and cry and put her arms around Tick, about crushing him, and say, "It feels so good to be home. I'm never going to leave again. We'll make it work somehow." Tick's ear would be so full of her tears, he'd have to shake them out so he didn't go deaf, and he would love her so much he would almost turn inside out. But shit. When the finale of the fireworks finally went off, and that dam went, busting out Axel's water plant, Tick would lose it all.

Nora had said, "No, really. Everybody will think it's a natural event. Rain happens. Floods happen. Just ask Lillian"—which Nora had been doing, every time she caught Lillian in public. "Raining hard, isn't it, Lilly," she said. "Tell us about the flood that washed out Jimmy Pete's townsite in the fifties."

But Tick said, "Fat chance. Axel doesn't believe in natural events. He'll get some goons out here and they'll haul our asses off to jail. The guy's a dog's dick, but he's not dumb. All he has to do when that flood hits is look around on the ridge and see the new cuts."

"People don't make floods," Nora had said back. "Even Axel knows we don't have that kind of power."

"But we do. We can make that water rear up and roar."

Tick put his head in his great hands. I gotta tell Annie Klawon how much I love her. I gotta tell her what I'm thinking of doing, and make her understand that it's all a mistake, and I'm sorry, and I didn't know what I had to lose. But I'm more afraid of that than dying. I'm his security officer—I could go to Axel, tell him everything, stop the show, cancel the party, take out the splash dam when everything's froze.

But then wouldn't dead old Kenny haunt me, har har all night long, "Eunuch," he'd call me. "Chicken-shit. Har." I would have a job, be working for Axel, and I'd be ducking like a crazy man with a ghost chasing him around, hitting him over the head with a two-by-four. Har. But I would have a job, and I would have a family, instead of going crazy in jail for ten years and then wandering the streets in Seattle, muttering like a drunk. But I'm no snitch. I might be a horse's ass, but I'm no snitch.

Back down to the bottom with another dead herring. Bump down, haul up. Bump down, haul up.

September 29

HIGH TIDE		LOW TIDE	
4:44am	14.2ft	10:37am	3.6ft
4:41pm	16.2ft	11:45pm	0.8ft

oho Day was promising to be one of Good River Harbor's finest days—fair, so far, with just a little breeze. The ferry was only a few hours away. Howard checked his reflection in the post office window to make sure he hadn't missed a spot shaving. He wished there had been a way to get a haircut, but at least he was clean—two dollars' worth of clean in Lillian's bathhouse. He stretched his back and smoothed down the tie under his Good River Products jacket. He thought maybe he was broader in the shoulders than he had been when he came to town. He walked back to check the window again. Honestly, if other people were feeling the same high excitement he felt, the whole town was ready to explode. The little bear he'd carved for Taylor was in one pocket. In the other pocket was his present for Jennifer—an alder bracelet, two circlets he'd carved from the same piece of wood, entwined and inseparable. It made him feel shy, how hard he had worked on it and how much he hoped she would like it. Hard to believe that Jennifer and Taylor were on the ferry at that very moment, watching the mountains slide by, looking out for Green Point and their first glimpse of Good River Harbor. He had emailed Jennifer to keep an eye out for spouting whales and bears pacing at the mouths of the rivers. Taylor would be telling her teddy bear to look, pressing his plastic nose to the steamy window.

Annie Klawon, big Tick's wife, was on the ferry too, coming home. Home for good, Tick said. Tick had Tommy and Davy down in his skiff, bailing and sponging, shining up the Evinrude Axel had loaned him, while he walked back and forth on the dock, retying the bowline, retying the stern, coiling his lines. Then he'd had his boys down at Lillian's while Howard was there, scrubbing them up. It had been quite a man's meeting. And Tick was all scrubbed up too, his beard as smooth as if it had been steam-ironed. Lillian had made sure of that, sending him back into the shower with some hair conditioner. In their hungry waiting, Tick and Howard and the pacing bears could be brothers. Is there any more primal joy, any satisfaction more deeply seated in a man's soul, than his family safe and together?

The town's brass band was warming up. On this occasion, it would be a banjo, a penny whistle, and the accordion. They riffed all over each other and ran up and down the scales, *Alleluia the great storm is over / tis a gift / when the saints / and may the circle / all the live-long day / the Lord loves his own and your mother is here.*

It was as raucous as any orchestra converging on A. The band would be first on the dock to greet the ferry. Everybody knew the band was playing to honor Annie Klawon and to kick off the Coho Days celebration, but Taylor would think it was great, like she was the queen.

Howard had done everything he needed to do for the party. The potato salad he voted for won first prize, and who could resist a patriotic salad with the eggs dyed red and the potatoes blue? Mike and Sherm, Axel's men, had finished stringing blue tarps over the boardwalk, tight as fore-sails. It was a glorious, flag-snapping, high-clouds day, so they probably wouldn't need the tarps for shelter, but it never hurts, the way the weather changes. That was a piece of good luck—that Jennifer's first view of Good River Harbor would be on a sunny day. There would be time enough for her to get used to rain.

Axel splayed himself over the top of a ladder, stapling the wires of Christmas tree lights to posts. The colors would be pretty at night, reflected on the water. Howard had to hand it to Axel. He had come around on this party, which took more . . . what would you call it? . . . *good sportsmanship* than Howard thought the guy had. Axel gestured to Meredith, probably telling her to hurry up and untangle the Christmas lights, which Axel should know is a job you can't hurry. The guy seemed beside himself with excitement.

Tick steered a two-wheel cart full of beer down from Lillian's. At the corner, he veered and ran the cart into the railing to avoid running over Tommy on his bike. Tommy was singing, as usual: "All I ever need is a song in my heart, food in my belly, love in my family. All I ever need . . ."

"Stop. Wait." Tick beckoned Tommy back. "What? Sing that again. Did Nora teach you that?"

"*All I ever need is a song in my heart*," and there was Tick, staring at Tommy with shining eyes and mouthing the words to the song. A glorious day indeed.

The ravens were lining up on the railings, hopping sideways, yawping, getting ready for the potluck. Mike and Sherm were hooking up propane for the grills. Nora had insisted that the Good River Products guys sign up for practically every committee, putting the site security guards on cleanup. That was fair enough, and Howard made sure they did. He put himself on the committee to judge the potato salad contest, but he didn't sign himself up for cleanup duty, which Nora thought was fine when he explained. He wanted to be able to take Taylor back to his little room and tuck her into the bed he'd made her from a fish box. Whether he could do that without crying, he didn't know, it had been that long.

Everything was ready for Tommy's concert. Axel's workmen brought out a table and taped on Tommy's cardboard keyboard so it wouldn't blow away. They got him a chair with a booster seat so he could reach the keys that Nora had drawn on. Tommy could sing while he moved his fingers, and Nora and Annie Klawon would probably be the only ones watching his hands. But still Nora had spent a full day tuning her piano, who knows why—that seemed to be her work in life, trying to get that piano to come into harmony with itself.

"Here is where I want to spend the rest of my life," Howard whispered to the post office window, and he was only a little surprised to hear himself say it. If he were the mayor of the village, he would appoint a special committee with only one job—to sit around in Lillian's, drink skunky beer, and imagine how you can live in a place without wrecking it. Now and then, the committee might have to pull the pants off a stranger. But other than that, thinking's easy work.

Imagine how to make a living—literally, a living. Imagine how to fish a channel without fishing it out. Imagine how to log the mountains without logging them over. Imagine how to make a potato salad so good it wins first prize, and then give it away, every bite. On Sisyphus's boulder wobbling in desperate balance at the top of a steep mountain, imagine how to sing in harmony. Just like Kenny said.

"What does she look like?"

Howard turned and there was Lillian, resplendent in her plaid Seattle raincoat, with a yellow nasturtium pinned in her hair. Despite himself, Howard reached his arms around her and pressed her bosom into his belt buckle. Could he hope that she would be part of his family too, an entrepreneur just like he was, a grandmother who would brush his daughter's hair back from her face and tell her to stand up straight?

"Why does everybody think they can hug me, just because I have a flower in my hair?" Lillian said. She pulled away and tugged down her raincoat, fore and aft. "I hardly made it down the boardwalk without getting my back disjointed."

Howard laughed. But when he considered how to describe Jennifer, he was so moved, he could hardly speak.

"She will have short blond hair. It will be wavy and unruly, because of the marine air. For the first few days in Good River Harbor, she will be wearing pink lipstick and jeans with the crease pressed in. She will be smiling. She will have a little girl by the hand."

≋≋≋

AXEL PULLED DOWN the front of his GR Products jacket, straightened his shoulders, and again walked the perimeter of the dock where the party was gearing up. Past the banjo player, practicing his licks. Past the accordion in its suitcase. Past Tick, who opened a bag of ice and poured it into a cooler. Axel's body was already buzzing, all senses on full alert, and the scritch of the falling ice made his spine shudder. He rolled his shoulders and turned away. But he stopped then and raised his head. He heard a sound he had not heard before in Good River Harbor, like ice, but like music. Was it coming from the cooler, or from the forest? He bent his head toward the sound. Then he strode down the ramp to Nora's trail. The music rang clearer, the closer he came. He slowed his pace. A few yards short of the opening in the woods, he slid behind a cedar and peered out. There was the bleeding stump of the old hemlock he'd felled. There was the pile of firewood he'd expected. There was Chum, snoozing like a schmuck. And there was Nora, seated with her back to him, playing her piano like a pro. Her hands dashed up and down the keyboard. The piano bounced with the force of her playing. The floorboards buzzed. The woods filled with music.

Axel grinned a slow smile. Final evidence; she was a concert pianist. The felon was almost in his grasp. One move against his construction site, and she was caught. His armpits prickled with pleasure.

Axel slid back behind the tree. The music—she moved her fingers and the very air sang. Single notes fell, fell, fell, while above them, small pops fluttered off descending scales. There was a sudden crash of chords, then another, and then it all fell apart and trickled down, whatever it was, this music. No sooner down than the music shot up again. It was like rain, it was like fire, it was like a thousand glass birds flying together from a cave, beating their wings so fast, so close, that when they smashed their wings together in flight, they made the sound of breaking glass, tinkling down, broken. Then up up, the shards of light, colliding, and falling in a cascade of music, all those silver feathers of music, falling in the sun. It was a revelation. It was a miracle, that music, the music that burst from the piano and filled the clearing with a clarity so sparkling that the trees might have been encased in ice.

When her hands were finally still, Nora leaned over the keyboard while the last vibrations shivered toward the sea. Axel exhaled. The wind shifted. Suddenly, Chum jumped to his feet as if he had been stuck with a stick and began to growl. Axel dropped to the ground behind a fallen log and pushed his face into the moldering dirt.

"What is it, Chum?" Nora leaned over to pat him, but his fur bristled under her hand. She grabbed his collar. "So. We have company." Judging from Chum's revulsion, it was either a bear or it was Axel.

"Hi, Axel," she sang out.

Axel held his breath. Wet moss was soaking his elbow and the length of his leg. A broken skunk cabbage was stinking up his jacket. He hadn't anticipated that crime-stoppers would get so dirty.

"Debussy. 'Feux d'Artifice.' Fireworks," Nora called out. "Now I'll play a piece just for you, and then you go back to town. I have work to do."

Work to do! Axel's heart raced.

"The piece I will play for you is 'Fantasie,' by Robert Schumann," Nora announced.

Axel crouched lower. A mushroom squashed on his cheek.

As Nora began to play, Axel crawled away from the clearing and walked slowly up the forest path through the saddest, loneliest music he had ever heard. He emerged into the looping twang of banjos tuning up and resumed his patrol. He did not hear the last notes of the piece she played. He did not see what she did next.

≋≋≋

IT ISN'T EASY to steer an old upright piano, each wheel rust-stuck sideways. Nora retrieved a hammer from the kitchen and whacked at each of the wheels until she got them pointed sort of straight. She put her shoulder to the side of the piano, braced her boots, and pushed. She had to cut her anchor line somehow and leave Good River Harbor, she knew this. She had to leave, and the piano had to let her go.

The piano creaked across the porch, veering to starboard. Nora smacked the front wheels back into line, aiming them for the plywood boards she'd set up as a ramp. She could have used some help—one to push and one to steer—but all help was gone. Finally, over the uneven boards, Nora muscled the piano to the edge of the ramp. The tide was out, and the water beyond the yellow rock-wrack, beyond the blue mussel beds, past the eelgrass, was calm. Across the channel, a line of clouds cut the mountains in half—shadowy spruce and hemlock by the water, patchy snowfields above the clouds.

Nora leaned into the side of the piano and pushed. Once the advancing wheels dropped off the porch, the piano rumbled down the ramp under its own weight, lurching from side to side as the plywood sagged and popped. Nora stood back and watched it go. It lunged off the ramp onto smooth granite and picked up speed, rolling toward the drop where the high tide had undercut the shore. The starboard wheel struck a rock. The piano cartwheeled onto the tideflat, smacked into the mud, and fell on its back.

The cabinet split diagonally, and all two hundred strings rang at once. A flock of gulls startled up, mewling. Ravens clonked in the spruce. Two eagles lifted, clattering the way they do, like stone on steel. Nora shook her head. Wouldn't you know. The universe starts with a single bell tone across the water, and this is how it ends—everything in creation crying out in one terrible chord.

Nora listened until the last of the piano's music faded away. Then she forced herself to turn her back on it. Behind the cabin, there was a bunch of punky firewood and rotted planks on a busted-up shipping pallet. She loaded up the wheelbarrow and hauled all the firewood down to the piano, then the planks and even the pallet. With the slats and scrap spruce, she built a pyramid against the piano. She rearranged a couple of sticks until she got it just right. Then she poured kerosene onto the pile. Closing her eyes against the sting of fumes, the sting of tears, she waited for the kerosene to soak in. When she held a match to a fir slat, a blue flame spread like water across the wood.

Kerosene starts slow, but once it gets going, even in wet wood, it burns hot. Before long, the fire was sucking air and roaring. The piano disappeared under oily smoke. Nora backed away from the heat. She pulled off her cap and wiped her forehead with the back of her hand. A few strands of damp hair stuck to her cheeks. Ashes flew at her like mosquitoes. She put a hand over her mouth, as if closing off her face would keep the smoke away.

Ravens swooped in on the rising air. Always, there are ravens at a fire, pacing, pacing, angry at the wait. With an oar, Nora shoveled embers to keep the fire tight, but then the oar began to smoke and she had to stir it in the sea.

The flames were so hot they turned the air above the fire to the trembling clarity of fresh water on salt. Through that air, snowfields shook on the mountains across the channel. Nora leaned on the oar and traced the ridgeline with wet and squinty eyes. Up there—that's where Nora would take hold of the prypole. She would feel its roughness in her hands, smell the sap still in it, feel its weight. She would wedge it against the fulcrum Tick had chosen. It was a worthy fulcrum, the resistance that would change everything—a granite boulder matted with green liverwort and specked with the orange lichen that marked a deer mouse's tiny river of pee. For a week, she had rehearsed how she would grip the pole with two hands, brace her legs against a ledge, and pull with all her strength. The lever would groan against the boulder and pop out the bottom logs. The whole barrier would twist apart then, and the force of all that water falling down the mountain would tear out Axel's dam. The salmon would be free to come home again. Nora closed her eyes. What would that be like, to be finally coming home?

The top of the fire let loose and crashed into the heart of it. Ravens hopped back. There was an eruption of sparks, then flames flared pink and green. Nora heard a muffled plink, a treble string breaking. Another plink.

"That blessed fire is playing my piano." Nora's hands were shaking. She tightened her grip on the oar. Single notes broke free, throwing sparks. Nora raised her head and listened to it play.

As afternoon came on, the tide leaked under the pyre and lifted the smoking coals. Nora sat on a log with the oar beside her and wept, while the tide pushed a current line of charcoal and ashes across the cove. Slowly, the cove filled almost to the top of Nora's boots. From wood smoldering under the tide, bubbles the size of ping-pong balls bobbed to the surface. For a time, they floated there, domes on the scum. When they finally popped, they let loose puffs of gray smoke.

The tide. It was time for the party. She put a gallon of drinking water in the front hatch of her kayak. In the back, just a blanket, a tarp, a loaf of bread, dog food. She tied the kayak to a root on the bank. At high tide, she would find it there, floating. Double-checking the knot, she whistled for Chum and turned to go. When she looked back, there were gray bubbles puttering up from the piano fire—smoke backfiring in random bursts from the sea, puffing smoke alongside a frond of bullwhip kelp.

"DIDN'T YOUR MOTHER teach you to give your seat to a lady?" Lillian said loudly. Half a dozen kids popped up and scuttled out of her way, ducking in and out of their dancing parents and coming to rest in a covey by the post office wall. Lillian eased herself onto a suddenly empty folding chair. The Coho Day festivities were still in full swing, but there is a limit to how much waltzing a lady can ask of any given set of knees. Axel's workmen were handsome, and they knew how to dance. Lillian had thought her feet would never be waltzing again. Probably wouldn't be waltzing tomorrow. But that banjo player really spiked up the music in the rest of the band, and why should she sit still when so many people wanted to dance with her?

All through the party, Axel stood off to the side by the post office gangway and scanned the crowd, like a secret service agent. Every time she danced by, Lillian could see him, standing alone and watching. Finally, she made up her mind. When the band began to play a waltz, she went over and stood in front of him.

"Will you dance with a woman who is old enough to be your mother?" she asked Axel. He glared at her. Lillian smoothed down her raincoat and said it again. "Will you dance with me?" He lifted one hand and put it at the center of her back. He took her hand in his other. She put her hand on his shoulder. It was the first time she had touched him in forty-seven years. His shoulder felt firm under her hand, and his hand, clinging to hers, was warm and damp. He smelled as musty as a newborn baby. Lillian felt an ancient ache in her breasts. And so they danced. Not like Fred and Ginger, but they danced. And all the time they danced, Axel said not a word. But his head bounced around, watching.

Meredith had walked up and down the potluck line, giving away grilled shrimp as fast as the postman could cook them. She is a pretty girl, Lillian thought. She'd been pretty from the day she was born. All she needed now was a grandmother to teach her about . . . oh, there was so much a grandmother could teach Meredith. Like, for example, rubber boots are not dancing shoes.

Howard had followed Meredith up and down the line, introducing his wife and little girl, as if the party was his wedding reception, and maybe that's how he felt, that kind of happiness. His wife was a pretty woman too. If she stayed, it wouldn't be long before she let her hair grow out to dark roots and traded her sandals for muckers. Annie Klawon was back, and if her spine isn't out of joint from being hugged so hard by so many people, she's a strong woman. She was home, and that was good and natural and the way the world ought to be.

It was moving and generous, Lillian thought, how his friends stuck close to Tick all afternoon. Who knows, maybe they'd all signed up for the Tick Committee. Whenever he opened a beer, took a swallow, and set the can down next to him, the can mysteriously disappeared and there would be Rebecca, pouring a beer into the sea. Or somebody else would say, we need you over here, Tick, and poor thirsty Tick would be scrubbing a grill or emptying the trash while his beer can bobbed on the tide. And here would be Rebecca, offering him a Coke. It might have seemed strange, that kind of solicitude, except this was Annie Klawon's first night in, and her friends probably thought she'd prefer him sober. And Tick—he was as nervy as Lillian had ever seen him, tripping over chairs, looking over the deck rail to check the tide.

The tables were cluttered with empty casserole dishes crusted with noodles, and a rim of frosting was all that was left of the giant cake. The town dogs nosed around underneath, licking between the planks of the boardwalk. That was disgusting, those long pink tongues.

"Get away," Lillian said, flipping her hand at the dogs. Half a dozen more kids edged off.

Lillian had to admit that Tommy's recital was the highlight of the party. It went off without a hitch. People clapped as he began When At Night I Go to Sleep, and their faces softened as Tommy pounded along through I pray the lord my soul to keep. When he paused to let his left hand catch up to his right, every single person in Good River Harbor, toddlers to grandfathers, mouthed the next words, and if it was a prompt or a blessing, who could say? Angels watching over me.

When the applause died down, Nora called out to Lillian for a song.

"A song," Tick shouted. Lillian took off her raincoat and walked to the front of the crowd. She had worn her purple dress with the lilacs on the bodice, just for this occasion. People started shouting requests. But Nora wanted "Amazing Grace," and that's what Lillian decided to sing. For the first verse, Lillian's solo voice rang the mountains. Then other voices joined in. It's a miracle really, Lillian believed, people singing in harmony, all those different voices singing different tones, and all the voices sounding together the slow, resonant chords.

"I once was lost, but now I'm found."

"Yes, Lilly," Tick said soberly. "Yes. A good and true song."

Lillian looked toward Nora, hoping she had liked the song, but Nora had melted back into the crowd.

As dusk turned toward darkness, the men began to rustle around to prepare the fireworks. People shifted chairs, pointing them at the channel. Blankets appeared from houses. The kids set their bikes aside and gathered cross-legged on the blankets. Sensing the climax of the evening, Lillian walked up the boardwalk to the bar. Of all the occasions in this town, this was the one that truly called for the gallon of good whiskey she'd been keeping under her bed. She did not know what she was saving it for, if she wasn't saving it for this town, this night.

It was a long haul up the stairs for those old legs. Lillian sat on her bed with her arms on her knees and caught her breath. From her upstairs window, she could see the dock and all the way down the channel across Green Point to the Kis'utch clamflats. A beautiful party, she thought to herself, and then inhaled sharply as she saw Davy drop into his skiff and row silently under the town.

"Uh-oh," Lillian exhaled, as she scanned the crowd for Meredith and did not find her.

A bartender can sweep her eyes over a situation and know precisely when something's not right—when a fight is about to start, or a woman is about to rag on her man. That silenced skiff and their disappearing teenagers were not right. The solicitude for Tick was not right. The list of committees was not right. "Amazing Grace" was suddenly terrifying. In fact, something was off about the whole party.

Lillian stuck her head out the window to get a better angle as Axel walked over to Howard. Poor, decent Howard was shaking his head no, gesturing to his wife and daughter, no no. No. But Axel spoke to him urgently and at some length. Finally, Howard nodded, walked over to Tick, who was just settling his big bulk on a blanket. Howard tapped Tick on the shoulder, said something. Tick also began to point and protest, his beard flapping no. He pushed Howard away with his shoulder. But Howard gestured toward Axel, said something more, and Tick finally let himself be steered toward the harbor, where the two men disappeared in the direction of the Good River Products skiff.

What in God's name?

Forgetting the whiskey, Lillian swept to the head of the stairs and hobbled back to the party as fast as her old legs would go.

≋≋≋

"THIS BETTER BE good, Davy McIver. If my dad finds us together, you and I are both dead meat."

Davy didn't know if it was good or not, this miserable mystery. Maybe it was good. Maybe his dad and Meredith's mom were up to something sneaky and important, something Axel would want to know about. That was the thing. Davy really could make good decisions. Axel had called him irresponsible, right there in front of his mom and dad. But wouldn't it be irresponsible if he learned an important secret and didn't tell? Or maybe the secret wasn't anything. Maybe Rebecca wanted help getting alpine plants or something. Raising a false alarm was completely irresponsible.

Axel's right, Davy decided. I am a complete jerk.

"Because if he finds out that we're together, I'm on the next ferry to Sitka, signed up for boarding school. That's what he said."

Davy didn't know that. This just got worse and worse. He wished he had never gone up that mountain, tracking Rebecca Hagerman. And if he had, he wished he had never left that note for Meredith. He should have been able to figure this out himself.

"Which might be fine with me, to get away from a dweeb like you."

Davy's head sank down between his shoulders. So why did she meet me here? Why is she sitting in the bow of my dad's boat, smiling while she beats me down? I'm beat down plenty already. For the first time since I sunk the boat, my family is happy. My mom is home. When I gave her a hug on the ferry dock, it felt good, her head on my shoulder, I'm that tall. "Have you grown another foot?" she said. "Just an inch," I said, but she was teasing me. We hung around together. Then I had to sneak away. My mom's home three hours, and I'm sneaking away to wreck it all. Just to show off for Meredith, that's what it is. Meredith, who calls me a dweeb.

It was dark and cramped, floating under the school. Their heads practically hit the stringers, and the tide was still rising. Davy wished the guys would get on with the fireworks.

When he had rowed out to the school to pick up Meredith, there had been plenty of room to sneak along under the houses. Not anymore. This was going to be a huge tide. Eighteen feet. He planned to get away from town as soon as he heard the first boom from the first fireworks. He figured, that way nobody would hear the engine noise, and if they did hear it, nobody would pay attention because the fireworks would be so cool, and if they did pay attention, they couldn't see the boat in the dark.

Davy would speed across the channel. He would tie the boat by the main channel of the Kis'utch River, where nobody would see the skiff. Then quick up to the ridge by flashlight to see what Meredith's mom and Tick had built with those downed trees, whatever it was. Maybe a hideout, he was starting to think, but what would Rebecca and Tick do in a hideout, except hunt. Or maybe kiss—a disgusting thought. He shoved it aside. Once he and Meredith had found the hideout or whatever, they would slide quick down the hillside, and nobody would know they'd been gone. Except if they solved the mystery. Then they would be heroes. Or maybe the mystery would be so terrible that they would have to keep the secret their whole lives, just Meredith and Davy forever, sharing a terrible secret.

"The trouble with you, Davy, is that you don't think things through."

"Oh for crying out loud, Meredith. Thinking things through is what I'm trying to do. Why do you think I asked you to come with me? To think things through. And what help are you? I think just fine except when you're around, and then I can't think at all. Forget it. Just forget it. Everything about this plan is nuts. Especially me."

There was silence between them.

"Okay," he said finally. "I'll row you to the beach at the end of the boardwalk, and you can get out and walk back to the party. Forget this ever happened. Forget everything. Maybe I'll see you around sometime."

If he lived to be a thousand years old, Davy would never understand women. His dad had told him that this is something a man simply cannot do. Meredith brushed back her bangs with her hand and looked at him with those big soft eyes. They were filling with tears.

"Are you breaking up with me?" she asked in a little voice.

There was a sizzling noise and a deafening report. Pink and yellow fountains of light sprayed into the night. Smoke twirled down from the first explosion, and then each twirl exploded, sharp as a hammer on gunpowder. The reports echoed in the cavern under the school. Meredith covered her ears. Thunder bounced back and forth between the mountains behind the town and the mountains across the channel. The skyrocket was followed by a burst of pink light that grew and grew until it turned yellow and fizzled away.

Davy yanked the starter cord. The motor caught.

"Dear God, let this be the right decision. Just once, let it be right."

He nosed the skiff out from under the school, pointed it at the waterfall, and gunned it.

THE BANJO PLAYER signaled to the fireworks crew and laid down another mighty lick. The postmaster touched a flame to a wick. The flame sizzled into the heart of the rocket. An aerial shell burst into pink and yellow bloom against the dark clouds. Its petals disintegrated into burning stars that arced toward the sea. A matching starburst rose from the black water. They met in a shower of sparks. Twists of smoke sizzled out of the center of the bloom. They detonated with a blast of white light and a sharp report. Annie Klawon reached over to cover Tommy's ears.

"Ooooh," he shouted, and shook his head free.

Three more balls of light arced almost to the top of the ridge. Three bursts of blue sparks lit up the whole clamflat. Clearly visible beside their skiff drawn up on the beach at the industrial site, Tick and Howard faced each other, opening and closing their mouths and shaking their heads violently as they flashed blue and green under the fireworks. Tick looked up the mountain, pointed, began to talk again. By now, he had Howard by the shirtfront and was yelling at him.

A skyrocket sizzled up and exploded into a fountain of rosy sparks that blew apart into more fountains—blue, pink, yellow. Ribbons of light crisscrossed the sky. Across the channel, Tick and Howard ducked their heads under the barrage. Pink waves rolled up on shore at their feet. At the harbor, the crowd exhaled excitement.

Annie Klawon stood up abruptly. She grabbed hold of Rebecca.

"What's going on?

"Tick!" Annie cried out.

Tommy clutched his mom and began to whimper.

A deep-throated rumble rolled across the channel and slowly engulfed the crowd in its black shudder. Under the construction lights across the channel, Tick looked up, grabbed Howard by the front of his shirt, and began to pull at him. He gestured wildly toward the waterfall. Howard resisted his pull, bracing his boots into the mud, and gestured as wildly toward the construction site. For a moment, they pulled apart and faced each other, the way wrestlers lean in, at that moment before the lunge. Then Tick lifted Howard into the air and slung him over his shoulder. With Howard's long legs teetering behind him like two-by-fours, Tick ran hard away from the river and scrambled up a rocky slope. The air flashed yellow and another skyrocket rocked the channel.

Through the thunder, a dark vee cut across a pink pool of light. Annie Klawon peered through the crowd. The vee was the wake of a boat, a small boat, a skiff, their skiff, with a person in the bow and, in the stern, another person, a person who surely was her son, her son who was steering straight toward the mouth of the Kis'utch River.

In the yellow glare of Axel's construction floodlights, a black paw of water reached over the ridge above the dam site. The flood crouched there, gathering its strength. Logs spun in the gleam of the advancing edge. Then the flood clawed through the last rocks and bounded down the mountainside. With great leaps from ledge to ledge, it batted away the rootballs of ferns and tore out young alders.

"Flash flood," Annie Klawon shouted. "No, Davy. No."

Tangled with ferns and alders in the advancing flood, a log tumbled and thumped in the torrent, caught a cut end, somersaulted, dove underwater, and leapt up again, spraying a skyrocket's orange glare. In a final black sluice, the flood smashed onto the alder flat. It crouched again and bounded toward the industrial site.

"Meredith." Rebecca's voice was more a breath than a whisper. In the chaos of the great roar, the construction lights blacked out. Darkness rolled with the echoing thunder over the channel.

On the wharf, people grabbed up children and walked slowly backward, as they knew to do in the face of a great beast. The last pink sparks flashed out. All color sank under the black waves.

"Light," Annie Klawon shouted. "We need light."

Every member of the fireworks team touched a lighter to a fuse. A skyrocket shot up and sprayed the air with silver flowers. A blue chrysanthemum blew itself to smithereens. Silver confetti streaked across the sky, laying down orange contrails. The flood itself became a fire, throwing pink sparks and shooting off reflected flares of blue and orange. A foaming orange wave smashed into the dam's plywood forms. Boards jumped into the air and dove back into the suddenly blue face of the flood. Trailing sparks, an arm of water swept the Airstream trailer off its blocks. The corporate headquarters of Good River Products, Inc. careened down a torrent of jittering colors. Roman candles crackled into the sky. Thunder rocked from mountain to mountain, shot through with reports from multibreak shells. With stars burning in its teeth, the flood advanced toward the incoming tide. When flood and tide collided, their contrary forces threw up a giant wave that roared toward the town, carrying logs and gas cans, boards and hellfire.

Davy's skiff slowed as the breaker rushed toward them. Then the engine roared, and Davy turned the boat so hard it raised a curtain of water. But the flood was faster than the engine. It caught the transom in one hard slap, and flipped the skiff. Two dark forms catapulted into the wave.

"Please," whispered Annie Klawon. She sprinted for the harbor.

She stood at the slip where their skiff should have been, but of course, it was gone. She ran for the Good River Products boat and did not find it there. Racing up the dock, she jumped into the Annie K.

≋≋≋

"CUT THE LINES," Annie Klawon yelled to Axel, as he pounded down the dock. He smashed the firebox, grabbed the axe, slashed the bowline with a single blow, and dashed back to cut the stern. He leapt into the front-loader as

Annie kicked it into reverse. With one hand on the wheel and her head out the side window, Annie shoved it to forward, pointed her bow straight toward the giant wave that was careening into the tide, and gunned it. Smashing into the flood, the Annie K's bow reared up, hung on the crest of the wave. Then the bow smacked down hard between walls of water, rocked and settled, and they were in the recoiling water behind the wave, moving like an icebreaker through the wreckage. Thunder rolled away and darkness fell around them as the last of the fireworks winked out. All Annie heard was the engine grinding and boards banging against the hull. All she could see were flashes of phosphorescence from the startled sea creatures themselves. She could not see her son. She could not find Meredith.

"The spotlight. Get the spotlight," she yelled.

Axel grabbed the handle and flipped the switch. A spear of light shot wildly over the seas. Floating plywood, five-gallon bucket, curl of kelp, corrugated metal roofing, sharp as knives. Back and forth the light swept, until it bounced off Davy and Meredith, found them again, and rested like a hand on their shining hair. Their heads rose and fell on the swash of the flood. Davy had one arm around Meredith and the other around a bobbing gas can. She flailed at entangling kelp and kicked away a desk drawer.

"Tie a line on that life ring," Annie called. "Heave it out and stand by to release the pins." So slowly, so carefully, through bucking lumber and floating lines, she fought to bring the boat close to Meredith and Davy. In the slapping, slopping chaos of the flood and tide, logs struck the bow, knocking the boat from its course.

"Grab the boat hook and get that crap out of the way," Annie shouted.

Axel poked at the logs to make a space, and suddenly there they were, Davy and Meredith, grabbing for the life ring.

"Release the pins." The apron clanked to the water.

Kneeling, Axel got hold of Davy's jacket but the jacket slipped from his grasp as Davy shoved Meredith to the edge of the apron.

"Get your leg up. Get your leg over," Davy shouted.

With Axel pulling and Davy pushing, Meredith rolled onto the boat and turned to haul in Davy. They lay panting on the deck. Blood trickled from Meredith's forehead. As Annie Klawon turned the boat and maneuvered through debris to the dock, Axel drew the children into the shelter of the pilothouse and pressed them both to his chest. This is how they rode to shore, in this awkward embrace.

Holding woolen blankets, hands reached down from the dock, and soon Davy was stripped of his wet clothes and engulfed in a blanket, bundled with Annie to share the warmth of a mother's body. Axel helped Meredith climb from the bow and soon she too was wrapped close to her mother's life-saving warmth, which everyone in Good River Harbor knew was the best thing for people who almost drowned, and for their mothers too. Stumbling in the blankets, Davy and Meredith let their mothers lead them home to their woodstoves and heaped quilts.

The rest of the mothers gathered their children and made their ways up the boardwalk to their homes, the spotlights of their headlamps bobbing before them like jellyfish in a dark sea. Shadows of their dogs wandered behind. Then it was quiet on the wharf, just a few people slowly putting away chairs or coiling strings of lights. Mike Sorensen snapped shut the latches on his banjo case, said goodnight to Lillian, to Axel, and turned to the work of his Cleanup Committee. Suddenly came a great hollering and hallooing from across the channel.

"Hey, you suckers. What about us? Me and my friend Howard need a ride home." Home, home, echoed the channel. There Tick and Howard stood, at the top of a rocky slope above the splintered construction site. Tick was waving an orange highway cone as if it were a megaphone. Howard flapped a yellow safety vest.

Mike Sorenson put down his banjo, hopped into his Good River Products skiff, and took off toward the clamflat. When the skiff nosed into the sand, Tick and Howard were standing together, each with his long arm draped over the other's shoulders.

They could not have seen that, not so far down the beach, a gyre of dark shapes circled in the deep water at the mouth of the Kis'utch. The circle flashed now and then when a salmon turned its side to the starlit night. As the flood-tide held, shimmering, at its peak, a ribbon of salmon unspooled from the spiral and turned toward home. Crossing the bar, each fish pushed a gleaming bow-wave upstream.

Back on the silent wharf, Axel sat down heavily on a bench, dropped his head in his hands, and began to shiver. Lillian, uncertain, sat down beside him. Then, because he was shivering, she took off her raincoat and arranged it over his shoulders. In her new purple dress, she sat tight beside him with her arm around his back. Because she was his mother and he was her son, she sheltered him as well as she could from the wind, which was just beginning to rise, the way the wind will sometimes rise when the tide begins to turn.

The black water of the channel shook under the small wind, then settled. All the stars in heaven reflected onto the water. The constellations swam there, the animals and ancient heroes, lifted and bent by the slow current of the tide. Far down the night-black channel, just where the tide turns past Bean Point, a kayak's silver wake moved slowly through the Great Bear, heading for Orion.

CODA

As the tide drained from the cove at Nora's cabin, a flock of crows banked sharply and dropped onto the circle of blackened mud where scorched rock-wrack still held on to the stones. They stalked stiff-legged across the soot, pecking experimentally at a bent, gray screw, a scrap of burnt leather, a charred timber. One tugged at a wire, hopping backward. When an eagle set its wings and carved over the cove, the crows lifted as one being, circled squawking, then settled again, jostling for space, tripping over the debris. Bolts with the nuts fused on them had fallen onto the cast-iron plate of the piano. They lay across a curve of tuning pins and busted-up wires, unsprung and brittle. In the mud some feet away was the brass pedal that sustains the sound.

ACKNOWLEDGMENTS

Over so many years, so many people have helped with *Piano Tide* in so many ways. Such good friends and family members—I hold you in my heart and thank you for your genius, your generosity, and your faith in a process that seemed to have no end. Deep gratitude to all of you:

To the people who read and responded to early drafts, John Calderazzo, Brook Elgie, Charles Goodrich, Kim Heacox, John Keeble, Hank Lentfer, Nancy Lord, Carol Mason, Erin Moore, Frank Moore, Jonathan Moore, and Vicki Wisenbaugh.

To all the remarkably generous and capable people who welcomed our family into their Southeast Alaska communities and homes, told us stories, taught us new skills and words, took us to sea and poetry readings, laughed and fished and feasted with us—all those friends on the VHF radio and the trails and the ferries. I will not name you, to save you any possible grief. You know who you are; I hope you know how much I love and admire you.

To concert pianist Rachelle McCabe, salmon ecologist Jonathan Moore, then-teenager Zachary Wisenbaugh, architect Erin Moore, naturalist Frank Moore, and all the other experts who shared their expertise—from how to tune a piano to how to swear like a teenager. To Richard A. Zagars, the incomparable Juneau artist who gave me the gift of his painting for the book cover. To Portland writer Brian Doyle, who grins at the mysterious chiming of our novels; we are born, he says, of the same "salt and song."

To my characters. Philosophy professor than I am, I had originally invented each one to embody a different theory of environmental ethics. But they soon told me that they had minds of their own, and free will.

They would do and think what they damned well pleased, which was way more complicated than I could ever learn—although they would try to teach me.

To Southeast Alaska, its denizens and its tides—the trumpeting whales, hidden coves, ticking barnacles—on every scale, in every weather, an astonishment of beauty and thriving.

For early sustenance and inspiration, thanks to the Wrangell Mountain Center, Fishtrap Writers' Residency on the Imnaha River, Playa, and the Spring Creek Project.

To those who have given always good advice, good will, and support in publishing, Laura Blake Peterson, Carol Mason, and Jack Shoemaker.

To my family, exceptional people who fill me with ideas, stories, love, and laughter. And especially to my truly wonderful husband, Frank. With his strong hands, deep intelligence, and generous love, Frank has built the foundation under every one of our shared dreams, including this one. Love and gratitude to you, dear Frank. Forever.